A mid the scuffle, Trinesh stumbled against the front wall of the Egg of the World. His outflung hands scraped along the row of little black knobs. . . .

"Kill us or not, it is already too late for you!" the captive woman spat. None of them had heard the outer door click shut. Only now did Trinesh sense motion. They were moving—the whole damned egg-thing was moving! His stomach told him that they were descending straight down.

"Ohe, commander of Tsolyanu—" the woman squirmed about in her captor's iron grip to gaze full upon him from dark, slitted eyes—"we are your prisoners, but shortly you will be ours. This thing, this sphere, is one of the Ancients' tubeway cars that travel beneath the world! Soon we shall emerge in my country!"

M.A.R. BARKER is a full professor at the University of Minnesota, in the Dept. of South and Southwestern Asian Studies, where he teaches the Urdu language, Arabic, and matters relating to India and Pakistan. He has worked on the background, history and lore of Tekumel since the age of ten. Since he got into war-gaming and role-playing games early, his crowded Tekumel sessions have been continuous from 1974. He writes:

"For those with an interest in the linguistics of Tekumel, a grammar and dictionary of Tsolyani were published in 1981 by Adventure Games, 1278 Selby Avenue, St. Paul, MN 55104. The sourcebook for Tekumel, issued as Volume I of "Swords and Glory: Adventures on Tekumel" by Gamescience, Inc., 01956 Pass Road, Gulfport, Mississippi 39501, should be in print by the time this novel appears; besides the history and cultures of Tekumel, it contains further information about the languages and scripts of the Five Empires. Several of the ancient scripts have also been printed as individual articles in the "Journal of Tekumel Affairs," 2428 1st Avenue South, Minneapolis, MN 55404."

FLAMESONG

M.A.R. Barker

DAW BOOKS, INC.
DONALD A. WOLLHEIM, PUBLISHER

1633 Broadway, New York, NY 10019

DAW Collectors' Book No. 643

First Printing, September 1985

1 2 3 4 5 6 7 8 9

PRINTED IN U.S.A.

1

The hall was cold, damp yet still redolent of the dry, dusty scents of the desert. Yesterday's heat had given way to pouring rain, the sort of sudden autumn storm that flooded valleys, caused landslides, cut roads, and drowned anything foolish enough to dwell in the ravines and gulches of this awful land. Today the skies had poured down water from dawn to dusk, and the last assault over the battlements had been conducted in a gray torrent that turned both friend and foe into misty shadows who slipped and skidded, cursed and struggled, and then died, upon the red-washed mud-brick wallwalks.

They had taken Fortress Ninu'ur just after sunset, and the rain stopped miraculously just in time to coincide with their shouts of victory—and with the dying cries of the last Yan Koryani defenders in the snag-toothed keep. The victors, soldiers of the Tsolyani Legion of the Storm of Fire, pushed on into the main hall. It was now empty, save for the bodies of the foe's nameless dead, and for the ashen rivulets that trickled down through the time-blackened roofbeams to mingle with the scarlet pools upon the flagging.

Trinesh hiKetkolel pulled off his helmet and looked around. The hall was not large: a room perhaps eight man-heights long, six across, and three high. The daises where its builders had sat to dine rose like little terrace-fields out of the water and the mess the foe had left behind. The Yan Koryani had been anything but neat. Scraps of clothing, *Dna*-grain husks, burnt-out embers from the fire they had lit in the center of the room, and myriad unnameable bits of flotsam littered the floor or floated like foundered boats in the water. There were no tapestries, no floor-mats, nothing to show that civilized folk had made this place a home as well as a fortress. The peeling mud-plaster of the walls displayed only obscene graffiti in the squarish, ugly letters of Yan Kor.

In these first days of autumn, in the month of Pardan of the year 2,361 after the foundation of the Second Imperium of the Seal Emperors of Tsolyanu, the Tsolyani armies lay locked in a seesaw struggle with the troops of Yan Kor and her northeastern ally, Saa Allaqi. The immediate objective was the conquest of this blighted buffer state of Milumanaya. Fortress Ninu'ur was about as good as anything Milumanaya had to offer.

Trinesh set his flame-crested helmet upon a half-empty sack of rotting *Dna*-grain, but there was no place to hang up his cloak, and he allowed it to slip off to lie in a sopping heap behind him on the floor. A vambrace came off, its padded lining soaked through and sticky, then the upcurving pauldron-collar, the gorget of valuable iron that his folk, the Clan of the Red Mountain, had gifted him, then the other vambrace. The straps of his *Chlen*-hide breastplate defied him; their leather was now wet and knotted in the buckles, as solid as the God-Emperor in Avanthar!

Trinesh leaned against the wall to spit blood. He had bitten the inside of his cheek when he jumped down from the wallwalk into the courtyard. An heroic wound indeed! He was almost too tired to curse.

Trinesh was a *Hereksa*, the commander of a *Kareng* of one

hundred men. His *Kareng* was one of the four in his Cohort, and the latter was one of the twelve currently fielded by the Legion of the Storm of Fire, the Tsolyani Twenty-First Imperial Medium Infantry. They were a new Legion, not yet a very good one, certainly not as skilled as the Legion of Serqu, "the Sword of the Empire," for example, but they were solid enough, reliable, and battle-hardened after six months of fighting.

The troops needed no further orders; they fanned out into the keep automatically. The *Tirrikamu* Horusel, the seniormost of Trinesh's five subalterns, took his *Semetl* of twenty and headed for the stair that led up from the far end of the chamber; Chosun and his *Semetl* would explore this story and any cellars below, while the other three *Semetl* searched the towers and the walls of the bailey. They had thrown dice, and those outside had lost. There was no joy at all in mopping up an enemy fortress in rainswept darkness.

Horusel's men finished removing the bodies of the slain. The Yan Koryani had fought well, but the Milumanayani— the tribesmen of the Desert of Sighs—were as useless to the foe as they were to the Tsolyani. As allies they were treacherous; as enemies they were—charitably—utterly craven. Trinesh had seen them scrambling away into the night, their leather desert-cloaks flapping about their scrawny legs, when his men had swept over the walls and down into the filth-strewn bailey. La! It was beyond humor—almost beyond contempt! Who needed friends like those sand-worms? They were as "noble" as timid *Ngi*-lizards!

One had to admit that the Milumanayani did have their uses. The Tsolyani had finally taken Sunraya, the old caravan city that was all the civilization eastern Milumanaya could boast. It had been hideously costly, and the war here in the northeast was by no means over. The legions of Tsolyanu should have been in undisputed control by now, but the Milumanayani tribes had delayed them, more so, almost, than the trained and well-equipped soldiers of the Baron Ald, who ruled Yan Kor. The foe—the Yan Koryani and Saa Allaqiyani regulars—could never have held this region by themselves, not with just the troops they could spare from the western front, where Tsolyanu's second great army advanced to close the trap upon Baron Ald's forces. The Tsolyani had ignored the tribes of Milumanaya, left them to whatever bribes and threats and bargains the Baron could offer them. A civilized people did not treat with wild creatures, after all.

That had been a mistake of epic proportions.

Many of the tribes had accepted the coin of Yan Kor. Others remained aloof, while some played at Guess-Me-Not with both sides. All of the sand-worms were deceitful, lazy, and ignoble; yet the Yan Koryani had made the most of them. Now the desert folk were always there; in every landscape— ostensibly as empty of life as the pinnacles of Thenu Thendraya Peak—there was always somebody: some damned scout, some desert-cloaked savage, some skinny child stinking of *Hma*-wool and *Hmelu*-beast fat, to watch and report. The Tsolyani had had to fortify their camps and guard their supply lines until they were well nigh as impregnable as Avanthar itself. The tribes were no threat in the field; a thousand of the gabbling savages would run before anything bigger than a *Semetl* of twenty. Yet they came back in the night, they raided, they stole, they spied, they burned supplies, they swore oaths and made truces, and then betrayed them again— and again and again until not even the gods knew who was who.

The Yan Koryani and the Saa Allaqiyani were "noble"; with them, one set the place and time for a battle, fought it, won or lost, and took the consequences. The tribesmen of Milumanaya practiced no such etiquette, nor did the flinty ravines of their sun-baked desert. How did one pacify a country made up of empty wastelands, mountains, sand, rocks, and savages who went around swathed top-knot to toes in stinking leather desert-cloaks? Not only was it impossible to distinguish friend from foe, but one could tell the men from the women only by stripping them sky-naked. Both then usually proved to be equally ugly, and the stench would stun a *Sro*-dragon!

Why the God-Emperor in Avanthar wanted this dreary wilderness back was clear enough; it had been abandoned— "mislaid" was perhaps a better word for the bureaucratic error in Avanthar—almost four hundred years ago by Emperor Neshkiruma, whose title, "The Cloud-Spinner," seemed apt indeed for that particular idiot. Now Tsolyanu would correct the oversight. Whatever the Empire lost it eventually regained, like the whore's virginity in the Epic of Hrugga.

Milumanaya was not the real goal, of course, Sunraya, its capital, might be useful as a staging base for troops and supplies, but the city itself was not worth the blood shed during the siege last spring. No, this arrow was aimed at Baron Ald of Yan Kor. Once that traitorous barbarian had taken the "high ride" upon the impalers' stake, the rest of the north—the squabbling Yan Koryani city-states, the sly-eyed people of Lake Parunal, the nomadic Lorun who lived in the marches of the far north, and even the nonhuman Pygmy Folk who had their underground cities in eastern Yan Kor—all would tumble back into Tsolyani hands as prettily as coins into a money-lender's purse! Saa Allaqi might be allowed to make a separate peace, but there would be no mercy for Yan Kor.

Difficulties—seen and unforeseen—had been the story of this Flame-accursed war: the Glorious Seal Emperor in Avanthar had given armies to two of his six currently acknowledged sons. Both had the same objective, but Prince Eselne was to advance up through the northwest, take the little buffer state of Pijena, and conquer the Baron's capital of Ke'er from that direction. Prince Mirusiya's forces were to do the same thing but by the longer and more arduous northeastern route from Thri'il, through the Pass of Skulls, into eastern Milumanaya, and up around from the east to the Baron's back gate. Prince Mirusiya's campaign had a useful secondary goal: a wedge driven up here would cut the Baron off from his Saa Allaqiyani allies in the farther northeast. Had that been all, Prince Mirusiya's task would at least have been equal to his half-brother's, but there was more: in order to succeed in his broader political goals, Prince Mirusiya must take Ke'er first, before Prince Eselne got there.

Prince Mirusiya worshipped Lord Vimuhla, the Master of Flame and one of the *Tlokiriqaluyal*, the Five Gods of Change, as did Trinesh and many of his Legion of the Storm of Fire. Prince Eselne followed Lord Karakan, the Hero of Ever-Glorious War, who belonged to the *Tlomitlanyal*, the Five Gods of Stability. Thus were two of the most powerful temples of the empire's ten major gods involved. It was common gossip that whichever of these two princes seized Ke'er first would be the likely winner of the *Kolumejalim*, the contest that would determine the next Emperor of Tsolyanu.

The stew-pot of political maneuvering had long been boiling, but it would bubble over in earnest once old Hirkane hiTlakotani, the current occupant of the Petal Throne, toddled off to Lord Hnalla's Paradise of Supernal Light! The other heirs—four more princes and one princess—would stir the fire as well, but, Trinesh thought, there were really only two cooks stirring this stew: Prince Eselne and his own master, Prince Mirusiya.

The eldest of the Imperial heirs, Prince Rereshqala, was said to have withdrawn from the contest to content himself with a villa on the southern coast, a coterie of sycophants, and an endless, meaningless round of ceremony and feasting. Not a bad fate, but hardly a glorious one. Prince Mridobu, who was third-eldest just after Prince Eselne, followed a different path to the Petal Throne: a staircase built of bureaucrats, offices, edicts, intrigues, and diplomacy. He was not to Trinesh's taste—nor to that of the warrior clans—any more than Rereshqala was. The youngest son, Prince Dhich'une, served as a priest in the Temple of mighty Sarku, the Lord of Worms and Master of the Undead, the least pleasant of the pantheon of Change. Rumor had it that Dhich'une had suffered some sort of mysterious setback last year and now sulked in his Temple's squat sanctuary in the City of Sarku in northern Tsolyanu. For folk who valued courage and battle, such as Trinesh' Clan of the Red Mountain, it would be hard to find a less appetizing candidate than Dhich'une, "the Worm Prince." Still, when one compared him with his sister, Ma'in Krüthai, or with Surundano, the new Prince recently revealed by the Temple of Thumis, God of Wisdom, Dhich'une did take on a certain warm and kingly glow! The Princess was a spoiled wanton, Trinesh' clan-elders said—and shook their collective heads. Poor Surundano did not even merit that response: he was a vapid nonentity, a minor clerk in the labyrinth of temple administration, before his backers had trotted him forth to make him a black counter upon the *Den-den* board.

The game might surge this way or that as the other players set out their pieces and cast the dice; yet all of those lesser blue and green and white counters would be swept away and popped back in the box. There were really only two black pieces on the board: Prince Eselne in the west, and Prince Mirusiya in the east. Barring a thunderbolt from the Ten Gods Themselves, it was one of these two who would next ascend to the Petal Throne in Avanthar. Trinesh hiKetkolel had already laid his wager upon Prince Mirusiya, the candidate of his clan and of his Deity.

And what was he himself in all this? Hardly a morsel of *Hmelu*-meat in the broth! Trinesh spat blood again and rubbed at the imprint of his helmet-rim across his forehead. He was no more than the very junior officer of a very small contingent in a rather humble Legion, sent to capture a very little enemy stronghold in a very useless land! Fortress Ninu'ur was one chunk of miserable *Kao*-squash in the stew. The Council of Generals had decided that it could not be allowed to remain as a threat to the southern flank of the Tsolyani line of march, and so he, *Hereksa* Trinesh hiKetkolel, had been ordered to go and take it. The first part had been easy—they had surprised the Yan Koryani in the rain—but the second half of the task promised to be harder. Who knew how many squadrons of green-armored Yan Koryani troops still lurked in the hills outside? —And how many ragged tribesmen sat tonight to lay plans for the retaking of this smelly, fly-blown, half-ruined sand-heap?

Privately, Trinesh held little hope of ever seeing his native city of Tumissa again, although he would never have admitted as much. What an officer cannot say to his troops may be whispered in prayer to one's god, the priests said, but in this case it was different: somehow he felt that ravening, fierce, uncaring Lord Vimuhla, the All-Consuming Flame, He Who Loves Conflagration and Red Ruin, would not understand . . .

"All taken, Sire," Horusel said from behind him.

Startled out of his reverie, Trinesh jumped and reached for his sword. It was not there; he had left it leaning against the wreck they had made of the door to the keep. He covered his embarrassment with sharp, efficient, military questions, the kind a good commander ought to ask.

"The outer enceinte? The upper floors? Any cellars where these sand-worms could stick their heads up their arses and hide?"

"Swept clean, *Hereksa*."

"Casualties? Prisoners?"

"Five dead in Fressa's *Semetl*; two in mine; two in Vinue's. Twelve or fourteen hurt bad enough to matter. No one else. —Prisoners?" He counted on his stubby fingers. "No Yan Koryani—they died to a man. A handful of Milumanayani: a half dozen warriors, a few women, some little ones."

"Tell the men to oil their weapons. Rust—" He stopped. Horusel hailed from the city of Penom in southern Tsolyanu, a place where everything rotted, molded, and corroded away overnight, where the biting insects were said to be as big as *Qasu*-birds, and where it was said that even gold rusted! No need to give Horusel such advice!

"A few of my *Semetl* want to offer flame-sacrifice, Sire—tonight. The Milumanayani are poor fare indeed, but they'll at least serve to show our devotion to the Flame Lord." Horusel watched his commander carefully, the planes of his seamed, hard cheeks as expressionless as slabs of stone. "Permission?"

Trinesh considered. Horusel was the staunchest supporter of the Temple of Lord Vimuhla in his *Kareng*; he had the special backing of their one assigned priest and a score of the troops. The priest, Chekkuru, belonged to the Vriddi clan of Fasiltum, moreover, and he was trouble: a member of the Incandescent Blaze Society, the inner circle of Temple zealots who took the commands of the God of Conflagrations quite literally.

Trinesh himself was a moderate: his faction held that the heady wine of religion should occasionally be diluted with the cold water of practicality. It was all very well to preach of burnings and ravagings and the Flame, but were not these events better enjoyed when they fitted in with the needs of this world—as well as the next, of course? Trinesh did not want to surrender too easily to the fanatics among his troops, but if he did not, they would complain that he was denying them the comforts of their faith.

"Have you wood for the sacrificial fire?" he asked at length.

The *Tirrikamu* hesitated. "A—a little, Sire. Some of the followers of the other Gods want it for cooking and to dry their clothes . . ."

Horusel knew which way Trinesh would decide; it was another gentle snare to prove that he, Horusel, was the more pious and hence better suited to command troops devoted to Lord Vimuhla and to Lord Chiteng, the lesser deity who served the Flame Lord as His "Cohort."

General Kutume hiTankolel, who commanded the Legion of the Storm of Fire, followed dread Lord Chiteng, but, people said, his primary deity really consisted of gold and silver coins. He would say nothing as long as things got done. It was lucky for Trinesh that their previous General, Lord Karin Missum, whose very nickname meant "Red Death," was no longer in charge. He had been promoted upwards—outwards, or sideways—because of his fanaticism, the rumor ran. Karin Missum would have ordered the Milumanayani captives burned just as soon as Fortress Ninu'ur was secured. Indeed, he would have had the Legion all heroes by now—and probably dead heroes at that! They had lost many good troops at the Battle of the Hill of the Stone *Serudla*, then more in the fight before the town of Mar, and still more when they swarmed over the walls of Sunraya. Piety might be "noble" in the eyes of the Gods and Their priesthoods, but when the record-scribes totted up their accounts, it was obvious that, like too much hot *Hling*-seed in the stew, religious zeal hurt more than it helped. No, Lord Kutume was *much* better for moderates like Trinesh—and for the Empire as well.

Trinesh temporized. "It's too wet tonight—too late, too much to do before we sleep. Some are wounded, and everyone is hungry. Keep your sacrifice—and the funeral pyre for our own dead—until morning. The sand-worms will burn just as well then. We had best look to ourselves now and leave Lord Vimuhla's needs till tomorrow." He raised a hand to cut off Horusel's protest. "Set Charkha and his *Semetl* at the gate—they made the lowest throw with the *Kevuk*-dice, did they not? Vinue's troops can patrol the walls. Fressa and Chosun will relieve them at half-night. Your people can stay here."

This last was a sop to Horusel's feelings: the old veteran was *Tirrikamu* of the first *Semetl*, while the others came lower down in the pecking order. Horusel's men would have the best and driest accommodations, and thus military propriety would be observed. The less grumbling, the quicker Trinesh would earn a promotion to *Kasi*—Captain—of a Cohort. His Clan of the Red Mountain would then do everything in its power to wangle him a promotion directly to General Kutume's headquarters staff. The General was said to be reasonable, provided one's clan made the proper gifts, and a moderate could find a safe harbor in his entourage. After that, why, who knew whither? Trinesh was still more than a little vague about his eventual ambitions. He was sure, however, that he did not want to remain a field soldier for the rest of his career. He was as certain of *that* as he was of tomorrow's dawn!

The *Tirrikamu* saluted, fist to breast, and departed. Trinesh sighed and looked about for a dry place to sleep. The cramped little rooms at the end of the hall were already filled with Horusel's people. Dineva, one of his female soldiers, had already got a fire going in one of them. She was a good trooper, one who ought to be promoted soon, a shrewd fighter, and reputedly as tough as a piece of untanned *Chlen*-hide. Nobody touched Dineva without an invitation. The camp wags had spent hours imagining what might happen if General Karin Missum himself had ordered her into his tent. The odds they gave were three to two in Dineva's favor. That particular bit of soldierly whimsy had never come to pass, unfortunately for the gamblers in the Legion.

Dineva rose and saluted him. "You want this place, Sire?"

"No—you people killed all the sand-worms and earned it for yourselves. Anywhere else?"

"Ai, there's a room on the other side of the hall—where the Yan Koryani officer slept. It's drier."

She had stripped off her armor and her soaking kilt. Trinesh eyed her angular nudity, but he was too tired. Not even the voluptuous curves of the Goddess Dlamelish herself could arouse him tonight! Moreover, he was no pretty-mannered city-soldier to favor his troops—male or female—on the basis of how well they danced on their backs upon his sleeping-mat. . . . And then Dineva was no great beauty either.

The room the woman had mentioned was indeed better, more private, and—to the point—dry. Trinesh's body-servant,

Bu'uresh, was already there, squatting before the sooty hearth and feeding its small fire with the papers and documents abandoned by the previous occupant. Who the Yan Koryani commander had been might never be known, but he—or she (the northern clans were matriarchal and employed more female soldiers than Tsolyanu did)—had certainly not been tidy. Scraps of yellowish *Hruchan*-reed paper were strewn everywhere: rosters, accounts, dispatches, orders, and all of the trivia of war. Some of the documents gleamed with gold and bright-hued inks, perhaps the commands of the Baron Ald himself. Had he not been so exhausted, Trinesh might have cared.

"Lord?" Bu'uresh looked up. "There's a little money here—silver, copper, a gold coin or two. If you want it. . . ." The rascal had probably already hidden away the bigger share for himself. Bu'uresh was a trifle *too* clever. He came from the western nation of Mu'ugalavya, and while the Mu'uga-lavyani were usually honest, slavery did seem to weaken that particular trait in a person.

"Keep it. What can I buy out here?"

Bu'uresh shrugged sleek, coppery shoulders. "Sand, Lord. Mayhap a Milumanayani chieftain's daughter."

Trinesh ignored his insolence. He squatted down upon the Yan Koryani commander's tattered sleeping-mat to remove the rest of his garments. The breast and backplates came off first, together with his belt of metal plaques and the tabardlike tasses that protected his thighs; then the stuffy, padded arming-jacket beneath; next the *Chlen*-hide greaves; then his soaking kilt; and finally his soft *Firya*-cloth undertunic.

He ran his fingers through his shoulder-length black hair, stretched muscles that ached from the burden of armor, sprawled his rangy body ("the pride of the clan-maidens of Tumissa," his schoolmates in the Temple of Vimuhla of his native city had jokingly named it) out upon the mat, and dragged another rolled mat over to cushion his head.

Something glittered there on the floor beneath the mat. He

looked closer—and was momentarily astounded to see his own triangular, sharp-nosed features staring back at him!

By the Three Fingers of the Flame . . . ! It was a mirror—a woman's little silver mirror. He picked it up.

This had never belonged to any Milumanayani desert harlot. It was beautiful: a dainty little trinket, its gold-inlaid back carved all around with unfamiliar Yan Koryani gods and heroes in low relief. There was some sort of symbol in the center, too: a stylized leaping flame. Whoever the woman had been, she must have served Lord Vimuhla, as Trinesh did, or whatever the northern equivalent of the Flame Lord might be. Moreover, she must have been as wealthy as an Imperial tax-collector: the thing looked like it might have cost a hundred *Kaitars*!

Interested now, Trinesh unrolled the other sleeping mat. There was a smudge of black *Tsunu* paste on it, the stuff women used to paint their eyes. He rubbed at it with his thumb. It was still greasily fresh. There was also a single long raven-hued hair caught amongst the coarse fibres of the mat. He sat up to find Bu'uresh standing by with a ewer of water and his little jar of scented *Puru*-oil, ready to massage him.

He held up the mirror. "Was Horusel done removing the slain when you came here?"

"Almost, Lord. Two or three sand-worms—put up no fight at all. A single Yan Koryani trooper. . . ." Bu'uresh's staccato Mu'ugalavyani accent made the deadly struggle that had just occurred in this room sound commonplace.

"No women?"

"None I saw. You want one of the prisoners—the sand-worms' hags? One of your lady soldiers—? Saina in Chosun's *Semetl* is not too bad."

Trinesh pretended outrage. "None of your affair! No more than I want you snuffling about between my legs, you . . ." He stopped, struck by a thought. "Send me Horusel—or one of his men."

The slave grinned but forbore from making the obvious jest connecting Trinesh with stiff, devout Horusel. This handsome, arrogant, young Tsolyani officer could be teased, but a slave must never go too far. Bu'uresh raised an eyebrow, went out, and returned with a soldier in tow: morose, long-faced Jirega of Horusel's *Semetl*.

"Where is the body of the Yan Koryani commander?" Trinesh began.

Jirega cast a glance toward the one tiny loophole in the western wall. "Outside, Sire. Dead. Enjoying the rain in his face." The man's tone hovered just barely within the bounds of military courtesy. He was one of Horusel's devoted followers.

"Who was he—she? What legion? What rank? You know their insignia."

The man scratched amidst the hairs of his pot-belly. "No one high, Sire. A man, an officer of their *Gurek*—as they name their Legions—of Niktanbo of Rülla. What they call a *Nümür*, I think—a commander of fifty. . . ."

"No Yan Koryani women? Courtesans? Female officers?"

"Ah, no, *Hereksa*." Jirega looked puzzled

It did not fit. Trinesh stumbled to his feet, tired joints cracking. "How well have you searched the cellars of his hovel—looked for hidey-holes in the walls?"

Jirega frowned. "Sire—*Hereksa*—we did the job. I—I don't think we missed anything. A pile of dirty grain-sacks, a wine-cellar without so much as an *Aqpu*-beetle in it, a—a closet or two. . . ."

Trinesh held out the mirror. "A *Nümür* of fifty owned this? Did he also wear the spangled skirts of a Jakallan dancing girl?"

Jirega blinked solemnly at the trinket, and the lines between his thick brows deepened. "No, Sire. No, of course not." He smiled, then, with all the toothy servility he could muster. "Oh, Sire, maybe a keepsake, a memento from his clan-wives?"

"*Chlen*-shit, man! This work? No piddling clan-boy from Rülla could afford this!" He pointed to the sleeping-mat. "Fresh *Tsunu* paste and a hair from a woman's tresses! There was a high lady here—recently, by the look of it. The road we came by is the only one in through the damned mountains, and no one escaped past us. Certainly no dainty trollop! No, there must still be somebody lurking somewhere in this hole!"

"Sire—"

Trinesh would be a laughingstock if this turned out to be a blow swung at empty air, but he had gone too far to back down. He said, "Get Horusel up. I don't care what time it is. Go over this worm-riddled ruin again—and again until you can swear upon your clan-father's tomb that no charming little Yan Koryani harlot is crouching in some oven or other, dagger ready to slit our gullets as we sleep!" He rounded upon Bu'uresh. "And you—! Don't burn any more of those damned papers—not until somebody who reads Yan Koryani looks at them! The Flame knows you may have destroyed too much already!"

He stood to watch Kirega depart at an undignified—and indignant—trot. Then he let out a long breath and began the slow process of putting his damp, sweat-stinking armor all back on again.

The great hall—which was hardly a hall, and certainly not great—danced with gusty torchlight when he entered it. Two of Horusel's soldiers dozed on the highest dais. Somebody had decided to turn the place into an infirmary, and the wounded slept or twisted restlessly beneath the driest blankets they had. Against the far wall, that nearest the door, two silent forms lay wrapped head to foot in blood-spattered sheets. A pair of the wounded had not survived. They would be added to the sacrificial pyre on the morrow, along with those already dead—and Horusel's prisoners.

The priest, Chekkuru hiVriddi, sat crosslegged beside the

bodies, his shaven head nodding in time to a mumbled litany to Lord Vimuhla. Those who worshipped one of the others of Tsolyanu's ten gods and their ten Cohorts would have to depart this life with whatever rites their co-religionists could manage. Chekkuru did not suffer unbelievers easily.

Trinesh expected to see Horusel, but it was Charkha, he who had been assigned to the outer gate, who met him instead. The *Tirrikamu* of the fifth *Semetl* towered over the rest of his troops, as thick through the chest as a *Mash*-tree trunk—and almost as devoid of brains, his men said. Charkha had his armor on, and the heavy one-handed war-axe that was the standard melee-weapon of their Legion swung loosely in his hand.

"Visitors outside, *Hereksa*," he said.

"Yan Koryani? Sand-worms? How many?"

"Tribesmen—scouts—maybe a score, maybe fifty. No regulars we could see. We potted one or two with our crossbows, but our strings were wet, and the men couldn't get off many shots."

"Spare strings?"

"Not enough. The rain would wet our extras. We didn't want to use more than we needed."

Trinesh spat. His cheek still pained him. "Double the watch."

Charkha grunted. "Already did."

He watched the subaltern leave. Then he returned to the business of getting the chin-strap of his helmet tied. The burgonet of the Legion of the Storm of Fire had cheek-pieces, an aventail of lappets and mail, and padding inside. It was hard enough to get on properly even when it was dry. The flame-crest was made of red-lacquered *Chlen*-hide and was permanently fixed to the helmet's crown, but he had removed the rain-bedraggled plumes. No matter; the gilding would tell his men who he was.

From where he sat by the wall the priest Chekkuru raised

his loaf-shaped bald head. "When you have a moment, *Hereksa*—"

"Now is good enough. What is it?"

"Sire," the man said softly. "Sire, these are noble dead—men who died in service to the Flame Lord. Persons who deserve respect. . . ."

Trinesh knew what was coming. "Of course. So?"

Chekkuru blinked at him, both eyes at once, like a *Chlen*-beast. "They should be cremated, Sire, before corruption can begin. Else do they go polluted unto Lord Vimuhla's Paradise of Ecstatic Flame."

"Not tonight. I already told Horusel that it all will be done in the morning—our dead, the prisoners, all in one sacrifice."

"I saw some beams in the shed in the courtyard. Not many, but enough—and a heap of straw for the savages' *Hmelu*-beasts. A pyre, now, tonight; that is what is proper." He laid a finger alongside his hooked, eastern, aristocratic, Vriddi nose.

Damn the man.

"No. Not now." The helmet at last sat snugly upon his head. "Morning will do. The bodies won't decay enough to summon Lord Sarku's Undead minions. Their souls will go on to the joys of the Flame."

" 'Wherever corruption and dead things dwell, there do Lord Sarku, Master of Worms, and his servant, Missum, Lord of Death, come forth to exult, to glorify putrescence, and to take possession forever . . .' " the priest quoted solemnly from "The Scrolls of Pavar." Musty texts larded with warnings and dire prophecies concerning the Gods and the Demon Lords of the Planes Beyond were Chekkuru's favorite reading matter. He conned those as avidly as Trinesh did the romantic odes of the Tumissan court-poets.

"Enough, man. As I say, all will be done properly at sunrise."

The priest gave him a sidelong glance but said no more. Trinesh saluted Horusel's guards in the little vestibule and clattered down the steps outside.

The night was as black as the inside of one of Lord Sarku's tombs. In a somber mood, Trinesh toured the gate, the three crumbling wall-towers—their ancient wooden floors so desiccated and riddled with *Oso*-beetle tunnels as to be perilous—and the battlements. Kashi and Gayel, Tekumel's two moons, might be up, but no one could have guessed it tonight: the sky was overspread with layers of scudding rain-clouds and fingers of drifting mist. The rock-strewn ravines and hillocks beyond the fort hugged their secrets to themselves, and the wind whispered of cold, damp things, of antiquity beyond remembering, and of hearts—human and other—full of hate and death. A thousand cloaked savages, a full Yan Koryani legion, might be out there for all the Tsolyani sentinels to see.

Something hooted and shrieked outside, far away. It might have been a *Zrne*, the terrible six-legged predator of the wilderness. It could also have been a signal. Trinesh shivered, even in his mantle.

"Sire," Horusel said from behind him. Trinesh jumped, and the *Tirrikamu* strove to repress a grin. The fellow was always doing that, a not-too-subtle way of discomforting his superior. One day Horusel would go too far! If the bastard were ever slain, Trinesh would see to it that Lord Sarku and his tomb-monsters would dine upon a sufficiency of corruption. He'd find some excuse not to cremate the man for a six-day!

"What?"

"*Hereksa*, we've found some Yan Koryani."

"What—? Where? How many?"

The subaltern didn't even have the decency to look apologetic; his expression was unreadable. "No idea of their numbers, Sire. They're hiding in the cellar, down in the well—back in a hole where we can't get at them."

Trinesh refused to give Horusel the satisfaction of hearing him groan. He turned, his aching legs as heavy as stone columns, and tramped back inside.

2

The cellar was not large: a single rectangular, windowless room beneath the main hall of the keep. The walls extended out in successive courses until they were joined by a flat capstone a man-height or so above Trinesh's head. The builders had not employed the true arch, a practice common among the petty warlords who had occupied the fringes of the Desert of Sighs after the fall of ancient Engsvan hla Ganga. A door opened off one of the shorter sides of the room, probably a store-cellar, behind which Trinesh could hear the captured Milumanayani moving about and murmuring amongst themselves. A child whined, and one of the adults shushed it.

Great Lord Vimuhla was said to delight in flaming human sacrifice, but Trinesh had always been too gentle—and, he had admitted to himself long ago in the temple school in Tumissa, too squeamish—to receive much spiritual benefit from the rite. Battle was different: it was "noble." One fought to win, and both Lord Vimuhla and His counterpart amongst the Lords of Stability, mighty Karakan, honored the warrior. If one were defeated and captured, there were just two options within the societies of the Five Empires: slavery or sacrifice. Ransom was sometimes possible for a prisoner of war who accepted slavery, but it meant coming home to face humiliation, and sacrifice was thus preferable for a "noble" person, male or female, human or one of Tekumel's nonhuman races, since it left one's dignity intact. A noncombatant was different in Trinesh's eyes. There was no glory in casting a woman or a child into the flames, not even the family of an enemy—no, not even a sand-worm's dirty relatives. He would do what he could to save the women and children from Chekkuru's warmly earnest little performance at sunrise.

The well occupied the center of the cellar floor, a circular shaft about a man-height across, surrounded by a low coping of mossy, green-stained bricks. Horusel's torch revealed only black depths; the water level was too far down to see. A rope swung limply from a bronze hook in the ceiling, its end neatly cut as with a sharp knife. There was no bucket.

Chosun, the *Tirrikamu* of the second *Semetl*, stood there, one booted foot up on the parapet. He waggled the severed rope-end at Trinesh.

"Hoi, *Hereksa*," he called jovially. "Sharp-toothed fish swim in our well."

"How many? How far down?"

Jalugan, one of the youngest of Chosun's troopers, glanced at the remaining rope. "About three man-heights, Sire. We had the bucket down. Someone sawed it—I felt it. Didn't see anybody, though."

"Cha! Anybody who goes down on the rope will be fish-food indeed!" The young soldier looked brash enough to try the feat, and Trinesh gestured him back. They needed all the men they had. "You'll be a nice haunch of *Hmelu*-meat dangling there while somebody sticks you with a spear out of a side-tunnel, man. Worse, your corpse will pollute the water."

"They may have spoiled the well already," Horusel said.

"Best get the troops above to collecting rainwater in helmets—pots, whatever we have, Sire. They can cut any bucket-rope we drop. We can't reach them with spears, and a crossbow won't fire straight down."

Trinesh hated to say so, but the veteran *Tirrikamu* was right. He gave the necessary orders.

There were still options; the easiest would be tried first. He leaned cautiously over the coping. "Ohe, down there," he called. "Any of you speak Tsolyani? Surrender and we'll see that you're not slain." He glanced up to see Chekkuru's heavy-lidded eyes watching him from across the parapet. It would be hard to keep any promises of clemency with the priest around. Cha! Let *him* go down there if he was so eager to be skewered!

There was silence.

"Go up to the shed in the bailey," he ordered loudly. "Get me a load of that damp straw—whatever else will make smoke. Lord Vimuhla may prefer roasted meat, but tonight we'll offer Him smoked sand-worm for dinner."

There was no reply from the well.

Trinesh sighed. The priest would get his flame-sacrifice—or at least a smoke-sacrifice. He snapped a command to Chosun, and the captives were led out of their storeroom and taken up above to one of the tower rooms in the bailey. Their Skeins of Destiny were still likely to be unpleasantly short; he could not just let them go, and Chekkuru would surely demand their unwilling participation in the Ritual of the Dawn of Flame in the morning.

Trinesh spent the rest of the night in the main hall, alternately dozing and staring at the floor. The fire below took a long time to burn itself out. Steam arose from cracks between the flagstones, and some of the shallower puddles actually bubbled. The flames must be drawing air through ventilation slots in the cellar walls, and the straw—drier underneath than it looked—burned merrily enough. If the gods willed, the ancient flooring would not collapse into the cellar! He was no architect to know about such things, but at least he had made sure that there were no wooden beams or posts supporting the cellar ceiling.

When Chekkuru came at dawn to demand the planking from a collapsed floor in one of the crumbling bailey towers, Trinesh could offer no logical objection. He pleaded exhaustion, however, and did not attend the sacrifice himself. Let the pious have their way. He also made no criticism when Chosun reported that the scrawny Milumanayani women and all of the children had squeezed out through a tower loophole and escaped in the night. Like himself, Chosun was somewhat of a moderate, although neither of them had ever discussed it with the other.

Bu'uresh brought him breakfast: *Dna*-porridge and wine liberally mixed with water, the best they had. The bailey shed contained several of the six-legged little *Hmelu*-beasts that everybody used for meat—and also for wool, along with the better stuff produced by their larger cousins, the *Hma*—only two were females and could give milk. It seemed best to save their animals until they really needed them.

"Fire's out, *Hereksa*," Horusel said. This time Trinesh was already on his feet. He had heard him coming.

The well-chamber was a blackened, smoke-stinking ruin. The place was silent except for the crackle of the dying fire. Three bodies lay crumpled amidst the embers, their charred garments marking them as Milumanayani warriors. They had doused their leather desert-cloaks with water and tried unsuccessfully to break through the heavy cellar door. Trinesh sent for the rope, and Jalugan, the youth from Chosun's *Semetl*, swung down into the shaft. He soon called up to say that a tunnel indeed led off horizontally from the well. It was empty. They passed a torch down to him, and he reported that as far back as he could see, perhaps ten or fifteen paces, there was no sign of the foe.

They made a rope sling, and two more troopers descended,

then Trinesh himself. A *Hereksa* had a duty to his men, after all. His eyelids felt like ground glass.

The passage was less than a long pace wide and barely high enough to stand erect. It slanted down in a series of concave steps cut into the solid rock. Trinesh was no scholar, but he did recognize volcanic stone: black and bubbled, filled with pockets of tuff and ash and all of the detritus vomited up from Lord Vimuhla's secret infernos below the earth. The enemy had attempted to put up a barricade some twenty paces farther on into the tunnel, but they had not found enough loose stone, nor had they been able to hang their desert-cloaks from the smooth ceiling. It took perhaps a *Kiren*—half an hour—to clear it all aside and move on. By this time most of the crossbowmen in Chosun's *Semetl* were with them, ready to deal with any Yan Koryani ambush.

They encountered no one.

Thirty paces beyond the barricade they came to a pit, an irregular, oval fissure in the slagged, ash-hued floor. The tunnel ended there, and Trinesh sent back for more rope, lanterns, and what trenching tools Fressa's *Semetl* had brought along. He need not have bothered. Their torches revealed a slope-sided, jagged crater about two man-heights deep. The irregular floor of this opened straight down into a vertical shaft, along one side of which rungs descended on into the darkness below, a ladder into the unknown. Both the walls and the rungs gleamed darkly silver, the color of age-stained steel.

Chosun held up a hand to prevent anybody from descending. "That's no water-well," he panted. The *Tirrikamu* was a big man, heavy-set and slow, not at all suited to explorations in caves. "A place of the Ancients, Sire. That's what it is."

"You are right," Trinesh replied. "We're already below the level of the well-water. I think we've left the softer rock, and now we're inside a sort of subterranean peak or dome of Lord Vimuhla's frozen flame-stone. It pushes up through the gravel and sand of the desert like a mountain in the midst of a lake. The epics say that Lord Vimuhla covered many of the cities of the Ancients with a blanket of fire when they defied Him before the Battle of the Gods at Dormoron Plain—''

''This flame-stone must then be very old indeed,'' Jalugan said from beside them. ''At home in Bey Sü our epic-singers tell of the sinking of the south—the Isle of Ganga and the end of the Engsvanyali Priestkings—and the rising of the north, where Yan Kor is now. They call it the Plain of the Risen Sea. To be older than that—as old as Dormoron Plain, if you are right, Sire—is ancient beyond measuring!''

The boy spoke truly. Trinesh decided to overlook his interruption, which under other circumstances would have been a breach of military etiquette. He turned to Chosun. ''What do you think?''

''We ought to send for the priest, Sire,'' the *Tirrikamu* grunted. ''He should know.''' He fingered the stained silvery walls of the shaft and shook his head.

The idea was eminently distasteful, but it made sense. A trooper was sent scrambling back up the tunnel to find Chekkuru hiVriddi.

Chekkuru came, pursed his lips, put a bony finger beside his nose, and cocked his head this way and that like a *Küni*-bird. ''You have come upon a holy thing, *Hereksa*,'' he opined. ''An entrance to Lord Vimuhla's fiery paradise beneath the world! To violate it is to call down demons and the anger of the Flame-Lord—''

''Oh, *Chlen*-shit, man,'' Trinesh sighed. ''Even I have heard of the metal places of the old ones, those who ruled Tekumel before the Time of Darkness. The epics are full of such marvels!''

''If you are so learned, why summon me?''

''Because I thought you'd know more. You've read enough to stuff the gut of a *Tsi'il*-beast.''

Chekkuru was not mollified. ''Fa, I have given you the benefit of my learning, but you choose not to believe. Do as you will; it is your throw with the dice!''

"If I send men down there and they die—either from demons or from Yan Koryani swords—yours will be the responsibility. The clans of the slain will come to you to demand *Shamtla*-compensation, and the Emperor's courts will gladly award it! You'll go to debtor's prison, thence to slavery—and how will you like kneeling at the feet of a fat clan-matron, a worshipper of bucolic Lady Avanthe, mayhap, or virginal Dilinala?" The others laughed, and some of the tension went out of them. Chekkuru did have his uses.

"I say no more," Chekkuru sniffed loftily.

Trinesh peered down into the shaft again. His previous solution ought to work here as well. "Send for more straw— boards, beams. Drop all of it down this Flame-accursed hole and toss a torch in afterward. Then cover the pit with water-soaked blankets. Any Yan Koryani at the bottom will smother as did their friends above." He cast a sly glance over at Chekkuru. "And if the place is inhabited by demons, why, then they must be Lord Vimuhla's *Hre-Niriu*, who are like sheets of living, raging flame; to them a little smoke will smell as sweet as temple incense!"

Jalugan left to carry out Trinesh's orders. The rest followed, Chekkuru in offended silence, carefully holding up the skirts of his pleated kilt to avoid the sooty walls. He resembled an old lady wading a mud-puddle.

The daylight above was another world. The skies still glowered, gray and misty as the robes of Lord Thumis, the Sage of the Gods. The rain had stopped, however, and from the flat roof of the keep Trinesh could see a dozen or so of his crossbowmen squatting here and there along the battlements of the bailey. Beyond Fortress Ninu'ur the desert was slate-gray and brown, an artist's charcoal sketch before the colors are applied. All appeared to be in order: no one had seen any Milumanayani scouts, and certainly no advancing columns of Yan Koryani.

Chekkuru's combined funeral and sacrificial pyre still smoldered in the courtyard. It reminded Trinesh of the stifling passage below and of the silent, deadly smoke that must already have done its work in the darkness. Suffocation was not a noble way to perish, nor was employing it a noble deed on Trinesh's part; yet how else to clear the fortress of the enemy? It was necessary. During a war, the Weaver of Skeins sometimes created very shoddy tapestries of fate for those involved.

Trinesh went to bed. —And awoke hours later to find Saina from Chosun's *Semetl* sitting crosslegged in his room, sorting through the captured Yan Koryani documents. Bu'uresh hovered behind her to assist.

Saina was a pleasantly pretty woman, round of face, and reasonably curved, though by no means young. A scar slashed down from one ear almost to her chin, and her nose was broad and concave rather than the straight, high-bridged paragon of beauty beloved of the Tsolyani poets, or the downward-hooked beak of the old aristocratic clans. Still, she was not ugly. It was said that Saina occasionally joined her comrades upon their sleeping-mats in return for lighter duties and even for coin, but Trinesh had never summoned her, nor was it really his affair. Like all of Tsolyanu's female soldiers, Saina was *Aridani*: a woman who declared before the jurists of the Palace of the Realm that she was independent of the strictures (as well as the all-enveloping, smothering protection) of clan and family. An *Aridani* was the legal equal of a male; she could be sued in the courts, hold Imperial posts, serve in the army—everything a male could do. Those who were not minded to declare *Aridani* status remained "good clan-girls," married at the behest of their elders, and enjoyed the security of a sheltered and dignified life in the clanhouse. Saina thus could do what she pleased as long as she kept up with her companions.

At the moment her immediate value lay in the fact that she hailed from the northern city of Mrelu and could speak and read Yan Koryani, though indifferently well. Fortunately, this was the language of the captured documents; had they been in Saa Allaqiyani, they would have been as illegible as lizard-tracks in the mud! Tsolyani and Yan Koryani were related to one another, though distantly, as was Milumanayani, the language of the damned sand-worms, but Saa Allaqiyani belonged to another family of tongues and was as alien to them all as fur to a fish!

"A visitor was coming, Sire," Saina said. "They were expecting somebody high." She held up a torn and slightly charred parchment. "Can't tell who because the end's gone." Trinesh cast a prickly glance at Bu'uresh, who managed to appear both innocent and sheepish at the same time. "Very high—the escort was a—a *Tokhn*, a commander of one thousand, an officer of about the same status as a *Molkar* in our army. Some other people are mentioned, but I can't riddle it all out."

"Nothing to say that the visitor left again later?"

Saina bent her dark head over the remaining papers. "Naught more, Sire."

The late morning light shone through the room's one loop-hole to transform her hair into a glinting, blue-black coronet of oiled steel. She had braided it and wound it round her head, both to get it out of the way and also to provide additional cushioning for her helmet. Trinesh had a sudden memory of his clan-sisters in Tumissa: Dlara and Shyal kneeling together upon a mat to sort out replies to some feast, Ebunan looking over their shoulders, giggling, hopeful that one missive would be from her current swain. It seemed like a different lifetime.

He dragged himself forcibly back to the present. "Ohe, and the metal tunnel in the cellar? Anything about that?"

"Maybe this: a copy of an old letter—it's dated last year before the Battle of Mar—to someone in their headquarters at Sunraya, about an important thing . . . Damn it all—" she swore jocularly and obscenely "—'See the enclosed attachment.' And that's not here." She saw Trinesh's eyes shift to Bu'uresh, who quailed. She hurried on. "More, I don't think a copy was ever kept—here's their symbol for 'secret dispatch.'"

He got up and began putting on his clothing. He felt her looking at him and wondered to himself whether one night he should indeed call Saina to his quarters. That would have to be left for later, however.

"Wait for me," he told her. "As soon as I've had a wash and some food we will go down to the cellar. There may be somebody there with whom you can practice your Yan Koryani."

Chosun and some of his troopers were already waiting for them at the end of the slanting tunnel. Trinesh bent and peered over into the metal shaft. The fire he had had lit there was nearly out—he must have slept half the day away. His eyes watered and he coughed. The place stank abysmally of smoke, and a few coals still glowed darkly red amidst the ashes. He pointed, and the soldiers began to climb down the metal rungs. They reached bottom—and had to dance a pretty step to get across the remaining embers without burning their boots. One man raised an arm to signal a further side-passage leading off from the shaft. Then he and his comrades disappeared into it, out of sight.

They waited, but no one returned to report. At last Trinesh descended to see for himself.

A short, metal-walled corridor led off horizontally from the base of the shaft. There was a double-leaved door there, also of metal, but it hung ajar on shattered hinges—not his men's work, Trinesh guessed, but Yan Koryani. The passage was featureless and empty, save for the remains of their fire: no bodies, nothing.

The chamber beyond was large: perhaps ten man-heights in length, seven or eight across, and three high. Chosun's men stood there, crouched in an awed huddle just inside the door.

They were staring not at the metal walls—nor at any enemy bodies, for there were none—but at what filled the center of the room.

A great silvery globe hung in the air before them. Perhaps a third of its bulk extended down into a black-mouthed shaft below it, a shaft that looked just big enough for the globe to fit inside, as a boy fits a kernel of *Dna*-grain into a reed blowgun.

The globe was gigantic. It must have been four or five man-heights in diameter, completely smooth, and as brightly polished as an egg laid only yesterday by some gargantuan metal bird. An oval outline, perhaps a man-height tall and half as wide, indicated some kind of door in the side facing them. Beside this, at waist-height, was a small, round indentation. Trinesh went closer to look. His eyes had not lied: the sphere—big as it was—actually hung in the air inside the mouth of the pit. He stared down into the hole and was rewarded by a dizzy view of metal walls that came together far beyond the reach of their light in the darkness below. This was a thing of the Ancients indeed!

Chekkuru arrived, looked, examined, mumbled a prayer, and then bustled over to them, eyes ashine with joyous zeal. "*Hereksa*," he crowed in an almost friendly tone, "we have come upon it! We have found it! Oh, we have a treasure here! The thing for which the wizard Subadim sought all his life, the goal of all the sages, the mystery revealed, the sublime and ultimate destination of all seekers . . ."

He stopped, spread his long arms wide so that his flame-orange robe swirled out dramatically about him, and intoned, "It is the Egg of the World!"

Even Trinesh could not find it in his heart to say, "*Chlen*-shit."

It was Chosun who broke the ensuing silence. "But—but was not the Egg of the World shattered when the gods fought amongst themselves at the Battle of Dormoron Plain? And did not Subadim the Sorcerer spend aeons seeking it thereafter on Thenu Thendraya Peak? And did he not later bargain a fragment of its shell to the Demon Tkel? And did not the wizard Metallja discover another piece and take it away with him to the Place of the Unstraightened City? So say the epics. . . ."

Chekkuru frowned. "There are other epics, man, and secret wisdom of which you know less than a *Dri*-ant does of the gods! There are the Scrolls of the Path of Burning kept in our temple in the forests of Do Cháka, the Stela of the Emperor Kanmi'yel Nikuma III, whose title is 'the Scourge of Vimuhla,' the Book of the Blazing Diagrams of Forever, the—the . . ." He ran out of dire citations and finished lamely, "In any case, there are many sources that say that the Egg of the World was *not* broken, that it was hidden by demons—that—"

"—That its yolk was made into an omelette within the skull of a certain priest!" someone snickered from the back of the room. Trinesh thought it was Saina.

"Enough of sacrilege! I shall make my report to Lord Huso hiChirengmai, the Preceptor of our Society of the Incandescent Blaze, himself!"

This had gone too far. "Respect the priest!" Trinesh commanded. "Show yourselves to be soldiers! Search this Flame-accursed hole! You, Jalugan, watch the door in that egg-thing! Let nothing come forth!"

Saina said, "Sire, come look here."

She stood in the center of the room, squarely in front of the closed hatch of the globe. She scuffed a foot in the dust. "Three squares of glass set in the floor side by side, *Hereksa*: this one's red, then a sort of yellow, then blue. You can see a little light down inside the blue one, flickering on and off like a lamp that's low on oil."

"What does it mean?"

"No idea— Sire. I've never heard the like of it. Why not ask the priest?"

"Chekkuru is now otherwise occupied."

Horusel and some of his stalwarts had just entered the room, and the priest was haranguing them upon the importance of carting this "Egg of the World" all the way back to Avanthar. As if they could get it out of here in the first place! The picture of Chekkuru rolling the great silvery ball along the rugged roadway back to the Emperor's Golden Tower was so funny that Trinesh snorted aloud, which earned him a puzzled look from Saina.

Chosun came over to report no Yan Koryani in the chamber and no other way out. There might have been footprints in the layers of dust on the floor, but their own men had already tramped through the place, and any such signs were obscured forever. The tunnel below the sphere was impossible: no rope was long enough for that! Chosun had also tried an experiment: he had dropped a torch into the shaft below the globe. It had never struck bottom, he said, but had tumbled and dwindled and disappeared into the depths as though the pit were a fathomless abyss leading straight out of the world into Lord Vimuhla's flaming paradises themselves!

"If there were any Yan Koryani here, they might've jumped into the hole, Sire," Chosun said. "That's their 'Way of Nchel,' their path of resignation: suicide, a way to end a Skein of Destiny that's too badly tangled in this life. Any who decided to live—and fight—must still be inside the egg."

The latter possibility had already occurred to Trinesh. Anyone who tried it ought to be dead of suffocation, of course. If the egg had ventilation holes, the smoke should have done its work; if not, the air inside must have exhausted itself hours ago. Could the globe have its own air supply? It was clearly magical, after all, and who could tell what the Ancients might have wrought?

"Horusel?"

"Here, Sire." The *Tirrikamu* strode forward into the torchlight.

"Station half a *Semetl* of crossbowmen where they can fire in through that hatch from two directions, five men on one side, five on the other."

He had to be sure. It was time for a final test.

When all was ready he summoned Jalugan. "Push the little indentation beside the hatch. Then fall flat—roll, get out of the way."

It was well that he took precautions. Something inside the globe clicked, and the hatch swung smoothly open. Jalugan had just time to yell a warning before sprawling down on the very lip of the pit. A flare of ravening scarlet radiance roared out from within the egg-thing, accompanied by a sizzling, screeching sound like red-hot metal thrust into a smith's tempering bath. Three figures came hurtling out of the hatch even before the light had died away to darkness. Trinesh glimpsed corselets of overlapping metal scales, helmets with nose-guards and back-swept crests, oval shields, and wicked, three-pointed spears that resembled fishermen's tridents.

Caught directly in the naked scarlet glare, the crossbowmen on Trinesh's right exploded into gray ash, their bronze buckles and accouterments splattering molten globules over the wall behind them. They did not even cry out. Chekkuru must have approved; it was a good death for worshippers of the Flame. Too bad the priest had not been included, Trinesh thought, but he could hear him squalling invocations somewhere in the dark.

There was chaos. The spell-caster, some sort of priest or wizard, stood gazing out of the hatch for a moment more; then he crumpled forward, four crossbow quarrels protruding from his back like the spines of a *Nenyelu*-fish. The three Yan Koryani soldiers were already locked in a confused, swirling, clattering melee with the crossbowmen, Horusel, Chosun, and several of Trinesh's axe-wielders. Men shouted, and torches danced wildly amidst the frenzy of battle.

He himself got his sword up just in time to parry a blow

from a fourth opponent who came leaping out of the egg-
thing over the sorcerer's body. This was no human but one of
the *Nininyal*, the Pygmy Folk, who lived in the arid northeastern wastelands of Yan Kor and were Baron Ald's loyal
allies. It was manlike, except for a short, heavy tail, as small
as a child, and furred all over. Its cruel, beaked jaw gaped
open to display sharp, peglike teeth.

The creature was almost too fast for Trinesh. He cut,
parried left, and slashed. He must have hit it because it
squawked and scrambled away toward Dineva behind him. It
seemed more interested in flight than in combat.

Dineva had her shield up, but the furry beast simply seized
the upper rim and swarmed over. The weapon it carried, a
weighted poleaxe barely the size of a human soldier's hatchet,
smashed down upon her helmet, but at that angle and range it
could not have hurt her much. She jammed her axe-spike up
into the creature's belly as it clambered over her shoulders,
and it squalled loudly, fell behind her, and struggled to rise.
Dineva kicked it, danced back to clear her head, and smashed
down with her weapon. It lay still.

Trinesh got in one more blow against the unshielded right
side of one of the Yan Koryani troopers. He thought that it
struck home, under the man's armpit instead of against his
breastplate, but he could not be sure. Then it was over. A
matter of seconds, and a half dozen of his comrades lay dead
or wounded, their bodies jumbled together with those of the
three Yan Koryani officers. The chamber still echoed with the
clash of battle, and it stank of blood and bowels and sweat.

Chosun emerged panting and red-faced from the press.
"May be more inside," he gasped. Perspiration glazed his
plump cheeks beneath his helmet.

"Careful, then!" Trinesh called. "They may have more
magic! You—and you—tend to the wounded—see if any of
the Yan Koryani still live!"

Jalugan and the crossbowmen edged toward the hatch as

they had been taught, in cautious patrol formation, three covering while the other two sprinted forward. One man crouched by the hatch and peered inside. He signaled for the rest to come up, and at last Jalugan waved for Trinesh to join them.

The only occupants of the egg-thing's single little room were two women.

The taller of the pair looked to be in her twenties. She was almost as long-limbed as Trinesh himself; slender, dark, and intense-looking, and attired in the same red-lacquered scale armor and maroon tunic as her soldiers. She had no helmet, and her long black tresses swung out like the wings of a bird from her flushed, high-boned cheeks. She held a curved sword, its blade thickened near the point and weighted like an axe; this she dropped when Trinesh would have advanced upon her. She spread her hands.

Jalugan stood watchfully before the other woman, a girl of perhaps eighteen summers. This one wore a chemise of deep scarlet cloth, an ankle-length skirt of black bordered with geometric designs in glittering red and green brocade, and a little skullcap of enameled and begemmed *Chlen*-hide: a pretty girl, not as luminously beautiful as the other but still lovely enough to set any bravo in Bey Sü to warbling odes in honor of her heart-shaped face and the arrows of her eyelashes! She was neither a soldier nor a priestess by the look of her. La, she reminded Trinesh of his clan-sister, Shyal! The girl shot a nervous glance at her companion and then she, too, let her hands hang open at her sides in surrender.

"Let me bind them, Sire." Horusel had entered the sphere behind them. "They may have weapons—may try to escape." He gave the women a broken-toothed smile, but his words were for Trinesh. "When you're done with them, you can pass them on to the men. And when they're finished, Chekkuru can earn us Lord Vimuhla's gratitude by feeding them to the Flame."

"There is no need for bonds," the older woman said. Her

Tsolyani was passable, but she spoke the language with the dark, burring accent of the north. "Do as you will with me—I am a warrior, and I will sing my death-song when the time comes. But let my maid, here, go. She does you no harm."

"Have you chosen your 'Way of Nchel,' then?" Trinesh asked. "You submit?"

"I will fight you with neither swords nor spells. On that you have my oath. I swear it—for both of us—upon my clan-mother's eyes."

Trinesh nodded and retreated a pace to make room for Saina and Dineva. "Search them, take any weapons and that one's armor. Watch for hidden daggers—and magical devices. Use force only if necessary. One of them is noble, I think: maybe the visitor mentioned in the commandant's document." He put on a fierce glare for Horusel's benefit. "As for our entertaining ourselves, that will not be allowed. Not with the warrior-woman, nor with the girl, not unless she be a professional harlot and is properly paid for her services. Else will you treat them with dignity. A heavy ransom will give you more ecstasy than would a year alone with either or both of these ladies."

"Sacrifices, then, Sire?" Horusel persisted. "If they can't be ransomed, I mean. Or if they or their clans refuse? We ought to honor the Flame-Lord. Chekkuru—"

The priest surprised him. From somewhere amidst Trinesh' soldiers, his voice came as clearly as a temple *Tunkul*-gong. "These persons must be held either for ransom or for more appropriate sacrifice, *Hereksa*. Look at their garments: scarlet armor and dark red kilt, the livery of the Legion of the Isle of Vridu, which lies off the northern coast of Yan Kor. Vridu is the center of the worship of the Lord of Sacrifice, who is an Aspect—or another name—of our own mighty Lord Vimuhla. These ladies thus deserve a high ritual in a great temple, not a bonfire in a mud hovel such as this place!" He paused.

"They might choose to enter the sacrificial flames voluntarily, their 'Way of Nchel,' to expiate the shame of their defeat here."

"I think," Trinesh said, "that it is time to name ourselves. I am *Hereksa* Trinesh hiKetkolel of the Legion of the Storm of Fire. My clan is that of the Red Mountain."

The older woman replied gravely, "And I am Belket Ele Faiz, *Tokhn* of the Legion of Vridu, as your priest has already guessed. I am of the clan of the Fishers of Vridu. This is my maid, Jai Chasa Vedlan."

"Sometimes they use three names when they're of high lineage, Sire," Saina murmured. "The first is their personal name, the second that of their mother's clan-ancestor, and the third is their father's, who is not so important in the north. The lineages they mention are good ones."

"You escorted a visitor," Trinesh continued. "Where is he—she?"

"Outside. Dead. The sorcerer, Qurtul Hne Tio. Your people slew him."

"And your mission here?"

She made a circular gesture. "This."

Dineva turned the woman roughly around so that she could reach the buckles on her corselet of scale armor. She made no protest. Saina ran her hands over the girl's body, then exclaimed and held up a little knife, a handspan long. The Yan Koryani ate with implements like this, rather than with their fingers.

Trinesh cleared his throat. There would be time for more questions later, and they had not yet inspected their prize, this egg-thing.

The chamber occupied only about two thirds of the globe; the two prisoners stood against a vertical bulkhead which Trinesh intuitively guessed to be the back of the cabin. The door-hatch was just forward of this on the right. The roof was curved, the room small and cramped, not quite three man-heights long and two wide. There must be a considerable space beneath the floor, however, since the ceiling was low enough to graze his flame-crested helmet. As they had surmised, the globe did seem to have its own air supply; he felt a continuous soft breeze upon his face from vents in the ceiling. Three rows of metal frames, like tall chairs or benches, were bolted to the deck, but their cushioning had long since fallen away to dust; the ages before the Time of Darkness were inconceivably remote. These curious seats looked uncomfortable to Trinesh, who was accustomed to sitting, eating, and sleeping upon reed mats spread upon the floor. Cushions and back-rests were common in Tsolyanu, but these chair-things were overly high: they were too small to sit upon crosslegged, and one's feet would hang down unpleasantly to rest flat-footed on the floor. Somebody—the N'lüss or the Ghatoni, he remembered—did prefer high seats like these. But then civilization had yet to reach those remote northern climes.

Along the front wall a rounded gray housing extended back toward the first row of benches, like a sloping waist-high table. The top of this contained a single row of ten bosses, little black knobs, rather like the rivets on a cuirass. Above this odd piece of furniture was a flat pane of gray glass, a poor sort of mirror, in which Trinesh could dimly see his own face. Three more such large mirrored plaques lined the side walls, and all around them were more rows of little studs interspersed with smaller circles and squares of transparent glass, within which delicate designs, lines, needles, letters, and unreadable numerals were visible. The Ancients had strange tastes in ornamentation!

The mirrors brought back an urgent memory. He spun around to face the older woman, whom Dineva had now stripped down to a soldier's tunic and short, knee-length skirt. Her armor and a dagger-belt lay in a heap beside her upon the floor.

"Where is your baggage?" he demanded. "We found nothing in the fortress above—no clothing, no personal articles save for this one little mirror here." He proffered it to her. She took it, smiled ruefully, and passed it on to her maid. Trinesh waited, but she made no further reply. He turned and called, "Hoi, Chosun—Horusel! Search the floor and that wall back there for hidden compartments!"

The captives were shoved against the left bulkhead. The investigation was quick, thorough, and very fruitful: a dozen little closets and chambers and niches and receptacles. Most were empty, although a few held enigmatic artifacts, certainly not of modern manufacture. Chosun discovered a large sliding hatch in the floor; this he opened to reveal a welter of housings, rods, metal tubes, and bars, none of them easily removable—or intelligible. Jalugan found the prize, however, a largish panel in the rear wall.

"Here's their gear, Sire—" he called.

It was almost the death of him. There was a scuffling noise, and the young soldier gasped and fell backward upon Dineva, his face a mask of blood.

Trinesh yelled something, he did not know what, and stumbled against the table along the front wall. His outflung hands scraped along the row of little black knobs. Horusel already had the older woman by the hair, bending her backward over his knees, his axe-blade hooked around her throat. The girl struggled in Saina's arms. There was pandemonium. Soldiers scattered, Chekkuru howled, Dineva struggled to her feet, and Chosun knelt to shield Jalugan.

Something appeared in the darkness inside the rear hatch, a vulpine, furred, beaked face: another of the Pygmy Folk!

"Hold, or this woman dies!" Horusel cried.

The grayish-white beak withdrew into the darkness of the rear compartment. The beast shrilled something in guttural Yan Koryani.

"Crossbows!" Trinesh ordered. He could see the little

monster skulking back in there, a double-bladed dagger, the weapon that had wounded Jalugan, gleaming in its three-fingered paw. He spared a glance for the young soldier: Chosun was caring for him.

"Kill us or not, it is already too late for you!" the woman spat.

None of them had heard the outer door click shut. Only now did Trinesh sense motion. They were moving: the whole damned egg-thing was moving!

His stomach told him that they were descending straight down.

"Ohe, *Hereksa* of Tsolyanu." The woman squirmed about in Horusel's iron grasp to gaze full upon him from dark, slitted eyes. "We are your prisoners, but shortly you will be ours. This thing, this sphere, is one of the Ancients' tubeway cars that travel beneath the world! Soon we shall disembark in Yan Kor."

3

The children were not allowed into the Pavilion of the Eternally Valiant. The vast, domed chamber at the top of the keep contained temptations, however, that no boy—or girl, in matriarchal Yan Kor—could resist: tattered banners, shields bearing the marks of blows struck for causes no one could now recall, spears, swords, axes, armor, and even a great *Sro*-dragon head, whose ebon glass eyes still glared ferociously, though it had been slain and stuffed long before their grandmother's grandmother had walked upon the green and black mosaic pavement of the hall.

Ridek, the eldest, was twelve, and he knew enough not to touch things. The table upon the low dais in the center of the room, for example, was littered with scrolls, books, chests, reed pens, and inkpots. A goblet of filigreed gold set with bosses of blue-green malachite lay overturned there upon a stack of parchments, buff and brown and creamy-white, all crinkly, their rows of letters smeared with sticky, dark red wine. Ridek could read some of the documents, but others were in cipher, in Saa Allaqiyani, his father's native tongue, or in one of the other languages of the Five Empires that he did not know. By twisting his head and craning, he could thus glean tantalizing snippets of battle reports, petitions from the clans, news of troop movements and supply columns, tidings of merchant caravans to strange lands, even letters relating to dark matters of espionage—a thousand things. But to move a single sheet a finger's breadth was to rouse the wrath of their father, the Baron Ald of Yan Kor. That was not an event to be desired.

Sihan, who was Ridek's brother and younger by a year, hissed, "If father finds us here, we shall all be impaled."

He had come up behind Ridek and now stood gazing down into the chaos on the table. Sihan would have liked nothing better than to poke through their father's papers for he had more scholarship than Ridek. Sihan was not very brave, however.

"Father does not impale people." Ridek glanced over at their sister, Naitl, who was six. Naitl cried easily and that could bring the servants or even stern Lord Fu Shi'i, their father's counselor. Somebody would eventually have to do something about Sihan; his fervid imagination was fast becoming a matter of concern to them all.

Naitl balanced on her father's broad, low stool of carven *Ssar*-wood to stroke the bejeweled hilt of the great sword that lay atop the litter upon the table. The weapon was splendid indeed, damascened and engraved; yet it held little interest for Ridek. It was a sword of state and not a real fighting blade. So far as he was concerned, its best use was to hold down papers against the breeze that rustled in off the Northern Sea through the pillared portico at the end of the room.

Ulgais, the youngest of the three brothers, raised his sleek black head to stare at one of the mosaic squares of the chamber floor. He often sensed things, although he had not yet seen his third birthday when his head would be shaved to make him into a real person. Now he was just a baby.

"He sees someone," Sihan stated darkly.

It was so. The air above the square shimmered, turned muzzy gray, and became a flickering oval. The children drew together to watch. The atmosphere thickened, and a being took shape there.

It was not a man. Skin of a deep bronze-red hue, with darker fur so short that it was like the nap of a carpet down its back and around its jaws and ears, a fanged bestial snout, six dark nipples on its belly, hands that had five fingers and a thumb, a costume that consisted of no more than a harness of straps and pouches: it was a Mihalli. Ridek, who fancied himself a warrior, took up the great sword. It was almost too heavy for him to lift.

"Hoi! It's only Aluja." He let the weapon fall again and ran around the table to greet the creature.

"Master Ridek! What do you here?" Like all Mihalli, this one spoke Yan Koryani with a lilting, musical accent. The gutturals and crackling consonants of Ridek's language seemed beyond its abilities.

The Mihalli were creatures of legend; few among the Baron's vassals knew that the old tales were true and that this nonhuman species still existed upon Tekumel. Fewer still were aware of the Baron's alliance with them and of their aid to Yan Kor. None, not even Ridek, could say what hold the Baron had over them, for the Mihalli were otherwise said to be so whimsically alien that none could fathom their purpose or name them as friends. They were great sorcerers; they traveled between the Planes; and they were shape-changers, able to take on the semblance of almost any being of their own size and hence move about freely in the midst of humankind in a variety of guises. Dangerous, strange, and yet—to Ridek, who had seen them come and go throughout his childhood—as familiar as his own brothers.

"You won't tell?"

"Father will impale us," Sihan muttered gloomily.

"No fear of that. We keep our secrets, eh?" The Mihalli

gathered Ridek up in its arms, and he inhaled the gamy, animal scent of its body. People said that the Mihalli were both male and female at once, but Aluja always acted more like a male than otherwise. Ridek wriggled free; he was no longer an infant.

"Father comes," Ulgais said. No one could say how he knew, but he was usually correct. All four of them scattered off into the nether regions of the hall, leaving Aluja alone upon the figured mosaic in its center.

The bronze doors boomed open, and two chamberlains entered to touch long tapers to the torches in the sconces along the walls. They were still at it when Ridek's father, the Baron Ald of Yan Kor, tramped into the room.

The man who styled himself *Arsekme*—"Baron"—of Yan Kor, was both tall and wide. "The Gate That Does Not Open," his present wife and the mother of his children, Lady Mmir Chna Qayel, styled him. Ridek was proud of his father: as thick through the chest as a fortress donjon and visibly almost as formidable, in spite of the encroachments of age. He had the longish torso and short, bowed legs of a Saa Allaqiyani mountain man, however, a feature Ridek was secretly glad he had not inherited. The Baron wore a square-cut black beard, but his head was shaved in the fashion of the chieftains of Saa Allaqi, one of whom he had originally been.

Ridek knew that story by heart: how his father had fled Saa Allaqi to avoid being slain by his brother who yearned to become *Ssao*—king—and had the ambition and the troops to do so; how he had served as a mercenary in the army of the terrible Seal Emperor of Tsolyanu; how the venal Tsolyani generals had betrayed him and left him to die upon Kaidrach Field; how he had sold his sword to the victors, the Yan Koryani, as a defeated mercenary had the right to do; how he had gone on to fight for Yan Kor and later to unify much of the north under his own banner; how he had offered the Tsolyani his submission and feudal allegiance—the original reason for his title *Arsekme*, "Baron"—in return for a measure of independence for the northlands; and how the Tsolyani had answered by sending expedition after expedition to crush him. None had succeeded.

Then came the terrible part of the tale, the part Ridek knew only through snatches of gossip overheard in Ke'er's cavernous corridors: how Ald had taken the Lady Yilrana of the High Clan of Ke'er as his mistress—she would have been his wife, but he was not so mighty in those days, and her clan-matriarchs spurned the match; how the Tsolyani general Kettukal hiMraktine had been ordered north to defeat Yan Kor, and how Kettukal had sent his sub-commander, Bazhan hiSayuncha, to besiege Ke'er when Ald was absent upon another campaign; how Bazhan had demanded Yilrana's surrender; how she had nobly—and naïvely—refused; and then when the citadel fell, how Bazhan had had her impaled upon a tall stake before the shattered gates, as the Tsolyani did to any stubborn rebel.

There was more: how, after the Tsolyani had left, Ald had returned to Ke'er and found her there; and how, still later, his allies, the nonhuman Pygmy Folk, whom the Tsolyani called *Nininyal* and the Yan Koryani *Nyenu*, both of which denoted "Little Ones," had captured Bazhan in an ambush.

What the Baron had done to Bazhan then was not part of any tale; doubtless it did not bear repeating.

The rest of the story was sad. Yilrana was dead. Even now it was obvious that the pain of her passing lay ever just below the surface of the Baron Ald's heart, a fanged shoal beneath cold gray waters. He cried out in his sleep, the servants whispered, though he had gone on to marry Yilrana's clan-cousin, Ridek's mother, Lady Mmir. The tides of time may sink a man's sorrows deep into the abysses of memory, but well do the sleep-demons know how to dredge them all up again! Some reefs do not wash away but cause the recharting of all of the courses of one's life thereafter.

Now Yan Kor was at war with Tsolyanu, and the Baron Ald would carry his revenge beyond Bazhan hiSayuncha to

those who had sent him: to General Kettukal hiMraktine, to
the proud aristocrats of Avanthar, and even to the Seal Emperor himself, he who had been Ald's friend before ascending
the Petal Throne of Tsolyanu. The Baron Ald was no un-
skilled clan-maiden, as his Lady Yilrana had been, to be
beaten by such as they! Not he! His enemies would run like
squealing *Hmelu*-beasts when he came. Ridek only wished he
were old enough to fight beside him.

Tonight the Baron wore a jerkin of dark green leather, a
short kilt embroidered with the emerald blazon of his wife's
people, the High Clan of Ke'er, and buskins of black-dyed
Vrigalu-hide. He tossed a long, jewel-encrusted rod down
into the clutter already on the table: the "Amethyst Scepter of
the Clans United." He must have just come from another
interminable meeting with his vassals: the clan-patriarchs,
the noble lords, the supreme pontiffs, and all the other high-
titled rulers of the petty principalities from which he had
cobbled together this present nation of Yan Kor.

He looked around, saw Aluja standing in the middle of the
hall, and grunted, "Ohe, Mihalli! News?"

"Some, Sire. The Tsolyani have reinforced the town of
Mar. Their Milumanayani puppet, Firaz Mmulavu Zhavendu,
has come over to our side, however, and his people will aid
us in its retaking."

The Baron picked up the goblet and peered underneath the
table for a wine-jug. He came up empty-handed. "That is
well. The bastard finally believes us: he's not to be Governor
of eastern Milumanaya after all. He slew his own father to
earn the post, but now the Tsolyani won't give it to him!" He
chuckled, deep in his throat. "That's very like them!"

"So it is. The Emperor has ordered General Kuruktashmu
hiKetkolel away from his Legion of the Lord of Red Devastation and given him the governorship Firaz coveted for himself."

"I know Kuruktashmu. Another of Lord Vimuhla's blazing
religious fanatics! Prince Mirusiya must be overjoyed—and
his brothers dismayed to the same measure! Mridobu in par-

ticular: he's probably chewing on the Petal Throne itself by now! Almost all of their eastern army serve Gods friendly to Mirusiya's Lord of Flame. Who will command Red Devastation, then?''

''Probably the one they call Karin Missum, 'the Red Death.' General Kadarsha hiTlekolmü of the Legion of the Searing Flame is to be promoted to Senior General of the eastern front, under Prince Mirusiya himself.''

''La! Some of the Prince's 'New Men': little folk who rose to power when he did. This Karin Missum is well nigh a foam-lipped maniac, a member of the Incandescent Blaze Society. Flaunt one Yan Koryani arse in his direction, and he'll snatch up a brand from the nearest campfire to chase it! We can easily lure him into doing something stupid. The other—?''

''A moderate, Lord. New at war, a man more suited to conning scrolls and dithering with theologians than commanding troops. . . .''

The Baron smiled lopsidedly. '' 'A weak bow soon breaks,' eh? They are like Mirusiya's other toadies, the greedy General Kutume and General Mnashu of Thri'il, who began his distinguished career as a market roustabout. Cha, we'll handle them!''

''Ah, Sire. General Mnashu has shifted to the party of Prince Eselne. He is being transferred to their western army. It is said that he could not stomach the zealots of the Incandescent Blaze. . . .''

'' 'A sharp axe cuts any tree.' We'll deal with them all.''

The Baron waved the empty goblet, and one of the chamberlains slipped out, his felt slippers making hushing noises upon the flagging. The other squatted in a corner, to all appearances a statue of emerald-robed bronze.

''So, Aluja? What of our battle-plan?''

The Mihalli's eyes were pupilless ruby orbs in the flaring torchlight. He—for want of a better pronoun—spoke in a quick, brusque tone, an unconscious imitation of a human soldier reporting to his commander. "Mirusiya's army is mostly in Sunraya. Your people stand ready to retake Mar and thus cut the Tsolyani supply lines. Mirusiya must send reinforcements to clear the road, but General Ssa Qayel—"

"Ohe. How is he? Mmir will ask." General Saa Chna Qayel was Lady Mmir's brother.

"Hot and sunburned, Lord." The Mihalli essayed a human smile. "He has prepared a trap in the mountains along the *Sakbe* road east of the Pass of Skulls. The Tsolyani must keep to that road, for their wagons cannot travel off of it—their *Chlen*-beasts would find only gravel to drink and thorn-bushes for fodder. Their legions are too heavily armored to deny you the hinterlands, and all Mirusiya has for scouts are his squadrons of flying Hlaka. Your Hlaka outnumber his and will drive them off. The Tsolyani will thus stay both blind and thirsty until the trap is sprung, and then your units will attack their column from every side at once and slaughter it. Thereafter General Kuruktashmu must come out of Sunraya or starve. He'll be caught in your pincers: your own troops down from Tleku Miriya in the west, and the Saa Allaqiyani from the east. The Milumanayani tribes—more or less united under Firaz Mmulavu Zhavendu—will harass them—"

The Baron would have spat but thought better of the time-hallowed sanctity of the hall. "I trust that sand-worm about as much as I do the Tsolyani! No, less! A little gold, and he tilts back into the Emperor's hand. 'The tree sways in the direction of the wind.' "

"He is useful—for now." The Mihalli turned his sleek, beastlike head to look at the doors of the chamber.

Someone else was coming.

It was Ridek's mother, Lady Mmir Chna Qayel. With her was another: a tall, exotic-looking woman of nearly thirty summers. This was the Lady Si Ziris Qaya, named "the Princess of the North," ruler of the Lorun tribes who wandered the desolate wastes beyond northern Yan Kor, all the way up to the Cold White Land where nobody went.

When she had first come to Ke'er the Lady Si Ziris Qaya had worn a beast-skin about her waist, a half-cape of silvery *Mnor*-fur, leather leggings—and that was all. She had perforce adopted the Yan Koryani court costume of loose overblouse and long, fringed skirt, but it was clear that she hated it. She had never quite surrendered to all of the dictates of the civilized south and still wore the wide cincture of *Zrne*-hide that marked her as a chieftainess of the Lorun. Her heavy tresses, too, were done in foreign fashion. They were as dark as anyone else's, but they were wavy rather than straight, and in the sunlight they glinted red instead of blue-black. Tonight she had bound them up in a net of glossy-green leather cords and did not wear the little skullcap of begemmed and enameled *Chlen*-hide that most Yan Koryani women favored.

She and Ridek's mother made an odd picture together: where Lady Mmir was small, wiry, slender, and dark, Lady Si Ziris Qaya was big-boned and fair—as fair as people ever were on Tekumel: a light-copper, ruddy-saffron hue, like a gold coin seen by candlelight.

Ridek knew, as did all Yan Kor, that his father slept with both of these women. Lady Mmir was his legal wife and a highborn clan-heiress in her own right, but Yan Koryani society was not monogamous. The clan-matrons ruled nearly everything and told the menfolk whom to marry; yet once wed, custom permitted any free person—male or female—to take further spouses, concubines, or temporary bed-mates as he or she willed. To display jealousy was a sign of weakness; it was not "noble." Lady Mmir therefore gracefully made the best of the situation and had become fast friends with this barbarian "Princess of the North." Outwardly, at least. Ridek could sense an underlying tension between them, just as Ulgais could "feel" the presence of sorcerous power.

If there was jealousy—and there was—it was not altogether sexual by any means. The Baron did not feel the same love for Lady Mmir as he had for Lady Yilrana; this present marriage was founded not so much upon devotion as upon mutual advantage. The High Clan of Ke'er needed his charisma to keep Yan Kor from crumbling back into a muddle of puny, squabbling city-states, just as he required the power of his wife's clansmen in order to maintain it. Lady Mmir was the brooch that pinned the cloak together. Once Ald felt himself totally secure, she could be replaced by any woman who could dislodge the memories of his lost Yilrana— improbable though that seemed—or who could serve his purposes better than Lady Mmir. If this fair-complexioned northerner managed to snip the threads that bound Ald to her, Lady Mmir would lose much—though not all, by any means. As senior wife, and eventually clan-matriarch, she would wield power as long as she lived. She bided her time.

The Lady Si Ziris Qaya might be shrewd, but the Lady Mmir was still cleverer. The Lorun woman must watch her step in Ke'er.

For now, the Baron's affair with Lady Si Ziris Qaya was good politics. Her uncouth tribesmen were indisputably loyal to her, and they were necessary to his war of revenge against the Tsolyani. How he got them was a matter of statecraft, not something to be criticized on such "ignoble" grounds as who slept with whom. Ridek could name at least a score of women who had shared the sleeping-mat of the Baron of Yan Kor. He himself was only twelve, but he could hardly wait until his fourteenth birthday, when he would become a man and his father would gift him with a concubine or two of his own. He already had his heart set on a certain Hris, the daughter of Lord Ku'arsh of Yan Kor City . . .

Ridek could not hear what his mother was saying, but she was laughing. Her eyes sparkled, and her heavy bracelets jangled as she recounted some bit of gossip. He heard the Lorun woman's lower, foreign voice purr something in reply. They had come to enjoy the night breeze, then, here at the very summit of the keep—and probably neither wanted the other to be alone with the Baron. For his part, Ald showed no favoritism but waved them both to sit upon the lower stools set around the table. He seated himself crosslegged upon his own higher chair. It looked as though it might be a long evening.

The Baron made a great show of sniffing the air. "Hoi!" he cried. "There are foes in this room!"

Lady Si Ziris Qaya flinched and stared about, but Lady Mmir only smiled. Ridek knew that his father had noticed that the sword of state had been moved from one side of the table to the other. He had the sharp eye of a *Küni*-bird—or of a Saa Allaqiyani mountain huntsman.

"Come forth! Else I shall have Aluja call up demons!"

Sihan sidled out into the light. The wretched craven was probably dribbling into his breechclout! Naitl followed, clutching Ulgais' hand. Ridek crouched lower behind the huge bronze Engsvanyali shield where he had taken refuge. He managed to catch Sihan's eye and sent him a fierce glare.

"No foes but friends, then!" Aid laughed. He bent to kiss Naitl and hoist Ulgais up to his massive shoulder. Sihan went to stand by Lady Mmir.

"Where, then, is your captain? Is not the warrior Ridek with you?"

Ridek felt a sinking sensation in his stomach, but all Sihan said was, "We only wanted to see the swords. Now you will impale us."

The Baron snorted. "Know that the High Lord of Yan Kor pardons your crimes!" He added Naitl to the burden already upon his shoulder. "If you three are here, then Ridek cannot be far away."

The Lorun woman approached and reached up affectionately to Naitl. Lady Mmir watched impassively.

"Your Ridek," Lady Si Ziris Qaya said, "he is the brave one—a *Thargir*, a 'young warrior.'" Both the Lorun and the Yan Koryani sent their adolescents, boys and girls alike, to learn the arts of warfare first as camp servants and later as skirmishers and slingers in actual battle. The Lorun started

this training somewhat earlier: by age ten or so their offspring
often saw service as scouts and foragers for their warbands.

"Ai, Ridek is ever the explorer, the adventurer. He will do
anything, dare anything. But he must answer when I summon
him. If he is here, he can go on squatting under some hauberk
or other—in considerable discomfort, I expect—until we are
done with our wine. When we go down to bed, I shall have
the chamber searched, and if he is found he will stay in his
room for a six-day! He still has something to learn about
'noble action.' "

Ridek bit his lip. That would certainly ruin the little tryst
he had planned with pretty Hris! There was no way out of the
hall save through those doors. He debated coming forth in
abject surrender but thought better of it. His father would not
respect that. Then, too, by the time they were ready for sleep,
the Baron might have forgotten to look for his errant son.

"Ridek makes a fine heir for your dynasty." Lady Si Ziris
Qaya smiled over at Lady Mmir. "A brave and heroic boy,
like mighty Hrugga himself. You must be proud of him."

Any answer was forestalled by the return of the chamber-
lain bearing a dusty clay jug of *Dronu*, the sweet, black
Salarvyani wine that the Baron favored. With him was Lord
Fu Shi'i.

Ridek had no love for this man. He had been his father's
friend since long before Ald went south to take service under
the Tsolyani Emperor, people said, but no one knew what
bound them together. Lord Fu Shi'i was small, taciturn, and
as slender and unbending as a staff of *Ssar*-wood. He affected
a loose, foreign-cut tunic of deep red *Firya*-cloth, tall leather
boots, and a circlet of silver about his cap of cropped,
dead-black hair. He came from no city and no clan that Ridek
had ever heard. Gossip had it that he hailed from the savage
lands of the far northeast, beyond Mudallu, beyond Nuru'un,
perhaps even beyond the Plains of Glass, where the world
ended. No one knew. Whenever Ridek questioned his father
about Lord Fu Shi'i he had received no more than a growl in

reply. His mother, too, only shrugged her slender shoulders and spoke of something else. That Lord Fu Shi'i did more than give his father counsel was well known, however: if anyone could call up demons, it was this strange, tight, sallow-faced man.

Lord Fu Shi'i sketched a bow to the ladies, but his words were for the Baron. "My Lord, there is a matter—" Ridek saw his eyes glitter as they shifted to Aluja. "Ah. It is good that you are here, Mihalli."

"Speak." The Baron Ald looked as though he desired nothing weightier tonight than a goblet of wine.

"My Lord—" His gaze flicked over the two women.

"Oh, come over here, then." Ald put the two children down and drew Lord Fu Shi'i after himself into the shadowed depths of the hall. They came to a stop very near Ridek's hiding place.

"The amulet, Lord. The one you had me give the Lady Deq Dimani when she left Ke'er to lead her *Gurek* of Vridu . . ."

"Well?"

"Its mate, Lord." He held up something small; Ridek could not see what it was. "The spark within it has shifted. Suddenly. Tonight."

Ridek had no idea what he meant, but he pricked up his ears at the name of the Lady Deq Dimani. No one who had seen her would forget her: the matriarch and absolute ruler of the Isle of Vridu that lay just off the Yan Koryani coast in the Northern Sea. She was a devotee of the Lord of Sacrifice, who was an Aspect of one of their own deities, Lord Vimuhla. Lady Deq Dimani moved as Ridek imagined the Master of Flame Himself must move: fiercely, smoothly, vibrantly, alight with internal fires of her own. The scullions whispered that the Lady Deq Dimani was another of his father's casual conquests, and there had been talk for a time that she might replace Lady Si Ziris Qaya in the Baron's heart—and perhaps Lady Mmir and even Lady Yilrana as well. Ridek himself had had disturbing dreams of her, though she was almost as old as his mother.

"Well?" the Baron was saying. "She was supposed to return to our lines at Mar. Just as soon as—"

"The spark did not just move across the face of the amulet, Lord. It *jumped*. She did not march back to Mar."

"A Nexus Point? A doorway into one of the Planes Beyond?"

"She has not left this Plane."

"Cha! Say what you mean."

"Some form of rapid transport. A thing of the Ancients is my guess: the tubeway entrance they found at Fortress Ninu'ur. An aircar. Something else. . . ."

The Baron pondered. Ridek could hear the bristly sound as he ran his fingers through his beard.

"We cannot have her absent when Ssa Chna Qayel attacks the Tsolyani reinforcement column. Her legion and that of her younger brother are crucial there, and the puppy won't move without his sister!" The scratching sound came again. "Can you trace her with that thing, then?"

"No, Lord. Not exactly. The spark did not jump far across the face of the amulet, but there is no way to tell which direction she took."

Ridek essayed a look around the embossed rim of the shield. He was rewarded by a glimpse of a flat, round wafer-like object of black stone in Lord Fu Shi'i's hand. Even from where he lay hidden he could see a tiny spark of amber flame glowing brightly in the center of the thing.

"We cannot await reports—no time to send somebody to Fortress Ninu'ur to ask after the Lady's health! Ohe, man! The timing of our assault is vital."

"There is a way." Lord Fu Shi'i paused. "Aluja."

The Baron gave a great, gusty sigh. "La, the Mihalli may be a master of Nexus Points and the Planes Beyond, but can he—she, it, damn it—home in on that telltale of yours?"

"We can ask. We have to ask, Sire."

Ridek heard the creak of leather, restless pacing, his father's angry breathing. He made himself into a small ball behind the shield.

Time passed. Then Lord Fu Shi'i's short, quick footsteps came rustling back. "Aluja says it is possible, though it has not been done before."

"Call him over. Have him focus his Nexus Point upon the spark. If Deq Dimani needs help, she shall have it—and if not, then Aluja can return her where she is needed. The woman exasperates me! She insisted upon dealing with this Flamesong thing herself—whatever it is!"

"You know her well, Sire. It is a thing of importance to her. Flamesong relates to her faith, to some archaic tenet or mystery of her Lord of Sacrifice."

"Sire," Aluja's lilting voice said from close by, "do you and Lord Fu Shi'i go and converse with your women. Let me have the amulet, and I shall manage."

There was silence. Then Ridek heard his father's laughter from across the long chamber, Mmir's merry reply, a soft comment from the Lorun woman. A goblet rang against the lip of a wine-jug.

Ridek peered out again. Just in front of him, no more than two paces away, a glimmering circle of muzzy gray light hung in the air, well nigh invisible in the shadows. Of Aluja there was no sign.

An idea dawned upon him. Here was another exit from the Pavilion of the Eternally Valiant, a way to avoid his father's wrath! He would go with Aluja! The Mihalli could return him later—indeed, could set him down anywhere he chose, in his own bedchamber where he could deny ever being near this wretched place! The rendezvous with Hris suddenly appeared much more possible again.

He dared not stop to consider the plan; the Nexus Point might vanish at any moment. He slipped out from behind his shield, took a tentative step.

Lady Si Ziris Qaya was looking straight at him over the Baron's brawny shoulder. He froze.

He realized, then, that she would not betray him. Her eyes narrowed, and she peered in his direction; then she bent over the table, pointed at some document there, and murmured a question in her dark, accented voice. His father rumbled a reply. Lady Mmir sat with her face half turned away from him, playing with Sihan and the other children.

He took another step, felt the tingling of Other-Planar power. He put a foot into the shimmering blankness within the shadow-gray oval.

The last thing he heard was Sihan's voice, quite clearly, like a gloomy, chiming, temple-gong. "If you are going to flog Ridek, Father, may I watch?"

Then there was darkness indeed.

4

"Let me put these two pretty *Hmelu*-lambs to the knife, Sire," Horusel growled. He stood with his feet apart, beak-headed axe still hooked about the throat of the woman called Belket Ele Faiz. His sun-bronzed features were yellow-gray in the pallid light that had come on automatically within glass circles in the vehicle's ceiling.

"No. They are needed. First to get that Pygmy-beast out of the storage compartment, then to instruct us in the use of this egg-thing. You kill nothing until I order it!" He had to take control, otherwise Horusel would surely snatch it from him. This was no ordinary military situation.

He looked past the *Tirrikamu* to the others in the crowded cabin. Chosun stood poised, sword in hand, against the rear bulkhead, while three crossbowmen—Trinesh recognized Arjasu, Balar, and Mejjai—crouched amidst the rotted chair-frames, their quarrels trained on the hatch behind which the Pygmy-beast still lurked. They belonged to Chosun's *Semetl*: moderates, praise to the Lord of Flame! Saina was helping

Dineva bind the wrists of the Yan Koryani officer's maid with a strip slashed from the girl's skirt. Jalugan huddled on the floor, a red-drenched rag held to his cheek. Of all of them, Chekkuru hiVriddi appeared the least anxious: he hovered around now behind Trinesh, inspecting the closed door of the machine with open-mouthed fascination.

"My maid here knows nothing. And I'll tell you the same," the woman named Belket Ele Faiz snapped. "Treat us as prisoners of war—for now."

"You do not deserve that courtesy! You broke the word you gave when you surrendered to us."

She sneered at him. "Not so! I swore to employ neither spells nor swords. I kept that oath. What the *Nyenu* did involved neither—nor did he act upon my command."

"Cha! Deception! I should hand you over to Horusel!"

"Do so. Rape us—kill us; then suffer what will be woven in your Skeins once we arrive in Yan Kor. Treat us well, and you will be held for ransom—or for honorable sacrifice, as you choose."

"For now you are *our* captives. We will speak of Yan Kor and sacrifices when the time comes. We Tsolyani have no love for your passive 'Way of Nchel,' and we may decide to fight on until we are all slain—"

"*Hereksa*?" Dineva interrupted. She had finished tying the girl and was starting on the older woman, gingerly avoiding Horusel's axe. "Chosun says he's ready to go in after the Pygmy-thing, Sire. With Arjasu's shield it should be no trick to push right in, dodge its dagger, and force it against a wall where Mejjai and Balar can kill it."

"There is no need of that," the Yan Koryani woman said. "Wait." She called out in her own language, and after a moment the creature appeared in the hatchway. His curious dagger skittered across the deck to stop at Trinesh's feet.

"He surrenders to you," she said. "We call him Thu'n— 'the Old One'—since none can pronounce his real name. He is a scholar of the *Nyenu*—the Pygmy Folk." She spoke to him soothingly in Yan Koryani. "I have told him that this shame will not last, that these cords will soon circle your wrists instead of mine and my maid's."

"That remains to be seen," Trinesh said. Things did appear very bleak. "Can you understand me, *Nyenu*—ah, Thu'n? You, girl? You must do as we say. Or else."

The maid nodded, and the *Nyenu*—damn it, that was the Yan Koryani word; Trinesh's people named them *Nininyal*—answered carefully, "I speak some Tsolyani." Its accent was horrible: whistling, mangled, and warbling, almost as though it spoke with two tongues instead of one. But it was intelligible.

"Then obey. We will not bind you. —Oh, cut the two women free as well—what harm can they do?" Horusel glared, but Trinesh stared him down. "Cha, man, half a *Semetl* of Tsolyani soldiers and unable to overmatch one noble lady, her maid, and a little beast?" From the corner of his eye he saw Chosun emerging from the rear storage compartment. "Anything?"

"A bag full of clothes, some documents, a purse of Yan Koryani gold—some of our Tsolyani *Kaitars* there too." He chortled. "Looks like our money's good even in the Baron's realm."

"Saina, look at the damned documents, will you?"

She pored over them, one by one. Then she shook her head. "All in cipher, *Hereksa*." The Lady Belket Ele Faiz curled her full lower lip in another sneer. Trinesh ignored her. Let her think him weak! He had no immediate need for the information.

Time passed, unguessable in the shadowless cabin.

Chekkuru hiVriddi gave a soft cry from behind him. Trinesh turned around—and gasped. The priest had done something: there had been a click and a hissing sound like liquid squirted from a wineskin.

Now there was a window in the wall of the cabin opposite the door!

Everyone babbled at once. Trinesh found himself looking

squarely at a man seated on the other side of the window. The man was dead—and had been so for a very long time. The face was a skull, the flesh mummified, the lips withered away from the bared teeth, the eyes no more than dusty sockets. The tatters of what once had been a tunic hung from yellowed collarbones.

Chekkuru shrieked something about undead servitors of mighty Sarku, the Lord of Worms, banged a fist upon the row of black studs below the window, and jerked his robe up to cover his eyes. At any other time the resulting vista of his hairy thighs would have been ludicrous.

The scene wavered, blinked, and became different: a great city beside a storm-dark sea, red tiled roofs lit by a dying, bloated sun, a maze of crumbling walls, broken-toothed towers, shattered rooms open to a sky piled high with lowering clouds . . .

It was Chosun, as unimaginative and stolid as Thenu Thendraya Peak itself, who poked a stubby finger at another of the little studs. Again the window changed: a room appeared, its furnishings of the same archaic, alien style as those in their cabin, a high table covered with glistening metallic sheets, like documents of some sort but all filmy and coated with a greenish patina. There were unidentifiable objects clustered beside them. Before anyone could speak, a slender, silvery fish swam across the picture: it flipped its feathery tail, and the metal sheets rippled and shifted in the wake of its passing.

Were there places, then, where people breathed water instead of air? Trinesh did not think so. Certain epics did sing of ancient cities sunk deep beneath the oceans of Tekumel, however.

"The view-portrayers still operate, my Lady," the *Nininyal* observed dryly. "You pressed the destination button that Qurtul Hne Tio had selected?"

Trinesh heard the hiss of her indrawn breath. "I—I pressed nothing. It was the Tsolyani—he backed into the console . . ."

The creature stared at her. Its beak opened and closed like a *Küni*-bird's.

"Alas, my Lady, then we may not be returning to Yan Kor," Thu'n said slowly. He touched the bulkhead with his three-fingered hand, and they all felt the soft humming of the egg-thing, the sensation of smooth, silent motion. "Whither we go and where we arrive are now in the hands of the Gods."

A long minute passed before they understood. The Yan Koryani woman herself said, "Surely you can tell us . . ."

The *Nininyal* dug a paw into one huge, gray-furred ear. He began to reply in the woman's tongue, but a threatening gesture from Trinesh made him shift over into Tsolyani.

"Not without Qurtul's skills. These were the personal vehicles of those before the Time of Darkness, and later of the lords of the Latter Times. Each can be given ten destinations—the buttons there on the box in front. They may be changed as the owner desires. A few scholars know how to do this—Qurtul was such a one—but so much has been lost. Without the names, numbers, or whatever the Ancients employed, of new objectives, a traveler cannot instruct the machine to take him thither. Even Qurtul did not possess such a list of destinations, nor, to my knowledge, does anyone else. —And even if one were found, no modern sage could read it. The languages of the Ancients are as forgotten as their sciences."

"And how did your Qurtul know which button returned you to Yan Kor?" Chekkuru hiVriddi put in.

"I think that he recognized a few of the ancient names by the shapes of their letters. Else he was as ignorant as you!"

"Then push another stud! Any one!" Trinesh cried. "I have no wish to visit that place where fish swim in what passes for air!"

"Who knows if we do indeed travel thither? The view-portrayers display not only the destinations of the car but also other places: a means of communication, more primitive than our sorcerers' telepathy, mayhap, but usable by any simpleton who can twist a knob.''

''Once we arrive, can we see what lies outside without opening the door?''

''Yes, if you know which picture is which. You might be gazing at a scene a thousand *Tsan* away.''

''What of returning?'' Saina asked. ''Can we not press the stud that takes us back to Fortress Ninu'ur?''

Thu'n pondered. ''Which button did your officer push?'' He scratched amidst the gray-brown fur of his belly. ''Moreover, Qurtul declared certain destinations to be perilous. The 'Enemies of Man,' the Ssu and the Hlüss, occupy various of the travel-stations; some are underwater or open upon sea-bottom ooze that is under vast pressure from above. Still other routes are blocked, and their warnings have failed over the millennia. We now travel at a speed we cannot imagine, and should we come to a rock-fall and not be turned back by the automatic signaling devices . . .'' He slapped one horny paw into the other.

The noise it made had a flat and final ring to it.

More time passed. Trinesh forbade anyone to touch any of the studs, particularly Thu'n. He mistrusted the *Nininyal*. The Pygmy Folk of Yan Kor had a reputation that included greed and treachery as well as scholarship.

It was Chekkuru hiVriddi who broke the silence. ''Hereksa. . . .''

Trinesh turned, a sharp comment about the irrelevancy of the gods to their present plight ready to his tongue, but all the man said was, ''The—the motion has stopped, *Hereksa*. Wherever we are, we have arrived.''

All was still.

Trinesh stammered, ''You—*Nininyal*—work the view-portrayers. Show us what lies without.''

Thu'n went to touch the studs below the glass square above the forward console and each of the three along the side wall as well. The one in front and two of the others flickered and displayed pictures. The fourth remained dark.

The rear device showed a landscape. Tekumel's two moons, reddish Kashi and green Gayel, cast weird double shadows upon mountains, tumbled boulders, and humped, desolate hills. Ravines and rocky gorges crisscrossed an empty plain close by. In the distance a tiny line of glittering blue lights danced across the landscape. The machine emitted a soughing sound, the keening of a despairing and mournful wind.

"Ssu," the *Nininyal* breathed. "Pray to all your Gods that this is not our destination!"

He turned to the other glass square on the side wall. It and the device above the forward console showed a different scene: a large cavern lit by smoky firelight, its vastnesses lost in the shadows beyond. Their "windows" gave an overview of the encampment; the egg-vehicle must have emerged upon an eminence of some sort. Several human figures were visible in the foreground. These stood or squatted around a campfire, some eating, others talking, a few huddled in sleep. Five or six worked with skinning knives over a huge and unidentifiable carcass. A woman, naked save for bone-white ornaments in her tangled hair, bathed in a circular pool nearby. Others stooped beside her to fill waterskins.

Below, a child ran out of the group by the fire. It came closer, halted, stumbled, and stared up in amazement. Then it scampered off screaming soundlessly, its stick-thin arms waving in terror. Some of the figures arose and pointed.

They had been seen. Here, then, was the reality outside, rather than the lonely landscape of the Ssu.

"Prepare yourselves," Trinesh commanded. "You, Thu'n, or whatever your name is, can you open the door?"

The *Nininyal* touched a stud beside the portal, and it swung wide. Trinesh gestured to the three crossbowmen to wait, and to Chosun to hold their captives fast. He poked his head out.

"Not Yan Kor, this," he reported to those inside. "Sand-worms—Milumanayani tribesmen—by the look of them." He ventured a backward glance. "Come out here, Saina. If they serve the Baron, somebody'll speak Yan Koryani."

Their egg-thing seemed to have emerged upon a flat platform. Idols, fetish-poles, and white-daubed ritual baskets lay all about. The cavern was dark, but an ocher and green double shadow high up along one wall indicated that at least a part of the place was open to the two moons. It was night here—as it must also be at Fortress Ninu'ur if their journey had taken as long as it seemed. Trinesh could just see the joinings of ponderous masonry blocks, barrel-shaped sections of fallen columns, like sections of white *Mnosa*-root, and half-finished partition walls of smaller stones and rubble. A hundred millennia might have passed since this place was whole. All was wind-worn and drifted over with sand.

"We seem to have popped out right on top of their temple!"

"No chance of them taking us for gods," Saina muttered without enthusiasm. "Even the Milumanayani are not that stupid."

Trinesh tightened his grip upon his sword hilt. "Maybe a little overawing will serve."

"Cha, I can smell them from here— No, it's a dead *Hmelu* just in front of our egg-thing. A sacrifice?"

"I'd rather not be the next one." Trinesh took a step forward. "Hoi, who speaks Tsolyani here?"

Those below stood frozen, gaping, murmuring, whispering. He sensed rather than saw the white gleam of bone-tipped spears, the leather slings, the clubs of spiky thornwood. He guessed the adults to number about fifty—maybe more.

"Yan Koryani? Anyone speak that?"

"Tsolyani is good enough," a voice called back. "I can do your talking for you."

One of the figures detached itself from the group: a man, garbed in the same dun-hued leather desert-cloak as all the rest. He set foot upon the eroded staircase that Trinesh now saw led down from their platform to the cavern floor.

"Your name?" Trinesh snapped. The fellow spoke Tsolyani perfectly, his accent as good as Trinesh's own. He was probably an escaped slave—a criminal of some sort, possibly a deserter from the army.

"I am Tse'e—'outsider' in the tongue of these folk."

Trinesh's suspicions were correct. No honorable Tsolyani would fail to give his personal name, his lineage-name if he had one, and his clan.

"And where is here?" Trinesh asked.

"La, honored guest, you do not know?" The man spread his arms wide, his voluminous cloak flapping out around him like the wings of a *Hu*-bat. "Why, here you are inside the Wall of Tkessa Tkol, down in the cisterns where there is still water, even though its noble builders, the Priestkings of Engsvan hla Ganga, have long since departed and left it all to the *Aya*, the great worms of the desert." He threw back his head and cackled. "Once this wall kept raiders and monsters away from the seacoast; now the rising of the lands has left it to shield us from the sun and the winds of sand!"

"His brain is as riddled as a log full of *Oso*-beetles," Saina whispered.

"Likely so." Trinesh did not take his eyes off the man, who was slowly edging his way up the stair toward them. "Ask within: has anybody heard of—what was it—the Wall of Tkessa Tkol?"

The Yan Koryani woman answered him. "I have read of it: an old place, a fortification erected by the Prefects of the North during the later Engsvanyali dynasties."

"But a wall? We're in a cavern."

"Probably the cellar of one of the guard-towers that stand at intervals along the wall. Some of these were as large as palaces, I recall."

Trinesh held up his hand toward the man outside. "Hold where you are! I must confer with my comrades." He left Saina to watch and ducked back into the cabin to confront

Lady Belket. "Well, woman? You seem familiar with this 'Wall.'"

"Not I, personally. But our agents come here to arrange passage south for our troops, when they go to fight the western army of your Prince Eselne."

"What sort of place is it?"

"There is no harm in your knowing." She pulled free of Dineva's grasp and pushed forward amongst the others to look up at him. She was almost of the same height, and he felt the softness of her breath upon his cheek. The effect was unsettling. "The Wall of Ṭkessa Tkol is more than two hundred *Tsan* long, as high as a *Sakbe* road-wall, and perhaps fifty—a hundred—paces thick. I am not sure. It served as a defense against raiders from what was then the sea. Its western end is anchored upon the ruins of the city of Ta'ure, and the Wall then wanders off eastward to vanish into the sands— who knows whither? We are still in the Desert of Sighs, in Milumanaya, but on the western side."

"Cha! Where are we in relation to Fortress Ninu'ur? Can we march back?"

"Not even great Hrugga of the Epics could survive that stroll! Several hundred *Tsan* separate you from your men at Fortress Ninu'ur, *Hereksa*, a little far to bawl commands." The Lady Belket moved closer in the crowded car, and her breasts brushed the hard *Chlen*-hide of his armor. "Go north, and you visit Akurgha, the Warlord of the oasis-city of Pelesar, the capital of this region—a wretched heap of mud-brick hovels and salt-sand. Go south, and you come upon our Yan Koryani legions—those who face Prince Eselne." She gave him a sly smile, her eyes glittering in the shadows. "Here is your chance, brave *Hereksa*: you are now behind Yan Koryani lines and in position to deliver a smashing rear attack, you and your half-*Semetl* of heroes!"

He did not bother to reply. Saina was summoning him back outside. The man had disregarded Trinesh' order and arrived at the top of the staircase.

He made an elaborate bow to Trinesh and another to Saina. "Ohe, ohe! Visitors! We have not had visitors for a very long time. A Tsolyani officer and his beauteous lady!"

Saina, bulky as any man in her grimy, sweaty armor, snorted.

Trinesh inspected the fellow. The firelight from below limned gaunt, hollow cheeks and a hooked nose that would have done credit to an aristocrat of the Clan of Sea Blue itself. The man's right eye showed only white, a sign of *Alungtisa,* the blindness that afflicted many desert nomads. Trinesh guessed him to be elderly: certainly more than fifty summers and possibly over sixty. His accent hinted at the central Tsolyani plain—Bey Sü? Usenanu? Katalal?—and his etiquette was fine enough for any courtier at Avanthar. He seemed to be a man of breeding, a member of a good clan, possibly even noble.

The tribesmen outnumbered them badly, and they would surely lose if it came to a fight. This man's co-operation was vital; he alone could translate and thus procure them food, water, and a place to rest. With proper courtesy, therefore, Trinesh gave his own names, clan, and title. He looked at the other expectantly.

The man said, "Tse'e. I am Tse'e. That is enough." He waved a cloaked arm behind himself. "These are the Folk of the Banner of Na Ngore." He pointed past Trinesh. "There, soldier!"

Both Saina and Trinesh swiveled to look. Among the clutter of feathered fetish-poles, broken stone images, and baskets of rotting sacrificial food, a tall staff loomed higher than all the rest. A dirty blue-and-white rag swung limply from it. Trinesh made a questioning sound in his throat, and the man named Tse'e waggled bony fingers mockingly.

"There, *Hereksa:* the standard of the Engsvanyali Priestkings! Not the original, of course—that became dust long ago—but a fair copy!" He spread his hands expansively. "Here you have them: the descendants of the Priestkings' soldiers, still on duty, still at Fortress Na Ngore, still waiting to repel the pirates of the deeps!''

What nonsense! Five—perhaps as many as ten—millennia had elapsed since the Priestkings' island of Ganga had slipped beneath the southern sea! The Second Imperium, the Tlakotani dynasty of the Seal Emperors of Tsolyanu, had arisen from the resultant chaos, and the Seal had now held sway for more than twenty-three hundred years! Still, truth or legend, this Milumanayani clap-trap made a good story.

Trinesh looked down at the sea of grim faces, narrowed eyes, and half-hidden weapons. He decided to humor the old renegade. With as much dignity as he could muster, he raised his sword and cried out the only Engsvanyali word he knew: the salutation with which Lord Vimuhla's priests greeted the god in the temple rituals.

"*Otulengba! Otulengba!*" Trinesh's memory failed him; he had never been much of a scholar. He finished lamely in Tsolyani. "We—ah—hail the defenders of the seas!''

From just within the egg-thing, he heard a derisive snicker from Lady Belket Ele Faiz and some snide comment from Chekkuru hiVriddi behind her. Then the tribesmen came surging up the steps, arms waving, weapons raised. Men shouted, women shrilled and gabbled, and children shrieked. He thought of resistance, then realized it was futile. He and Saina were surrounded, overwhelmed, plucked at, grasped, and handled. He could not see the others, nor the madman Tse'e. In a swirl of bad-smelling desert-cloaks and skinny limbs, he was manhandled down the steps, across the cavern, and over to the campfire. Faces reeled before him, hands, eyes, tangled braids that stank of rancid *Hmelu*-fat. He found himself seated upon a block of stone, encircled so closely by jostling bodies that he could barely breathe.

Tse'e forced his way through the mob. "Welcome, *Hereksa*," he cried. 'You have done well indeed—better than the nonhuman Shunned Ones, who were our last visitors to arrive by tubeway car!''

Trinesh would have asked about those "Shunned Ones," but other questions were more urgent. "What will happen to us?"

"Why, you shall be fed, given water, and guested with all of the pomp these heirs to the throne of Ganga can provide. You shall remain here—or you may walk home through the desert. I advise against the latter, not now. The sands can be crossed only during the colder months."

It was now Pardan. Two months of autumn remained before Tekumel's short—and still hot—winter season. Such a wait was unthinkable.

"We shall trouble these people for only this one night," he declared. "Then we depart in the egg-thing in which we came."

Tse'e looked uncomfortable. "You will not be allowed to set foot upon the station-pyramid again. It is a sacred place."

"We shall fight our way back up there if need be."

"You are outnumbered by four—five—to one. Be patient, *Hereksa*, and join in the life of Na Ngore, as I have done. If you are determined to leave, a time will come when the hunters are absent and you may regain your vehicle by some ruse. Even if the car has been summoned away, you can call another, you know."

Trinesh had not known. "How?"

"Three glass plaques are set in the floor before it, though they are likely buried under rubbish and baskets of offerings. Step upon the red one if no car is present; the yellow plaque lights when a vehicle is on its way; and the blue glows when a car is at hand and ready to depart."

A young boy appeared to thrust a cup sloshing full of liquid into Trinesh' hands, a cup that suspiciously resembled the cranium of a human skull.

"Drink it, man," Tse'e urged. "They will not slay you once you have drunk their water and tasted of their food." A shallow bowl that might once have been the bottom of a clay pot was laid upon his knees. "Eat! To refuse is to insult your hosts! Do not fear; tonight it is *Hmelu*-meat and not that of 'one who serves.' "

"What—?"

"You do not know? How little we Tsolyani care for the social niceties of our neighbors! The Folk of Na Ngore practice a custom that is not followed even by other tribes in the Desert of Sighs. Look, soldier, this is a harsh and deadly land. Food and water are scarcer here than *Chlen*-dung in the Emperor's Golden Tower. When a citizen of Na Ngore is old, wounded, or ill, he offers his body to his fellows. A quick knife across the throat, and the tribe has bone for its spears, a skin from which garments are made, hair to weave into other apparel, sinews to bind blades to shafts, a skull to use as a basin—a thousand other useful things. Naught is wasted. His flesh is also added to the stew-pot, so that his *Vanh*—his Spirit-Soul, what we Tsolyani call the *Baletl*—departs happy in the knowledge that even in death he serves his people."

There was an outraged squawk from somewhere close by: Saina. Trinesh jumped to his feet, the platter slipping from his lap to smash upon the floor. He ignored the buzz of angry voices this evoked.

"Now you look, old man—Tse'e, or whatever name you hide under! We will not tolerate—"

A thin, sun-blackened hand pushed him back. "Learn something else, *Hereksa*! The Milumanayani freely give all they have to anyone who needs it. They demand the same courtesy in return. Here no person has the right to possess more than another—not permanently, not with the same nice legalities of ownership that obtain in our land. Some girl has probably taken a fancy to your soldier-woman's armor, tunic, kilt—whatever. If she refuses to share, she will be seized and beaten. That is the law. Afterward, if she needs those items again, she has only to demand their return. The same applies to you; the only reason that you still have your weapon and your harness is because I am talking to you. It is impolite to interrupt a conversation!"

He spoke to the others around Trinesh and went away. A moment later he returned with Saina, scratched, a little bloody, and as furious as a *Zrne*-beast whose lair has been defiled by human-smell. She wore only her stained, dirty under-tunic, and she clutched a crumpled ball of brown-black leather to her ample breasts: a desert-cloak.

Trinesh leaned over and spat resignedly. "Do as they ask," he called to his companions. "Later I think we can get it all back." He sighed and began to remove his armor, passing each piece in turn to the eager hands stretched forth to receive it.

5

I t was very dark.

Ridek could smell pitch, fragrant and resinous, like a *Tiu*-tree after the spring rains. There was also the scent of grass, growing things, damp wetness, and an underlying odor of something acrid and strange. He realized that he was cold, and he shivered.

Just ahead of him, amidst a tangle of brushy vegetation, a luminous circle hung in the air. It began to fade even as he watched.

He knew what he had to do: he gathered himself, tensed, and sprang toward it—into it . . .

. . .Into brightness. The sun blazed down upon him. But it was an ugly orange-red instead of the familiar yellow orb of Tekumel. He fell, rolled, and sat up gasping. He had almost tumbled down a steep, rock-strewn slope! He lay still for a moment to catch his breath, then squinted over the edge.

Aluja stood there below in a hollow, surrounded on every side by towering pinnacles of red-veined rock. The Mihalli held Lord Fu Shi'i's amulet in one hand and a translucent, bluish globe in the other. He took a few tentative steps in one direction, then returned and stalked off in another; he halted, looked about, then paced around in a gradually widening spiral. He appeared wary—confused?—and seemed to be seeking something.

Ridek staggered to his feet, dusted himself off, and began to descend the slope. He opened his mouth to call out, but Aluja whirled without warning and did something to his globe. A beam of sapphire light, as brilliant as a lightning flash, sprang forth from it, and the scarlet veining upon the boulder in front of him writhed and vanished without a sound. Ridek stared. The Mihalli turned to his right and fired again, then again. The words of greeting died in Ridek's throat. The red tendrils were not part of the rock. They were alive—and clearly dangerous!

He glanced down. Beneath his own feet the porous stone crawled with threadlike strands of viscous red, like the blood vessels in the white of a person's eye! A tendril crept up to caress his boots with speculative interest, then surged forward. Others followed, little knots and fibers wriggling along over the grayish rock.

Ridek would have cried out, but it was too late. Only a dim oval swam in the air where Aluja had been.

He yelled the Mihalli's name then, but to no avail. The little threads began to wind their way up his calves. Others squirmed after them, as tight to the surface of the rock as hair upon a man's head. He jerked his left foot up, and the tendrils tore and popped. He did the same with his right foot, but the filaments inching about his left foot returned with greater agility than before. Above, the angry tangerine sun hung in gory splendor in a brass bowl of sky, a gentle breeze touched his face, and he could hear the cheerful noises of insects in the pulpy red-black trees beyond.

"Aluja!" he yelled. "Aluja!" The fuzzy gray oval shrank down to a dot and disappeared.

Ridek had always thought himself brave. He would not let these vein-things defeat him! Still, terror reared up unbidden to choke off his shouts, and he was surprised to find his eyes blinded with tears. Grimly he wrenched his feet free a second time, but it was more difficult. Again, and it was still harder. Soon he would tire, and they would swarm over him. What to do? He forced calmness upon himself, tensed his muscles, and jumped as high and as far as he could. There was a sward of russet-red grass—or what looked like it—a few paces away. If he could reach that . . . !

The scarlet thread-things spoiled the attempt. He ended asprawl upon the lip of the rocky slope, feeling warmth and a horrid, rhythmic pulsing beneath his outstretched fingers. His hands hurt, and he dragged them loose. Their palms were bloody, as though cut with sharp sea-coral. His boot-tops were no longer visible, and he felt the gentle, crawling palpation of the thread-things moving up his thighs beneath the white *Firya*-cloth tunic his mother had given him that morning.

He could endure no more. "Aluja!" he howled. "Help me!"

A shadow swept over him from behind. "Aluja," he gasped with relief.

But it was not the Mihalli. A nightmare loomed there, a blackish-yellowish-greenish thing made up of many pods and spindles and glistening sacs, a monster out of half-remembered baby-dreams of terror.

Ridek fainted.

And awoke to scream again. He lay upon his back, his limbs wrapped with squishy russet bindings like strips of ghastly seaweed, his body a mass of itching and torment. He could not move. A saw-toothed feeler approached from above and behind his head to caress his face. It passed down over his bulging eyes and crawled along his cheek toward his mouth. He struggled but his raw throat refused to scream, and he gagged and choked. Mercifully, he fainted once more.

Consciousness returned amidst wavering, tenebrous shadows. He tried to cry out, but a hand—a humanoid hand this time, slender, red brown, and six-fingered—rose before his eyes to reassure him.

Aluja—beloved, familiar Aluja—swam into view. Ridek could only hold out his arms—he found them now free and unfettered—and moan.

"Oh, Ridek! That you should have followed me!"

"How—? I saw you go . . ."

"The demons who dwell upon this Plane summoned me back. Lord Nere and his creatures owed a debt to me, as now do I to them."

"Lord Nere—?"

"The master of the Fiftieth Circle of the Planes Beyond. Here—" A ladle of something hot and honey-sweet appeared before Ridek's lips. "I had not intended to pass unbidden through his domain, but it was needful. . . ."

There were too many questions. Ridek drank gratefully and slept.

He opened his eyes, and for a moment the terror of the thread-things overwhelmed him all over again. He sat up—and saw not one but three of the gangling, stalklike monsters who had come upon him before. He screamed, involuntarily, and Aluja rose gracefully from the floor where he had been sitting.

"Peace, boy. These are Lord Nere's 'Many-Bodied.' They rescued you and hence deserve your gratitude."

How did one thank a creature that resembled a series of bladders and puffy, bloated pods strung together in no discernible order with mucid sinews supported upon several sets of mismatched legs?

"We must decide what to do with you," Aluja was saying. "There is no time to return you to your father now, nor do I dare tamper with the Planes of Time and put you back before—or even shortly after—you left. To leave you here is also quite impossible—'' Ridek was grateful for that ''—and to carry you with me upon my mission is madness. Your father has a hold upon some of us Mihalli that enforces our service and prevents us from harming his purposes. Now I am torn, indeed.''

Ridek could only whisper, ''I came to be with you.''

''I know. I must think upon it.'' Aluja touched Ridek's brow. ''You seem well enough. Lord Nere's servitors are unfamiliar with your human internal workings, yet all appears in order. You have only to regain your strength. Rest.''

He did not want to rest. He struggled to his feet and found that he was naked, his feet and hands covered with a labyrinth of tiny bluish lines, like the *Aomüz* tattoos that a Livyani noble wore to display his rank, his clan, and his religious affiliation.

The Mihalli saw his expression and said, ''Those will pass. You will have no scars.''

Ridek felt a rush of relief. Then Hris' piquant features rose incongruously before him, and he wondered a little regretfully what she would have thought of a hero returned from the Planes Beyond, all scarred with mysterious markings . . .

Aluja essayed a smile. ''Your boots and clothing are there, quite restored, though with materials that would confound your Yan Koryani artisans. There is also food. Lord Nere's creatures have scoured their world for sustenance you can digest.''

Suddenly he was ravenous. The bilious-looking blue gourd Aluja laid before him contained round, black granules that popped in his mouth and filled his nostrils with pungent fragrance, like *Ngalu*-berries but sweeter. There were also a thick, ocher-hued cake that he did not like and a melon-thing that tasted of roasted meat mixed with nuts and spices. He wolfed down most of it.

He looked around. The room—if such it was—consisted of curved surfaces, odd holes, and amorphous lumps of no obvious purpose. Symmetry seemed to be in ill repute here. All was of one piece, reddish-gray in color, and strangely veined—unpleasant memory!—with darker striations of black and brown and maroon. Three of the "Many-Bodied" sat— stood?—just beyond the flat protuberance that served as Ridek's bed. They remained motionless, save for the rhythmic in-and-out of various of their drooping, purple-mottled sacs. He looked for something like a conventional face but found none. There were indeed wrinkled white patches that might be eyes, orifices that could serve as mouths, round knobs that were perhaps organs of other, alien senses. He could not tell. In the end he gave up. Whatever—and however—the "Many-Bodied" were, Aluja had said that they had saved his life.

He sat down again upon the oddly resilient couch. The dark brown coverlet did have a curiously elastic feel, now that he thought about it. He watched for a moment as Aluja spoke, if that was the proper term, with his hosts, then lay back.

This time it was only the sleep-demons who seized him all unawares.

A blink, a moment, a dream of Hris—her face queerly commingled with that of a taller, older, more strikingly beautiful woman: the Lady Deq Dimani?—and then he was awake, Aluja's hand upon his shoulder. There was more food and an egg-shaped basin of yellow glass that held water in which to wash. As he dressed, he noticed that the marbled markings upon his hands and feet were already growing fainter; a whisper of disappointment crossed his mind.

"You are ready," Aluja said. The Mihalli held out a knurled stick of what looked like polished black wood. "This is the best I can manage within the time we have. Carry it wherever you go, for it contains magic: a spell of warding against blows and anything else that would strike your person violently. It is no defense against slower-moving perils, however: fire, gases, and the like.''

Ridek hardly heard him. ''Then I am to go with you?'' he cried. ''Not return to Yan Kor?'' He was greatly cheered when Aluja nodded. The prospect was too exciting for thoughts of danger. He hefted the staff. It felt better as a weapon than a device of sorcery, for it was very like the quarterstaff used by the Saa Allaqiyani. They had developed it into an art, called *Kichana*, of which the Baron Ald was an acknowledged master.

''It is the only way,'' Aluja said thoughtfully. ''You must accompany me. But you will stay back, well in the rear, and you will obey my every command as though it were your own heart's wish! You will not stray, nor will you speak, nor interfere, nor attempt any feat of bravery.''

Ridek was offended. ''I have already been instructed in the elements of soldiery! The first lesson is obedience.''

''See that you remember that when we cross the Planes. There are things worse than Lord Nere's scarlet threadlets and the 'Many-Bodied,' and we have a long way to travel.''

His curiosity would not be denied. ''You—we—go to rescue the Lady Deq Dimani?''

''So you heard! As big-eared as a *Nyenu*! Cha, boy! Yes, it is she whom we seek.''

''Why? What has happened to her?''

''Nothing, perhaps.'' Aluja sighed and fished Lord Fu Shi'i's amulet from one of the pouches of his harness. ''This is a 'linking amulet'; the Lady wears the original, and its mate—this duplicate—then keeps track of her movements.'' Ridek saw that the surface was covered with intersecting lines and whorls, like the astrolabe of an astrologer. ''You see this spark? It was there when she was at the town of Mar—'' the Mihalli's peculiarly jointed brown finger touched a spot upon the stone ''—and now it is here, not far away, but it moved too quickly and suddenly to indicate a march on foot. She could only have made that journey with the aid of some artifact of your ancestors, the technology of the human Ancients.''

"The war-council spoke of Mar—"

"Bigger and bigger ears! She was to travel from there to a small castle—a stronghold of no account—behind Tsolyani lines: Fortress Ninu'ur."

"Why?"

"Your father's troops discovered an important site beneath that place: a travel-station of the Ancients' transport system that once ran like *Shqa*-beetle tunnels beneath the surface of Tekumel. Did your teachers tell you of the tubeway cars?"

They had not, but Ridek said, "Certainly."

Aluja eyed him. "Well, they are—useful. Your people built them long ago, when this world was very different. Some still operate. If one knows their mysteries, one can travel at great speeds—far faster than the fastest messenger can run—to many places beneath Tekumel. If those destinations are unobstructed, one can them emerge—"

"—With soldiers, to strike the enemy in the rear!" Ridek's eyes shone as the idea took hold. "Spies, scouts, agents—assassins—!"

"La! You are as devious as your father," Aluja said. His fanged mouth opened in a human grin, but his ruby-red eyes did not smile. "In any case, the Lady Deq Dimani escorted a few of her scholars to Fortress Ninu'ur. It was of urgent interest to her—exactly the sort of thing she would dare."

"But why did *she* go? Surely there were others?"

A shadow crossed the Mihalli's features. "She would see for herself. Then, too, she had a second target: a part of her mission of which I know little. There are caverns near Fortress Ninu'ur, the Caves of Klarar. Legends say that a great store of relics from before the Time of Darkness is hidden there. More, the local folk tell of a ruined shrine somewhere in the hills close by Fortress Ninu'ur, a temple once dedicated to the One Other. Have you heard of that deity?"

Indeed, the priests of Ridek's temple school had never discussed that dread being, but the acolytes told tales of Him at night in the dormitories. The One Other belonged to the dark, to the terrible Pariah Gods who stood outside the Engsvanyali pantheon of the ten Gods and Their ten "Cohorts," the Demi-Gods who served Them. That pantheon had been codified by the Priest Pavar of the Isle of Ganga, and it was upon his humble theological foundation that the Priestkings of Engsvan hla Ganga had erected the mightiest empire to exist since the Time of Darkness. Now Pavar's Gods were worshipped throughout the Five Empires—all save in heretical Livyanu—but the Pariah Gods were anathema; their sects had been stamped out millennia ago, their temples leveled, their devotees slain, and their doctrines cast down into oblivion. Ridek knew of three such outcast deities: the One Other, the One Who Is, and the most hideous of all, the Goddess of the Pale Bone—She Who Cannot Be Named. There might be still more. The Pariah Gods were unknowable, inimical to humankind and to the allied nonhuman races—even to the First Races of Tekumel, the hateful Ssu and the Hlüss.

Did the Pariah Gods exist? Were they as real as Pavar's ten deities? The epics—the great "Lament to the Wheel of Black" in particular—stated that during the Time of the Gods, when humankind was young, the One Other had joined with nine of Pavar's deities to combat the tenth, Lord Ksarul, "the Doomed Prince of the Blue Room," at the Battle of Dormoron Plain. If this were true—and every priesthood in the Five Empires declared it so—then the Pariah Gods were as real as any other of the Engsvanyali pantheon.

The dormitory myth-tellers were probably no worse informed than the rest of humankind, all save a few savants at the very center of Lord Ksarul's involuted hierarchy. Ridek was hazier than most; he had never been interested in the legends of the gods. That was Sihan's forte, one in which Lord Fu Shi'i provided ample tutelage!

Aluja brought him back to the matter at hand. "In any event, I am not sure whether the Lady Deq Dimani visited the Caves of Klarar, or whether she found that shrine which was her real goal—"

"What reason would she have for seeking such a—a place of ghosts and horrors?"

The Mihalli's reddish-brown mane rippled as he sat down beside Ridek. "To acquire a thing she knows of through the arts of the priests of her Lord of Sacrifice. He is the same as Lord Vimuhla of Pavar's pantheon, whom your people also worship. She told your father that the followers of the One Other had stolen that thing away long ago and hidden it in their shrine."

"Why—? What is it?"

"As far as I am aware, it is a force of great power: perhaps an artifact, perhaps a spell, or even a demon-being. She named it 'Flamesong' and declared that it is the tool with which the Tsolyani can be defeated once and for all, finally, easily, and without further loss to Yan Kor."

"Oh, Aluja! Not magic! The palace servants say that my father has already suffered misfortunes aplenty from sorcerers and wizards and the lying promises of creatures from the Planes Beyond—" Ridek stopped, his hand to his mouth. "I am sorry, Aluja. I meant no offense to you."

"None taken. We Mihalli do dwell upon many Planes—often at one and the same time, and in ways you cannot comprehend—but we are as much flesh and blood as you." Aluja wrinkled his beast-snout in distaste. "Your father argued with the Lady Deq Dimani regarding this matter—I know because I was present. He ordered her to let 'Flamesong' alone. The hilt of such a magical weapon sometimes wounds its wielder more grievously than its blade does its foes."

"She refused?"

"Of course. The Lady is—ah, headstrong, willful, the sole matriarch of her island of Vridu since she was a girl. Your father had stronger expletives for her. The Lady Deq Dimani

answered that this 'Flamesong' belongs to her Lord of Sacrifice, that it is harmless to Yan Kor, and that it will win your
war with Tsolyanu as surely as a *Sro*-dragon gobbles up a
Hmelu! She swore that this flower conceals no thorns, no
twisted bargains with monstrous powers, no oaths to the Dark
Ones that would grant them entrance into Tekumel's Plane . . ."

"What if she is wrong?"

Aluja pondered. Then he said, "You are young, but you
have dwelt at the very heart of affairs in the court of Ke'er.
You comprehend what I say—more, perhaps than your father, who worshipped his Yilrana and now loves Yan Kor,
and who mingles both together in a venomous cup of blind
revenge upon the Tsolyani. You may be wiser than he,
Ridek—wiser than Lady Deq Dimani as well, in spite of your
youth. Her loyalties are to her island, to her fierce and fiery
God, and to her own hatred of Tsolyanu—a stream that flows
from some wellspring of which I know nothing. If she is
wrong, then she—and perhaps all who dwell upon your Plane
with her—will require our assistance indeed."

Ridek had another thought. "My father should have had
her escorted by an army to obtain this 'Flamesong'—at least a
legion of soldiers and a host of his mightiest sorcerers. He
should have dispatched Lord Fu Shi'i himself!"

"Only the Lady Deq Dimani can master 'Flamesong.' It is
a thing of her ancient, secretive faith, and she would not
allow meddling by the followers of any other god. Even your
father is ignorant of its details." Aluja looked down, the
glowing rubies of his eyes concealed. "As for Lord Fu Shi'i,
it were better that he be involved as little as possible . . ."

Ridek waited, but the Mihalli said no more. They sat
together in that curious room that resembled no room upon
Tekumel and looked out at the alien, burnt-orange-hued sky.

"And now some power of the Planes Beyond has carried
off the Lady Deq Dimani?" Ridek waved down Aluja's
words of denial. "I read it in your face."

"I think not—really! Rather some device of the Ancients, some accident."

"Whatever—whoever." He began lacing his boots. "Come, Aluja. We go to aid the Lady."

The words had a noble ring to them. Ridek did not understand why the Mihalli answered him only with a gentle smile.

6

The skins stank, but at least they offered some comfort. Trinesh had acquired them by simply pointing and by giving up his *Chlen*-hide vambraces in return. What their new owner, a scrawny Milumanayani warrior, would do with the embossed and lacquered arm-guards of a Tsolyani legionary was not immediately evident.

It was easy enough to get one's belongings back. A few gestures, some shouting, and a little helpful translating from the renegade, Tse'e, seemed to suffice. During the course of the long evening, Trinesh had had three helmets, two different breastplates—one Saina's—and so many spears, clubs, desert-cloaks, baskets of foodstuffs, pots of ghastly local liquor brewed from cactus-pods, and other miscellaneous marvels that he could not recount them all. He had also acquired a slightly rusty steel sword—rare and valuable, even in its present condition—and several scraps of Yan Koryani armor and military gear. The Baron's agents had indeed been here. Trinesh fondly hoped that they had enjoyed the same orgy of trading and counter-trading to which his own people had been subjected.

Tse'e said this happened every time visitors arrived at Na Ngore. Things always quieted down afterwards. As soon as the novelty of owning a set of fancy pauldrons or a pair of greaves wore off, their new proprietor was often willing to hand them back, usually for no consideration in return. Profit was not involved: it was pride of possession that mattered, and there was as much raucous bickering among the tribesmen themselves as between them and their guests.

Trinesh rolled over. The cavern floor was lumpy in spite of his pile of skins and desert-cloaks. He still had the steel sword—he must ask for his iron gorget-piece back tomorrow as well—two spears, a Yan Koryani dagger in addition to his own belt-knife, a jug of water, and a flat basket filled with dark brown tubers that resembled *Hmelu*-turds. He had no way to cook the tubers, but if they had to stay here for any length of time, he could always demand a pot from someone. He hoped he would not have to risk any more of the locals' dubious stew.

The rest of their party was scattered all around the cavern. He heard Chekkuru bleat an outraged and pompous reply to some tribesman's importuning. The priest had provided amusement at least: he had refused to give up his vestments until a gaggle of women playfully held him down, kicking and squalling, and wrested them violently away. Horusel had begun by swearing to surrender nothing and to die fighting instead. He had then done battle with a swarm of warriors but had had brains enough to use only the flat of his sword, praise be to the Flame Lord! He was not stupid enough to think he could win, and eventually he shouted for a truce and grandly bestowed his legion cloak upon the bravest of his opponents. The Milumanayani were delighted. Horusel then joined in the spirit of the thing, took it all as a joke, and ended with a great store of armor, weapons, and food. He squatted now atop his loot, munching something and bantering with Dineva. Chosun, on the other hand, was shy for a big man, and his success was less spectacular. He and his crossbowmen sat crosslegged close to the fire, a few of the sand-worms' starveling wenches with them, and the resultant festivities were only now winding down. No one had troubled poor Jalugan; his wound was deep and painful, though not serious. Saina had taken him as her own special charge, and the two of them now lay together amid a heap of desert-cloaks not far away. Trinesh wished the injured youth whatever joy he could find in the arrangement.

Most of the Milumanayani were still awake, off in an open area of the cavern floor, probably holding council to discuss their unlooked-for guests. No need to worry, Tse'e said: there would be no treachery now that Trinesh and his party had shared food, salt, and water with their hosts. The tribesmen were currently making a great uproar: loud speeches, heckling, catcalls, and applause. Trinesh wondered what it was all about. He must ask Tse'e in the morning.

The Yan Koryani woman and her maid had not been bound again. The only direction of escape was the egg-thing, and there was no need for harsh measures. Trinesh did order them closely watched; it would be stupid to let the women and their little Pygmy-beast steal their sole means of returning to Fortress Ninu'ur, leaving them stranded in this Flame-forsaken place! He stood up to look. Yes, there they lay beside Dineva, Thu'n in a furry huddle on one side, the Lady Belket Ele Faiz curled up on the other.

He searched for the Yan Koryani girl—what was her name? Jai Chasa Vedlan—and finally saw her sitting apart from the rest, not far from his own sleeping place. She had not fared well; the womenfolk had demanded her pretty, feminine apparel, and at one point she had been stripped as naked as her mother had borne her. Saina had then provided a desert-cloak, as well as a gaudy skirtlike garment woven of *Hma*-wool and what was probably human hair.

The Milumanayani had not bothered the women. That, at

least, was a mercy; it had probably saved lives, particularly in Dineva's case. Though the tribes of the High Desert cared nothing about the ownership of property—their possessions were so few and life so hard that sharing them actually made sense—they did have a powerful sense of personal privacy. To rape a woman or slay a comrade was to start a feud that might last centuries and result in many deaths. War-captives were something else: they were indeed enslaved, but even then their females were never raped. A slave had to work— though no harder than others in the tribe—but slavery was less onerous here, and the refined cruelties of the Five Empires were thankfully missing. If any raping was done, it would likely be one of Trinesh's soldiers who would do it and not the Milumanayani. Dineva, Saina, and the two captives were as safe in Na Ngore as children in a temple of Dilinala, the virginal Cohort of the Goddess Avanthe.

One puzzle kept pricking at Trinesh's mind: the behavior of Lady Belket's maid, Lady Jai Chasa Vedlan. There was nothing overt, nothing really wrong, but he could not understand her reaction to the evening's chaffering and ribaldry. She smiled, petted the children, ate sparingly, and said so little that he would have thought her mute if he had not known otherwise. The girl appeared bored to the point of listlessness, as indifferent as a gladiator at a festival of flower-fanciers! Was she then a devotee of Dra the Uncaring, the Cohort of Lord Hnalla, Master of Light? Dra's followers affected total inaction, disinterest in the things of this life, and an ennui that surpassed rational comprehension. Upon consideration, he decided this could not be so, for then she would have been of no use to Lady Belket.

The Lady Jai was lovely, far superior to the trollops who followed along in the wake of the army. He had not known such a woman since he left Tumissa—not since a certain junior priestess of the temple of the Goddess Dlamelish had introduced him to various inner mysteries . . . La, he put *that* memory firmly back where it belonged and thought of something else!

His mind refused to abandon the topic of women, dredging up a vision of Lady Belket Ele Faiz with which to torment him instead. She was more beautiful than her maid. But then she looked as though she were too clever, too sophisticated, too wise in the ways of the world, to succumb to any pleasurable urges of his! She was undeniably fascinating, as alluring as any of the heroines of the epics! She was, however, a trifle too old for him. (Though only by a few years at most, his little inner voice niggled. He popped a lid upon *that* thought, too, before his voice could accuse him of bashful cowardice!) In the epics, the women were always younger than their lovers, he reminded himself. That was poetic tradition, and why did traditions exist if not to impart wisdom? The Lady Belket Ele Faiz was not for Trinesh hiKetkolel.

He grunted, rose, and went over to the Lady Jai. There was no use even pretending to himself that his motives were innocent.

She had not donned the desert-cloak Saina had acquired for her but had draped it carelessly across her lap. The dancing, dying light of the fire turned her breasts into ruddy globes that compelled desire as the bards said the candle demanded the sacrifice of the *Karai*-beetle in its flame. Those breasts, Trinesh noted, were high and well rounded, their nipples dark in the shadows, like her unbound tresses themselves. A length of curving, golden thigh showed beneath the folds of the cloak, but she made no effort to cover herself, as many other women of prudish Yan Kor would have done. She paid him no heed.

He stood before her for a long moment, then asked, "You are comfortable?" He himself was not.

"As far as possible." Her voice was low, accented, and musical. With just a subtle change in intonation it would have been seductive. She looked away.

He tried again. "Do not fear. We shall not let them harm you."

"Thank you."

"Nor shall we Tsolyani. I do not let my troops make war upon women."

"That is noble of you." Her voice was colorless. Did it conceal sarcasm?

He sat down uninvited. "What duties do you perform for your Lady Belket?"

She raised her eyes. They were large and long, almond-shaped, slightly tilted, as black as polished onyx, and luminous with glints of yellow firelight.

"I am her maid. I dress her, groom her, perform little services. No more." Was that last phrase stressed more than the rest?

"You are far from home. What is your city?" Why was the woman so laconic? So difficult? Perhaps she hated all Tsolyani—had she lost a lover, a clan-brother, or somebody in the war?

It was unthinkable, Trinesh believed firmly, that any woman could really dislike him. He would have cheerfully conceded that this might be no more than the natural confidence of a reasonably handsome young man of good clan and lineage, but he would also have pointed to the numerous successes he had already enjoyed, enough to make him an acknowledged expert on women among his clan-brothers and the fellow-subalterns of his legion. Oh, he had met women who were not attracted to him—for whatever reasons—but in the case of this Lady Jai Chasa Vedlan he did not sense "an arrow without a target," as he called it. No, there was something odd about the girl's behavior, almost as though she were asleep or drugged. He peered closely at her face but could see no signs of narcotics.

"I come from Dharu, the city we call 'the Forge of Yan Kor.' "

"You're not from Lady Belket's Isle of Vridu, then."

"No. From near the mouth of the River Vri, on the coast of the mainland. We are fisher-folk. Our clan is related to hers. Both serve the Lord of Sacrifice."

At least she was talking! Perhaps she was only shy. (As was Trinesh himself, his inner voice sniped, nastily and without provocation.)

"So do we, though we name Him differently: Lord Vimuhla."

"I know."

"Tell me of your people. What is it like there, in Yan Kor?"

She sighed and gazed full upon him. For a moment Trinesh thought he had won past her defenses. Then she pulled aside the desert-cloak so that he could see the full glory of her gleaming, coppery limbs. She had not troubled to put on the crude skirt Saina had secured for her, and his eyes traveled of themselves down from her breasts to her slim and silky belly, and thence to the dark triangle between her thighs.

She said, "If you are going to rape me, soldier, please do so quickly, for I am tired and would sleep."

He could only gape. "No—no—" he stammered. "I shall not—cannot—"

"Here." She pulled herself up onto her knees. "Kiss me. Get it over with." She shut her eyes tightly, as does a felon who anticipates the thrust of the executioner's impaling stake.

Astonished, he backed away and pulled the shreds of his dignity about himself like a beggar's ragged mantle. "No, Lady. I mean no insult. I take no woman who does not desire the taking."

"So you say." Her lips were parted, but her expression was one of utter unconcern. "Do as you will. I make no resistance, yet you will have no joy of me. I do not feign apathy only to discourage you from lying with me. My response is genuine."

"I believe you, Lady," he said with formal courtesy. He

had now regained a scrap or two of composure. He got to his feet. "Sleep well."

She drew the cloak back over her body for warmth and let her long tresses coil down over her cheek.

Trinesh could not resist one last question, one of supreme importance to his youthful ego: "Tell me, Lady, what is it that causes your disinterest? Do you hate us Tsolyani? Or all men? Or am I personally so displeasing . . . ?"

He thought he heard her sigh again. Her voice came, muffled and indistinct, from beneath the cloak. "None of those. The response you seek has been shut away from my heart; I can no more give love—or share in pleasure—than a *Chlen*-beast can fly." She said no more.

Trinesh turned on his heel and strode away. He felt thwarted and foolish, and this made him furious. He had almost attempted exactly what he had forbidden Horusel and the others to do, and yet the girl had parried him as neatly as a master swordsman knocks aside a novice's clumsy thrust! Cha! As the Tumissan proverb put it, "The best weapon is that against which your adversary has no defense!" It was a long time before he fell asleep.

He was awakened by the exile, Tse'e.

"*Hereksa*, I have news for you. The Folk of Na Ngore still hold council, and—"

"And what?" Trinesh felt of his aching limbs, rubbed his eyes, and yawned. The cistern-pool was inviting. He needed a bath.

"They deliberate. Here, all who dwell at Na Ngore—men, women, and even those children who are old enough to comprehend—vote upon every issue that affects the tribe as a whole. Nothing is resolved without unanimity."

"Foolish," Trinesh grumbled irritably. "How do they ever arrive at a conclusion?"

"Often they do not. They continue the debate until all are agreed, though sometimes the tribe splits, and the factions go their separate ways."

"They do not come to blows?"

"Rarely. Disagreement usually results in no more than inaction: if there be no consensus, nothing is done. The legends say that this was the reason that these people remained at Na Ngore when the rest of the Priestkings' garrison departed, and the sea dried up and became the desert it is now. They quarreled and argued whether to go or stay—and still they are undecided after all these millennia!" The old man cackled gustily.

"Madness!" Trinesh was awake enough to take interest. "La! There are times when I question the rightness of our own Tsolyani system—a God-Emperor, whose every whim is law—but this insanity makes Tsolyanu seem a veritable paradise!" He stopped and gave Tse'e his full attention, for the renegade's expression bore a shadow of grimness. "Quickly. Tell me how this present council concerns us. Should they plan to add us to the stew, they must be ready to count our Tsolyani votes—and we vote with our swords!"

Tse'e cleared his throat. He glanced down at his bare, dusty feet. "Since you dwell here now, you do have the right to vote. But no harm comes to you. That is not what they discuss."

"Say it, then."

"They have learned that three of you are Yan Koryani. When the Baron's agents came here—you have seen evidence of them—they treated these people harshly: slew some, tortured others. . . ."

"By the Flame, why? Give these creatures your armor, and they love you more dearly than your clan-mothers!"

Tse'e threw back the cowl of his desert-cloak to rub his balding head. "They fell out over the use of the cistern. The Yan Koryani would have brought a large contingent of troops hither and reserved the water for themselves."

"Did you not mediate, as you did for us?"

The old man frowned. "I am still a Tsolyani. I admit that I

did not argue very ardently for the Baron's people, though they wished it earnestly enough to beat me.''

"I see. What do they want? We will not give up our prisoners.''

"It were better that you do. Several of the folk claim the right of vengeance, and that is proper within their laws. Most of the others have agreed, though there are several who say that these are not the identical Yan Koryani who oppressed them.''

"The latter view is correct.''

"In Tsolyanu, when a felon cannot be apprehended, does not the Imperium punish his family, his clan, and sometimes even his friends for the crime? The principle is the same.''

The renegade was right. Tsolyani justice was not that dissimilar, though more complex in its workings. Trinesh said, "Why, then, have we not paid enough *Shamtla*-compensation to make up their losses: our weapons, our armor, even the clothes off our backs? Let these savages be satisfied!''

"There is no concept of *Shamtla* here, *Hereksa*. Property counts for naught, especially in cases of personal grievance. No, the Folk of Na Ngore are fixed upon punishment.''

"This cannot be." The Yan Koryani were prisoners of war; they might possess useful information. General Kutume was parsimonious, but he did reward services of value!

"No?'' Tse'e's good eye was hooded and sly. "Why do you care? These are Tsolyanu's sworn foes, *Hereksa*. If they die, you should rejoice. It relieves you of any danger from them. Later, you—and perhaps I with you—can regain the tubeway car and slip away.''

"It is not noble!" His determination was suddenly as unbreakable as mighty Hrugga's sword in the epics.

"Do you then care so much for the girl? Oh, I saw you go to her last night! And for the rodent-faced *Nininyal*—and for a Yan Koryani general?''

Trinesh opened his mouth to make an indignant reply, but

visions of Jai Chasa Vedlan's smooth and sensuous limbs obstructed his reason, arguing between his sense of duty as a soldier, and the Lady Belket's exquisitely patrician features—

What had the wretch said about her? A general?

He echoed the thought. "A general? What—? Who?"

It was Tse'e's turn to marvel. "You did not know?" Trinesh' expression told him, and he began to laugh. "La! La, brave soldier! A gigantic *Akho* in your net instead of a minnow! You have captured a high one indeed. The woman is the Lady Deq Dimani, General of the Legion of Vridu!"

Trinesh goggled at him. "But she said—"

"She duped you, of course. I know her. I saw her—" He broke off and began again. "Here you have a chance to see one of Yan Kor's cleverest officers out of Tsolyanu's path forever!"

Trinesh was not listening. He pulled the desert-cloak about him, shouted for Horusel and the others, and plunged off across the cavern.

The council was apparently still in session, although many of the children were asleep upon the hillocks of drifted sand that served as seats, and some of the adults, too, lay dozing here and there. The business of governance in Milumanaya was obviously fatiguing. He stopped and waited until the rest of his party came up, and the Milumanayani had bestirred themselves. Then he ordered his comrades forward through the tribesmen's ranks.

The three Yan Koryani were there already. They stood nude before the assembly, their wrists bound up behind their heads, and ropes of prickly thorn-fiber looped about their necks. The Lady Belket Ele Faiz—the Lady Deq Dimani, if Tse'e spoke truly—looked upon him stonily. Her features were set and pale. Thu'n did not raise his head, and Jai Chasa Vedlan gazed absently into the distance, like a child compelled to attend a debate on esoteric theology.

Trinesh wheeled upon Horusel. "Who let them be taken?"

The *Tirrikamu* hawked up phlegm. "Some of the sand-

worms' women came and led them away. We thought they
would bathe them, feed them. . . . How were we to know?''
He did not meet Trinesh' eyes.

There would be a reckoning later. Trinesh said icily, "Go
and cut them loose.''

Tse'e put out a hand. "No, *Hereksa*. They are judged.
Now they will be punished.''

"How? This humiliation? Or is there more?''

Tse'e scratched beneath his desert-cloak. "More. They are
to die, *Hereksa*, and it will be no easier for them than it was
for those their countrymen slew. The customary method is
harrying. At first it will be like a game, with much jesting
and laughter. The womenfolk will drag them to and fro
around the cavern; then they will strike them and stone them;
then their mouths and other orifices will be stuffed with
cactus-thorns; then will come burning with hot coals and
piercing with—''

Trinesh would hear no more.

"Stop!'' he cried. "None of this will be done! These three
are noble folk. They are prisoners of the Imperium, and they
are under my protection!''

Of all of the passions of humankind, the lust for vengeance
was one of the darkest and yet most universal. Tales of
Milumanayani atrocities were as common as *Chri*-flies in the
Tsolyani barracks. The women were said to be the instigators
and the tormentors in the tribes of the Desert of Sighs; once
unleashed upon a hapless victim, their cruelty was indescribable.

"Sire—'' Horusel began in a conciliatory tone.

"Shut up! I ordered you to go and free them. Give them
desert-cloaks or whatever you have. Then bring them here
and form a circle about them!''

The tribesmen had risen to see what transpired. Now they
murmured among themselves.

Trinesh seized Tse'e's bony arm. "Did all of them vote for
death?''

The man considered. "Not all. Some did not agree. Yet

they were persuaded to abstain out of respect for those whose kinsmen the Yan Koryani slew. An abstention is not a negative vote. No one now urges any course other than punishment."

Trinesh thought to see a subtle rift among the tribesmen: some were clustered on one side of the open space, the rest on the other. Only a few sat or sprawled independently of these two divisions. He addressed Tse'e. "Tell those who are resolved upon death to stand there on the left, those who would release the captives on the right. We will take another vote."

Tse'e glowered but spoke as Trinesh directed. The Milumanayani appeared puzzled. Some giggled and jested; others displayed irritation; and everyone chattered. In the end they did as they were told. The majority moved to the left, and only a few went to the right. A sizable number remained in the middle, whispering and staring. Trinesh looked them over. Then he said, "Tell me the words for 'I vote to free them.'"

The renegade's scowl became a glare. "In the name of all the gods, *Hereksa*, WHY? Leave well enough alone—" He saw Trinesh's face and hastily added, "Say *lupazhes tezha'i*. That is what you want."

Trinesh waited until all were attentive. Then he turned to Horusel and the rest and said, "We are about to participate in a tribal council. We will vote for the release of these prisoners. Say these words after me and walk to that group there on the right." He pointed, then uttered the phrase Tse'e had given him.

The others stumbled over the foreign syllables. Only Chekkuru and Horusel stood silent, resentment mirrored in their faces. Trinesh had known this would happen. He eyed his subordinate and snapped, "I gave a command, *Tirrikamu*. Argue it and Balar there shoots you dead. Balar!" The crossbowman hesitated but cocked his weapon and inserted a quarrel. He pointed it, shakily, at Horusel's breast. "And you, priest. You are under military law as long as we are in the field. This you know. Arjasu, your bolt will be for Chekkuru hiVriddi! Mejjai, stand ready in case either misses.''

This brought compliance of a sort. Chekkuru scuttled over to join Trinesh, and Horusel followed more slowly. One day they must settle this matter, but not now. Trinesh repeated the Milumanayani words, louder this time, and raised his hand to orchestrate a ragged chorus of the same from his followers.

''Now,'' he said pleasantly to Tse'e, ''we have no unanimity, and what is not completely agreed cannot be done. So you said yourself. Tell them that we are immutable in our resolve. We will hear no more arguments.'' He tossed his belt-knife to Chosun. ''Horusel seems unable to hear my order. I shall see to having his ears cleaned later. You go and cut our captives free.''

Voluble protests arose, but Tse'e patiently repeated the same phrase over and over. Then it was done, and the two women and the little *Nininyal* were unbound and allowed to stagger over to stand beside Trinesh.

''I thought you would be happy to see us slain,'' Lady Jai Chasa Vedlan said. She permitted Dineva to wrap a desert-cloak about her shoulders.

''Why?'' He glanced over at the other woman. ''Because your Lady here lied to us? She who is no lowly *Tokhn* of one thousand but a high general, not some nonentity named Belket Ele Faiz but the High Lady Deq Dimani herself, Matriarch of the Isle of Vridu!''

The Lady turned her perfect, oval face to look upon him. ''So you know? The one called Tse'e told you?'' She donned the soldier's tunic Saina held out to her. ''I was right,'' she said to Thu'n. ''He did recognize me.''

''My Lady did not lie!'' It was the first time Trinesh had heard any spark of emotion in Jai Chasa Vedlan's voice. ''Her personal name *is* Belket Ele Faiz! Deq Dimani is her accession-name, just as your Tsolyani Emperors take haughty titles when they sit upon the Petal Throne!''

"Fa! Thus far we have had nothing but clever subterfuges from your 'noble' Lady!"

"What would *you* have done?" the girl shot back.

"Leave off," the Lady Deq Dimani said. She had regained most of her equanimity. "We are still a long way from Tsolyanu, and the Weaver must weave a strange skein indeed before I am dragged in chains before your God-Emperor Hirkane hiTlakotani in Avanthar. Now we had best look to our skins. These sand-worms seem displeased with your voting."

It was so. A single large group had formed to listen to the haranguing of a gray-locked elder. Some slipped away to return with weapons. A woman interrupted to rant and gesticulate.

Tse'e said fearfully, "I warned you. They vote to slay us all."

"Tell them that we vote against that course of action," Trinesh answered.

"What! You are mad! Back away and ready yourself to die!" The old renegade spoke to the tribesmen, nevertheless. "They vote to expel you from the Folk. When this is done they will slay you."

"Say that we vote to remain within the tribe." Trinesh experienced an odd cheerfulness. Either this fanciful stratagem would work, or it would not. If not, they would fight. If they lost, they would die as soldiers.

Chaos ensued. Some tribesmen shouted, others wrangled. Several of the older men stalked off in disgust. An infant piddled in the sand and yowled; one of the women rushed to rescue it.

"Tell them that every action of the Folk will henceforth require a full discussion and a vote. No one shall eat, drink, cook, fill waterskins, hunt, sleep, relieve himself, or perform any other task until we, the community, have heard the proposal and voted upon it."

One of the younger warriors rushed forward. The crossbowman Mejjai lifted his weapon, but Trinesh shouted an order to desist. The Milumanayani halted in bafflement.

"Inform that man that violence against a fellow-tribesman is a breach of the law. If he attacks, he becomes a felon and is liable to punishment!"

"I admit that I am surprised by your cleverness, Tsolyani," the Lady Deq Dimani declared. "Still, they will soon become frustrated, and then we are dead."

Trinesh did not take his eyes from the Folk of Na Ngore. "Wait, Lady. I have one more arrow to my bow. Translate for me again, Tse'e." He flourished his newly acquired steel sword. "Fellow dwellers, servitors of the Priestkings of Ganga! Know that we, your co-tribesmen, have a proposal of our own to lay before you!" He glanced at Tse'e and growled, "Put my words eloquently, renegade; else you remain to face their wrath!" The old man rolled his good eye in despair but stepped forward. He waved his arms, declaimed, and made dramatic gestures. "Ah, good. Now: tell them that a certain wise and noble member of our party—" he bowed toward Chekkuru hiVriddi "—is a priest of great holiness. He commands us to re-enter the egg-thing there, and his sanctity will keep our sinful laymen's feet from defiling the glory of your—our—temple. Say that this pious priest is upon a mission ordained by the gods, and we are his soldiers! The Folk must now return all of our arms and gear; otherwise we face certain defeat at—at the hands of monsters who will consume us and then come bounding through the tubeway to slaughter the Folk of Na Ngore."

"*Hereksa*, you are brilliant," someone breathed. It sounded like Saina, but it might have been the Lady Deq Dimani.

Tse'e spoke at length. Their audience consulted, and at last the gray-beard arose to address them.

"He says they now vote upon your plan, *Hereksa*," Tse'e said.

"Good. I am confident of the outcome. Tell us the words so that we may do our civic duty as well."

The vote was, not surprisingly, unanimous. A child who did not seem to comprehend the issue was unceremoniously slapped into full concurrence. Trinesh marshaled his comrades into some order and marched off to the temple platform, accepting weapons, bits of clothing, and armor from those within reach as he went. No one objected.

"And what happens," Chekkuru asked, "if some of their young bravos decide to accompany us upon this divine mission you have laid upon me?"

"Let them," Trinesh responded. "Our car is too crowded. They must summon a vehicle of their own in which to follow. Are we to blame if the ten studs of their conveyance are set for destinations different from ours?"

7

I t took the Folk of Na Ngore only moments to realize that their quorum no longer included their unwelcome guests. By the time Trinesh's party was halfway across the cavern, the Milumanayani were already belling in full pursuit. Army discipline kept the Tsolyani together, however, and they were almost at the top of the timeworn steps of the tubeway platform before the first warriors reached the open space below it. Arjasu and Mejjai picked off two of these, but Balar missed his target. The foe then retreated precipitately to the shelter of the low, ruined walls that crisscrossed this section of the chamber. Whoever had built these partitions and for whatever purpose, they now provided excellent cover for their owners.

"Save your bolts," Trinesh ordered. "Into the egg-vehicle!"

Chosun, the last inside, pressed the door-stud in the very face of a determined rush by a score or so of their erstwhile fellow-citizens.

"When they find the depression by the door we'll have

them in our laps," the big man panted. "I see no way to lock it."

Trinesh dragged Thu'n forward. "Which button takes us back to Fortress Ninu'ur? Come, I think you know!" He jabbed his steel sword into the creature's abdomen for emphasis. It must have hurt but was not meant to pierce the skin. They needed the *Nininyal*.

"Not I, Tsolyani!" Thu'n gasped. "I swear it! Our sorcerer said only that one button would take us to Yan Kor—though which city I know not. Another may be set for Fortress Ninu'ur since the car was waiting there when we discovered it. I am an historian and no scholar of machines—that was Qurtul's work."

"Cha! Push any button!" Horusel demanded. "The sandworms batter at the door!"

The sacred number of Lord Vimuhla was three. Trinesh muttered a prayer and depressed the third stud.

Nothing happened. The forward view-portrayer continued to show contorted Milumanayani faces just outside the eggthing's curved metal shell. One came close enough to squint into what must be the device's external lens, treating them to a view of a large and angry eye. The cries of the Folk did not penetrate the vessel's walls, but the thumping at the door became louder and better organized.

"The third must be the destination button for this place," Thu'n offered unnecessarily.

Trinesh pushed the second stud.

The sensation of motion was immediate and welcome. Missiles thudded upon the roof of the car as it dropped down into the vertical tunnel whence it had emerged in Na Ngore. Chekkuru hiVriddi uttered a voluble paean of thanksgiving.

Trinesh looked about and counted. All were present, including Tse'e.

"We have no way of knowing whither this vehicle takes us," he said. "I suggest that we now swear upon our various gods to abandon our hostilities and cooperate. When we reach a destination belonging to one or the other of our sides, we become enemies once more. Thereafter we decide to fight or surrender according to our Skeins of Destiny. Let there be no more perfidy until that time comes.''

All muttered assent. Trinesh glared fiercely at Horusel and Chekkuru, but even they seemed willing enough for a truce.

"Now we see what arms, clothing, and food we have. Each shall reclaim his or her own belongings—including these Yan Koryani.''

There was nervous laughter as each item was brought forth and exchanged. The results were not too discouraging. The crossbowmen had perforce left their shields behind, but they had zealously clung to their weapons—the Folk did not use crossbows and showed no interest in them. Balar had a hand-axe as well. Trinesh and Chosun both possessed swords and belt-knives, Horusel his axe, Saina a saw-toothed bone spear, Dineva only a club, and Jalugan nothing. The renegade, Tse'e, displayed a slender steel poniard in a sheath strapped to his thigh, its hilt bearing the markings of some Yan Koryani legion.

Chekkuru surprised them all: from beneath his desert cloak and what portions he had recovered of his priestly vestments he withdrew the Lady Deq Dimani's sword and Thu'n's double-bladed dagger. These he handed back to their owners.

Armor was a problem. Nothing was complete, but there were enough pieces to make up three composite harnesses. Trinesh commandeered one for himself, gave the second to Chosun, to whom it had mostly belonged, and let the Lady Deq Dimani have what remained of her own elegant equipment. The rest he returned to the others. He was delighted when Horusel reluctantly surrendered his own iron gorget-piece; he had thought it lost for good!

The deep pouches of their several desert cloaks provided a heap of tubers and several strips of dried and salted meat. Chekkuru pronounced the latter to be *Hmelu*-flesh. Trinesh had his doubts, but he kept these to himself; hunger would make almost anything palatable, even the last contributions of "one who serves."

The motion of the car continued, silent and after awhile almost imperceptible. The view-portrayers showed only blackness. Trinesh forbade Thu'n from fiddling with them. Who knew what might thus be alerted to their coming?

He had laid one bothersome question aside during their flight from Na Ngore. Now he had time to ask it. He rounded upon Tse'e. "You recognized the Lady Deq Dimani, did you not? And I think she knew you as well. The need for pretense is past, and I will have your real name and any other relevant truths from both of you!"

The renegade looked away. "I am Tse'e," he said softly. "Only Tse'e."

The Lady Deq Dimani leaned against the rear wall next to the Lady Jai Chasa Vedlan, who seemed dazed. "He revealed my identity to you, *Hereksa*," she said, "and one bad turn deserves another. Would you know his true name?"

"Please . . ." Tse'e murmured. "It no longer matters. . . ."

"I shall tell you." She rose and made a mock curtsy. "Make obeisance, *Hereksa*! You address Prince Nalukkan hiTlakotani, the youngest brother of your Seal Emperor!"

Her words left a widening pool of stunned silence.

"When I was a little girl this man came to seek refuge upon our Isle of Vridu," she continued. "My mother turned him away—"

"No," Tse'e pleaded. "Say no more—already it is too much. . . ."

She went on, relentlessly. "His eldest brother, Mursun Dlekkumine, was born to Prince Hetkolainen during the reign of their grandfather, the Emperor Arshu'u, 'the Ever-Splendid.' Hirkane, who now sits upon the Petal Throne, is the second of Hetkolainen's heirs, and this 'Tse'e' the third and last. In the year 2,291—Thu'n, am I not correct? You know the reckonings better than I—Hetkolainen became the Seal Emperor under the throne-title 'He Whose Glory Never Ends.'

His offspring were given commands in the great armies their grandfather had raised for the conquest of the north. When Hetkolainen died in 2,345 neither this wretched 'Tse'e' nor Hirkane sought the throne: Hirkane 'renounced the Gold,' as your idiom has it, and took no part in the *Kolumejalim,* 'the Rite of Choosing of Emperors.' That left the oldest and the least suited, Mursun, to rule. He perished in 2,346 without issue, and if he is remembered at all, it is only as 'the Weak.' Thereupon the priesthoods and the Servitors of Silence came to Hirkane and begged him to think again, to seek the Gold. It was either that or no emperor at all—an interregnum, a struggle between more distant claimants, or even a civil war, with the north in chaos, and with Mu'ugalavya in the west and Salarvya in the east eager to pick up any counters dashed from the board.''

"Lies!" Chekkuru cried. "Once an heir renounces the Gold, he or she can never stand for the *Kolumejalim* again! Moreover, there is no Nalukkan in any list of Imperial genealogies. . . ." His eyes narrowed as though he remembered something.

She shrugged and made a scornful gesture. "Genealogies are easily forgotten—or altered—or expunged entirely. As for the rest, do you not say, 'Even the sun can be moved if the gods so will'—and, 'Where power exists, there are deeds?' The jurists of Tsolyanu searched in their lawbooks and discovered that, indeed, one who refuses to join in the *Kolumejalim* may not come forth later to contest *that* reign. But no law prevents such an heir from entering into any *subsequent* competition. Hirkane hiTlakotani was thus technically eligible. So also was Prince Nalukkan hiTlakotani, who styles himself 'Tse'e,' but—"

"This cannot be!" Chekkuru shouted again, "Treason—" Trinesh shushed him.

"—Prince Nalukkan had omitted to renounce the Gold when Mursun Dlekkumine stood for the Petal Throne."

"What?" Trinesh's face showed honest puzzlement. "That

meant that he had to join in the *Kolumejalim*! An Imperial heir who does not abandon all claim to the throne *must* participate. Should another candidate win in the contests set by the priesthoods, all of the losers die! Only by renouncing the Gold in advance can a Prince or Princess avoid the competition entirely and remain alive! This—this 'Prince Nalukkan' should have perished when Mursun Dlekkumine was anointed in Avanthar—''

"You have said it. For whatever reason, he did *not* give up the Gold. His life is forfeit if he is caught." She laughed, deep in her throat. "Bow to your Prince, *Hereksa*; then execute him as a felon condemned by the highest tribunal of your land!"

She extended one hand, palm up, to Tse'e, daring him to gainsay her.

Tse'e shook his straggling locks. He looked as though he would again plead ignorance or deny her altogether. Then he sighed and said, "She is right, soldier. I am as she says."

"But the *Kolumejalim*—?" Chosun puzzled.

"I did not renounce the Gold—for reasons which are mine alone to know—but chose instead to flee. All that is an epic no bard will ever sing, but I will admit that in the beginning I planned to return at the head of an army—certain factions would have assisted me—but Mursun Dlekkumine perished. Some say he died of *Zu'ur*, the vicious drug supplied by the Hlüss. Thereafter Hirkane became Emperor all too swiftly—a good and efficient Emperor, which was something I had never anticipated. He knew, of course, that I had not renounced the Gold, and I was compelled to seek refuge first in one northern city-state, then in another, until his agents had winkled me out of almost every sanctuary. It was during that time that I visited Vridu. Later the Baron Ald unified the north, and the only remaining refuge was that in which you found me: wretched Na Ngore in the Desert of Sighs. Oh,

escape to still more distant lands was possible, of course—
beyond Salarvya to the Nyemesel Isles, or to the forests of
Tane that lie west of Mu'ugalavya and the Plain of Towers—
but I hoped to return to my homeland. I am still a Tsolyani,
no matter what tongue I speak or what garb I wear. . . .''

Chekkuru would have interrupted, but Chosun gave him
such a glare that he desisted.

"Hear the rest of it, priest," the old man said. "There
were times when I wanted to surrender—to die. But the
Weaver had spun the threads of my Skein of too stout a stuff.
When at last I found Na Ngore, I discovered that I had
become more severe than any Tsolyani judge: it was I who
condemned myself: not to death but to life. I refused the
condemned man the final thrust that gives eternal peace. I
lived, yes, but it was a life more arduous than any prison, a
mindless round of hunting, eating, sleeping, and growing old
as a barely tolerated 'guest' of the Folk. Never did they
accept me as one of them, nor did I desire that. My dreams
were always of Tsolyanu and of Avanthar." He faltered.
"I—I would die at home; yet that is denied me except upon
the impaling stake as a traitor to the Empire. There are some
things a man cannot endure—not the pain of execution, I
swear to you, but the ignobility, the shame. Can you understand that, *Hereksa*?"

He stopped. Then he said, "That steel sword you carry
was mine, a memento of the days before I came to Na Ngore,
when I still yearned for armies and power and a triumphal
return to Avanthar. Among the Folk I had no need of it. Now
I ask you this favor, *Hereksa*: as a servant of the Imperium,
as a Tsolyani—as one whom I have aided—put its blade to
my throat and end this Skein! Do this thing, *Hereksa*, and an
Imperial Prince is in your debt. . . .''

"Slay the traitor!" Chekkuru snarled then, and Horusel
echoed his words.

That decided it for Trinesh, of course. "No. Listen, Tse'e,

or Prince Nalukkan, or however you—'' he broke off to search his memory; he had learned the thirty-odd Tsolyani pronouns for "you" in the temple school, but he had never before needed the one reserved for an Imperial Prince! He gave up and went back to the simple, honorific *Tusmidali*. "Ah— you, however you would be known, you have aided us, and we are grateful. Yet I cannot grant your wish, nor shall I allow any of these others to do so. We still need your skills and your knowledge of the Desert of Sighs. Let us not speak now of treason and dying and executions and laws! It is my turn to implore you—''

Chekkuru trembled with anger. His hands opened and closed spasmodically, as though they gripped the old man's throat.

The Lady Deq Dimani shook her long, raven hair back from her face. "I think that there is another, special reason that your priest here would see this 'Tse'e'—this Prince Nalukkan—dead, *Hereksa*. Have you heard of the revolt of the Vriddi clan in 2,340? So? Chekkuru hiVriddi may not recall an Imperial Prince named Nalukkan, but every Vriddi knows the name of the commander, the young *Dritlan*, who was sent to put down that rebellion, to level Fasiltum, their 'City of the Chiming Skulls,' into the dust, and to see their leader, the Lady Elara hiVriddi, and her followers cast into the Emperor's dungeons or given the 'High Ride' upon the impalers' stakes. The officer entrusted with those pleasant duties was named Nalukkan, though few may now recall that his clan-name was Tlakotani."

Chekkuru screeched and launched himself upon the man who called himself Tse'e.

Trinesh did not think. He brought the hilt of his sword down upon the back of the priest's shaven skull with a satisfying thump. Horusel's iron-hard fingers clawed at his shoulders; then other hands, feet, and fists pummeled, clutched, and battered against his armor, until he found himself buried beneath a press of bodies on the smooth, gray deck. He had no idea whom he struck or why. Boots and bare feet shuffled around his head, and he heard yells, grunts—a milling, struggling, cursing chaos. Somebody kicked him, painfully, in the thigh. Then one of the view-portrayers shattered, and shards of glass rained down over them all.

Hands plucked the weight from Trinesh's chest. He lay upon his back, the little cabin lights wheeling giddily above him. Another body was removed from his legs. He heard further blows, shouting. Chosun's florid features swam before his eyes, and he was roughly hauled erect.

Chekkuru hiVriddi lay doubled up on the blood-smeared floor. The priest was neither dead nor unconscious, for he moaned and put cautious fingers back to explore a gash in his scalp. Trinesh looked for Horusel and saw him pinioned beneath Mejjai, Balar, and Saina; it took the three of them to hold him. Dineva must have supported Horusel and the priest, for Jalugan and Arjasu stood watchfully before her. The Lady Deq Dimani had apparently been involved as well; she was bruised and disheveled, her tunic torn. Tse'e and the girl huddled against the cabin walls. Only Thu'n was missing; the little *Nininyal* had probably dived into the rear storage compartment once more.

Tse'e—Prince Nalukkan hiTlakotani—pointed a trembling finger at Lady Deq Dimani. "Why?" he cried. "Why have you undone me so? What harm did I do you that you parade my shame before these people?"

The woman's cheeks were flushed, and she panted for breath. "And why not? Did my mother fail to tell you when you came crawling to us for sanctuary? Were you asleep when your tutors chanted the glories of your ancestors? Did you never hear tell of the Legion of the Searing Flame? No? One of your own Tsolyani Legions! A thousand years ago that Legion suffered disgrace—through no fault of its troops— and the Flame-accursed Emperor Metlunel II, whom you

Tsolyani stupidly honor as 'the Builder,' drove it into exile—near eight thousand loyal soldiers, their families, their clansmen—! Did no bard sing to you of their sufferings, their wanderings in the northlands: how they lived among the Lorun and the Yan Koryani, how they were hunted by the dreaded Shunned Ones, how they—''

"But what connection—?" Trinesh got out.

Her eyes flashed at him. "Cha, another poor scholar! Have you never considered the naming of my Isle of Vridu? Of the River Vri eastward of it, on the mainland amid the forests?" She touched one finger to her throat. "We, most mighty Prince, are Vriddi too! We are descended from the exiles of the Legion of the Searing Flame, the kinsmen of those you massacred in Fasiltum, the cousins of the 'rebels' your soldiers slew. Do not your annals brag of 'rows of impaling stakes as numberless as the pillars of high-vaunting Avanthar'?"

Saina said slowly, "May be as may be, Lady. But the Vriddi of Fasiltum are loyal citizens now—mostly, anyway. Who can keep a hatred alive for so long? And, for the sake of the living, WHY?"

"What can you know of tradition, woman—you, who are probably descended from some lowly clan whose greatest glory is its claim to have swept latrines for a thousand years? Cha! We Vriddi remember a glorious past that stretches back before Engsvan hla Ganga and the First Imperium of the Bednalljan kings to the Dragon Warriors of ancient N'lüss! Millennia! Aeons! An age is like a second to us! You may forget, but we do not! As for 'loyal citizens,' do you Tsolyani not say, 'Once the Zrne is slain, the Hmelu graze in peace'?"

She wheeled back to face Trinesh, the dark curtain of her tresses swirling out about her cheekbones. "Just now I swore to commit no violence, Tsolyani. Release me from that oath. Give me leave, and I carry out the sentence this craven butcher's brother—your Seal Emperor—passed upon him!''

Trinesh found himself praying that they would reach their destination—any destination—that something would occur to interrupt the hatred now boiling up so virulently among them. Nothing of the sort happened. He drew a ragged breath and tried to run his fingers through his hair, but his nails scraped the flanges of his helmet instead; he had forgotten he had it on.

Damn the woman! Damn them all!

"No!" he shouted. "No! There will be no killing. Not this—this Prince, not Horusel, not Chekkuru hiVriddi, not you, Lady. No one! We swore, and I hold you to your oaths! The only execution will be that of the one who breaks that word. Upon that you have *my* oath! I still command here.'' He raised the Prince's sword. "Is there any who disputes me? It is better that we fight now—my skill against that of any would-be mutineer! If enough of you disagree, slay me and squabble over the spoils! Then, I think, you will all be dead by the time this car reaches its destination! Now we need each other more than we need Missum, the Lord of Death!''

For a moment the balance swung this way and that. Then Chosun stepped over to Trinesh. His three crossbowmen followed, as did Saina and Jalugan. Dineva wavered but came to stand beside Saina. Horusel snorted in disgust, but some of the fury had gone out of him, and he held up his hands in grudging agreement. Prince Nalukkan nodded to Trinesh. Only Chekkuru and the two Yan Koryani women remained.

"You do have my word,'' the Lady Deq Dimani admitted. "That is a thing I do not break. Come, Jai.'' She murmured to the girl in Yan Koryani and called out to the *Nininyal*. "You, too, Thu'n. All is done here—for now.'' She lowered her curved sword.

Chekkuru hiVriddi still nursed the bloody lump upon the back of his loaf-shaped skull, his expression cold and unreadable. "Think, *Hereksa*," he said with finality. "You hold the temporal power, but there are others greater by far. What you do may not please your God."

No one debated him. Yet peace seemed more useful at this juncture than strife, whatever the tenets of the Flame Lord might preach.

8

Their second journey in the egg-vehicle was longer than the first. No one wanted to revive the deadly tensions of the past hours, and they thus limited all conversation by mutual consent to the simplest amenities. They rested, ate, and rested again. There was no water, however, which was worrisome, particularly if they emerged in some still more remote area of the Desert of Sighs.

Trinesh appraised his little force covertly from the shadow of his helmet's beaked visor. Chosun he could count on; Horusel, too, was a sensible man and a skilled fighter, if one got past his fanaticism and his obvious little plays for power. Dineva was equally good, with Saina not far behind. The three crossbowmen, fellow travelers only because of the whim of the Weaver of Skeins, appeared shaky but still in reasonably good spirits. Balar was young and brash, a burly, roughly handsome rogue from the mountains near Hekellu in the far northeastern corner of the Empire. He fancied himself a mighty lover, and even now he lounged beside the Lady Jai

Chasa Vedlan, gallant words no doubt spilling from his tongue like honey from a spoon. Too bad he was not as good at soldiering! He'd have made *Tirrikamu* if he had spent as much time with his crossbow as he did with his doxies, his drinking, and his gambling. The Lady Jai ignored him as completely as she had Trinesh. Stocky Mejjai was utterly average: the barracksroom jokers were wont to say that even the Goddess Dlamelish Herself could spend an aeon alone with Mejjai and never remember his face. Arjasu, on the other hand, was the best trooper of the lot. A ten-year veteran, he was tough, hard, and experienced at everything from mountain skirmishing to siege warfare. If it came to a fight, Arjasu would be the man to have at one's back. Jalugan, now, might pose a problem: for all his bravery, he was very young. More, the slash Thu'n had given him must be growing painful, and there was no telling whether the boy would harden like *Chlen*-hide in a tanner's chemical bath, or whether he would crumble under the stress.

Chekkuru hiVriddi sat whispering with Thu'n. That would have to be stopped; the priest had already shown his willingness to aid the Lady Deq Dimani against Tse'e—Prince Nalukkan hiTlakotani—and Trinesh dared tolerate no further confidences. The Lady herself sat crosslegged, her back against the rear wall of the cabin, ostensibly dozing as a good soldier does when there is nothing to do. Tse'e squatted as far from her as he could get, beside Chosun near the forward console.

They were all both relieved and apprehensive when the car finally sighed to a halt. Trinesh permitted Thu'n to twist the knobs beneath those view-portrayers which still functioned—the one broken in their recent scuffle was that which had not worked anyway—but only blackness was visible without. One of the controls produced a hum, amid which a repetitive chiming, clanking note boomed forth like the knelling of a bronze gong. Thu'n fussed with the knob; the hum disappeared and the ringing was reduced to no more than the tinkle of dripping water.

"A lightless burrow beneath the earth?" the Lady Deq Dimani said. "Not a good place for us, not without lamps or spells of illumination."

Trinesh silently agreed. He pressed the fourth destination stud.

There was no way of calculating the length of their travel. Trinesh tried to count his pulse-beats but lost track when Jalugan interrupted to ask a question. His stomach told him that he was already hungry, but its complaints were not significantly louder when the motion of their vehicle ceased once more.

The glass squares revealed yet another cavern. A strange strip of flickering yellow light ran along the ceiling and glittered from rows of dully shining vehicles much like their own. Horusel would have opened the door for a quick look, but the others urged caution. It was well that they did so: a great machine rolled restlessly to and fro in the shadows there, a thing of wheels and coils and metal spars and winking red eyes.

"A *Ru'un!*" The Lady Deq Dimani breathed. "The automatons of the Ancients."

"Yet like none described in the epics," Chekkuru exclaimed. He had been morose and silent since their quarrel, but now he seemed sufficiently interested in new mysteries even to forget the lump Trinesh had raised on his skull.

"This, too, is no place for the living," Trinesh remarked to no one in particular. "I press the fifth stud."

The car sped off again.

This journey took still longer. It ended with a red light flashing upon the panel to the right of the destination buttons. An authoritative voice squawked words in an unknown language.

"Lord Vimuhla speaks," Chekkuru opined gravely. "That red light is the color of His Supernal Flame!"

The forward view-portrayer revealed a tunnel which ended in a jumble of dark shapes. The two side-viewers showed smooth, curving walls of a blue-black substance. All of the light seemed to come from some source atop their own vehicle. The voice repeated its message with greater insistence.

"Press another button, *Hereksa*," the priest said. "We stand outside the gates of the Flame Lord's sacred paradise beneath the earth!"

"If so, then this is your chance to enter, thus avoiding the need to die on this Plane before taking up residence here!" Saina said. The others laughed at Chekkuru's discomfiture, and even the Lady Jai smiled.

"More likely a collapsed passage beyond," Thu'n declared. "If you want to give thanks, then offer it to your ancestors who created such excellent alarms and restraints!" He himself pressed the sixth stud before Trinesh could intervene.

The air in the little cabin grew thick and foul. Trinesh thought to detect a smell of burning, but he could see no fire. This doubtless reinforced Chekkuru's identification of their last stop, but previously nothing had penetrated their car from outside. It worried him.

"Food, Sire?" the crossbowman Balar asked. With a flourish, he proffered a squat cylinder of silvery metal, the flat top of which he had ripped off with a knife to expose a thick, brown paste inside.

"Where did you get this?"

"From one of the little compartments in the wall." Balar pointed.

Trinesh inserted a finger, tasted, and spat. "Fa! Either it is poisoned by age or else it is no food at all!" The stuff had a ghastly oily flavor, worse than any nostrum brewed by the apothecaries. "Did you eat of this concoction?"

"Not I, Sire. Not much, anyhow. But—ah . . ."

"Go into the storage compartment!" Trinesh bellowed. "Quickly! Thrust your finger down your throat and vomit it back out again—all of you who ate it!" His own mouth burned. He fumbled in the pouches of the nearest desert-cloak for something with which to kill the taste and came up with a strip of dried meat. Even the flesh of "one who serves" was preferable! If this were indeed edible, then the "food of the Ancients" was less appetizing than the venomous purplish vegetation folk named "the Food of the Ssu"!

The substance was too thin and watery to be grease such as the carter clans used on the axles of their lumbering wains. It might be fuel for their car—smiths, jewelers, and other crafts-men employed various arcane substances to fire their furnaces—but he had seen no orifices through which the machine could be "fed," nor was he fool enough to poke about in the compartment Chosun had discovered under the deck. La, for all they knew, the Ancients might have greased their beards with it, as the N'lüss tribes did theirs with *Hmelu*-butter!

They spent the next hour or so listening to Balar and Mejjai retching in the rear compartment. Arjasu had tasted none. The pair eventually appeared, much chagrined, their lips red and blistered, to squat miserably on the floor at the rear of the cabin. They seemed undamaged otherwise, for which Trinesh was grateful.

He dozed, then awoke to find Saina's hand upon his arm. "We're somewhere, *Hereksa*. We've stopped."

The scene outside was one of great beauty, though forlorn and dolorous. Their vehicle stood upon the lip of a precipice overlooking the ruins of a city. The forward view-portrayer showed a floor that ended abruptly in a jagged crevasse. Beyond this, separated by a deep, purple-shadowed canyon, rows of empty windows, eroded walls, and shattered case-ments climbed up a hill in tiers like the gray battlements of some time-besieged fortress. The roofless buildings and black tunnel-mouths resembled a nest of *Dri*-ants—but a nest that contained no life. All was dead, decayed, and tumbled into chaos. Sparse undergrowth clawed up to drag the mighty towers down; silt and rubble choked the thoroughfares; and only brambles and sad, black-leaved *Aika*-plants used the esplanades and filled the fountains now.

The side-portrayers displayed the same scene but from an angle that held more promise: they showed the cavern behind the crevasse, a huge, pillared chamber that ran off into darkness. The place was artificial, made by humankind—or by some other sapient species—and it contained machines, housings, walkways, ladders, and enigmatic devices. Most important, one of the panes depicted a second egg-vehicle, identical to their own, hanging above a circular shaft no more than ten paces away! Its door-hatch was open, and fat, gray canisters lay piled neatly in the foreground. There were no signs of living beings. The car and its surroundings appeared as deserted and melancholy as the city across the way.

They waited, but nothing changed. The cavern remained as still as an artist's picture.

Trinesh had just laid his hand upon the door-stud when there came a thudding upon the car's roof. He jerked around to peer into the view-portrayers. All three still showed the same scene. Yet there was a difference: their pictures were now sliced into griddings of small, neat squares.

It took him a moment to recognize those squares for what they were: the interwoven mesh of a net, a huge snare that must have dropped upon their vehicle from above!

He managed to shout a warning; then their car tipped, rolled, and deposited them all in a heap upon what had just been the ceiling.

They yelled, struggled, and fought back up to their feet only to slide down the walls again as the car slowly righted itself. It seemed to possess an internal equilibrium of its own. The netting spread and strained but held fast. The scene outside tilted back from shattered stone roof and sapphire sky to the ruined city and the cavern.

There was no sign of the fishers who had netted them.

"We are taken, Tsolyani!" The Lady Deq Dimani pulled herself up against Trinesh's chest. At any other time this might have been pleasurable.

"Brace yourselves!" he called. "Whoever has us will

either open the door or roll us on over the cliff." In the latter event they were all lost, but he saw no reason to mention it. The neighboring car was nearer now, as though their own vehicle hung from a crane that slowly bore them away from their entrance tunnel.

Thu'n clawed his way to the destination buttons, pushed one, then another. He was rewarded by a stink of burning and wisps of smoke from beneath the cabin deck.

The situation demanded urgent measure. "Here!" Trinesh ordered. "Chosun, open the floor-hatch you found! You—Balar—find a cylinder of that stuff you tried to eat! We may be able to restore power to our car!"

They scurried to obey. The enigmatic tubes and containers beneath the sliding hatch-cover were as before, but smoke drifted up from them, and the smell of fire was stronger. Trinesh saw a small door, like that of a miniature baker's oven, in the top of one of the housings. This he pried up, burning his fingers as he did so, to reveal a popping, fizzing, sparkling mess of flat, black plates upon which complex diagrams and runes were engraved in silver. Here were the sorcerous tablets that powered the car! He knew enough about magic not to touch them. Tiny arcs of crackling light dazzled his eyes.

Arjasu slapped a dull-gleaming cylinder into his outstretched palm. Trinesh dug out a dollop of its brownish contents and dropped it down amid the little plaques inside the compartment. If the machine required fuel, he would offer it some!

Dense vapors emerged, and more lightnings flashed.

"Push another button, Thu'n!" Trinesh shouted. He slammed the little door shut and backed away.

The smoke became worse, and they coughed. "Thu'n! Damn it!"

"I pushed everything," the little *Nininyal* wailed. "Look!" A dozen red lights glittered now upon the control panels. The disembodied voices of ancient spirits began to howl, lecture, and preach from everywhere at once.

The Lady Jai sank to her knees to gasp for breath.

"We have no choice." The fumes gagged Trinesh, too, and he felt dizzy. "We leave the car—fight whatever awaits outside—ready yourselves—!" He plunged over to the door and pressed the stud. Nothing happened. A bright red light below it caught his eye: another button there. He jabbed at that, and the door swung wide.

The netting blocked the opening, but Trinesh slashed the rough, elastic stuff apart with his sword. It groaned and tore away to reveal gray beings swarming about the base of their car a man-height below the threshold. More were emerging from hiding places behind the machines and housings in the distance, and others swung down from the walkways that crisscrossed the ceiling. The air smelled of musty cinnamon, and a high, sweet chiming, like many sets of wind-bells tinkling all at once, met his ears.

"Ssu!" The Lady Deq Dimani screamed. "Ssu!"

Trinesh hardly heard her; the cables of a gigantic block and tackle hung within his reach, and he seized one of these to swing down over the mob toward a clear space beyond. There were no Ssu near Trinesh's home in the western regions of the Tsolyani Empire, and the storytellers' tales had been less than accurate about the "Enemies of Man."

This was fortunate for his morale.

He faced one of the squat gray beings perhaps three paces in front of him. The creature lunged to slash at him with a jag-edged sword as he regained his feet. The blow missed by a finger's breadth. He scrambled to get his balance and assessed his opponent.

The Ssu was a head shorter than he. Four wide-spraddled legs extended out from the twisted column of the torso, and its two upper arms ended in hands that had two long fingers and a shorter thumb. The head was oval, the face only vaguely human: there were two eyes, round and black-gleaming, and nostril slits but no nose. The mouth consisted of a vertical ellipse. It was the thing's skin that was the most repellent: it resembled mottled gray parchment peeling from a roll, the ends loose and ragged, very much like the winding sheet of a corpse long in the grave. The musty cinnamon smell was overpowering.

The creature emitted an arpeggio of fluting, chiming sounds and struck again. Trinesh parried automatically, advanced, made another parry, and found himself back underneath the spherical shell of their car hanging in the net above his head. He saw an opening and riposted. The Ssu recoiled, a bit of its cinnamon-fragrant skin tearing off to float down between them like a wisp of gauze. To his right, a second human form came leaping down into the fray, then another and another. He heard Chosun's cry of "The Flame!" and Horusel's deep, answering "Hai!"

A ring of gray-mottled faces confronted him. He ducked, parried, and cut. One of the Ssu went down, its hands scrabbling at a flood of dark ichor spurting from amid the rags of loose skin hanging from its breast.

"The other car!" Trinesh shouted. "Over there!" He swung at a new adversary, and the shock ran up his arm as his blade bit home. It felt as though he had chopped into a dead tree-limb.

Something slowed him, prevented him from recovering for yet another blow. The ebon eyes of the Ssu before him loomed larger and larger. By Lord Vimuhla's Three Tongues of Fire! He watched in surprise as his hand turned of its own accord to lower the sword it held. His jaw went back to make his throat an easy target above his iron gorget.

He had no control over his body!

There was a twang from the car door above, and pallid, white lids slid down to shroud the glaring black orbs before him. The Ssu crumpled, the feathered butt of a crossbow quarrel protruding from its abdomen.

"Let them not look you in the eye!" the *Nininyal* shrilled from behind the crossbowmen in the open door.

The marketplace storytellers had been particularly remiss in omitting any mention of the hypnotic powers possessed by the "Enemies of Man."

He recovered to find four others by his side: Chosun, Dineva, Horusel, and the Lady Deq Dimani herself. He could not see the rest, but he heard the intermittent snap-twang of crossbows from above him. The press before them was so congested that their foes had little room to strike. He yelled the command to form his party into a wedge. They must traverse the few paces that separated them from the other car quickly; else they would be overrun and buried!

"Get down here!" he bawled. "Get the girl—everybody!"

There was no time to look back. He snarled the order to advance and sensed that his comrades heard him. Someone behind him screamed and fell against his leg. He reached down with his free hand to clutch at a human arm, but it was dragged out of his grasp, and a horde of chiming, cinnamon-smelling monstrosities surged over the body. Who it was he had no way of knowing.

He brought his blade down upon one of the peeling gray skulls. The Ssu threw up its arms, and Trinesh snatched the creature's sword as it fell. He tossed it blindly behind him. Some of his people had no weapons for close combat, and they would make good use of it. More Ssu went down before the sweep of Horusel's axe. An opening appeared, and they pushed into it. Another two paces and they would be at the second vehicle's door.

A higher, ringing bell-note sounded. The Ssu facing them began to retreat.

"They summon sorcerers!" a voice panted in his ear. He glimpsed the Lady Deq Dimani there, her scale corselet splattered with dark liquid.

"On, then!" he howled in reply. "Now!"

They moved forward, smashed aside those foes still in their path, and clambered up into the second car. There were Ssu there, too, but Horusel and Dineva slew them almost before they had had a chance to react. A hatch similar to that of their own vehicle was open in the floor, and odd-shaped instruments lay scattered about beside it.

"If they have ruined the controls—!" Thu'n squatted down to see. "I cannot be sure—it looks as though they attempted to change the destination settings. Thus did Qurtul do—"

"Shut the door and push the Flame-accursed button!" Trinesh did not wait but himself dived for the control-board. Someone—Dineva, he thought—slammed the hatch.

The silence was sudden and astonishing.

The car lights came up. Trinesh fumbled with the knobs beneath the forward view-portrayer and saw their first vehicle, smoke belching from its doorway, a patch of sky with ruins beyond, and a cavernous hall that now seethed with gray Ssu. No living human forms were visible in the swirling mob outside. Three-fingered hands clawed and pounded at the hull, and he prayed that those at the door would not be too clever about pushing the stud in the depression beside it.

He poked a thumb at the leftmost stud on the control console.

Their foes seemed to rise with the swiftness of birds, while they themselves fell downward into darkness. Bodies plummeted past the view-portrayers, apparently those unfortunates who had been on the roof or close enough to the lip of the tubeway tunnel to tumble into it.

Trinesh looked around. Chekkuru hiVriddi was there, and he suppressed a momentary pang of some emotion akin to regret. Dineva knelt beside Saina while Chosun applied a bandage. The *Tirrikamu* grinned and signed that the wound was minor. Thu'n stood at the controls, the Lady Deq Dimani with him. Both strove to console the Lady Jai; she did not seem to be hurt, but she was trembling and terrified. The girl was no warrior. Balar and Arjasu squatted on their haunches at the back of the little cabin. They were good soldiers, already inspecting their crossbows, counting quarrels, and murmuring in matter-of-fact tones to Tse'e—Prince Nalukkan.

Horusel and Mejjai emerged from the rear storage compartment, blood and blackish ichor streaking their harnesses.

Jalugan was missing.

They would grieve later, when there was time.

"I think," said Balar, "that we have seen Ssuyal. In Hekellu we have tales of great human cities there, deserted places occupied now by the 'Enemies of Man.' "

Trinesh's attention was elsewhere. He gazed down at the forward console. An inscription had been painted above each destination button, doubtless the terminal to which that stud would send the car. Sadly, these labels were in the tongue of the Ssu: dots, whorls, and circles, as illegible as a spattering of raindrops upon a pavement!

Once more their journeying lay solely in the hands of mighty Lord Vimuhla. Trinesh sighed and looked to his own bruises and scratches.

Their vehicle was already far away in the lightless tunnel when the forward view-portrayer suddenly bloomed with a flower of incandescent brilliance. Back in the city of the Ssu their original car seemed to fly into pieces. Its dying was as dazzling as the heart of the sun. The glass immediately went dark, leaving them to blink and rub their eyes in astonishment.

Whatever had caused the explosion, it struck them all as a pleasing and proper offering to the Lord of Flame.

9

"Leave it alone," Trinesh said. "All of it. We open nothing, eat nothing, drink nothing. Whatever cargo the Ssu stored here, it cannot be friendly to us."

Horusel and Dineva had ransacked their car, and a jumble of canisters, tubes, and other bric-a-brac lay now beside the implements and devices left by the Ssu. The tools were of human manufacture, but their controls and knobs had been modified to fit Ssu hands. Not even Thu'n knew what they did, nor did they dare test them now. Trinesh almost had to fight Horusel all over again when the man pointed a tube-like instrument at the wall and would have pulled the lever protruding from its handle. Experimentation could come later when there was less danger.

Trinesh caught a signal from Chosun and put down the lensed box he was inspecting. The *Tirrikamu* sidled over and whispered, "Sire, the girl slipped something to the Yan Koryani woman. She hid it in her tunic."

The view-portrayers were useful for more than the displaying of pictures. Trinesh followed the big soldier's eyes and saw the two women mirrored in one of the dark glass squares on the side wall. They sat with their heads together, apparently resting. He made a silent gesture to Chosun.

He waited until the *Tirrikamu* was in position, leaning against the rear bulkhead behind the Lady Deq Dimani. Then he moved to stand in front of her.

"May I see what the Lady Jai gave you?"

She frowned. "What does she have left to give, *Hereksa*? Only her own body—and that you almost took in Na Ngore." As though in echo of her mistress's words, the girl extended an alluringly curved thigh from beneath her desert-cloak. Trinesh refused to let himself be distracted.

"Must I search you, Lady?"

"I gave her nothing!" the Lady Jai said. She sat up so that his eyes traveled down the column of her throat and into the open collar of the desert-cloak she wore.

"My Lady, please. I want no—"

The Lady Deq Dimani raised her left hand, fist closed, as though she were about to give him something. Her other hand slid out from inside her tunic like an *Alash*-snake's striking; it held a small object, dark and round, the size of a *Dlel*-fruit pit.

Trinesh yelled, dodged automatically, and batted at her wrist. Then Chosun's great weight dropped upon the woman from behind. Whatever the object was, it flew free to strike the bulkhead and ricochet into Saina's lap. The Lady Deq Dimani struggled, kicked, and cursed in her crackling northern tongue until Chosun captured her flailing arms. Tse'e—it was hard to think of him as Prince Nalukkan—pinioned the Lady Jai similarly, though the girl made no resistance. He was not gentle; it was clear that he had no love either for the Lady Deq Dimani, who had betrayed his identity, or for any who served her.

"Hold, man! No harm to them!" Trinesh was more shaken than he cared to admit. He knew full well what the object had been: an "Eye," a common type of sorcerous tool employed by the Ancients. He had seen real ones in the temple school in Tumissa, and the markets were full of hawkers who peddled fakes to the credulous.

There were many "Eyes": some fired beams of energy that could kill, others performed tasks, and a few did things that no modern scholar could comprehend. What today's sorcerers achieved with spells, the Ancients before the Time of Darkness had done with machines. Both drew power from the Planes Beyond, moulded it, and formed it into energies, substances, and even such complex manufactures as food and drink. A spell was subtle and could be modified by a skilled sorcerer; an "Eye" produced only the one effect its maker had built into it.

"You found it in one of the compartments!" Trinesh accused the Lady Jai. "Your mistress here would have seen me dead—perhaps all of us—rather than share it for our common good!"

The Lady Deq Dimani glared into Trinesh' eyes from no more than a hand's breadth away. Her lips were drawn back from sharp white teeth, and her breasts heaved with fury. "I could have used it on you before, Tsolyani, as you and your ruffian stood at the console! I did not. I swore peace with you until we reach some destination where we can go our separate ways. That oath I kept. Yet nothing in my vow prevents me from acquiring weapons or acting otherwise as I see fit. I am not under your command, *Hereksa*. I am a general in my own right, a ruler, a matriarch, a. . . ." She ran out of breath.

"You parse logic admirably, my Lady. Now do you want to be bound again, or will you amend our compact to include cooperation—full and complete—until we mutually agree to end it?"

She clenched her fists and turned her face away. Dineva began methodically cutting thongs from the hem of one of the desert-cloaks.

"Very well," the Lady conceded. "Perhaps you are not wrong. I agree."

"And the Lady Jai? The *Nininyal*?"

"They too." She spoke briefly in Yan Koryani. Trinesh spared a glance for Saina, who nodded to indicate that nothing untoward had been said.

"So be it. Now what is this 'Eye?' "

"I know not," she replied coolly. "There was no time to learn."

Lord Vimuhla roast the woman! She could have blown out the wall of their car! He had heard enough tales of "Eyes" to know of their perils, and so, doubtless, had she. Fortunately she had not had the time to fire it. Perhaps she herself was not sure what she would do once she had drawn it out of her tunic.

He took the "Eye" from Saina and inspected it. The size and shape of a human eye, it had a round, black spot on one curved surface and a tiny stud on the other. A square indentation below the stud showed two symbols, unreadable and alien. The priests of the temple school had mentioned those, too: they were numerals indicating the charges remaining in the instrument. Sometimes later owners added inscriptions noting the function of an "Eye" as well, but this one was unmarked, smooth, grayish-blue in color, and as enigmatic as the visage of a god.

"Can anyone read these squiggles?" Trinesh asked. "You, Chekkuru? You, Thu'n?" Both shook their heads in negation.

"We must try it out on the next Ssu we meet," Chosun observed genially. "Thus may we learn its purpose."

Trinesh said no more but put the "Eye" away in his belt-pouch.

He returned to the forward console. Thu'n awaited him there, and he signaled to the creature to activate the view-portrayers. The one above the destination buttons, that which had shown the death of their first car in the city of the Ssu, still had no picture at all. Successive turns of its knob revealed more dark caverns, another dimly lit way-station filled with burned and ruined vehicles, a place of white crystal that the Lady Deq Dimani said was ice—cold and bitter ice, like that upon the summit of Thenu Thendraya Peak—and more blacknesses.

The three side-portrayers showed other scenes. There was a jungle, dripping and looped with vines, amid which a single monolith of mould-splotched stone towered like a venerable sentinel in the green-lit gloom. The city of the red-tiled roofs appeared again, followed by a vista of elegant gardens, neatly kept flowers, trees, and many-hued buildings of no recognizable nationality. Golden beings strolled to and fro in that landscape. They were humanoid but not human: more of the Ancients' automatons, the *Ru'un*.

"Oh, let us go there, *Hereksa*," Dineva said. Her homely features were wistful and almost pretty in the shifting play of reflected light. Trinesh smiled and touched her arm. She did not draw away, and he thought that she must be very close to the breaking point. Tough, veteran soldier-woman that she was, her endurance had to reach an end sometime! He suddenly realized that he himself was in no better condition. Another moment and they'd be in one another's arms! Cha! He straightened up.

"Our journey is not in our hands," he said. "If the Ssu managed to set the destination buttons, then we travel whither they will. If not, our fate lies in the hands of the ancient owner of this car."

"Or rather in the hands of Lord Vimuhla," Chekkuru intoned.

Trinesh did not disagree. They could only wait.

Again the hours drifted by, uncountable in the never-changing light within the car. They rested, slept, and tended to their bruises. Thirst became a problem, as, to a lesser extent, did food: if Trinesh's stomach were typical, they must soon find something more appetizing than the sand-worms' tubers and stinking dried meat!

So familiar had their car's soft humming become that they were disoriented when it stopped.

Thu'n played with the controls and miraculously managed to produce the same scene on all four view-portrayers of their new car at once: a hall of many columns, beyond which the hot blaze of sunlight shimmered upon stone flagging. The architecture was unfamiliar: truncated columns, like upside-down staircases, towered up from small, drum-shaped bases to ponderous capitals lost in the shadowy groining of the ceiling. Carvings swarmed over every visible surface: geometric patterns, arabesques, fantastic and baroque rosettes, an eye-wrenching labyrinth of intricate sculpture so elaborate that it seemed tasteless.

"Do we go out, *Hereksa*?" Horusel asked.

"No one awaits us—human or otherwise." Thu'n peered from one view-portrayer to the others. "There, on the right, in the open court behind those columns, do you see that coping? Mayhap the rim of a tank or pool . . . ?"

Trinesh gave swift orders, formed up his party, and opened the door. No Ssu or any other horror could keep him from water now!

The hall was empty of life; only a tepid breeze wandered idly between the hulking pillars. There were no furnishings or tapestries, and their car hung in the air above its tunnel-entrance in the exact center of a stepped platform. Waist-high screens of pierced, pink marble, as dainty as the lacework of a clan-maiden's bridal coronet, enclosed this platform. Past these they saw that the hall was an open portico, surrounded on all sides by a broad plaza paved with white, buff, and black stone in a complex mosaic design.

There were not one but four pools, each exactly three man-heights square, set with geometrical precision in the middle of the courtyard on the four sides of the central building. More to the point, these tanks contained cool, welcome, delicious water! Trinesh tried in vain to slow the exodus, but nothing availed; not shouts, not orders, not even physically collaring poor Mejjai, the last to emerge from the car.

He gave it up and joined his comrades. Let them all be eaten by monsters! He, too, needed first a drink, then a bath.

The plaza was empty, not a stick or a leaf anywhere, the intricate mosaic flagging as hot beneath their boots as a griddle-plate. The court was further enclosed all around with marble walls some three or four man-heights high: an open-topped, square box surrounding the portico in the middle. Every one of the four walls contained two doorways, one in each corner. Holes in the stone lintels and sills showed where door-leaves had once closed these apertures, but they were empty now.

More sculptured geometric patterns occupied every available space: the panels of the walls, the door-jambs, even the undersides of the lintels. There were no inscriptions, and not one of the carvings depicted a living being, not an animal, a bird, or a tree. To an inhabitant of the Five Empires used to murals, bas-reliefs, and friezes displaying all of the rich tapestry of religion and legend, this was unsettling if not actually ominous.

No one came to disturb them, but Trinesh posted Arjasu as a sentry just in case. The rest drank, bathed, and rinsed out their filthy garments in the breast-deep, blue water. Only when they were finished and rested did he let them examine their surroundings.

The place was more than ornate; it was splendid, a palace, a marvel of the sculptor's art, albeit graceless and vulgar. The columns of the colonnade were perhaps three man-heights tall. Above these were entablatures of overhanging architraves and cornices, all scalloped and crimped into a welter of garish, frilly, little designs. Still higher, the roof of the colonnade rose in a series of domes, cupolas, and flamboyant vaultings to culminate in a tall spire. The entire structure was blanketed, top to bottom, with dainty carvings. It reminded Trinesh of the ultimate masterpiece of some effete—and slightly mad—pastry-cook.

The parapets of the courtyard walls, too, were pierced with tiny holes in an exquisite geometric fretwork. Balar declared that, given a rope and some sort of hook, he could climb up and see what lay beyond before they ventured into the unknown darkness behind any of the courtyard doors. Saina suggested knotting garments together and tying one end to Trinesh's sword to serve as a grapple. He had no wish to lose the weapon, however, nor did Horusel or any of the others offer theirs. They did have the odd-shaped sword he had seized during the battle with the Ssu; Saina had caught it, and it now lay with their other possessions in the car. The thing was useless, its hilt too small and too alien for a human hand and its balance as awkward as a tree-branch. Still, he decided, such feats of mountaineering could wait until they had explored this level.

Trinesh spread his clothing and quilted arming jacket to dry upon the baking pavement. He found himself watching the Lady Deq Dimani as she bent to don her steaming tunic once more. It was enough to turn a man's loins to Lord Vimuhla's blazing fire-stone! She wriggled into the garment, and the view was lost—more the pity! She saw him looking and turned her back upon him self-consciously.

The Yan Koryani were said to be the most prudish of the peoples of the Five Empires. Yet, just beyond her mistress, the Lady Jai continued to sit upon her soggy desert-cloak, her long, damp tresses coiling down over her shoulders, as nude and lovely as a copper-gold statue of the Goddess Avanthe Herself. Perhaps Dilinala, Avanthe's Cohort, was a more fitting comparison, Trinesh thought ruefully: Lady Dilinala had no interest in men either! The girl wrapped her arms around her knees and put her head down upon them as though to doze, her appearance of bored lassitude unchanged.

Dineva and Saina splashed and swam in the pool with Chosun while Mejjai, Balar, and Arjasu stood guard in turn. The Tsolyani cared little for male-female modesty, and, indeed, few would covet Dineva's hard and leathery frame. But Saina now. . . .

He cursed himself silently. They had more urgent problems.

He squinted against the sun and saw Thu'n and Tse'e squatting in the shade of the portico. He tried to think of the wizened old exile as Prince Nalukkan hiTlakotani but gave it up; Tse'e was Tse'e. Beyond those two, Horusel was just donning the last piece of his armor, the only one of the party to do so. Chekkuru hiVriddi was missing, but then Trinesh remembered that he had gone off to bathe separately in the pool on the far side of the colonnade. The priest still had his arrogance, his fine Tsolyani sense of dignity: a member of a high clan never bathed in the company of his social inferiors. Damn him—and all his hawk-faced Vriddi clan-brothers—anyway!

"Time we looked about," Trinesh remarked to Horusel. He was having trouble with the soggy lining of his helmet again. He dropped it and picked up the Prince's steel sword. Nothing suggested a need for armor here; they had seen no one. The place was as deserted as one of those lightless caves to which their egg-vehicle had carried them.

The *Tirrikamu* grunted assent, and they made a slow and cautious circuit of the walls. Trinesh peered into one of the doorways and discovered a short corridor. Three paces, and this gave into a long, narrow passage parallel to the courtyard wall outside. Arbitrarily, he turned to his right. Another rectangle of hot, yellow light was visible down there: the other door in from the courtyard. He walked along the passage to discover a single dark opening on his left, exactly in the middle between the two courtyard doors. Two paces beyond the latter, the corridor ended in a right-angled turn; he rounded this to see two more sunlit doorways on his right and an identical shadowy opening in the center of the left wall.

"Follow this corridor," he ordered Horusel. "See if it runs completely around our plaza. I go to look into one of those left-hand doorways."

Within the inner passage the light dimmed rapidly to darkness. His boots squelched in something gritty yet soft, and an acrid, acidic smell made him wrinkle his nose. He thought he heard a faint chittering above his head. He halted. *Vur*-bats, or their larger cousins, the *Hu*-bats? Or something worse? Throughout his childhood his clan-brothers had stuffed his head with tales of the nighted creatures of the catacombs beneath the ancient cities of Tekumel. There were the *Kayi* who floated in the air like bags of gas to drop tentacles down upon the unwary; then came the *Biridlu*, creatures resembling velvet capes, who hung from the ceilings of tombs and swooped to crush their victims in their muscular folds. . . .

He made an unceremonious retreat. After all, without a torch or a lamp, he might have plunged over into some idiotic pit or staircase!

Horusel met him as he emerged. "All the same, *Hereksa*. A square corridor all around the courtyard. I poked my head into one of those side tunnels, too: four paces, and you're in a parallel passage that seems to run all around the first one—a square surrounding a square—and full of *Hu*-bat shit. I need another bath."

"We return to the others," Trinesh directed. "Let's see if Balar can get to the top of the wall or up onto the roof of that central confection." He had no desire to go back into the darkness, not just yet—not until hunger got the better of him!

With the Ssu sword as a grappling hook and a rope cut from their desert-cloaks, the crossbowman scrambled up onto the enclosure wall. His head soon reappeared above the parapet.

"Sire, the roof is flat for ten paces or so," he reported. "Then there's another coping, and beyond it a second courtyard on three sides of this one. It's walled, too—facing ours—and then more domes and turrets behind that."

"People?"

"None in the courtyard or the buildings beyond, Sire. No sign of life."

"Doors? Gates?"

"One directly below me, Sire: an archway. But I can't see into it. Opposite in the far wall there's a matching gate—closed, I think."

"What's on the fourth side?" Trinesh asked. "Which direction is it?"

"Behind you, *Hereksa*." Balar pointed over their heads. "You look straight down the wall and a cliff below it—" he paused, obviously pleased to save his most portentous tidings until last "—into a valley. There's a river down there—a wide one with a shallow ford across it—and beyond is a city: houses, roofs, temple towers, a big square filled with merchants' awnings—woods and fields all around. There are little boats on the river. Sire—and people! Human beings!"

Trinesh was the first up the rope. If only this were Tsolyanu and not Yan Kor! Doubtless the Lady Deq Dimani prayed for the exact opposite.

It was as Balar had said. The city was unknown to any of them, however, and they bickered over its identity. Chekkuru counted what he thought were twenty temples—the Gods and Cohorts of Pavar—and stated that it was surely a medium-sized town in eastern Tsolyanu. Horusel and Saina disputed him; they pointed to four sprawling, castle-like buildings of brick and dark wooden beams grouped about the main marketplace, and declared these to be "the Four Palaces of the Square" of some city in Mu'ugalavya: Tlar, possibly, or Khu. No one knew of any rivers near those places, particularly a stream that flowed east to west, and the range of blue-misted hills to the north was wrong for either. Chekkuru began a long, wrangling argument, and Trinesh had to step in as tactfully as possible to say that none of them had ever been in Mu'ugalavya and one theory was as good as another.

Arjasu and Tse'e proposed yet a third identification: one of the towns on the eastern shores of Lake Parunal, in Kilalammu, mayhap, or Jannu, or Mudallu beyond. This suggestion met with opposition from Balar, who had grown up in Hekellu on the eastern frontier of the Imperium and had heard travelers' tales of the squalid little states of the far northeast. Arjasu turned to Thu'n for confirmation, saying that the Pygmy Folk dwelt closer to those regions than Hekellu and ought to know, but the *Nininyal* only shrugged and denied any expertise in human urban architecture. Chosun simply shook his head, and Mejjai grunted phlegmatically and retreated into the shadows of the central portico to sleep.

Trinesh privately wanted to agree with the old exile but could not bring himself to say so. He spared a sidelong glance for the two Yan Koryani women; their expressions told him nothing. This might indeed be a smaller city in Yan Kor, or in one of its allies, Pijena, Chayakku, or Saa Allaqi. If so, their worries had only just begun.

He would have to warn his own party.

They were too high and too far for their shouts to be heard in the city across the plain and the turgid, muddy river. A desert-cloak waved upon Saina's spear-shaft might be seen, but then why alert the inhabitants to their presence? There must be some way down through the palace—temple, citadel, or whatever this building was—and it seemed better to meet their unknown hosts on their own terms. Trinesh left Arjasu upon the roof to observe and ordered the rest down to take counsel.

"We have water aplenty," he said when they were assembled, "but little food. No one is seriously injured, and I see no reason to signal to the city-folk just yet." He shot the three Yan Koryani a hard look. "I propose that we find some way over into those other sections of the citadel. We must also examine our car and its contents for anything useful."

"Including the 'Eye,' " the Lady Deq Dimani said sweetly.

"Ai, the 'Eye,' too."

He left it at that. Later, as Kashi rose to wash the swarming carvings of the enclosure wall with ruby moonlight, he set forth a roster of sentries and watch-times. In this he included the Yan Koryani, but each would always be accompanied by two Tsolyani—oath or no oath! Chekkuru was put to devising suitable funeral rituals and an elegy for poor Jalugan, while Tse'e, Thu'n, and Trinesh himself inventoried their possessions.

10

The following morning Trinesh brought out the "Eye," stood at what he hoped was a safe distance, and pointed its iris at a wall. He depressed the stud. Nothing resulted, and his audience laughed—a trifle nervously. One of the symbols on the "counter" changed, but that was all. The device was either out of order, or else its function was undetectable by human senses. He thought, half seriously, of trying it upon the Lady Deq Dimani herself, but then matters were not urgent enough to warrant a possible accidental execution!

It went back again into his belt pouch.

The contents of the car were more interesting: a dozen of the flat, silvery-gray canisters; a jumble of metallic discs that might be buttons or possibly coins, though they were too light to be silver or gold; three little boxes with glass circles and lenses upon them, and short, stiff, metallic cords that ended in odd pincer-like clips of unknown purpose; the long tube Horusel had almost triggered; a squat, black cylinder with a hole in one end; and four metal bars with handles. One of these last ended in a crescent-moon of bright metal, perhaps a religious symbol, while the remaining three had spatulate tips that could be honed down to serve as daggers. A heap of miscellaneous parts and pieces completed the lot.

Trinesh experimented with the tube-device, but pulling its lever produced only a loud click, and he laid it aside. Two of the other items proved to be of greater interest. The first was the cylinder: when its handle was squeezed, a finger-like flame appeared from the aperture in the tip. The other useful item was one of the boxes; this had a transparent stud that lit up with a soft yellow radiance when one twisted its knobs. They now had fire—though no fuel for cooking—and also a lamp to light their exploration of the passageways around the plaza.

It was thus that Trinesh learned the bad news. Horusel and Chosun returned all besplattered with *Hu*-bat dung to say that there was a third corridor all around the second. As in the first and second rings, this had exit doors to some presumed fourth and outer corridor as well—or perhaps to the second courtyard beyond—but those doorways had been sealed up with huge blocks of stone mortared together into a solid barrier that only siege-tools could breach!

Whoever dwelt in the city did not welcome visitors arriving via the tubeway cars!

They could still use their makeshift rope and grappling hook to descend into the courtyard beyond the surrounding building of corridors. Balar, however, had the foresight to toss one of the canisters down there before descending himself. The container had hardly stopped rolling when a myriad tiny, whitish lizard-things with spiny tails and a dozen sets of legs poured forth from crevices between the stones to snarl and worry at its metal shell with all the fury of enraged *Zrne*-beasts. The canister remained undamaged, but Trinesh doubted whether their boots, sandals, and bare feet would prove as durable.

The longer they watched the lizards' performance, the less friendly their unknown hosts seemed.

There ought to be a solution—something other than getting back into the vehicle and trusting their Skeins to the mercies of the Ssu or its previous owners, those nameless Ancients who had built it. They would have to try that route if they could not get across the outer courtyard, but the destinations shown by this car's view-portrayers lacked appeal. Moreover, Trinesh argued, who would build a great citadel, a masterpiece of masonry and sculpture, with no way in or out? There was probably a secret door or a tunnel beneath some flagstone that bypassed the lizard-things' courtyard. Whatever the reasons for sealing off this area—Ssu or other unpleasant guests, presumably—those were human beings down there, and Trinesh's ragged little party posed no threat. Why harm helpless travelers?

He resolutely refused to think of slavery, sacrifice, or various other unsavory practices of the societies with which he himself was acquainted.

They had time. He set his people to devising ways to deal with the lizard-things. He himself tried the "Eye" upon them, but they only stared up at him from unwinking, bright green eyes. None of the other devices did any better. Arjasu opened one of the canisters from the car, poured its oily contents down into the courtyard, and rejoiced as a dozen of the monsters ate of it and died. Their fellows soon swarmed over the corpses, however, and even the skeletons disappeared. Trinesh then set fire to the brownish grease in yet another container; this produced black smoke but almost no flame, and the lizards evaded it easily. There had to be a way!

By the end of the second day they finished the last of their tubers and dried meat. With plentiful water and no strenuous activity it would take them several six-days to starve, but Trinesh had no intention of waiting for that unhappy dénouement.

Indeed, there had to be a way.

Three more days passed, each hungrier and less pleasurable than the preceding one. The Tsolyani and Tse'e spread their desert-cloaks as sleeping mats in a single small area of the first ring of corridors, while the two Yan Koryani women kept their distance around the corner. Thu'n chose a place farther down that same passage, and this moved Trinesh to post one of the sentries inside the portico itself. There must be no unscheduled—or unaccompanied—departures via the tubeway car! Chekkuru took up separate residence across the plaza apart from everyone else and devoted himself so enthusiastically to his rituals that his chanting became a single, monotonous, sing-song drone in the background. No one spoke much, there was little to do, and they grew increasingly morose and surly. Trinesh found himself yearning for the rough camaraderie of his Legion and wondering who had taken command after he had vanished. Even the rigours of army life took on a mellow, remote, sparkling quality that trickled away like the last dregs of sweet Tumissan wine from a flagon.

It was Tse'e who eventually discovered food.

On the morning of the sixth day after their arrival, he awoke Trinesh from a vision—daydream or sleep-dream, who knew?—of spiced *Jakkohl*-meat and succulent *Khaish*-root stew. The old exile's hands overflowed with a darkish substance that dribbled brown juices upon the mosaic paving. He grinned and thrust a fragment into his mouth.

"No—!" Trinesh cried in horror. "Don't! We are not reduced to eating—*that*—yet!"

Tse'e blinked at him in puzzlement; then he cackled. "Not what you think, *Hereksa*! This is *Ozhain*—fungus! It grows wherever one finds darkness and *Hu*-bat dung or other carrion! The outer corridors are filled with it. The Folk of Na Ngore consider it a delicacy."

Whatever it was, its appearance and texture were strongly scatological. Fortunately, it did not have the fragrance to

match. Trinesh sniffed dubiously and was reminded of a
damp cellar. His stomach made urgent demands, but his
gorge threatened to rise in revolt. Still, it was better than
starvation—or departing once more in the tubeway car. He
accepted a piece, put it to his lips, and found it moist and
unpleasantly spongy. The taste was not bad: like *Dna*-porridge
mixed with sea-fish and seasoned with swamp water.

"Eat, *Hereksa*!" Tse'e chortled. "As nourishing as anything served to the Emperor in Avanthar! This *Ozhain* is
somewhat different from what we had in Na Ngore, but it is
food! Now we do not starve! There's enough to feed a
legion—and if you leave a little, it grows back!"

Trinesh looked past him to see a ring of grinning faces.
The others had already been informed. He took more of the
Ozhain from Tse'e, hobbled up to his feet, and grandly
declared a feast-day.

Saina scorched some of the fungus over the tiny flame of
their cylinder device, improving its flavor considerably thereby,
and they ate their fill for the first time since leaving Fortress
Ninu'ur. Their mood lightened, became first genial, then
raucous, and finally culminated in off-key folk songs from
Saina and Arjasu, followed by epic poetry (with histrionic
gestures) by Chekkuru, and a Tumissan love-sonnet from
Trinesh himself. Even the Lady Deq Dimani joined in with a
Yan Koryani lyric, her voice as dark and melancholy as her
northern seas. Trinesh felt giddy, silly, raised above all the
world like a God! This *Ozhain* must contain a drug, he
decided; it was either that or the effects of a full stomach after
several days of fasting.

He looked across the circle to the Lady Jai; she smiled
tentatively at no one in particular. Both Gayel and Kashi were
up, hovering just above the black-silhouetted fretwork of the
parapet, and her eyes were pools of green and red moonlight.
Balar, next to her, proffered a fresh tidbit of *Ozhain* and
murmured something in her ear. She made no response but
stared vacantly out into the darkness. The young crossbow-

man might fare no better with her than Trinesh had, but he was persistent: he continued with further whisperings and little attentions. The Lady Jai returned him a faint smile.

Jealousy swept over Trinesh in a thundering wave. He felt his cheeks blazing, and raw fury welled up into his throat. Who was this Balar! No more than a swaggering animal, a member of a clan of no importance! He was a subordinate, a common soldier!

Trinesh's fingers slid all of themselves to his sword-hilt. He struggled for restraint and forced them away again. Saina sat beside him, and he was next amazed to find his startlingly independent fingers sliding over to caress her smooth thigh. It was like the hypnosis of the Ssu! Her small, callused hand came down unseen in the darkness to close hard upon his and lead it on to softer and more interesting locales beyond. She wore nothing but the desert-cloak she had acquired in Na Ngore, and when its folds were pulled aside . . .

Scarlet lust blinded him, and he sucked in a ragged breath. He turned to her and realized that in another moment they'd be coupling together on the floor before everybody, like the chief entertainment at a Jakallan orgy!

Then someone brushed between them and broke the spell: the Lady Deq Dimani.

"Your pardon, *Hereksa*," the Yan Koryani woman purred. "It is hot, and I would swim before I sleep . . ." Her voice sounded distraught, choked, and shaky. "Come, Jai." The girl followed her, one silken calf gliding against Trinesh's arm as she passed.

Trinesh gasped for air, found nothing but the fire-smoke and the baked-fish smell of cooking *Ozhain*, and staggered outside to the nearest pool to lave his forehead with cool water. The veil of lust receded from his eyes; the feast was over.

He sought a place apart from the others and lay down. Yet the sleep-demons refused to come, and his head whirled with streamers of fragmented thoughts. He must be insane, drugged by the *Ozhain*! He could ill afford to lose control now.

He looked up to see Saina standing before him, her desert-cloak hanging open from her sturdy peasant shoulders.

"You wanted me, *Hereksa*?" she asked tonelessly. The question was deliberately double-edged.

He found that he did.

Later he lay beside her, relieved of his passion but still thrumming inside with a roiling turbulence to which he could put no name. She turned her broad, pretty face to his and licked her full lips. He knew that she would have him begin all over again.

"Tomorrow we leave in the tubeway car," he muttered shakily. "If we stay here, there's naught to eat but the mad-man's fungus. Mayhap he's too senile to feel its effects, but the rest of us will suffer more of this delirium!"

"And is that wrong?" Her wide, flat nose nuzzled his cheek, and she sketched skillful kisses along the line of his jaw.

"Yes—no . . ." Lust awoke again in his loins. He drew away and sat up. "Damn it, woman! It's well enough for two or three of us! But what of the others—you cannot serve us all—!"

"There's Dineva. She does as she pleases. Tonight I think that her pleasures include Horusel—or Chosun—or both." She pulled her desert-cloak up to cover her heavy breasts. "And the Yan Koryani: those two may act the haughty princesses now, but after a day or two they'll join in with a will, you'll see."

"You—you don't think that the Lady Deq Dimani and the Lady Jai are lovers?" The question had been in his mind for some time.

"Them? I doubt it. I've seen enough during my army days to make me believe otherwise. La, I suspect that officer-woman is as hot-blooded beneath her dainty armor as any harlot in the temple of Lady Dlamelish."

Naked passion returned once more to becloud his vision, and he cast about for a less dangerous topic. "Listen! Along with this—this sexual joy, there's another side to *Ozhain*: jealousy—rage—hatred! I almost slew Balar tonight! We'll fight, kill, murder each other over you women or any other stupid pretext. Not one of us will ever see home again! Do you understand me?"

She paid this argument no heed. "We can manage—share," she mused. "Many men have more than one wife, and many wives more than one husband. Dineva and I alone can manage the lot of you—even without the accursed Yan Koryani and her pretty pet!"

"Think, Saina! Who serves Chekkuru hiVriddi? What of the damned *Nininyal*?"

"The priest is married to his god. If he needs a woman, Dineva and I will each eat a fistful of fungus and see who surrenders to it first!" She giggled. "And I doubt that the Pygmy Folk are interested in human females."

"The Flame burn it all!" he shouted, not caring who heard. Anger engulfed him, and he wanted to hit her, beat her, kick her senseless. It must be the *Ozhain* again. He dug his fingernails into the intricate molding of the wall beside him. "We have a duty to return alive—bring back this Lady Deq Dimani, rejoin our legion, fight the Flame-scorched war! We can't stay here forever rutting like *Chlen*-beasts!"

"Cha!" she pouted and made a face. "The army'll do without us. We can spend our time here exploring, learning, finding a way out of this building—not even our miserly General Kutume can deny the rightness of that. We need the relaxation. And what's the harm in enjoying ourselves—?"

Despairingly, he tried one last tack. "And the results? Children—babies born here in this empty ruin of a palace?"

"Well, we would have to think of that sometime." She considered. Then her face brightened. "I have a supply of *Lisutl*-root in one of my pouches, *Hereksa*, enough to keep all of us women safe from pregnancy for a month—maybe two or three. After that, though. . . ."

He saw that this argument had reached her.

"I am right," he said. Some of the vapors had cleared from his brain. "We're all alive and healthy tonight, but who knows how many of us will live through another day—a six-day, a month—of eating that vile stuff? No, we leave as soon as we can get ready tomorrow."

"It is yours to say, *Hereksa*." She turned to leave.

Her dark-cloaked shadow was abruptly limned in scarlet as a flare of ghastly red light burst forth upon the roof above them.

They both cried out and threw their arms up to shield their eyes.

"Up there!" Trinesh yelled. "The rope! Quick!" He fumbled for his weapon, as blind as a *Hu*-bat in the sunlight. He heard the pounding of footsteps, boots, clattering, shouts.

"We're attacked!" Chekkuru screeched from somewhere in the dazzle.

"Who? where—?" That was Arjasu's lighter, calmer voice.

"Sorcery!" Dineva called back. "Or a fire-missile from a mangonel!"

Trinesh had no idea how he reached the roof. The spinning blotches of ruddy flame before his eyes dwindled away as his vision returned.

"Careful—!" There was a snicking sound to his right as Arjasu cocked his crossbow. Mejjai crouched watchfully in front of him.

"If they're coming up over the battlements—" Arjasu began. His words trailed off in puzzlement.

The roof lay empty before them.

"Who was posted up here?" Trinesh demanded. "Whose watch was it?"

"Chosun's," Horusel grunted.

"Not mine," the big man snapped back. "Balar's."

"Where in Lord Vimuhla's sacred Flame is the bastard?"

Dineva moved past him on silent, bare feet, as cautious as a *Jakkohl* in a farmyard. "Chosun sent Balar off to his duty a *Kiren* ago."

"Sire! Look here!" Horusel crouched by the far parapet, that which overlooked the city. He pointed at the low retaining wall.

They stared. A section of the stone fretwork was charred and smoldering, the upper courses actually melted and sagging like hot wax. The very flagging of the roof itself was blackened for a good man-height in every direction all around! Horusel touched a bare toe to it and leaped back with an oath.

The stock of Balar's crossbow lay just within the burnt area, little tongues of flame still licking up from the wood. The bow itself was gone. Beyond, at the base of the parapet, a heap of embers crumbled and drifted in the cool night breeze. A puddle of yellow metal gleamed there amidst those ashes.

Balar had worn a ring and an armlet of gold.

Trinesh had all of his senses back. He strode over to a cooler part of the wall to look down. Only unrelieved darkness met his eyes. He turned around and counted heads. Arjasu, Mejjai, Chosun, and Dineva stood in a wary huddle. Horusel crouched in front of them, his axe in one scarred fist and his feet spraddled in fighting stance. Thu'n and the Lady Deq Dimani waited farther back. Saina guarded the rear, watching the rooftop across the other side of the courtyard. Chekkuru hiVriddi's bald head presently appeared above the parapet where their grappling hook hung; the priest was puffing and out of breath from the climb. Below him, Tse'e called up a question in his cracked, aged voice.

"Where is the Lady Jai?" Trinesh asked.

"I am here, Tsolyani." She glided out from behind her mistress. She had not stopped to don her desert cloak.

As she came up to Trinesh, he saw that her eyes sparkled, and her cheeks were flushed with excitement. Briefly he wondered if she was one of those women who take their pleasures from violence rather than the gentler arts of love. It was the first time he had seen her so animated, but he felt no inclination to admire her beauty, not now.

"Were any of you on this roof—with—with Balar?"

They eyed one another and shook their heads. "He was on watch alone, as you ordered, *Hereksa*," Horusel said.

Chekkuru came up. "Lord Vimuhla—" he intoned.

Trinesh quelled him with a furious snarl. "No god did this, priest! No flame-demon flew up here to strike Balar down!"

"The crossbowman may have tried some experiment of his own with one of the tools of the Ssu," Thu'n put in. That seemed more plausible.

Trinesh felt for the "Eye" in his belt pouch, but his fingers only slapped against the naked skin of his belly; he had been too busy with Saina to think of clothing. The device must be below, with his garments.

What a sight they must be: hardly soldiers at all! Horusel had managed to don his helmet and portions of his harness, but he made a ridiculous picture in his breastplate and greaves without a kilt. Most of the others either wore desert cloaks or nothing at all, although everybody did have a weapon. That, at least, was useful! Nor could Trinesh play the camp drillmaster and burn the ears off his motley followers, not when he himself was one of the prime culprits! The blame might lie with Tse'e's stinking fungus, but that was no excuse for this dismal failure of Legion discipline. What must the Lady Deq Dimani think of the Tsolyani army? At least she had her tunic on, if not her boots and armor!

"Tonight we double the watch," he commanded stiffly. "And in the morning we shall account for every item—every bit of metal. If Balar was fool enough to play with the devices of the Ssu, he deserved to have his Skein ripped from the loom! We will discover who or what was responsible."

His little inner voice chided primly, "It is *you* who are responsible, Trinesh hiKetkolel! Who permitted the feast? Who posted one sentry alone on the roof? Who left the accursed Ssu implements unguarded in a heap upon the court-yard pavement?''

That was really unfair! Trinesh would have debated the matter with himself, but someone put a hand upon his elbow.

''Too late for any such measures, *Hereksa*,'' the Lady Deq Dimani said. She pointed out into the night.

Below, where the city glimmered in the double moonlight behind the lead-gray sickle of the river, a cluster of orange lights twinkled and danced. More arrived with each passing moment. Then they swept out across the ford and over the plain toward the citadel, a trickling stream of sparks, like molten metal dribbled from an alchemist's crucible.

''We are seen, Tsolyani, and now they come for us,'' the Lady Deq Dimani stated. She did not sound overly dismayed.

11

Fortunately for Ridek, Aluja was the first to emerge into the blasted, charred landscape. The Mihalli leaped back through the gray-glittering Nexus Point "doorway" so rapidly that Ridek, behind him, was knocked skidding and slithering into the greenish mud of the Nameless Plane.

"Something—" Aluja panted. "We cannot—" He stank of scorched fur and smoke, and he slapped at a spark caught in his short mane.

"What is it? Fire—?"

"Ai, everything is burning there! I must think. . . ."

Ridek brushed mud from his soiled tunic. It was a hopeless task; he gave up and plumped himself down upon a slimy boulder. He was tired, his feet hurt, and the excitement of adventuring on the Planes Beyond was fast wearing thin. Home—and even his father's inevitable wrath—had begun to take on a certain longed-for, roseate aura. A day, even an hour, ago he would have scorned this as cowardly and "ignoble," but fatigue, the passage of time, and their increasing distance from home brought forth wicked little worries that pricked at the edges of his consciousness.

It reminded him of the time he and Hris had borrowed a skiff and sailed out to Njekka Shoals. The initial thrill had given way to myriad anxieties soon enough. First there were the deceptive tides that surged all around the fanged, sea-girt rocks; then came the wind and scudding rainclouds; and when night fell his elementary navigation failed him utterly. He was never so glad as when the lights of Ke'er Harbor finally hove into view around Bayantla Head. He kept up a brave face, but he suspected that Hris saw through it. Six girls as pretty as Hris Alni Ku'arsh would not get him out onto the Deeps again, not until he had more seamanship!

His last stop with the Mihalli had been more amusing than dangerous: the tense throng of cloaked tribesmen, the dark cavern, the stench of drying skins and rotting sacrificial meat, all had been frightening at first. This, however, was the perfect occasion for Aluja's shape-changing talent, and Ridek had not been surprised when he took on the semblance of a skeleton muffled head to toe in tattered cerements! La, it would have been comical were it not so serious! Ridek himself had hidden in the shadows among the tribe's crude religious emblems and baskets of smelly tubers while Aluja strode out upon the temple platform to harangue the Folk of Na Ngore in their own tongue. The Mihalli had served the Baron in the Desert of Sighs for many years, and he spoke the language almost as well as he did Yan Koryani. The tribesmen's reaction to this apparition, "my all-purpose ghost," as Aluja styled it, would make great retelling if they ever got back to Yan Kor! A mind-touch with the Mihalli's blue-glowing globe, a thing he named the "Ball of Immediate Eventuation" (whatever *that* meant), evoked a detailed and sorrowful recitation of grievances concerning certain recent fellow-citizens. The Lady Deq Dimani, her maid, and a creature who was probably one of her Pygmy Folk advisers had indeed arrived in a tubeway car, ostensibly prisoners of a half dozen Tsolyani soldiers. They had departed again similarly—and good riddance! The facts were unclear, but they did include breaches of tribal etiquette, poor social attitudes, and the loss of eight warriors who had journeyed off in a second tubeway car upon some "mission" and had not returned. The behavior of guests had greatly degenerated, it seemed, since the age when Aluja's "ancestor" had lived. The Mihalli commiserated, uttered mournful cries, and vowed immediate pursuit. It was all he could do to prevent the rest of the Folk from joining them, hot with rage and bent upon definitive vengeance.

Ridek returned to the matter at hand. "You saw only fire?"

"Ai, a place that is all flame—not the energies of an empty Plane, but a real fire, a building or a cavern. Nothing could live in that holocaust. If the Lady Deq Dimani and her captors are there, then they are—" Aluja hesitated; he tended to forget that his companion was a twelve-year-old boy. Didn't humans protect their offspring from the knowledge and the sight of death? He was not sure.

"Dead?" Ridek said scornfully. "I have seen dead men before." He had, indeed, but only from a distance: the elaborate funeral of Lady Mmir's clan-uncle a year ago, two felons who had committed such enormities that the Baron's council had had them impaled, Tsolyani-style, and the body of a fisherman washed up on the sands near Ke'er. He was no stranger to death.

But then he had not really seen all that much of it either.

Aluja arose and daintily plucked murky yellow leaves from his fur. He forbore from mentioning the charred bodies he had glimpsed: not human, but smaller, four-legged, two-armed, and still redolent of musty cinnamon. The boy would surely have heard tales of the Ssu.

"We can remain here for a while," he said. "This Plane is harmless, and it lies within a region that is fertile with sorcerous power. There must be other Nexus Points nearby that will permit us to see the same place from a safer distance." The Mihalli began to revolve, around and around, as Ridek had seen him do before.

Ridek had learned much of the topography of the Planes Beyond during his sojourn with Aluja. There were "fertile" zones in which the "skin of reality" was so thin that one could almost feel the presence of neighboring Planes like a breeze from nowhere upon one's cheek; there were also "barren" regions where the "skin" between the Planes was as thick as the hide of a *Chlen*-beast, no Nexus Points existed, spells did not function, and only the stored power of "Eyes" and other devices operated—if they worked at all. Many of the Planes were featureless voids in which nothing lived; others boiled with inchoate energy; some contained creatures, peoples, and whole universes much like Tekumel's; a few were home to beings so powerful and so inimical that not even the Mihalli dared set foot within them. Then there were the Planes of Time, the Planes of Death and the Afterlife, and the Planes which were the paradises of the Gods Themselves: a multifarious, kaleidoscopic, muddled, confusing cosmos of worlds, beings, things, and powers, all floating like many-dimensional bubbles within the infinite matrix-ocean of reality. . . .

Of all of the races of Tekumel, only the Mihalli could traverse the Planes and recognize their orientations and interrelationships. Had Ridek been a Mihalli child, Aluja could have diagrammed their patternings for him, but he was human and hence limited to the fragmentary insights attainable through words alone. The Planes were like the pages of a book, Aluja said, but a book whose leaves did not lie only in a sheaf one on top of the other; each page, each sheaf, extended into infinity sidewise, horizontally, vertically, forwards, and backwards, all at the same time!

Luckily for Ridek, he lacked even a smattering of theology or philosophy, else he would have been thoroughly confused. As it was, he accepted Aluja's dissertation uncritically—and, for the greater part, without enthusiasm. He had never shared Sihan's interest in things arcane, nor did he have Ulgais' natural talents with Other-Planar powers.

Where they were now was a "Nameless Plane," an innocuous but dismal place. The sky was a dull, sad umber, the vegetation yellow or purple-black; the air stank like an apothecary's beakers; the soil consisted of gray-green muck; and the horizon was perpetually obscured by tatters of gray-brown mist. Not at all prepossessing! There was life of a sort: flat, eyeless lumps that crawled sluggishly across the spongy rocks and mud-slick clay. Nothing harmful, Aluja assured him, but distinctly unpleasant all the same. This Plane had no inhabitants and no name; it was a nonentity in a universe filled with more exciting things.

"What else did you see?" Ridek persisted.

"Nothing—nothing of interest, anyway. It was too bright: flames, a mass of molten stones, like the heart of a fire-mountain."

"If the thing—your amulet—says the Lady Deq Dimani is there, then she must be dead." He did not want that fate for her, and he added, "Perhaps she is farther away, not in that building, but somewhere nearby?"

"The amulet homes in upon her closely," Aluja answered. There was no use raising false hopes. "Here, I'll show you." He took out the device, peered at it, and went suddenly silent, his long beastlike jaw agape. In rueful tones he said, "Ai, boy, I grow old! I should have looked at this before putting my head so trustingly through the Nexus Point door! See, the spark is gone again: from near the upper meridian of the circle to the southeastern quadrant. The Lady has already left the place of the fire!"

"Back to the cavern? Your 'ghost' may not convince those folk a second time—nor the Tsolyani soldiers."

"Not the Desert of Sighs. The spark has moved across the face of the amulet to a new location."

"Then we must follow?"

Aluja nodded.

Suddenly it was too much. Ridek slumped against the boulder, childish tears welling up from nowhere. "Oh, Aluja, I want to go home! I *must* go home!"

The Mihalli was amazed. He had not realized! What was worse, he had no idea how to comfort a weeping human child! He remembered that Ulgais and Naitl liked to be picked up, stroked and caressed, but when he attempted this now with Ridek, he was met with struggling limbs and threshing fists. He released the boy in astonishment.

"I must go home—to Yan Kor! My father— It must be daylight—hours after we left—my mother will worry—"

"Hours?" Aluja was still more puzzled. "I told you, but you must not have understood. Some Planes are temporally slower than others: Lord Nere's, for example. Days have passed upon Tekumel. . . ."

"*Days?*" The tears became a storm.

It took a long time for the tantrum to cry itself out. Aluja sat silently beside the boy and waited. Humans were inscrutable.

When he was calm again Ridek said, "You—you will not tell anyone that I cried, will you? The Lady Si Ziris Qaya says that the boys of her people—younger than I by a year or more—go for days in the forests as scouts and messengers. They even fight sometimes as *Thargir*—skirmish troops. I would not have her—or my father—know."

"No, of course not." Aluja was bewildered. When one hurt, one cried, screamed, yelled, or whatever suited the occasion. Why others should not be told was mystifying. Yet if it meant so much to Ridek, he would do as the boy asked.

"Then let us go home, to Yan Kor." Ridek used the black staff Aluja had given him as a crutch and got to his feet. He was suddenly aware of the alienness of the Mihalli beside him, the eyes like marbles of scarlet glass, the subtly inhuman posture, the downcurving fangs that would have terrified any other human. It seemed important to make his needs very clear. "You must understand: my parents must think me dead, and they will grieve. I have to go home. Now. When they find out that I am alive, they will be relieved—but very angry.''

He did not want to think *how* angry.

Aluja acquiesced with a sinuous shrug. He was familiar enough with humankind to have seen parental grief, and the boy was a burden anyway. He inspected a patch of scraggly saffron vegetation, then turned to face the cloud-draped hills in the distance. ''The route to Yan Kor lies there: three Nexus Point doorways distant, perhaps twenty paces of actual walking. Can you manage that?'' He did not know how much endurance Ridek still possessed.

The boy surprised him yet once more: he sniffed disdainfully and snapped, ''Of course!''

They traversed a Plane of sandy hillocks, a second of black glass shards that shifted, clashing and tinkling, beneath their feet, and then a place all covered with fuzzy white bushes, like a field of *Firya*-plants from the fiber of which the weaver-clans made cloth. On this last Plane they halted in the midst of a thicket of puff-covered, dazzling white fronds, while the Mihalli consulted the amulet and his blue orb.

''Wait,'' Aluja said. ''My senses tell me that we are very close to the Lady Deq Dimani. One doorway leads to Yan Kor, and one in that—direction—goes to the place where she is now.''

''I suppose you want to go to her, now that we are this close?''

Aluja strove for a look that the boy would interpret as apologetic. ''We are so near. And she is my first concern. Your father ordered it.''

''I only wish I had the power over you that he has!'' Ridek flared. ''Damn my father!''

''Someday you may wield that power in his place,'' Aluja replied with enigmatic precision. He did not elaborate. ''Yes, I would see her, but no more than a glimpse, a moment of your time—and Tekumel's. Enough to be able to tell your father her situation. Then if I require assistance to get her back—"

"Soldiers? More Mihalli? Wizards?" Excitement flickered up in spite of Ridek's urgent need to return home.

"A Nexus Point door is small. Only one person can pass through it at a time, and so much energy is needed that I cannot maintain one for long—"

Aluja would have continued, but the boy brusquely waved his black staff and grumbled, "Oh, go ahead."

Three paces through the cloud-white vegetation, and the familiar iris of a Nexus Point doorway gaped open in the air before the Mihalli. Aluja motioned him to stay where he was, thrust his muzzle through, and after a moment entered it completely.

Ridek waited in impatient silence. A minute passed, then another. And another. He pulled a puff of white fiber from the nearest plant and found it sticky and sweet-smelling. He was hungry, but he dared not taste it. He sat down, the staff across his lap, and looked about. The sky was also white, as blank as new parchment, the pearly, puff-covered branches motionless and uninteresting, the soil an ordinary, prosaic brown. He sifted dry dust through his fingers. Nothing moved.

There was a tramping, crunching sound. It was far away, but it seemed to be coming closer.

The white bushes were too tall for him to see over. The landscape became suffused with menace: the terror of the invisible. He watched the Nexus doorway, but Aluja did not reappear. There was nothing to climb, no vantage point to give him a view, and he moved closer to the Nexus door to assure himself that he could get through before it vanished— never again would he be trapped as he had been on Lord Nere's ghastly world! The black oval (was it really black or was it some color that human eyes could not perceive?) hung unchanged in the muggy, stifling air. He poised himself before it.

The tramping approached. He thought he heard a voice, a

human voice! It said something gruff and commanding in a foreign tongue. Was that a glitter of silver over the fluffy top of that bush? A spear point? A helmet crest?

He waited no longer but gulped a breath, held it, and plunged through the Nexus Point as a swimmer dives off a cliff into the sea.

His knees and outstretched hands struck metal, and he let himself roll. It was nearly dark on the other side of the portal, and it took long seconds for his eyes to adjust. Except for an abrasion or two, he was undamaged. He sat up, then let out his pent-up breath in a gasp of relief: Aluja stood there, back to him, peering through what looked like a lattice of dull bronze.

The Mihalli whirled at the noise. "I told you to wait!" he hissed.

"Men were coming—creatures, anyway—soliders—"

"You should have stayed! The guardians of the Pale Legion rarely leave the paths in the Garden of the Weeping Snows! They would have passed you by!"

That was unfair! How could he have known? Ridek made a rude sound.

Aluja seized his shoulder roughly, and for a shocked moment Ridek thought the Mihalli was about to strike him. Yet he only hustled him back across the chamber, giving him just time to see that the place was quite small, entirely covered with metal, and crisscrossed with protruding rivet-heads in diagonal patterns. Three walls were covered with solid plates; the fourth was blocked from the ceiling almost to the floor with heavy bars. A cage? A cell?

There was something worrisome about Aluja's crouching stance, the way he held the "Ball of Immediate Eventuation" in one six-fingered hand. He sought about in the air, snarled something in his own tongue, then shifted back into Yan Koryani. "Now you are trapped too, boy, like me!" he cried, "The Nexus Point is closed from this side!"

"What? You—we—cannot . . . ?"

"No, whatever this place is, it is impervious to sorcery. A 'dead zone' where other-planar power cannot come! Here I am as blind and helpless as you—as a human."

Ridek ignored the comparison. "How can the Nexus Point be closed from one side only?" The extent of their predicament began to dawn upon him.

"The walls, ceiling, and floor are metal—and metal dissipates the energies of the Planes Beyond unless it be specially shaped to act as a channel, a conduit! Why do you think sorcerers wear no armor, no weapons or jewelry—even carry few coins? The Nexus Point in the Garden opens into this place, and this metal then prevents a mage from departing. Probably this prison also contains damping spells to keep its victims from using sorcery to open the door or blast down a wall—a nice trap for those who journey with the powers of magic!"

"What about the door—the bars—?"

"Locked. Without magic or the tricks of the locksmiths' clans, we remain here until our hosts come to see what prey is caught in their snare."

Ridek thrust his head through one of the spaces between the bars. He looked left and right and saw a longish corridor that disappeared into the darkness in both directions. Just opposite, high up in a bracket on the wall, was a lamp: a strange little transparent globe that glowed a steady yellow. The wall itself was covered from top to bottom with a low relief of writhing geometrical designs. He craned his neck and was rewarded with a glimpse of more barred cages on the same side of the passage as theirs. He put his head through the bars closer to the cell on his right and wriggled around until he could squint into it.

A body lay sprawled there; elongated bones of mottled ivory shrouded in the stained remnants of a robe or mantle, a shattered device of corroded black stuff, the dried and cracked remains of a leather harness, and a skull.

That skull was not human: it was melon-shaped, a flattened

sphere, ugly and sinister. The eye-sockets were long vertical ovals, and he could see no holes for nostrils. Where the lower jaw and the teeth should have been, there was only a single rippled, jointed, bony column: a neck and throat but no mouth!

Shakily he reported to Aluja. The Mihalli said nothing but closed his scarlet eyes and squatted down.

This did not reassure Ridek in the least. "Who is—what was—that creature?" The answer was important.

"A Shunned One, I think," Aluja replied grudgingly. "A race that dwells in the northeast of your land of Yan Kor. They live in sealed cities and cannot breathe our air for long."

"It was left here to perish?"

"So it would seem. That, in some wise, is encouraging. The Shunned Ones hate humankind. Whoever dislikes them may be friendly to us." Aluja lowered his long head to gaze down at his orb once more.

They waited, but no one came. Nothing.

Ridek examined the little cell more carefully: it was exactly three of his paces wide and four deep; the rivets were as immovable as the crags of Njekka Shoals; there were no furnishings, no toilet facilities, not even a bucket for water. He was reminded that he was both hungry and thirsty.

"What do we do?" he demanded in exasperation. "Sit here and die?"

The scarlet eyes blinked at him. "What else? —Yet I think that our coming must trigger an alarm somewhere." The boy looked as though he were about to cry again, and Aluja hastened to add, "Someone will come. This place is in decent repair; it's not a dusty ruin, not a lost dungeon beneath some deserted city. Mayhap I can bargain: trade some service for our freedom."

He did not sound overly hopeful.

12

Ridek squatted down upon the hard metal floor. He intended only to rest, but the sleep-demons seized him instead. He awoke to a raging thirst and a hunger that would have made fish-heads and *Dna*-grain gruel—the fare his tutors gave him when he was lazy about his lessons—a veritable feast of the gods!

He tried the door again, reached an arm around to fiddle with the lock, and did his best to squeeze through the bars. All to no avail. The space between the lowest horizontal bar and the floor looked more promising: it was a few finger's-breadths higher than those above it. He glanced over at Aluja, but the Mihalli was asleep.

He lay flat, huddled himself small, and thrust first his arms, then his head, and finally his shoulders through one of the holes. It was a tight fit. The rough surface of the bars scraped away skin, but he wriggled, panted, and pushed. His upper body was out! The rest was easy. After all, had not he and Sihan explored the warren of secret crawl-ways behind the fireplace in the Great Hall in Ke'er? Sihan had ended stuck as tight as a stopper in a bottle and eventually had to be rescued, screaming and half-dead with terror, by their father's masons. But Ridek had made it!

He crawled the rest of the way out into the passage and scrambled up. The black staff lay within reach inside the cell, and he pulled it through after him.

"Aluja!" he called softly. "Aluja!"

The Mihalli was on his feet in one single, fluid motion. They both knew that he was too large to follow.

The boy was overwrought, as well he ought to be, and Aluja had to wait until he grew calm enough to listen. "Look, Ridek," he said, "you are the master of our Skeins now. You must leave me and get help: find the owners of this place, those who have prepared this trap, and obtain their cooperation! Say that we wish them no harm, that we are not like the Shunned Ones, the Ssu, or others who would do them ill. Tell them that we would only return to Yan Kor, and that I would willingly perform some service in return for our freedom. These things you must do."

The boy was precocious for his age; indeed, he was clever even for a Mihalli child, although Aluja would never have claimed as much to any other member of his own species. He reached into his belt-pouch and withdrew a small, round, dark object. This he put into Ridek's palm.

"Here is an 'Eye,' a tool made long ago by human sorcerers. My 'Ball of Immediate Eventuation' is too complex for you, but this you can use as soon as you are away from these metal walls. This is the 'Excellent Ruby Eye'; point it, press this stud on the back, and your target is put out of phase with the temporal currents of this Plane—"

"I don't—"

"Never mind, then. It emits a flare of red light and 'freezes' its target in time. One so struck becomes a statue, immovable, untouchable, as solid as Thenu Thendraya Peak! You can leave him thus for as long as you wish: a moment, a day, a thousand years. You understand? The victim is not dead; another push of the stud releases him from stasis. If he were attacking you with a sword, he would emerge to finish the blow and do exactly what he had planned to do before the 'Eye' took him.'' He watched the boy's face. Clever or not, Ridek could hardly be expected to understand all this. Yet there was no other course.

"Don't worry, Aluja. I—I shall find the key—return with food—get you out—" Ridek looked as though he might cry again, and Aluja reached through the bars and took him into his arms. This time the boy offered no protest.

Arbitrarily Ridek turned to his right. The corridor was long, the other cells empty and dust-filled. Here and there more of the yellow lamps made eye-hurting mazes of the carven geometric patterns on the walls and the ceiling. Some of these curious little lanterns were dark; others were broken off entirely. No matter what Aluja thought, whoever owned this place did not visit here often.

Aside from his own cautious, scuffling steps, there was no sound. The passage was as eerily silent as one of the Empty Planes. He came to an open door, passed through, and peered down into a shadow-hung circular stairwell. The gods knew what awaited down there! A strange, bittersweet odor wafted up, and he backed away. His premonitions were sometimes almost as accurate as Ulgais's.

He retraced his path, came to Aluja again, and told him what he had found. The Mihalli could make no suggestion as to what might have been at the bottom of that stair, but he was emphatic on one point: Ridek must find a way *up*, not down.

Two more of the cells were occupied in addition to that in which the Shunned One lay. Both occupants were human and both were dead, one a very long time ago, the other recently enough to give off a noxious stench. Ridek did not pause to see. He was close to the outer limit of his endurance now; any more and he would tilt over into panic.

The passage ended in another door, as massive as a sepulchre-stone. It was open, however, and beyond he glimpsed a second stairway. Blessedly this led up. One, two, three turns around the newel-post, and he came to a landing where a second door barred his way, its panels of crude, black wood. It opened at a push, and he saw that its outer side was elegantly carved in more geometric patterns, a fanciful design of whorls, zigzags and triangles.

He found himself in a room, large and ornate, the walls and floor done in a mosaic of red and black tiles. High in one wall a stepped embrasure led up to a narrow slit that let sunlight into the chamber: beautiful, clean, bright sunlight, as welcome as rain to summer crops! He could not climb up to see out, but it was enough to know that he no longer wandered in some subterranean dungeon.

There were more doors, all open, another stairway up that was broader and still more elaborately sculptured, further rooms and hallways. Ridek paused to remind himself of the way back to Aluja.

He emerged into an airy upper portico of pillars and pierced balustrades of polished, blue-veined marble. The floor of this chamber drew his attention: it was divided all along its length into narrow pathways separated from one another by little carven curbings. Each level was raised a finger's breadth above the one next to it, and every one was a different color. The outer, lowest walkway was of black basalt, the higher one beside it red, then green, then yellow, then white, and finally blue—a beautiful, rich azure, like the lapis lazuli his mother wore on feast days. From the topmost walkway—dais? —the colors descended again in reverse order until one came back to black.

Ridek was familiar with the significance of daises. His father and mother occupied higher platforms than did the clan-matriarchs and their consorts, and these in turn were set above the seats of the lesser courtiers of the Baron's household. The Tsolyani were said to be still more formal. Yet here one had what amounted to a series of parallel walkways, all differently colored. It was unlikely that they were just architectural embellishments: they could have a ritual purpose, or they might serve to separate the various strata of society. In the latter case, he wondered, how did one cross the room: from the black pathway on one side to its mate on the other? Halfway along the empty, silent portico he found the answer: a set of narrow, oblong apertures in the floor. A glance told him that a steep little stair led down on one side, through a short tunnel, and up again to the walkway of the same color on the other. Only the central, blue pavement continued unbroken. Of course!

He was still examining these odd arrangements when he heard a noise. The steps of the staircase leading up out of the tunnel beneath the red walkway were tall and narrow; he banged his shins and cursed.

It was enough. He was seen.

Two people had come in at the far end of the chamber, both upon the lowest path, the black. One was a boy of about his own age, the other a girl. They wore only short kilts of some coarse, soot-hued fabric bordered with white embrasure designs. Ridek stared, and the pair stared back.

They might have been twins: both were shorter than he by a handspan, slender and wiry-looking, with long, glossy-black, curled tresses caught up with gleaming copper pins. The girl wore a necklace of copper plaques; aside from the clearly visible difference in their sexes, they were as identical as a person's two eyes.

Their costumes were unlike those of any nation Ridek knew. The girl's small, high breasts were bare, but her kilt was not cut in Tsolyani fashion. They might be Livyani, but he had heard that those odd southerners wore even fewer garments than these two—and tattooed themselves from head to foot as well! They were certainly not Mu'ugalvyani nor from some other northern land; those nations preferred more clothing. They were also not likely to be Salarvyani if the

emissaries he had seen at the court of Ke'er were any crite-
rion: those folk were sallow, hairy, and partial to garish,
multi-colored robes. Ridek was also intrigued by the staff—
tool? weapon?—the youth carried: a sort of complicated halberd of dark gray metal. Was it steel? Iron was so rare on
Tekumel that his father had spent years searching for enough
to equip his own personal legion, the *Gurek* of the Mighty of
Yan Kor.

Surprise was mutual. The girl pointed, whispered, and
made little fluttering gestures. The boy hefted his axe-sceptre-
thing and gawked at him open-mouthed.

The girl motioned and said something like, "*Tii pa
denketü'ü.*" The language sounded like the singing of a bird,
all rises and falls, and ending on a final warbled high note.
She pointed down at the black pathway upon which she and
her companion stood and indicated that Ridek should join
them. A warning? He might be standing upon the color
reserved for nobles, priests, or the gods themselves, for all he
knew!

Ridek himself was noble, the heir of the ruler of Yan Kor
and all the north. Something in this pair's attutide hinted that
they might be slaves or serfs. He decided that he would *not*
come down to their level. Instead, he stepped up onto the
central blue walkway.

If only princes walked upon azure, then Ridek Chna Ald
would have nothing less!

The girl cried out in her strange, chirping language, and
the boy echoed her. Both made importunate gestures. Their
meaning was clear enough.

Ridek strode toward them, Aluja's "Eye" clutched surreptitiously in his left hand, the black staff in his right. The boy
lowered the halberd-thing, jabbed a finger toward Ridek's
tunic and boots, and muttered in awed tones to his companion. Then both of them bowed.

He felt as though he had just won a signal victory!

A shrill, scolding voice called out from farther away among

the squat columns. Others replied, deeper and more resonant. He heard laughter and the clink of metal. Then both the boy and the girl knelt, their attitude again all too intelligible; someone of high station was coming. Ridek began to have doubts about the wisdom of his bravado, but he had cast the dice and now must stand by his wager.

They had not long to wait. A dozen men and women in sable-hued kilts swept toward him along the black walkway; then armored soldiers in blue, white, and silver livery upon the red; elegantly garbed courtiers and chamberlains upon the green; older and more venerable persons in costumes as colorful and iridescent as *Kheshchal*-birds upon the yellow; and two plump, pale-skinned, elderly matrons in gowns of thin, pearl-gray gauze bespangled with brilliants upon the white.

No one occupied the blue walkway upon which Ridek stood.

The party halted in confusion. One of the old ladies said something to a suave, middle-aged gentleman on the yellow path just below her; he passed the message on to a functionary upon the green, who gave it to a gilded officer on the red, and thence to a purposeful-looking, stout woman upon the black. She addressed the boy and girl, received a murmured, humble reply, and transmitted it back up through the hierarchy to the two occupants of the white tier. By the Sword of Karakan, Ridek thought, a conversation must be an all day affair here!

The group stared at Ridek, some smiling and giggling, others obviously impatient. The black-kilted woman stepped forward with great self-importance and snapped something in their sing-song language. She waited.

"I am Ridek Chna Ald, Prince of Yan Kor," he replied. Whatever came of this, he would not disgrace his parents' lineages! The situation did not really appear threatening, and he began to take heart. Then he saw what hung at the servant-woman's broad, black, leather belt: a little whip of knotted silken cords. The backs of the boy and girl kneeling before him bore faint traceries of scars. This did not bode well.

The woman tried again. One of the courtiers spoke in what sounded like a different language, and after him another. Ridek repeated his name and titles. He strove to appear proud and commanding, but he could feel his masquerade fraying around the edges. These were adults, foreigners, and—for all he knew—tyrants, fiends, or cannibals! His legs were as weak as reeds, and perspiration trickled down his forehead into his eyes. He dared not wipe it away.

The taller of the two women on the white pathway made an imperious gesture, and a black-clad youth raced off on silent, bare feet. Hunger, thirst, and—to be honest—stomach-queasy fear vied for Ridek's attention.

There was a jangling, chiming noise. Over the high-piled coiffures, plumed headdresses, and fantastic helmets of the party Ridek saw the servant returning with a powerfully built man who wore a kilt of vertical stripes of many colors. A lacy net of little chains hung like a cloak over his torso and jingled around his bare knees. Strangest of all, his face was concealed beneath a golden mask shaped like a *Sro*-dragon's head.

The mask had no eyeholes. The servant led this individual along by the hand.

The others upon the lowest, black walkway made room; the masked man—slave? servant? captive?—approached to within five paces of Ridek and raised thick-fingered hands that looked as though they belonged to a soldier or a gladiator. He spoke in a different tongue, one that Ridek recognized.

It was Engsvanyali, the language of the Priestkings of Engsvan hla Ganga, as dead and dusty as the Scrolls of the Priest Pavar himself!

Ridek had never been good at the classics. He was still struggling to formulate a greeting when the man addressed him again, this time in Tsolyani. He had mastered enough

Tsolyani to reply—but not much more, to the despair of his tutors and Lord Fu Shi'i. The man made dramatic gestures and said something else in a guttural, mushy-sounding tongue, possibly Salarvyani. Of this Ridek knew nothing at all.

The man's next words were in Yan Koryani! His accent was foreign, barbarous, and sounded as though he had learned the language in the lowest stews of one of the eastern cities: Tleku Miriya, Krel, or even Ngakü on Lake Parunal. No matter, it was as musical as the hymns of the gods to Ridek's ears!

What he said was utterly incongruous, however: "Piss on you, whoever you are, answer me before the *Gaichun*'s lady here has us both castrated! You must speak a tongue somebody can understand!"

Ridek stood speechless. He almost dropped the "Eye."

"Hear me, you son of a *Chlen*-turd." the translator declaimed in loud, formal tones suited to a herald announcing the divinity of an emperor, "I'm supposed to be telling you the ever-living, ever-copulating titles of the two old *Hu*-bats behind me there on the white. From what these arse-kissing slaves say, you're in trouble. Your tunic and boots and hair-do all sound like the Five Empires—mayhap Yan Kor—and if you can understand me, then say so—prettily and quick! And get your clumsy feet down off the *Gaichun's* shit-smeared blue walkway!"

"You—you. . . ."

"No, I'm not Yan Koryani. My mother was a whore in Jakalla in Tsolyanu, and who my fart-eating father was I neither know nor care. A slaver bought me for two copper *Qirgals*, and I worked in the mines in Fasiltum till I was nineteen. Then I was sold to an owner who tried to make a batch of us slaves into a private army. He armed us with crossbows and trained us so well that we slew his overseers, stole his sister-kissing treasury, and ran off into the mountains of Kilalammu. From there it's a longer story than I've time to tell. But here I am, Okkuru son of nobody, with no lineage and no clan, yet still First Translator of the Governor of the Realm!'' He paused to bow again. ''Now it's your turn. Say something, may the gods fry your balls for eggs! Tell me who you are and what you're doing here so that I can pass it on to the *Gaichun*'s old crone and her beloved hair-teated sister!'' He turned and made a flourishing, jingling obeisance before the two matrons upon the white pathway.

''I—I am Ridek—'' It no longer seemed like a good idea to say that he was the son of the Baron of Yan Kor. There were such things as hostages, ransom. . . .

''Ridek who?''

He temporized. This vulgar slave probably knew nothing of Yan Koryani lineages. ''Ridek Chna Ald. I am a—a traveler. I came here by accident—by sorcery . . . I mean no harm.''

The man named Okkuru tilted his head back, and Ridek realized that he could see out from beneath his mask. ''A child! A traveler? A story I wouldn't believe if Lord Hnalla, Master of the Gods, came down and whispered it in my ear while buggering my arse!''

''If—if we could only sit down. I'm tired—hungry.'' It was becoming too much.

''Wait. Let me make up a charming tale for the old biddy.'' The translator spoke at length, arms waving and chain harness tinkling.

One of the chamberlains put forth a hand, and a soldier strode forward. The translator said something else, and the man stopped, hand upon his sword-hilt, to look back at the old woman questioningly.

''I told them you were a sorcerer, a prince in your own country,'' the translator muttered. ''Act like it.''

''But—''

The elder of the two women raised a beringed finger. The slave boy who had first met Ridek advanced toward him upon the black walkway, bowed, and indicated the gold-flecked white stone of the next lowest path.

"Only the *Gaichun*, the High Governor, is allowed up where you are," the translator declared. "The old harridan forgives you. Now come down to her level. She'll allow you that until things get clearer."

Ridek obeyed, his legs so rubbery that he feared he would collapse. The two fingers' breadths of distance between the blue and the white walkways seemed like three man-heights.

"Now kowtow politely. That's it! The boy, Soruhi, will take you to a robing room, then on for some food. You've got to be properly costumed in order to eat here, and nobody dines in front of anybody but slaves—too much danger of defiling your precious status! Your betters would be insulted if you sat down with them, and you yourself ought to be scandalized at the thought of feeding with anybody lower! Understand me?"

"Yes— But—" One urgent question still loomed large in Ridek's reeling, exhausted mind. "Where am I?"

"As Lady Dlamelish loves fuzzy-arsed virgins! You don't *know*?" A muffled guffaw emerged from beneath the golden helmet; the translator bent his head back, tilted the mask up, and blinked at him in amazement. "Why, boy, this here is Mihallu!"

Ridek was dizzy, fatigued beyond measure. "Mihallu? Where the Mihalli live?"

"Mihalli? Who—? The ancient race? Not so, lad! These folk are human, the descendants of the Engsvanyali conquerors who slew the last of those magic-mucking monsters! A Mihalli in Mihallu?" The man's laughter echoed within his mask-helmet, and the courtiers behind him twittered and snickered. "Not unless it's dead, skinned, and spread for a carpet! There's a ten-thousand-year-old order from the Priestkings of Ganga to slay any Mihalli on sight!"

Afterward Ridek had no recollection of reaching the little white and gold room the old woman—the *Gaichun*'s Lady—provided, the bath given him by a squad of chattering servants,

the ceremonies of dressing, the formalities of eating behind
a lacquered wooden screen, the questions, and the final rituals
of getting into bed.

All he knew was that Aluja would surely die if he so much
as hinted at the Mihalli's presence here in this warped mad-
house of a country.

13

Streaks of mist-gray dawn smudged the horizon by the time the line of waving torches reached the base of the citadel and surged around its western bastions, presumably toward some entrance in the buildings beyond the outer courtyard. It was hard to discern who and how many had come up from the city, but Trinesh guessed about a hundred. They were apparently all humans, although Gayel's last greenish moonlight hid everything but their cloaks, the glint of helmets, and the sheen of spears.

Whoever their accidental flare had attracted came well prepared.

Trinesh and his comrades inspected their possessions once more. Every item was in place, including the "Eye" Trinesh had confiscated from the Lady Deq Dimani. They could only conclude that Balar must have found another of the Ancients' deadly instruments and kept it hidden for himself. He had paid for his avarice.

There was one last decision to make, the most important of

all: should they leave at once in the tubeway car or stay and face the force climbing up from the city? Chekkuru and Horusel urged departure, but the others were willing to see who would arrive. Tse'e and Trinesh argued that they could always fight a delaying action and retreat into the tubeway car if matters became difficult, but the Lady Deq Dimani expressed doubts about thier chances once the strangers reached them. This only made Trinesh all the more adamant.

To their left the spires and cupolas of the tubeway car portico first became pale blue and then as dainty pink as a confection of *Dmi*-sugar in the dawn-light. The city still slumbered in deep shadow in the valley to the north. If the gate in the lizard-court was indeed the only way into their area, the rising sun would be full in the eyes of anyone coming through it or shooting from atop the parapet above it. Their defensive situation was as good as they—and the Weaver of Skeins—could devise.

What of the lizards? Whoever crossed the outer courtyard must first deal with its ugly denizens. There might be a concealed tunnel into their section from the buildings beyond the lizard-court, and Trinesh set Tse'e and the Lady Jai to watch within. The rest he posted upon the rooftop. Arjasu and Mejjai had their crossbows, but Balar's was gone. Two crossbowmen, with perhaps fifteen quarrels apiece, could not stop a hundred foemen for long, but it was the best they could do. The Lady Deq Dimani suggested using their boot-laces as slings—rounded pebbles were plentiful upon the roof—but those advancing up from the city gleamed with metal armor, and sling-stones would likely be as effective as thrown sandals.

They made their dispositions and waited.

At last the sun struggled up through the dawn mists to reflect blinding, ruddy glitter from a solid phalanx of blades, helmets, and shields arrayed along the parapet across the lizard-court. A poor chance of victory!

It was time to decide: fight, flight, or parley. Trinesh took a final hurried poll and opted for the last—to be followed speedily by the second if need be.

Someone shouted from across the way: a high, authoritative male voice.

"*Hereksa*," Chekkuru muttered. "He speaks Engsvanyali!"

"The armor!" the Lady Deq Dimani exclaimed. "Like the harnesses of the Priestkings' soldiers in the murals!"

It was true: the many little bosses, spikes, and knobs protruding from the pauldrons, the chaised wasp-waisted breastplates, the visored and crested helmets, all resembled the book-paintings in the library of Trinesh's clanhouse as closely as though copied by a master armorer.

"We have not traveled through the Planes of Time," said Chekkuru nervously. "We saw no Nexus Point doorways—those I would recognize." Thu'n nodded agreement.

"Can you answer him?" Trinesh asked the priest.

Chekkuru blinked. He poked his shining bald skull a hand's breadth above the parapet and struggled with the ancient language. He might know his litanies by rote, but as an Engsvanyali conversationalist he left much to be desired.

"Ohe!" the voice called again. "Do you speak Tsolyani? Yan Koryani? Salarvyani?" Whoever their hosts were, at least they could converse!

The weapons across the way included crossbows. Trinesh abandoned any hope of armed resistance and clambered up to lean on the gritty coping.

"We are Tsolyani, most of us," he yelled back. "Who are you?"

The man across the courtyard was portly, middle-aged, and pompous by the sound of him. His entire head was covered by a mask-helmet made in the semblance of some fanciful beast-monster: a complex headdress of gold-chased silver, the eye-sockets picked out with red gems. Tall *Kheshchal*-plumes trailed down behind to spill over scarlet vestments like those of a priest, distinctly clerical though unfamiliar. Another stood shading his eyes beside him: an armored soldier who looked as though he had stepped out of an Engsvanyali tomb-relief!

"I," said the red-robe, "am Chunatl Dikkuna, High Priest of Lord Karakan in this Province of Mihallu. And this," he indicated the officer, "is Lord Tekkuren Chaishyani, First General of the Seekers of Indelible Victory, the Thirty-Fifth Legion of the Empire of the Priestkings of Engsvan hla Ganga."

"As Lord Vimuhla burns bright!" Chekkuru gasped. "*Hereksa*, the histories say that the Thirty-Fifth Legion marched off to conquer the east in the reign of Bashdis Mssa VII, 'the Dispenser of Bounties'! They never came back. These people have been dead for ten thousand years! Either these are the Planes of the Departed, or else we have traveled back in time, Nexus portal or not!"

"Make no defense!" cried the priest of Karakan. "You have intruded into the First Palace, the House of Ancestors, the Many-Chambered Sanctuary of the *Gaichun*, who is Governor and master of this land! Show no enmity, and you suffer no harm. We come now to take you forth from there."

They could only stand and watch as the soldiers—Engsvanyali or whatever they were—opened the gate in the opposite wall, threw down handfuls of a brownish powder that sent the lizard-things scurrying away, and advanced to the base of their own building. Efficient, black-kilted serfs trotted across with picks and mattocks to smash down the wall blocking the doorway. Then troops armed with antique halberds and cumbersome, clattering winch-crossbows came to surround them. Finally the splendid personage identified as General Tekkuren Chaishyani followed to pipe orders in some twittering language that was neither Engsvanyali nor any tongue they had ever heard.

No one touched them. A lesser officer gingerly gathered up the tools and instruments heaped beside their tubeway car. More workmen pried up a square of pavement in front of the car's hatch to reveal three glass squares, one blue, one yellow, and one red. Another dignitary peered into the car, then slammed the door shut and stamped upon the red plaque.

The car sighed and descended into its tunnel to disappear from sight.

Their captors inspected Trinesh's ragged party closely but did not disarm them. Instead, they formed ranks and escorted them out through the lizard-court, now sparkling with amber crystals that crunched underfoot and gave off a harsh, acrid smell; then into the labyrinthine buildings they had seen from their courtyard roof; on through barely glimpsed, empty halls and chambers, and out once more beneath a portcullis of verdigris-coated bronze; down a grassy roadway of time-hollowed granite blocks; and across the plain to the river. This they crossed in a splashing mob. The soldiers gestured for them to keep to a path marked by poles in the center of the ford. There were probably deeps on either side, judging by the flotilla of coracles and lateen-sailed small-craft that hovered nearby to watch. Trinesh had a brief view of dusty fields where children ran shouting after lumbering *Chlen*-beasts; clumps of overspreading, leafy *Gapul*-trees around mud-brick huts so old they seemed to have sprouted out of the earth itself; then more fields, larger houses, standing crops of red-leaved *Dna*-grain, and occasional awestruck farm folk.

Thus they came to the city.

It was more of a small town, once walled, a humped, untidy mountain of dawn-blue domes and rooftops in the shadowed valley. The ramparts were in disrepair, many of the merlons fallen away, and the gate itself was propped open permanently with a balk of timber. A single soldier leaned over the battlements to yawn and scratch himself as they entered. Within, the streets smelled of charcoal smoke, food, and spices; women squatted before their doorways to grind *Dna*-grain; and children scattered before them, screaming and laughing like little brown *Küni*-birds in flight.

It was so much like Tsolyanu! The faces of his comrades told him they felt the same.

Somewhere behind the jumbled tenements a *Tunkul*-gong boomed to summon the devotees of some god or goddess to the morning rituals. Trinesh almost expected to look up and see Tumissa's prowlike fortress frowning westward toward Mu'ugalavya from atop its mighty crag.

Yet this was not Tumissa, nor was it Tsolyanu. These people wore black kilts and did their long hair in elaborate loops and braids fastened with copper pins. When they spoke it was not Tsolyani but some singing, musical tongue, full of unfamiliar vowels and glottal catches. Their skin was more sallow, a brownish-yellow instead of the coppery gold of the Empire, and their faces were narrow and triangular, with long, thin noses and pointed chins, rather than the high cheekbones and broad foreheads of Trinesh's own clansmen.

More sightseers joined their procession at every step. Most were men, but there were women too, all attired alike in short, black kilts with little distinction between the sexes. The children grew from a mob into a pushing, chattering horde.

Visitors, then, were an uncommon occurrence here.

One other difference struck Thu'n so strongly that he trotted up beside Trinesh to mention it. Unlike Tsolyanu or any other of the Five Empires, the crowd contained not a single nonhuman of any species, nor did any of the throng approach within ten paces of the little *Nininyal*. Amid all the noise and confusion Trinesh tried to think of some place on Tekumel where no nonhumans dwelt. Nothing came to mind. Wherever humanity lived, there were the allied races as well: the little Hlaka fliers, the pouched and baggy-looking Pachi Lei, the Pe Choi who resembled tall insectoid statues of white and black chitin, the reptilian Shen, the gruff and bumbling Ahoggya—squat cylinders with four arms and four spraddled legs and four pairs of eyes, one pair on each side—and a half dozen others.

No, this was not a familiar place at all.

The sprawling market square they had seen from the citadel was bright with tents, panniers of unknown fruits and vegetables, and bolts of cloth. The streets were paved with slabs of white quartz and black basalt, the buildings were higher and better kept, and the occasional trees were obviously maintained for both beauty and shade. Their procession (now more a full-fledged parade) halted in milling confusion before one of the four palaces Horusel and Saina had thought to be Mu'ugalvyani. Trinesh had an impression of domes, spires, buttresses, cornices, and inward-leaning walls slanting up to tiled and gabled roofs. Then they were hurried up a broad staircase into cool, incense-fragrant dimness. Gold gleamed here and there within a cavernous vestibule, and as his eyes adjusted, he saw more of the geometric carvings, squat upside-down columns, pierced screens of polished red wood, ornate furniture, and tapestries woven in muted tones of indigo, maroon, and amber.

There was something odd about the floor of the hall: it was divided into a bewildering maze of raised daises, platforms, and delicate walkways of several hues. Little foot-bridges led over differently colored areas to connect with their own shade again on the other side. It resembled one of the bureaucratic office-chambers in Tumissa, where the status of each scribe and official was defined by the level of the dais upon which he or she sat. The feast-chambers of the great Tsolyani clans were similar, the highest station being reserved for a gilded replica of the Seal of the Imperium, the symbol of the omnipresent Emperor, with places for lesser guests set upon descending tiers of daises, like broad steps, that continued down to the floor where the common folk ate. The Tsolyani view of cosmic order demanded this physical yet abstract display of the hierarchies of society. Trinesh thus comprehended the arrangement at once, although the use of colors was strange. These raised pathways did not end at the doors of the chamber, however, as their Tsolyani counterparts did, but meandered on out into every hallway and corridor as far as he could see.

Chunatl Dikkuna, the priest of Lord Karakan, emerged from the throng to scrutinize them. He said. "You will walk only upon the black areas until the High General assigns you your positions." The officer thus mentioned stood farther back; his small, pinched, soft-looking face wore a pained expression beneath the spiny crest and towering plumes of his antique helmet. That headdress must weigh as much as a small child!

Both the Lady Deq Dimani and Horusel would have spoken, but Trinesh forestalled them. "I am a soldier of the Tsolyani army," he said, "a *Hereksa*."

"A general? A captain?" The priest eyed him with interest.

Trinesh was not close to being either. He phrased his reply carefully. "Sire, I am a military commander. Our rankings presumably differ from yours."

"This Lady?" The priest inspected Trinesh's companions. He seemed sophisticated enough to know grain from chaff: lower-class troopers, an odd but clearly peripheral nonhuman, and three nondescript tribespeople—Tse'e, Chekkuru, and the Lady Jai. Aside from Trinesh himself, only the Lady Deq Dimani had the look of quality—and authority—about her.

She saw what was needed: an immediate assertion of rank and class. "I am the sole Matriarch of Vridu, an island in the northern sea off the coast of Yan Kor. I am also the High Priestess of the Lord of Sacrifice, whom you may know as Lord Vimuhla—"

"Vimuhla? One of the *Tlokiriqaluyal*, the Five Lords of Change?"

"So He is." She raised her strong, squarish chin. She might be bedraggled and hungry, but Trinesh thought her very beautiful.

The priest undid the catches of his closed, gold-chased headdress and pulled it off. The face beneath the gem-encrusted mask was less imposing than the serpentine monster it de-

picted: clean-shaven, with the bluish jowls of one whose
beard requires two razorings a day, thick eyebrows joined in
a solid bar above close-set eyes, and a thin, weak nose that
ended in a red-veined bulb just above fleshy lips. His skin
was pale ivory, smooth and unmarked save for a telltale
crinkling about the eyes. Trinesh guessed his age at about
fifty, but he could not be sure. This Chunatl Dikkuna looked
Salarvyani, though subtly different from those whose trading
caravans brought black *Dronu*-wine and bales of gay-striped
fabrics to Tumissa.

The man frowned and ran begemmed fingers over his
sweat-gleaming bare skull. "Lord Vimuhla is not favored
here, nor are any of the Lords of Change. Were I to tell the
High General, he would order you—ah—degraded to the
black *Klai Ga*, the walkway of slaves and commoners." He
smiled ingratiatingly. "Yet there is no need to say more than
one wishes, of course. 'A good huntsman tests the wind
before approaching the prey,' eh? Lord Hnalla rules this land,
and after Him Lord Karakan; Lady Avanthe is beloved for
Her attentions to the crops, the yearly river-flood, and the
animals; then come Lord Thumis and Lord Belkhanu. These
comprise the five *Tlomitlanyal* of Stability. The Lords of
Change have Their temples, too, but those are small and
mean—of no power."

"Then it is time you—" Chekkuru began hotly. Horusel
himself put a scarred hand upon his shoulder, and the priest's
protest ended in a squeak.

"Enough," Trinesh interrupted. "Where are we? You must
know that we came here by chance via the tubeway car. We
intend no harm."

"This is Mihallu, the easternmost province of Engsvan hla
Ganga, the glorious Empire of the Priestkings—"

"How can that be?" Trinesh did not know whether to be
amazed or angry. "Do you tell us that we have crossed the
seas of time? Engsvan hla Ganga is ten thousand years gone,
the Isle of Ganga itself sunk beneath the waters of Msumtel

Bay, the northern sea risen to become a plain! The Priestkings lie drowned, and their dominions are no more than ink-tracks upon musty parchment!''

''Let us discuss these matters in a private place.'' The priest nodded judiciously at the throng pressing about them. ''I will explain. There are things you must know.''

It seemed best to obey. Chunatl Dikkuna spoke to the High General, who waved a curt hand and stalked off surrounded by his entourage. The priest then led the way across the hall, indicating that they should remain upon the black walkway, the lowest. They passed beneath an archway and halted in a smaller side chamber filled with flat stools and folded wooden screens stacked against the walls. Chunatl Dikkuna himself paused just within the door to stand upon a single raised tongue of green stone that extended out into the black tiling with which the rest of the floor was paved.

''An antechamber adjoining the feast-hall,'' he remarked apologetically. ''It will serve until matters are plainer.''

''What will you do with us?'' The Lady Deq Dimani's cheeks were flushed; she must still be smarting from this priest's cavalier rejection of her deity.

''Listen, and you will be well treated.'' He raised a monitory finger. ''Know that I myself am a foreigner here. I come from the city of Jgresh in Salarvya, and I was not always called by the Engsvanyali name of Chunatl Dikkuna. My parents were of the Gürrüshyugga clan—the lords of much of the southeastern coast of our nation—and my original name was Horrükhü Jaggäsh. I journeyed hither as a physician seeking herbs and elixirs—''

''What has your personal history to do with us?'' The Lady Deq Dimani was impatient enough to be rude.

''Peace! Hear me! I was raised a worshipper of our Salarvyani Goddess, Lady Shiringgayi, but I—ah—improved myself vastly here by taking on not only an Engsvanyali name but also the profession of a priest of Lord Karakan. My knowledge of his doctrines is admittedly casual, but still it exceeds that of the locals as the sea is greater than a river. Most of the hierophants of Mihallu can neither read nor write, and their wisdom is limited to chanting Engsvanyali catechisms by rote—of which they understand less than does an Ahoggya of the ballads of the bards!"

Trinesh drew up one of the low stools and sat upon it. To Lord Vimuhla's icy hells with etiquette! "These folk did not know you? They have never seen a Salarvyani?"

"You have to understand. Mihallu is isolated, cut off as no other place is cut off; to the south are the jungles, mountains, and fierce savages of Rannalu—all of whom I eluded to get here. Go north, and you come to Moringana Massif, even denser forests, and the wild lands of Mudallu and Nuru'un. To the east are the Plains of Glass, a barren desert that makes all else appear as lushly fertile as Lady Shiringgayi's loins by comparison, while to the west are the barbarians of Jannu and Lake Parunal."

"Lake Parunal?" the Lady Deq Dimani cried. "I know of it! We have only to cross it to reach Saa Allaqi and Yan Kor."

"Madam," Chunatl Dikkuna replied sadly, "you are now in Ninue, the capital of Mihallu. The River Naru rises out of the mountains bordering the Plains of Glass; it flows westwards for two thousand of your *Tsan* to reach Ninue; thence it journeys on for another thousand *Tsan* before it debouches into Lake Parunal. This valley of Mihallu is only three or four hundred *Tsan* across from north to south, but it would take half a lifetime to walk it end to end!"

"And Lake Parunal is still eighteen hundred *Tsan* from Vridu," Tse'e added with malicious good humor. "A few hours in the Ancients' tubeway car but years on foot!"

The despair that seized Trinesh was like the gloom of thunderheads over a summer landscape. Tumissa—home—was farther away than the paradises of the Immortal Gods! He changed the subject. "But this— this matter of the Priestkings— Engsvan hla Ganga?"

"To these people Engsvan hla Ganga is very much alive," answered the priest. "That is the key to Mihallu: the Engsvanyali Empire still lives. The Priestkings' legions expelled the nonhuman Mihalli who dwelt here aforetime. They then settled this land with humans from the tribes roundabout and established their rule for millennia thereafter. That same rule continues here to this day. According to these folk, the Priestkings' Isle of Ganga never sank. Their 'High Governor' —the title of *Gaichun* is a corruption of the Engsvanyali word *Zhaitolan*—claims his mandate directly from the Priestkings' chancery! All is ostensibly as it was before Pavar's island disappeared beneath the waves."

"Madness," Trinesh breathed. "They do not know? Are there no merchants—travelers—to break the sad news to them? After ten thousand years?"

"They know. But they do not admit it. Ganga lies halfway across the continent, a legend, a history, a fable. The fiction of its existence must be maintained, for Mihalli government and society rest upon it, nay, cling to it like leeches to a *Nmatl*-fish! It gives these folk their justification to rule!" He pursed his lips. "Merchants? Ai, at this moment there are a dozen Salarvyani caravan-masters in Ninue, such as he who rescued me from the jungles of Rannalu, and a few wanderers from other lands to boot. All must pretend to the existence of Engsvan hla Ganga. To do otherwise means imprisonment or a decree of death."

"But these folk are *not* Engsvanyali," the Lady Deq Dimani exploded. "I have seen the Priestkings' portraits—statues, coins, paintings in books! These people look no more Engsvanyali than Thu'n here!" She ran her fingers through her thick mane in exasperation.

"True, true, Lady. Racially these folk are no heirs of Ganga, yet every lordly house claims descent from some Engsvanyali lineage or other. You saw General Tekkuren? He traces his ancestry back to a Chaishyani ancestor. Tankolel, Ssaivra, Ssanmirin, Chagotlekka, Ketkolel, Mraktine—their peerage reads like a roster of the legendary heroes of Dormoron Plain!''

"The language?" Trinesh puzzled. "We heard no more Engsvanyali after you first addressed us."

Chunatl Dikkuna gave him a regretful smile. "I probably speak less Engsvanyali than you do. The common tongue here is Tka Mihalli, a language of the Aom family, related to Saa Allaqiyani and the dialects of the northeast. The locals throw Engsvanyali words into their speech as a Jakallan cook tosses hot *Hling*-seed into a stew—the more one uses, the higher one's status."

"Let us speak of ourselves," the Lady Deq Dimani persisted grimly. "What happens to us? We came by the tubeway car, and we are *not* Engsvanyali. Do we change our names and religions? Do we tell these lunatics that we serve the Priestkings, though only sea-monsters now sit upon the throne of Ganga? Shall we pretend to this fantasy, this relic, this parody of the past?"

Chunatl Dikkuna stroked his nose. "That is for you to choose. You may stay on here as I have done, or you may walk home. They will not permit you to regain the tubeway portal—that lies within the old palace, the Many-Chambered Sanctuary of the *Gaichun*."

Trinesh thought of something. "Why was that place deserted? Does no one live there?"

"They say it is inhabited by ghosts. The halls swim with ancient sadnesses . . .''

"Cha!" Chosun snorted.

"Oh, if you prefer more mundane reasons, then know that the present *Gaichun* is old. He does not enjoy the height, the climb, the crossing of the river, and the distance from his cronies here in the city. There are political urgencies as well. He therefore resides in the Palace of the Realm, with his clan-cousin who holds the title of High Prefect."

"So that is what we saw: the four palaces!" Chekkuru exclaimed. "We ourselves still follow the Engsvanyali system in Tsolyanu: four 'palaces' which govern the realm under the central authority of the God-Emperor in Avanthar! The Engsvanyali divided their administration into the 'Palace of the Realm,' the 'Palace of the Priesthoods,' the 'Palace of Ever-Glorious War,' and the 'Palace of Foreign Lands,' We continue their pattern in Tsolyanu, and so do they here.''

''True, but here the Palace of the Realm is occupied by the *Gaichun* and his adherents, that of the Priesthoods belongs to the clans which provide the hereditary hierophants of the temples, that of Ever-Glorious War—in which you now stand—is home to the descendants of the Priestkings' legionaries, and that of Foreign Lands is empty, a ruin, ever since the civil war a century and a half ago.''

''You speak as though the Four Palaces were all independent powers,'' Tse'e put in. ''Yet all are supposed to be the arms of the Imperium. They should not be fiefdoms!''

''Time and distance blur all things. In Mihallu, the Palaces are not completely autonomous, but they do maintain a certain nice aloofness. The *Gaichun* is ill-disposed toward his generals, and the priesthoods love neither. I shall instruct you in local politics later, as need arises.''

''This could not happen in Tsolyanu,'' Tse'e scoffed. ''The ruler—the Emperor, the High Governor—would have only to command, and tradition and religion would come thundering down upon his foes as surely as Thenu Thendraya Peak crushed the Demon Qu'u in the Epic of Hrugga! The army would oust any rebel generals—''

''What army? Here we have generals but no troops! These people have never seen a battle! The Thirty-Fifth Legion, the 'Seekers of Indelible Victory,' contains no more than a few score of Lord Tekkuren's relatives. The other nine Engsvanyali legions posted in Mihallu are similar: clans of inbred aristocrats and popinjays. They war only with one another, with the tribes of Rannalu, or with the chieftains of the states to the north. My master, the High General, cannot tell the hilt of a sword from its blade! There are Illustrious

Scribes who cannot read, Supreme Pontiffs who do not know one God from another, Refulgent Chamberlains who have no functions and hardly a chamberpot to piss in! Reports are prepared daily to be forwarded to Ganga, carried by runners all the way to Arbala, a city in Jannu on the shores of Lake Parunal over which Mihallu has yet some sway. No reply ever comes back, of course. Doubtless even now some Chief Scribe of the Supernal Household scribbles the news of your arrival and requests instructions from far-off Ganga.''

''A joke!'' Chosun cried. The others muttered agreement, but no one laughed.

Chunatl Dikkuna remained unruffled. ''Oh, true. Each month the ship-captains of Lake Parunal are paid to pass on coffers of documents to the High Governor of Chai Aijjakhan—what you now call Saa Allaqi. I suspect they throw them into the lake to be perused by the fishes and the nonhuman Nyagga who dwell beneath its waters. But the Saa Allaqiyani cheerfully accept the taxes and treasures our noble *Gaichun* forwards to the Priestkings! Those they do not refuse!''

This was insanity. Trinesh sat in stunned silence, but Saina giggled. ''I do not fancy myself a slave. Better an Engsvanyali noblewoman! I do not look well in black.''

''If you fit into the High General's purposes, woman, you may indeed end as a Mihalli aristocrat as I—and others— have done.'' Chunatl Dikkuna eyed her with great seriousness. ''I can aid you: the High General requires new stones for the wall of power he builds to contain the *Gaichun*. You may well fit into his design.''

''We are not stones or bricks,'' the Lady Deq Dimani snapped. ''Neither mortar nor cement!''

''All pieces must fit into the plan. Either that or be discarded.'' The Salarvyani favored her with another smile. ''Peace, Madam, please! At least allow the architect to unroll his scroll. You and your soldiers—''

''Not *my* soldiers—''

''Forgive me. Whoever they are. You and these soldiers

may fulfill some of the High General's needs. Then no harm will come to you, and if all goes well, he may even permit you to return home. These smelly-cloaked tribespeople here are naturally another matter."

"They are not such at all." The Lady Deq Dimani moved to stand beside the Lady Jai. "Their attire is an accident of travel."

"Even better. The soldiers will likely be allowed to walk upon the red *Klai Ga*. Priests use the green or the yellow, depending upon their Circles. Courtiers are allowed the green, high persons the yellow, and princes are dignified by the white. Once a color is assigned you must keep to it. Never leave it to step upon any other hue."

"What?" Horusel gasped. "How does one visit the markets? The latrines?"

"Within the palace each walkway leads to all facilities appropriate to that rank of society: bedrooms, privy chambers, dining halls, corridors, and stairways to the upper verandahs where one may take the air. As for markets and the city outside, one employs slaves—who may walk upon the streets or even the naked earth—or else one travels thither in a litter floored with one's color, never letting one's feet touch the ground unless a carpet of the correct hue be spread there first. The highest praise that can be engraved upon a Mihalli nobleman's epitaph is: 'Here is one who never strayed from his color.' "

"Is there no limit to this foolishness?" the Lady Deq Dimani jeered. "We are tired, hungry, thirsty! If we are guests, then perform the duties of a host. If we be prisoners, then at least give us food before we are taken to your slave-pits!"

Chunatl Dikkuna exhibited remorse. "Your pardon, my Lady of Vridu. I am remiss. But you must know the custom of the land; else you would indeed end your Skeins in some hole—or worse. Now we are ready to progress to Lord Tekkuren's audience. There is no question of slave-pits, particularly if you let me serve as your interpreter. My role is, alas, crucial. Were you to deny the existence of Ganga, it would go hard with you. If you were to speak Engsvanyali to the High General—a tongue he must pretend to know but does not—he would be discomfited, which would be unwise. And so with other customs, usages, and fine points of etiquette.''

One more thought occurred to Trinesh. ''And what,'' he asked, ''do we owe you for this timely aid, my Lord Priest?''

The other spread his arms ingenuously. ''Why, 'naught but a smile and a wave of the hand,' as we say in Salarvya.''

Dineva had heard the expression. ''Ai, 'a smile of acquiescence when you ask for favors later, and a hand that waves riches into your purse.' I think we know this priest, eh, *Hereksa*?''

Chunatl Dikkuna rocked his head gently from side to side, the Salarvyani expression for an agreement clearly understood.

14

They had little opportunity to admire the gilded, baroque elegance of the High General's audience chamber. Chunatl Dikkuna donned his golden mask once more and assumed the role of translator. The Engsvanyali, he said, had their interpreters wear masks in order to conceal their identities, a practice recommended in the one hundred and fifty-third stanza of the Paean of Psankothoth of Nirukkai. He quoted:

"And Charkhuvra the Interpreter heard naught save his mistress's voice, spoke naught but her words, and saw naught, even through the dark-lit windows of his adoring soul."

Many, Chunatl went on, took this text literally and gave their translators masks with no eye-slits at all. The father of the present *Gaichun* had been still more conservative: he had ordered his spokesmen blinded *and* masked. Such piety was rare nowadays, fortunately for Chunatl and his colleagues in Ninue.

No one ventured to comment.

Trinesh would have launched directly into an explanation of their presence in Ninue, but Chunatl Dikkuna motioned him to silence. The High General must first display hospitality. A wave of the hand, and they were told that food would be provided as soon as the audience was over. Another wave, and they were awarded clothing, armor (hurriedly rummaged from some unguessably wealthy storehouse: Trinesh's harness was silvered steel!), and quaintly antique costumes for the Lady Deq Dimani and her maid. Elegant *Chlen*-hide swords, short, heavy, and embossed with the arms of Ganga, were offered the soldiers, but Trinesh chose to wear Tse'e's steel blade instead, even for ceremonial purposes. The old man himself, Chekkuru, and even Thu'n were presented with garments according to their stations and tastes.

Still further waves, and they were assigned their *Klai Ga*. Trinesh was granted the red, with his troopers to follow him there in strict order of rank. Chekkuru hiVriddi was allowed the green because of his clerical status. The priest held out for the yellow, saying that the Vriddi were as noble as any lineage on Tekumel—and older than the Priestkings themselves by a good dozen millennia! Lord Tekkuren only displayed bad teeth in a polite grin; Chunatl had likely made a selective translation.

When the Lady Deq Dimani's turn came, she disdained to argue for the white and accepted the yellow walkway. She did protest when Lord Tekkuren would have placed the Lady Jai upon the black, as was proper for a lady-in-waiting. After all, as she said, the Lady Jai Chasa Vedlan was of high clan and lineage in her own right.

Lord Tekkuren sniffed and waved the girl over to the green walkway.

There was no precedent for Thu'n, but the High General

seemed pleased to have the little *Nininyal* as an oddity at his court; he waved his pale, plump hand once more and sent him over to the green as well.

Only Tse'e remained, in reality the noblest of them all. Trinesh begged the old man to declare his real name and status, but this he declined, muttering that he had been a Milumanayani tribesman too long to care for worldly dignities. He compromised and accepted the green *Klai Ga*, however, when Chunatl pointed out that he would otherwise end his days apart from his companions in some scullery. Lord Tekkuren, for whom this debate was not translated, appeared nonplussed until Chunatl told him that this strange guest was traveling incognito—an arrow that struck closer to the mark than he realized.

The matter of their religions was thornier. Chunatl suggested a ruse. The Salarvyani would "misunderstand" when the party was asked its sectarian affiliations: he would hear "Vimuhla" as "Karakan" and would so translate to Lord Tekkuren. Trinesh, Chekkuru, and the Lady Deq Dimani were horrified. Deny their religion—or allow someone to mistake it? Ignoble! Chunatl argued that the sin of mistranslation would be his alone, but the others vehemently refused. The Salarvyani grumbled something about *Chlen*-brained pride but amended his plan: when asked which God they worshipped, each person would not name "Vimuhla" but rather that Greater Aspect of the Flame Lord whom he or she personally favored. The local clergy were blissfully ignorant both of Lord Vimuhla's eighty-seven Greater Aspects and of Lord Karakan's fifty-six. If one answered "Orkutai the City-Destroyer" or "Esseng of the Scintillating Bolt of Desolation," who would be the wiser? The Aspects of the two War-Gods sounded similar enough to permit such obfuscation. The idea kept their honor intact, but it still smacked of dishonesty: "as close to ignobility as one might shave an egg," Chekkuru complained. The Salarvyani insisted that his stratagem would be accepted without question, and eventually they let him have his way. The High General beamed and made welcoming gestures. It was obvious that Lord Tekkuren wished them no harm—for whatever reasons.

Trinesh decided that the time had come to seek certain urgent answers. He whispered to Chunatl, "You said that the High General has a use for us?"

"Let the formalities run their course, Tsolyani. 'Make a splash and frighten the fish.'" Chunatl turned his glittering beast-head back to his master, who had launched into a lengthy peroration.

"The fish had best take the bait or the fisherman goes to sleep," the Lady Deq Dimani murmured wryly.

"Patience. He comes to the meat of the fruit," the Salarvyani replied. He nodded, making the flowing *Kheshchal*-plumes of his headdress bob and shimmer, and bent forward. "Yes. Yes. Oh. That is how he plays the piece, then!"

"Tell us," the Lady Deq Dimani hissed.

"He believes that you are connected with the invasion."

"The *what*?" Trinesh gasped. He heard muffled exclamations from his comrades behind him, and the Lady Deq Dimani made as if to rise.

"The invasion. La, he breaches all etiquette by immersing you in politics before dinner! A clue as to your importance, at least."

"The Flame broil your greasy—!" Horusel clenched scarred fists. Trinesh quieted him with a glare.

"Let him speak on. I'll clarify as I translate." Chunatl eyed the veteran *Tirrikamu* with trepidation.

The High General obliged almost at once, tossing his helmeted head to accompany the singing intonation of his strange language.

Chunatl said. "Two six-days past, runners brought news of the landing of a great ship at Arbala. It contained many soldiers, and its captain, a lake-pirate named Harchar, bore a *Tilunatl*: one of those decrees once issued by the High Chancery of the Priestkings upon plaques of gold. This particular document gives the bearer—this Harchar—the Governorship of Mihallu, replaces the present *Gaichun*, and urges all citizens to obedience and loyal duty."

"A *Tilunatl*?" the Lady Deq Dimani said, puzzled. "How? The Priestkings have been dead for millennia—? A forgery?"

"Mayhap. Or a genuine artifact looted from some tomb."

"Even these lunatics must be able to detect a counterfeit," Trinesh sneered. "And if it is authentic, then it must contain dates, names, and places that do not tally with what these folk think to be the facts. Who would believe such flummery?"

"Many, Tsolyani, many." The ruby gems of Chunatl's mask glowed as he shook his head. "The folk of Mihallu are devoted to tradition and to their myth. Some there are who wish to see the *Gaichun* toppled. They would acclaim Captain Harchar's *Tilunatl* were it written upon a dried *Chlen*-turd. The *Gaichun*'s supporters will reject it, of course: it would take trumpeters from the heavens and a choir of the Gods Themselves to make *them* comply! Already the lines are forming. The lords of Arbala, of Mshechar, and of a dozen towns along the road to Ninue have gone over to this invader. A change of dynasty facilitates the making of new alliances, the breaking of old ones, the settling of enmities, and the gleaning of wealth and power out of chaos."

"Then there will be war?" asked Chekkuru. "The *Gaichun* will raise troops? Surely he must win! How many can a pirate-captain bring?"

"Troops? Not so. The High General, here, opposes the *Gaichun*: no aid will be forthcoming from Lord Tekkuren. The priesthoods are hostile to both. Already they send missions to placate this Captain Harchar, charlatan though he must be. The *Gaichun*'s clansmen are few, his enemies many."

Trinesh felt as though he floundered in a pool filled with darting minnows. He reached out and snatched at the biggest one: "But—yet—what has this to do with us?"

"You see no connection? Think! In the midst of this turmoil you arrive in a tubeway car, within the heart of the *Gaichun*'s most hallowed palace, brought hither by the magic of the Ancestors! The High General is certain that you come directly from Ganga, from the Threshold of Immanent Glory itself. Either you are here to defend the *Gaichun* and preserve the present order, or else you come as harbingers of his doom, to see that he be properly overthrown and replaced. Lord Tekkuren fervently hopes it is the latter: he is sincere in his devotion to duty and good government."

"And if the former?" the Lady Deq Dimani asked.

"Then you are rebels, foes of the new *Gaichun*—and of the High General's party. Rebels against Ganga and the Priestkings. Rebels who have fortuitously fallen into the hands of a loyal servant of the Engsvanyali Imperium. Lord Tekkuren will then take steps to—ah—deter you."

Trinesh consulted with his companions and found them unanimous. "Tell the High General that we are indeed here to see to—to the peaceful transfer of power to this new *Gaichun*," he announced. "If we must be involved, then let it be with the High General and this mountebank ship-captain. One aberration is as good as another."

Chunatl Dikkuna spoke, and the High General chirruped, nodded, and smiled.

"He raises a related matter: he perceives that you are divided into two groups, one perchance hostile to the other. He would know what this portends."

The Salarvyani's face was invisible beneath his mask, but his tone conveyed a warning: Lord Tekkuren Chaishyani was shrewder than they had guessed. Both Trinesh and the Lady Deq Dimani spoke at once, and the High General scowled. Chunatl shushed them and said, "He says that if one faction supports the new *Gaichun*, then the other must logically oppose him. Say something, anything, and let me speak for you."

"Tell him—for now—that this is a political matter which relates to us alone," Trinesh essayed cautiously. He sensed the Lady Deq Dimani's baleful gaze upon him. "Tell him that our differences concern us—and the high and secret policies of Ganga—and we ourselves will deal with them." The Lady Deq Dimani relaxed and sat back upon her dais once more. He spared her a mute glance of gratitude.

The Salarvyani spoke, and the High General grinned and chirped. He arose, signed to the servants, and twittered to Chunatl. The audience was at an end.

The red *Klai Ga* wound out of the hall, down a stairway, through corridors overflowing with florid garniture, and into a marble rotunda with warlike scenes from some Engsvanyali epic painted all around its ceiling. Servants trotted along beside them upon the black walkways, bowed, and set up screens of carved and lacquered wood like those they had seen when they first entered the palace. None but slaves ever dined together, Chunatl informed them, and each was to eat apart from the others. The special dining costumes proffered them were splendidly hideous.

A gravely silent, black-kilted attendant led Trinesh into one of the screen-cubicles so created and indicated a couch heaped with cushions. The pictures in the Engsvanyali manuscripts in Trinesh' clanhouse showed that the Priestkings lay at full length to dine, but Trinesh was unused to that position and seated himself crosslegged instead. The man made gestures, looked puzzled, and departed. Others entered to place a low table before him upon his red dais; then they, too, retired, always keeping humbly to the black *Klai Ga*. Still more servitors brought perhaps two dozen tiny bowls, each containing a different delicacy. He recognized grilled and shredded *Jakkohl*-meat, a stew of *Kao*-squash and roasted fowl, broiled fish (or was it lizard or some other reptile?), flat cakes of reddish *Dna*-bread upon which pungent *Hling*-seed had been sprinkled, poached eggs that had been replaced in their shells, wrapped in gold foil, and embellished with bright green legumes—and several more. A blackish jelly he did not touch, nor the fried white grubs in savory sauce, nor the little crustacean coated with red glaze and incongruously crowned with a tiny silver diadem. The meal was so ostentatious, so rich, so sugared, so spiced, and so decorated that Trinesh hardly knew what was edible and what was ornament—like the bumpkin Fekkumu in the Epic of Hrugga who ate the flowers out of the centrepiece! The beverages were similarly varied. There were ten miniature flagons full of various wines, liqueurs, juices, and essences. He had no idea which was supposed to be drunk with which dish and so settled upon three wines that he liked and ignored the rest.

The twenty-seven articles of cutlery totally baffled him. As soon as the servants had left him to eat in lordly solitude, he abandoned all pretext and used his fingers, as was the Tsolyani practice.

He struggled for restraint. He had seen hungry soldiers unexpectedly confronted with food before, and the results had been both memorable and unpleasant. Even so, he could not help stuffing himself.

Afterward they were shown to separate apartments off the central rotunda. Each consisted of a bedroom, an adjoining bathroom, and a still smaller chamber featuring only a low bench of sculptured white marble. The purpose of this last item became clear upon inspection, and Trinesh spent the next few minutes marveling at the complex pumps and valves that washed away whatever one put into the receptacle beneath the seat. A bronze tap beside the thing provided water for cleansing oneself. None of the Engsvanyali epics had described such luxuries as internal plumbing.

The sleeping arrangements were equally unfamiliar. Instead of a bed-mat upon the hard floor, the custom throughout much of the Five Empires, the chamber contained a curious double couch, one half red and the other black. The significance of this became apparent when a slight, thin-faced girl entered upon the lowest walkway. She bowed and waited beside the black side of the couch.

Trinesh was not unused to women. He grinned, and the girl undid her kilt and posed before him. He might have done more, but fatigue and rich food had unmanned him utterly, and a smile was the most he could manage. He was even too bemused to wonder how any coupling might be done without his crossing over to her color or she to his.

He never found out. He spiraled down into sleep.

A single, dreamless hiatus and he was awake again. The taste in his mouth and other urgent necessities told him that many hours had passed. The girl was gone. He used the marble bench and wandered out into the rotunda hoping that someone would show him how to fill the bathing pool. Black-kilted servants sprang to their feet, copper hair-ornaments jingling.

One pointed and said, "Chunatl Dikkuna."

The Salarvyani awaited him upon the green walkway at the entrance of the rotunda. He seemed upset, and Trinesh almost forgot and went to join him. The attendants' faces warned him of his impending gaffe, and he halted upon his own red *Klai Ga* just in time.

"Look, Tsolyani—*Hereksa*—or whatever you call yourself, we have trouble!" The priest was so perturbed that he had begun without even the honorifics expected in Tsolyanu, much less those required here in this etiquette-shackled land.

"What?" Trinesh rubbed his eyes to clear the last sleep-demons from his brain.

Chunatl Dikkuna squinted at the impassive attendants, settled his robe about his shoulders, and beckoned Trinesh closer. "We are overheard," he breathed, raising his eyes piously toward the ceiling. Little niches were visible there above the rococo frieze that ran along beneath the murals:

listening posts. "They may not understand Tsolyani, but they will note that we have talked."

"What occurs? What time is it?" Trinesh felt as though he were immured in a dungeon. This entire complex of rooms had no windows: the only illumination came from many-branched oil lamps set upon tripods by the walls.

"You slept a full day. It is evening again." The Salarvyani rasped his fingers across his blue-shadowed chin. "There is a matter of urgency."

"Water first. My mouth tastes like the workroom floor in an embalmer's shop."

Chunatl signaled to a servant, who brought Trinesh not water but a draught of some sour beverage, like half-fermented wine. It made things surprisingly better. "We are overheard? By the High General's people, you mean—your master's agents?"

"They—and others."

"What others? Here, in the High General's own palace?"

"Yes, the *Ochuna*, 'the Serpent That Winds Within.' I shall explain." Chunatl waggled beringed fingers. "Every room, every corridor, has its spy-holes: a maze of tunnels and passages that runs beneath much of Ninue. Together these comprise the *Ochuna:* a means of spying upon everybody and everything. The High General, the priesthoods, the *Gaichun*—and perchance others—have the use of it—"

"How? Why not seal off these passages? Or post assassins to deal with unwanted listeners?" His head still boomed like a temple gong.

"Such actions would be discourteous—and impolitic: 'Swat one of my *Chri*-flies, and I swat one of yours.' By unwritten agreement the *Ochuna* is safe to all. The High General's watchers sometimes stand side by side with those of his foes. There is no 'color' there; a priest, a slave, a noble, or the *Gaichun* himself—all may travel the *Ochuna*."

"More madness." Trinesh sucked at the goblet. "Every

plot, every assignation is common knowledge then? Is there anything in Mihallu that is not crusted solid with ceremony?" His wits were returning. "What is this trouble you mention? What occurs?"

"In the afternoon men came from the *Gaichun's* palace with a writ commanding the presence of the three Yan Koryani. The two women were taken, but the little nonhuman refused to go—"

"*Taken?*" Trinesh did not understand. "They are my prisoners! Taken where? To the *Gaichun's* palace? For what reason?"

"Your prisoners no longer, the Yan Koryani woman said. Yet I think that even the *Gaichun* will not dare detain them; they are Lord Tekkuren's guests and must be returned."

The priest's oily tone only infuriated Trinesh the more. "The Flame burn you all! They are *my* captives; the High General should never have let them go. He had no right!"

"Peace! Not so loud. Some of those above may understand Tsolyani. The High General had no recourse against a writ from the Priestkings' Governor. Calm yourself—and enlighten me: why would the *Gaichun* want the Yan Koryani woman and not you? Whom does she know here in Mihallu? In the *Gaichun's* palace?"

This made as little sense as the rest of this mad country. "Know? Here? No one. Nobody."

"Don't dissemble with me! Our people in the *Ochuna* tell me that she was taken to meet some unknown visitor. We cannot discover who. Lord Tekkuren worries. It is not desirable that he should worry."

"Do you question my word? She is as far from home as we are! For her to know anyone here would be a miracle of the gods!"

The priest twisted at the lappets of his vestments. "You think not? I shall show you. No, wait—do you speak her tongue?"

"Not I. But Saina does—the younger of my two *Aridani* soldiers." Chunatl's anxiety was contagious.

"Get your woman and come."

Trinesh found Saina asleep upon Chosun's couch. He woke them both, put a finger to his lips, and indicated that they should dress. Chunatl Dikkuna appeared in the doorway, the impropriety of stepping upon the red *Klai Ga* forgotten.

"No armor. It would make noise. —Yes, wear your sword-belts. Hurry!"

He led them out of the rotunda and into the shadowy corridor, looked left and right, then touched a boss amid the welter of carvings upon the wall. A black rectangle yawned before him.

"The *Ochuna*," he intoned. " 'The Serpent That Winds Within.' "

He would have slipped into the dark aperture, but Trinesh seized his stiff collar and snarled, "The rest of my people come too! We will not be separated!"

"Impossible. They stay here. The *Ochuna* is not for a rabble of blundering foreigners! Bring only the woman who speaks Yan Koryani. The others will be safe. I swear it by the Goddess Shiringgayi's thirty-six motherly teats!"

Trinesh considered. The Lady Deq Dimani's doings interested him as much as they did Lord Tekkuren. No, more! Promotion, reward, even a "Gold of Glory" from the Petal Throne, all depended upon his returning to General Kutume with the Lady Deq Dimani meekly in tow. If she eluded him now, all those hopes would vanish.

"Very well. But your life is surety for my people—and we take both Saina and Chosun here. Arjasu and Mejjai—my two crossbowmen—will guard the *Nininyal;* I doubt whether the Yan Koryani would depart without him."

Trinesh awakened the others and gave orders. Then he, Saina, and Chosun stepped over the high sill into the black opening. The panel grated shut behind them. The darkness inside was a palpable weight upon his eyes, and the place had a fusty, bittersweet smell, like a root-cellar in which dried *Dlel*-fruit are stored.

Trinesh felt the Salarvyani's sweat-damp fingers on his wrist, and Saina's small, callused hand upon his other arm. He wondered momentarily if Chosun had enjoyed her company as much as he had. More, he wondered which of them *she* preferred. ("Ignoble!" his little inner voice carped at him. "Great matters are afoot, and all you think of is your groin? Fa!")

Chunatl Dikkuna lit no lamp but followed tiny discs of phosphorescent stone set into the walls at intervals along the way. The reason became clear when Trinesh's outstretched fingers scraped against some crackling, brittle substance covering the wall beside him. It felt like a carpet of dried grass. He jerked back with a muffled curse.

"*Shon Tinur*," Chunatl whispered. "A black fungus that grows upon every wall and surface in the *Ochuna*. Even if we had a lantern we would see only blackness—no corners, no stones—just black upon black, like a sepulchre draped in velvet." Chosun grunted, and the priest added cheerily, "It's harmless—no fear—though it is full of little beetles that bite. . . ."

The Salarvyani seemed to know the way: like a blind beggar who returns to the same corner each day, Trinesh thought. The dots of pale green radiance led them onward, down a narrow stair with risers so high that Chosun almost fell, through corridors where their shoulders brushed against the fungus on both sides, and into chambers in which only the trail of glowing discs kept them from tumbling into unseen pits and pools.

"Five hundred and forty-five, forty-six," Chunatl counted. "Ohe, up this little stair, and we are there."

Up and up, around and around. They came to a peephole, as bright as a beacon after the suffocating, ebon depths. Someone waited there, a figure muffled in a cloak, proof against both the chill and the biting beetles. Trinesh realized that he was cold: they had come a long way underground. He pressed against Saina for warmth and found her pressing back, too eagerly perhaps to attribute entirely to their surroundings.

The man was one of Lord Tekkuren's watchers. Chunatl spoke to him in Tka Mihalli, and he made room at the peephole.

At first Trinesh could make out nothing. It was like looking through a hollow reed at an artist's palette or into a woman's jewel-casket. Colors swirled below there, gay-hued fabrics, the glitter of silver and gold, eye-wrenching patterns of parquet, mosaic, and glazed tile.

He stood back to let his eyes adjust.

"You see her? The Lady. Over there, on the yellow *Klai Ga.*" The Salarvyani's breath upon his cheek smelled like perfume sprinkled over spoiled meat.

They gazed down into a broad hall from a vantage point perhaps three man-heights up in one of the side walls. To the right were columns in the upside-down-step style; beyond these was the night sky. The left-hand wall writhed with the ubiquitous geometric patterns, and along its base were the highest platforms and walkways of the *Klai Ga.* Directly across from them three tall, trapezoidal doors were flanked by soldiers in the white, blue, and gold of the Priestkings' livery. The room was three-sided, then, with the fourth open for air and light: the sort of rooftop portico the Engsvanyali architects had favored as audience chambers long ago.

The blue dais against the rear wall was occupied by a man who must be the *Gaichun* himself. A beehive helmet and upcurving shoulder-pieces of filigreed gold hid the Governor's face, but his hands and his posture told Trinesh that he was very old. Two elderly women in gowns of gauzy, silvery puffs and flounces reclined on couches directly below him upon the white *Klai Ga.* The lower daises and walkways swirled with soldiers, courtiers, functionaries—a hodge-podge of colors and archaic costumes. There must be a good two hundred of Mihallu's noble-folk down there.

Trinesh, however, had eyes only for the Lady Deq Dimani.

She stood at the very edge of the yellow walkway, and she embraced a short, slender youth in iridescent green upon the white. The newcomer's shoulders shook as though he wept. He was so small: at this distance he looked to be no more than a child!

"You see?" Chunatl scolded. "You see?"

"Who is he?"

"You don't know?"

Trinesh was piqued. "How should I? For all I can tell he might be a god—or mighty Hrugga himself disguised as a dwarf! Or the *Gaichun*'s son!"

"Cha! 'Sarcasm ill becomes a noble soul,' as the proverb has it. There is the Governor's heir over yonder—by his mother, the taller of the old women on the white. No, it is not Prince Tenggutla Dayyar. Few would willingly embrace *him*."

The Prince at whom this remark was aimed glanced to his right, toward them. Trinesh saw a face of pale ivory, black half-moon brows, a receding, dimpled chin as blue with close-shaven stubble as Chunatl's, and long, delicate fingers that twined restlessly upon his lap. He wore a tight-fitting tunic of yellow brocade, an ankle-length skirt-like robe of many little panels, and a collar of glinting green beryls. Unlike most of the others, his head was bare, his oiled, ebon curls held in place with huge golden pins sculpted in fantastic shapes. More jewels winked in his earlobes, at his throat, and in the septum of his short, hooked nose. Even the space between his lower lip and his chin had been pierced for a labret of blue sapphire. The Prince's costume dated a good two thousand years later than those of his mother and the other woman beside her. These present-day Mihalli seemed to care nothing for historical accuracy; as long as something was demonstrably Engsvanyali, they copied it indiscriminately.

Prince Tenggutla Dayyar smiled toward someone directly

below Trinesh's vantage point. He peered but could see only the top of a woman's head, a lady upon the green *Klai Ga.*

It was enough; he would know the Lady Jai Chasa Vedlan anywhere.

Chunatl jostled Trinesh aside to make way for Saina. "Listen, woman," he said, "and tell me what they say. Find out who the boy is."

She squinted, put first her left ear and then her right into the little aperture, and strained to hear.

She shook her head. "It's Yan Koryani. But it's too low, too far, too much noise."

Trinesh thought the Salarvyani would shake her, a dangerous thing to do to Saina. "Who, by Shiringgayi's glorious loins? Who?"

"How do I know?" she flared back. "Wait." She listened again. "No—yes—a name? 'Aluja?' Who is Aluja? The boy? It's not a Yan Koryani name. Somebody—Aluja? —is in a prison."

The *Gaichun* chose that moment to sign to those upon the black *Klai Ga.* Horns blared and gongs sounded. An orchestra of flutes, drums, and bells struck up a clashing, barbaric melody that was anything but Engsvanyali. The Priestkings would have thrust their divine fingers into their godlike ears!

Chunatl groaned. "Now they will go to the feasting chamber. Afterwards they will return to enjoy dancers, jugglers, and recitations of the epics—performances as bad as any you will find on Tekumel. We shall not have another opportunity. Oh, may Shiringgayi's black hole swallow them all!" He turned to the High General's watcher, but the man only shrugged. "There is nothing to do but go back. You will have to question her and ferret out the identity of this princeling yourself. Lord Tekkuren will be magnanimous. If you fail, he will be otherwise."

Trinesh watched the Lady Jai cross the long hall, gracefully avoiding the throngs of chattering courtiers in her path. She stopped before the white *Klai Ga* and made obeisance to the young man in green. Whoever he was, his importance to the Yan Koryani was apparent. The two women stood to speak with him as though they were alone in the hall.

A flash of glitter caught his eye. Prince Tenggutla Dayyar had risen also. He murmured to someone near him, a hulking man who wore an eyeless mask and a costume of swinging chains: another translator. The two of them approached the Yan Koryani. The Prince said something, the interpreter spoke, and the Lady Deq Dimani smiled. Then a black-kilted major-domo bustled up to lead them off through the central door in the far wall where they were lost to view.

Only Trinesh noted the long, thoughtful look the Prince cast after the Lady Jai Chasa Vedlan.

15

The others were waiting in the rotunda. A conference was in order. Trinesh drew everybody together and indicated the listening posts up under the ceiling. In a whisper he and Saina related what they had seen.

Their comrades listened, argued, and conjectured, but no one could suggest an identity for the Yan Koryani boy. He seemed too young to be a soldier, an emissary, or a merchant-traveler. He was certainly of high clan; his status upon the white *Klai Ga* was proof of that. The Lady Deq Dimani appeared to know him, which was another point in favor of his importance. Anything further was guesswork.

The name "Aluja" was equally enigmatic. Saina swore that it was not of northern origin, but Chekkuru surmised that it might be from Jannu or one of the other little states roundabout. Could this Aluja be an ambassador and the boy his son? Perhaps someone—the *Gaichun*, the priesthoods, or some third faction—had popped Aluja into prison but left the boy free?

"Likely he stepped on the wrong color," Horusel threw in sourly. "Yet what's the purpose of a mission to this Flame-scorched hole anyway? The Baron Ald will get no troops from Mihallu. Ahoggya mercenaries might be possible, now. When we were in camp at the Pass of Skulls we heard the Salarvyani were sending some of those dirty beasts up through Kilalammu and Jannu to join the Yan Koryani. . . ."

"Unlikely," Chunatl retorted. "No Ahoggya has ever set foot in Ninue. It is much too far to the east."

"The Ahoggya fight for pay," Tse'e said. "If these people are mad enough to send taxes and tribute to Ganga ten thousand years after its demise, perhaps the Baron has found a way to wangle a tithe for himself as well?"

"Gold. That's likely it, *Hereksa*." Horusel's armor creaked in time with his pacing.

"Gold?" Chunatl pursed his lips. "Perhaps. But not to pay Ahoggya. I myself am a Salarvyani. A Yan Koryani mission that involves Salarvya would be known to me, and then I would not need you to identify the princeling. Others of my people here would have informed me."

Horusel grimaced. "Mayhap they trust you as much as I do."

The priest bridled and would have answered hotly, but Trinesh intervened. "Leave be. Ahoggya mercenaries are only one idea. Without facts we are no more than philosophers gnawing at paradoxes."

Chunatl made a clicking sound with his tongue. There was nothing more to be done. If the High General was displeased, so be it. Surely Lord Tekkuren had better-placed agents within the *Gaichun*'s household itself?

The Lady Deq Dimani reappeared about noon, dark smudges of fatigue beneath her heavy-lashed eyes. She went straight into her sleeping apartment followed by the Lady Jai, who bore a cloth-wrapped bundle that clanked when she set it down. Gifts, probably, Saina muttered to Trinesh: jewelry and baubles from the *Gaichun* or from the unknown Yan

Koryani prince. The girl shut the door, leaving them staring after her.

The morning passed. Trinesh gave orders, and Horusel and Arjasu padded off to reconnoitre the palace. They returned within a *Kiren* to sketch a plan in a puddle of wine upon the marble floor. The red *Klai Ga* rambled through halls and corridors, they said, up a grand staircase to a flat roof covered with trellised vines and potted plants, and into rooms crammed with ornate furniture and oddments: walls of statuary, shelves of colored glass vases and decanters that shone like jewels in the sunlight, and a whole chamber filled from ceiling to floor with scrolls and books. A few of the black-kilted slaves hovered about, but no one had hindered them.

Thu'n emerged for the afternoon meal. Tse'e, who had taken a liking to the creature, would have begun a conversation, but the *Nininyal* was not disposed to talk. The others bathed, ate, rested, and dawdled the afternoon away beneath the awnings of the roof garden.

Boredom, Trinesh thought, would become a problem. They were well fed and comfortable, but otherwise things were much the same as they had been in the Many-Chambered Sanctuary. Already Chosun paid court to one of the serving wenches; Arjasu stroked his crossbow and sharpened the heads of his quarrels; and Chekkuru, Dineva, and Horusel mumbled and plotted together. Saina said nothing, but Trinesh felt her eyes ever upon his back. Tse'e obtained a scroll from the library-room and sat crosslegged to read it. The old man had changed back into his Milumanayani desert-cloak; it was more comfortable than the stiff and complicated costume the High General had provided. Mejjai, who rarely spoke, drank everything the slaves offered, methodically and earnestly, as though he planned to stay drunk for the rest of his life.

How many days until this Captain Harchar arrived to seize the *Gaichun*'s throne?

Trinesh wondered if they could survive until then.

At sunset two officers in resplendent blue, white, and gold

livery appeared to summon the Lady Deq Dimani to the Governor's palace once more.

Trinesh found her buckling on the gold-inlaid dress armor the High General had bestowed upon her; she preferred this to the uncomfortable Engsvanyali frills and veils and starched collars now—or rather, still—in fashion among the women-folk of the *Gaichun's* court.

He confronted her. "You are still my prisoners. Captives of war. Whatever these locals say."

"Would you use that little sword, Tsolyani?" She flicked a contemptuous finger not at Tse'e's blade hanging from his belt but at his lower abdomen. She seemed almost happy, more amused than annoyed. "Will you bind us with bed-clothes? Gag us with napkins? These messengers bring a writ commanding our attendance at a fete of essences tonight. Their authority supersedes yours, I think."

"Tell them that you cannot come." Trinesh was adamant. "You are indisposed."

"Nonsense." She made as though to pass him by, and he seized her shoulder. A single rippling motion and she was free, off behind the two astounded functionaries. "Hands that touch me belong to dead men, *Hereksa*. Would you fight me? My sword skills are likely better than yours—or do you prefer to wake with one of these copper hairpins driven through your eye and into your brain?"

"You are still our captives, Lady. We outnumber you, and we are the better armed."

She made a face. "Your pompous little High General may not permit fighting between his guests. And the *Gaichun* would be wroth indeed."

"Wroth? Who? Why?" It was Chunatl Dikkuna, silent upon slippered feet behind her. The two messengers turned, bowed, and held out a document inscribed upon sapphire-dyed parchment. They gabbled in Tka Mihalli.

The Salarvyani fingered the plaques of his pectoral and dithered. Then he brightened. "It says here, Madam, that you, the Lady Deq Dimani, Matriarch of Vridu, are commanded to the *Gaichun*'s feast. I see no invitation for your maid, nor for this—this being here." He wrinkled his nose at Thu'n. The Salarvyani pointed with their noses.

"They are included, of course. My entourage."

"Not so. That is not the way of it."

Trinesh suspected otherwise, but the stratagem might serve. Let her go by herself. Intuitively he sensed that she would abandon Thu'n but not the Lady Jai.

For the first time the Lady Deq Dimani displayed anger. Her nostrils flared, and spots of color appeared on her cheeks. "Ask these gentlemen," she said evenly, "who is invited—and who stays."

Chunatl beamed. He knew the language; she did not. A few chirruping words, a query or two, and the *Gaichun*'s escort snatched back the document to peruse it for themselves. Chunatl twittered at them. The senior of the two men scowled and gestured to the Lady Deq Dimani.

"He says that you are named here. No others. You may depart, but the girl and the nonhuman stay."

"Only until I reach the *Gaichun* and obtain writs to summon my comrades." She gave Chunatl a furious look. "And, Salarvyani, I can match whatever these Tsolyani carrion have offered you. More. If you fear that the High General will be displeased—that I plot with the *Gaichun* against him and this rogue, Captain Harchar—disabuse him. I care nothing for your plots and politics."

Trinesh opened his mouth to ask her who the boy in the *Gaichun*'s palace was. He thought better of it. Chunatl Dikkuna was already wavering; sweat trickled from under his turban-like headdress to stain his scarlet collar. More discussion, and he might surrender. The Lady Deq Dimani could be very forceful.

"Agreed." Trinesh made a show of reluctance. "But she goes alone."

The Lady Deq Dimani said something guttural in Yan

Koryani, and Jai Chasa Vedlan retreated into their sleeping chamber. Could she lock herself in? Trinesh had noted no bar or chain upon his own door. He nodded to Mejjai, who went to stand guard. Arjasu and Dineva advanced upon Thu'n, but the *Nininyal* only raised his furry paws in exasperation and marched back into his room. The next move belonged to the Yan Koryani woman.

She gave them all a cold stare. "Two *Kiren*, Tsolyani. Then my companions join me." She departed, the *Gaichun*'s bewildered emissaries trailing along behind.

"And now, *Hereksa*?" Saina asked.

A very good question indeed.

"The Yan Koryani woman is right, you know," Chunatl Dikkuna said. "The High General cannot refuse the *Gaichun*'s direct command. If she is wanted badly enough, he may breach all etiquette by ordering her and her people brought to him. After that. . . ."

"We would not see them again," Horusel finished.

Trinesh fumbled with the buckles of the unfamiliar armor Lord Tekkuren had given him. "We must have her. That is firm." He held out a hand, palm up, to silence any debate. "The High General and the *Gaichun* want her because of their feud and their fear that she may have something to do with the pirates' invasion. We Tsolyani need her for different reasons. She may be able to work us harm here if she is free and in league with some Yan Koryani mission. Moreover, she might wheedle the *Gaichun* into letting her reach the tubeway car; she then returns to Fortress Ninu'ur—or to Yan Kor—to lead her legions against ours. If that happens, we fail as soldiers: we are shamed and ignoble. If we bring her back, we are heroes, and the Petal Throne rewards us."

"Little likelihood of her getting home from here!" Horusel snorted. "Let all three Yan Koryani hide under the *Gaichun*'s kilt. When this Captain Harchar comes, we'll persuade him to aid us. They're as much danger to him as to us. If he has the wits of a *Shqa*-beetle, he'll help."

"How do you know?" Chekkuru cried. "The man may be a tyrant whose followers will slaughter all parties indiscriminately. Or he may already be in the pay of the Baron Ald. Or she may so gull him with her pretty face that he chooses her over us!"

"Or she may be able to do something with the boy—and this 'Aluja'—to defeat the pirate!" Saina added.

"Any one of those Skeins bodes ill for us," Trinesh said. "I say we act now, on the side of this Lord Tekkuren Chaishyani, who has at least befriended us. We are soldiers; Captain Harchar, whoever he is, will recognize that and desire our assistance in this assassins' paradise. Let us aid him in advance: seize the Yan Koryani so that the *Gaichun* cannot employ them against him!"

Chunatl Dikkuna clutched at his shaven pate. "I cannot allow any action unless the High General commands."

"The Yan Koryani are our prisoners—rebels against Ganga. Tell him that."

Horusel was unconvinced. "Let them go, I say. We can't hold them against the *Gaichun*. We're outnumbered, and High General Tekkuren has neither troops nor power. Free, they can do us little injury here in Mihallu, nor is there any way for them to return to Yan Kor. We can always retake them if this Harchar proves congenial, but hanging onto them now is like grasping a fistful of fire-ants." He looked to Dineva and Chekkuru for support. "If you want the truth, our best course would be to slay the girl and the nonhuman beast and be done! Then give the so-noble Lady—and her princeling—the same treatment when next we see them!"

This was no time for a breakdown of command. Trinesh thrust out a fist and counted on his fingers. " 'Every soldier's cart has four wheels: gold, promotion, glory, and more gold.' We gain all four by taking this Yan Koryani virago back with us. If we must remain in Mihallu, then Lord Tekkuren is best suited to roll our cart for us. He wants the Yan Koryani held—not dead! Save your massacres for the battlefield!"

"The *Hereksa* is right," Saina declared. She stood up. "Why not move the girl and the *Nininyal*? Imprison them elsewhere as hostages against the Lady's return?" She whirled upon Chunatl. "Some hidden dungeon, man—in your *Ochuna*—with the High General's consent as soon as you can get it, naturally."

"I—"

"Quick." She looked to Trinesh for agreement.

Chekkuru hiVriddi stepped forward to speak. He had to be stopped. It was likely that he would side with the Lady Deq Dimani: he had already made his sympathies for his distant kinsmen on the Isle of Vridu all too plain. For Chekkuru, ties of blood and religion took precedence over national loyalty, money, glory, and probably everything else. Trinesh made a sharp gesture to cut him off. "Saina's idea is best," he said. "Well, Chunatl Dikkuna?"

The Salarvyani wavered.

"The *Gaichun*'s people will soon be at the gate," Trinesh continued. "We save the High General's guests from his enemy the *Gaichun*, a man who will swiftly either be unemployed or a rebel against Ganga. Come, priest, you must know of some hidey-hole where we can keep the girl and the *Nininyal*! It is in your master's interest!" He grinned and parroted the Salarvyani's own words. " 'Lord Tekkuren will be magnanimous. If you fail, he will be otherwise.' "

"There is a place. . . ."

"We go. Arjasu, Mejjai, get the Lady Jai. Horusel, Chosun, see to the *Nininyal*. Saina, stay close to Chunatl. Tse'e—Lord—and you, Chekkuru, come with me. Collect your gear."

Horusel and Chekkuru exchanged glances, but the others scattered to obey. Then they, too, went to retrieve their belongings. This was not the time for rebellion.

Tse'e laid a hand upon his arm. "No injury to the girl—or to Thu'n!"

"Not unless need be." He snatched up the silvered helmet Lord Tekkuren had gifted him and slashed off its long plumes.

Less ornament and it would make a serviceable battle-helm. "Both are valuable to us—and my clan-elders never taught me that it was noble to slay helpless women and scholars."

He did not mention the satisfaction it gave him to frustrate Horusel and Chekkuru hiVriddi—nor, his little inner voice pointed out, his odd reluctance to see the Lady Jai Chasa Vedlan come to harm.

"Now!" Chosun cried. Wood cracked, hinges squealed, and Trinesh heard the *Nininyal* yelp a protest. No sound came from the Lady Jai's room. Trinesh was relieved to see her presently emerge between Arjasu and Mejjai, as composed as ever. She said nothing.

"Here," Chunatl panted from the corridor. The panel leading into the *Ochuna* hung ajar, and he waved them into the darkness.

Judging from their stumbling, clattering, cursing progress, their second trip through the *Ochuna* would soon be table gossip throughout Ninue and probably the rest of Mihallu as well. There was no help for the racket.

"Two hundred and twenty-three," Chunatl counted off the green-glowing discs. "We turn here. A line of three, then twelve, then a lever." Trinesh heard the rustle of the ebon fungus, an exclamation as the beetles inhabiting it avenged the intrusion, and then a sighing noise. A whisper of a breeze brushed icy fingertips across his cheek.

"A hall, five discs, a door to the right—" Something clanked and chattered: a chain? "This chamber is not known to many. Inside, Tsolyani."

He stood aside to let them pass. Three paces, and Trinesh ran headlong into a bristly wall that crackled and scratched. The *Shon Tinur* fungus! It was less than a finger-breadth deep, and he bumped his nose upon rough stone. He gagged, backed into Saina, and spat. A thing like a hot needle jabbed his arm, doubtless one of the invisible beetles. He jerked away and struck Arjasu's crossbow. The man swore; he had carried it loaded, and the quarrel must have been jarred from its groove. Others banged into them both.

Hubbub. Then stillness.

"Chunatl? Priest?" That was Tse'e.

"I am here." The reply came, muffled and indistinct, from behind them.

"Where in Lord Vimuhla's incandescent Paradise—?"

"Outside. You are within. The door is locked." Metal clanged again.

"Traitor!" Chekkuru hiVriddi screeched. "Perverted slave of the hairy-bellied whore-goddess of Salarvya! Heretic! Is this how you repay our aid? Our affection?" Trinesh heard Dineva attempting to quiet him.

Someone kicked and thumped the door; it sounded distressingly solid.

"Forgive me," Chunatl pleaded. "You are all safe here, Tsolyani and Yan Koryani alike. I told you that I must consult the High General—he must say what to do. Your discomfiture will not last long. As soon as the danger is past, the Yan Koryani woman returned, and the *Gaichun's* agents frustrated, you will be released—taken to some better refuge, given freedom, kindnesses, and dignities once again." They heard his ragged wheezing. "Be patient, Tsolyani, and think not too harshly of me. What I do is for the best."

"Ohe, for you, of course!" Dineva spat.

He made no reply. The pit-pat of his slippers echoed away down the corridor.

"A light." Trinesh fumed. "Dineva?" She always had flint and tinder in her belt-pouch.

A spark flared, and flame sprang up.

Tse'e's shadow blocked off the flickering glow. "Here: a strip from the scroll I had brought to study."

Their prison measured about five paces square. One of the side walls contained a second door, smaller than that by which they had entered. Chosun pushed at this, and it opened to reveal a cubicle no more than two paces wide and perhaps three long. The walls and floor sparkled, shimmered, and surged with a myriad tiny movements. The big man let out a bleat and backed away. The motion subsided as water drains down into sand, and they looked only at *Shon Tinur* fungus.

"Beetles!" Saina shuddered. "The place is alive with beetles!"

The faint breeze blew from within the second cell, where a jagged hole in the far wall led off into blackness. Mejjai stooped to see, then exclaimed, "Hoi, *Hereksa*! Bones. Someone tried to escape—" He called for the light, knelt, and jumped up again swearing in the rustic accents of western Tsolyanu. "Beettles! Kneel down, and they're over your boots and into your legs like needles!" He cursed again; then: "Poor wretch. Got a stone out of the wall. Crawled through. Beetles ate him."

So much for the fate of the unknown prisoner.

"Back out," Trinesh ordered. "Here, by me. Scrape the fungus off this wall, off the floor around us. Use your swords—armor—anything hard. Don't put your hands in the stuff!"

At last they stood in a cleared space by the outer door, out of breath but only slightly bitten. Trinesh put the Lady Jai, Tse'e, and Thu'n into the midst of the party; their footgear was of little use against the insects.

They waited.

The light went out, but Trinesh ordered the rest of the scroll saved for later. Rustlings filled the darkness. Someone squeaked and batted furiously at an unseen tormentor. Trinesh set Chosun, Arjasu, and Horusel to digging and hacking at the door. They reported slow progress.

They waited again. Occasionally they stamped their feet, and the clicking, buzzing noises subsided. When they stood still the insects swarmed back to the attack.

Sitting or lying down was impossible. The best course was a close huddle, with those on the perimeter tramping and kicking just often enough to discourage the little monsters. This could not last; fatigue, thirst, and plain, unadorned fear would eventually take their toll.

Chunatl Dikkuna had much to answer for, whatever his motives.

More waiting, immeasurable as the wind, cold as the abysses of the Flame Lord's deepest hells. Phantoms and colors appeared before Trinesh' eyes against the sable backdrop; when he blinked they became coruscations of fire, dancing ghosts, all of the terrors of a child haunted by the dark. He tried to think of Tumissa's warm sunlight, the faces of his clan-sisters, home. . . .

He was startled out of his reverie. Something touched his shoulder, crept across the plates of the High General's fancy dress-cuirass, and fumbled at his cheek. He reached up instinctively and caught a hand; the fingers were slender and soft: a woman's. Dineva? Saina? No, their hands were callused. Whether by accident or design, it must be the Lady Jai. Was it too much to hope that she desired this contact?

The door-chain rattled, and the hand was snatched away.

Light poured in upon them.

It was not Chunatl Dikkuna. Torchlight made a cascade of gold of the swinging chain trappings of the masked interpreter Trinesh had seen in the *Gaichun*'s audience hall. Behind the curve of his beast-mask they glimpsed the barbuta-helmets and inlaid armor of the Governor's household guard.

"Ohe." The translator tilted his head back to see. "Point your crank-sticks somewhere else!" The man spoke like a slave, a southerner, probably from the stews of Jakalla. "Crank-stick" was Tsolyani army slang for any crossbow, whether cocked with a lever, a stirrup, or a winch.

Arjasu sidled over to one wall, Mejjai to the other. They needed no orders.

The Lady Deq Dimani had won, then. Trinesh' heart sank. She had persuaded the *Gaichun* to send a real escort this time, and they were likely her prisoners. Horusel made as though to seize Thu'n but found Tse'e in his path. The Lady Jai stood next to Trinesh, an easy hostage. No need to threaten harm to her—yet.

"Here, now, friends!" the interpreter said in his deep, rough voice. " 'Hasty spoils the spell,' as the magickers say. No swords. No crossbows. No stick-me-quick daggers!" Brawny arms emerged through the curtain of delicate chains hanging from the collar around his neck. His hands were open, the fingers stubby and knobbed. There were old, white scars upon his wrists: the man had indeed been a felon or a slave.

"Better," he said. "Here you see Okkuru the translator, servant and personal buggerer to the dung-plastered *Gaichun* of Mihallu. A commoner once but now as mighty as a king in this outhouse of a country!"

Trinesh said, "I am Trinesh hiKetkolel, *Hereksa* of the Legion of the Storm of Fire. My clan is Red Mountain."

"Fine folk. Near the top of the middle and just below the lowest of the top." The assessment was exactly correct, but the man's genial tone was subtly insulting. In Tsolyanu one did not speak ill of another's clan, not unless one was prepared to fight a duel or pay *Shamtla*-compensation.

"Get on with your task," Trinesh growled stiffly. "Do we fight these pretty little soldiers you bring? Let us be at it!"

"Fight?" Okkuru jingled his chain harness. The gems of his dragon-mask twinkled scarlet and amber. "If you like. But first talk to my most noble, impotent, worm-prick master here." He sniggered. "I call the dungball every obscenity I can imagine and tell him they're Engsvanyali honorifics. At this moment he's cowering behind me around the corner, dribbling brown into his shoes and scared out of his perverted wits. Speak sweetly to him, and mayhap there'll be no call for blades and bolts."

"Let him come forth. We offer no harm."

Arjasu and Mejjai lowered their weapons, and the others

stood back. Trinesh noted that Saina had taken a stance just behind the Lady Jai; Horusel and Dineva guarded Thu'n. He had no idea how valuable the pair would be as hostages if their captors had *not* been sent by the Lady Deq Dimani. They might be no more than feeble white counters upon the *Den-den* board. Yet any play was worth a try.

The translator shuffled aside with an elaborate genuflection, and they gazed upon Prince Tenggutla Dayyar.

"Greet him with all honor," Trinesh muttered. "I think we are about to meet a new player." He bowed and then, as an afterthought, gave the youth a military salute. That ought to please him!

The Prince squinted at them, rubbed his hooked beak with a long fingernail, and lisped something in singing Tka Mihalli. The blue labret between his lower lip and his chin probably interfered with his speech. Such uncomfortable jewelry had not been the fashion for thousands of years.

"His mother was a raddled whore, his father a Salarvyani catamite who cuckolded the *Gaichun* while he was busy with little boys," the translator proclaimed in richly ceremonial tones. "He says welcome."

"What does he want?" It was cold, and his insect bites stung. Trinesh would suffer no more formalities—and this Okkuru's jibes at the expense of his betters were growing irksome. At home such a cheeky slave would have been marched off to the market to be sold as field labor by now! He sensed that Chekkuru and probably Tse'e felt the same.

"La, he'll get to it. It takes this get of a mold-slime's mother a full four *Kiren* to perfume his pretty curls each morning."

The Prince spoke, and Okkuru said, "He wants an agreement with you."

"Us? What can we do for him?"

"Why, get your honorable selves out of his country. He has enough troubles as it is: kill off his father, his mother, and his aunt; maneuver the High General into open treason;

and fiddle the priesthoods until they end either as his puppets or slaughtered. He wants no interference from Ganga, or from the Yan Yoryani boy, who's become a sort of pet in the *Gaichun's* household, or from the Yan Koryani princess—''

''Or from Captain Harchar, I presume,'' Tse'e said.

''None likely from that quarter,'' Okkuru chortled. ''The last we heard from Arbala, the brave pirates had hopped back aboard their boat and left.''

''What?'' Chekkuru cried. Everyone echoed him, even Mejjai.

''Oh, ai. The noble Prince here had his agents tell the ruffian just how far it was to Ninue. All the dangers along the way. The mighty armies that would squash his hundred sailor lads as you'd crush a nest of *Shqa*-beetles. The poisons, the plots, the wicked folk of Mihallu—in league, naturally, with the ancient Mihalli, the nonhuman monsters who dwelt here before the Priestkings came. Ohe, the great Captain Harchar took a day or two to loot Arbala—stinking, hairy hole—and then fled with his little twig quivering betwixt his legs. Likely he's off plundering easier ports by now.''

''So the great invasion is over. Does the *Gaichun* know?''

''Not likely. The Prince pays the messengers better than his dear father ever did.''

Trinesh hissed between his teeth. ''And we are inconveniently in the Prince's way. Why not kill us where we stand?''

''Now, now, Lord.'' Okkuru strove to sound reassuring. ''He wants you gone without a fuss. The Prince thinks you're from Ganga, and he would have no trouble with the Priestkings—no legions pouring up out of the tubeway car to haul him off to explain why their emissaries vanished.''

''So. What must we do?''

''Get the Yan Koryani princess, the boy, and the one other person, a wizard named Aluja who's the boy's teacher, and leave. The lad claims this Aluja can help the *Gaichun* defeat every foe from here to the Plains of Glass. This doesn't sit well with Prince Tenggutla. You get rid of the lot, and you walk free."

"Back to the tubeway car in the Many-Chambered Sanctuary?"

"Ai, and his piss-dripping highness will help you there as well." He turned and warbled in Tka Mihalli. The Prince blinked and gave them a dazzling smile—literally. He even had little diamonds set into his front teeth.

"I told him you were willing and ready to go, now that the new *Gaichun* doesn't plan to take up his post. The governorship isn't supposed to be hereditary, but here it's been so for centuries. If the old turd dies. . . ."

"To the point," Tse'e demanded. "What aid can he give us with the tubeway car?"

"Well, now." The translator jangled his chain-harness and beckoned to one of the guardsmen, who advanced to lay a stack of thin metal discs, like breast-pendants about a palm's breadth in diameter, into his hand. Okkuru held one up so that they could see the whorls and squarish letters incised upon it. "The Prince says every car has a little slot under the front housing—the box with the ten knobs on it. Slip one of these into the hole, and the car goes to the ten places on the disc. Change it, and you're off to ten new destinations."

Tse'e asked wonderingly, "But the symbols—no one can read the languages of the ages before the Time of Darkness . . . ?"

"True. But these folk took this set off a dead wizard they trapped somehow. By trial and error the magicker had found where every little mark took him, and he scratched the modern names on the discs in Classical Tsolyani. He must have come here that long ago—"

"A fortune!" Thu'n marveled. "The temples would pay—"

"Shut up," Trinesh snapped. "Look you, Okkuru or whatever your name is, why do this for us? What's the Prince's price—and yours?"

The helmeted head bobbed from side to side. "I told you

what this twig-sucking degenerate wants—that and mayhap a
little extra *Dmi*-sugar in his mother's milk. As for me, I want
to go with you. I've had it in Ninue. Being a noble lord in
Mihallu is lovely for them as like total boredom, but I'm still
young, and with the fortune I've amassed here I can live out
my days back home in Tsolyanu.''

"An escaped slave!" Chekkuru made a sharp downward
gesture. "The impaling stake!"

"Oh? Mayhap in Fasiltum, mayhap even in Jakalla. But
who knows me in Tumissa? Mrelu? Thraya? I've a yen to see
the Empire again, and money makes folk blind, even to
these.'' He displayed the pale cicatrices upon his wrists.
"More than one slave has bought his freedom. Like they say,
'Money sings, and the bureaucrats dance.' ''

Tse'e glanced over at Trinesh. "Some of the hunted can
indeed be forgotten," the old man murmured. "Others cannot.''

The Tsolyani exchanged jubilant glances. Trinesh said,
"Tell the Prince that we agree. We'll do what he asks.''

"Hold." Horusel glowered. "With a little help we can
take the Lady Deq Dimani and the boy. But this wizard—
Aluja—?"

"Your kind friend, Prince Tenggutla here, also offers you
an 'Eye' to replace the one the little Salarvyani and his
dirty-arsed High General stole from you when they confiscated the things you had in the tubeway car—and your personal property."

Trinesh snatched at his belt-pouch. His money and toilet
articles were there, but the "Eye" was missing! The slavegirl
they had sent him had done more than just sleep on the black
couch!

"Never mind, soldier. This one's probably better: guaran-
teed against wizards, magicians, and catamites!''

"Oh? What does it do?"

The blind eyes of the dragon-mask glittered. "He says he's
not sure. Nobody's used it for a century or two. But it's

supposed to 'repeal the powers'—that's what the record in the *Gaichun's* trophy room said.''

Trinesh reached for the ''Eye''; Horusel for the discs. Okkuru whipped them both back out of reach. ''Ai, lords, there's still the sweetening.''

''And what may that be?'' Saina raised her sword again.

Trinesh had a premonition that he knew what the Prince would ask.

''The girl. The furry little sewer-worm wants the girl. That one there, beside your captain.''

Trinesh had been right. He cried, ''Never!'' at the same time that Horusel grunted, ''Take her and welcome!''

The two men glared at one another.

''The Lady Jai is a prisoner of war—'' Trinesh began, but Horusel interrupted with an angry sweep of his sword.

''We've had enough, *Hereksa!*'' the older man rasped. ''All I'm taking anyhow! You can dandle some other doxy when we get back to the Legion. This Prince what's-his-name wants her, he gets her! Fair trade for the discs, the 'Eye'-thing, the Lady, the boy, the *Nininyal*, and the wizard! Home and reward, you said? Well, so it shall be!''

''I say no,'' Trinesh rapped.

''Don't bother, *Hereksa*,'' the Lady Jai said softly. ''What he—or you, or anyone—does to my body makes no difference. He can do as he likes for an hour or two. Just so I can return to my Lady Deq Dimani. . . .''

''No—''

''Yes!'' Horusel said. Dineva and Chekkuru echoed agreement.

Even Saina lowered her weapon. ''If she doesn't mind, then—''

''No hour, alas,'' the burly translator said slowly. ''He wants her for permanent. To stay with his other womenfolk.''

''Now that I forbid!'' Trinesh cried in fury. ''She—''

The Lady Jai addressed Okkuru directly. ''And what if I make no resistance but give him no joy? Among his other eccentricities, does this Prince take pleasure in coupling with a limp sack of *Dna*-flour?''

Okkuru tilted his mask back to reveal a coarse, flattened nose and tiny, shrewd eyes. ''Why—? If you don't do as he wants, he'll strip you bare naked and stuff you into that little cell there. After you've danced for the beetles for a time, you'll sing, whistle, or play music to whatever tune he calls! Don't be a fool, girl! I know this sweaty little monster! Take my advice: he'll only pester you for a little while. Then he'll forget and look for some new toy. Life in the *Gaichun*'s palace may be dull, but it's not too bad.''

''She goes with us.'' Trinesh had endured all he could. He looked to the others for support. Tse'e, Thu'n, and Saina were clearly with him. Arjasu watched with the cool gaze of the professional soldier who cares neither one way nor the other. Mejjai said nothing.

Chosun rubbed his paunch and shuffled his feet. ''Uh—*Hereksa*, best let the girl weave her own Skein, eh? She'll have to make do. We can't keep her against all of those soldiers out there.'' The big man refused to meet his eyes.

The Lady Jai came to stand before Trinesh. ''I will stay with this Prince, Tsolyani. Do not fear. I may yet be able to persuade him to let me leave with you and my Lady.'' Her eyes glinted flame in the ruddy torchlight.

Trinesh did not want to think of the limp, damp hands of the creature in the doorway caressing her smooth limbs, her breasts . . . His little inner voice would have spoken, but it was drowned out by the pounding of his heart. He swung around, sword raised.

—And discovered something hard and sharp against his throat. Dineva's dagger scraped against the collar-flange of his breastplate. She could use the knife, he knew. But would she?

''We want to go home, too,'' she pleaded in his ear. ''The girl's not worth the death of any of us. And she's willing to stay. Don't turn this into a mutiny, *Hereksa*. Please!''

"Kill him! Kill him!" Chekkuru squalled. "He offends the Lord of Flame—refuses sacrifices—disdains the gods—makes sport of their servants—!"

Chosun swept an arm around in a broad arc, and the priest's voice shut off as though chopped with an axe. "I'll not see him slain! Take him alive, get him out of this wench's power, get us home—but no harm to the *Hereksa*! He's never been unfair to us."

Trinesh slid his fingers up along his breastplate, found Dineva's thin, sinewy hand, and gently pushed it and the knife away. "This lies between Horusel and myself," he said. "He is the one who leads this dance."

He planted his feet and began to circle. "Translator, tell your people to make room. Chosun, Saina, see that we are not disturbed by the priest or anyone else. Come, Horusel, you know the penalty—and the shame—for mutiny." The words of the dueling masters in the Red Mountain clanhouse came back to him, and he added formally, " 'Let our swords be our advocates, the Lord of Flame our judge!' "

Confidence buoyed him up; Horusel was a veteran, the survivor of more barracksroom fights than anyone could remember, yet he was no duelist. If Trinesh could stay beyond his reach and use Tse'e's slender steel blade as his teachers had instructed him, he ought to win.

They exchanged tentative parries. Prince Tenggutla Dayyar scuttled out of the way, eyes ashine and lips drawn back. Blood sports must be rare in Mihallu, Trinesh thought fleetingly. Another blow, a downward parry. Their hilts clattered and locked together. The older man flung out his left arm, a dagger glittering in his fist. Trinesh knocked it aside, shoved, leaped back, then in again. His blade clacked and skipped across Horusel's breastplate to tear a lappet off the man's right shoulder-pauldron. It did no real damage. He blocked a following swing and jumped away once more. He realized that he was holding his breath against all of his preceptors' sternest warnings. He let it out in a warcry, thrust left, dodged a riposte, and slashed low and right. Horusel's embroidered Engsvanyali kilt began to change from white to red along his left thigh. Was this to be so easy, then?

The *Tirrikamu* was no fool; he knew both his weaknesses and his strengths. As they turned, he reached out, cuffed Saina with his clenched dagger-hand, and sent her sprawling over onto Trinesh. Without pausing he leaped in after her. In this kind of brawl he would be the victor.

Trinesh wasted a long moment shouldering the woman aside; no time to see to her now. He stumbled backward, out through the door. To grapple with Horusel was almost certainly to die.

Something sharp pricked Trinesh in the right arm, just above the elbow where his mail sleeve left off and the vambrace began. Amazed, he spared a glance to his flank.

Prince Tenggutla Dayyar crouched there just outside the door, eyes bright with gleeful malice. He clutched a tiny needle of a dagger in his beringed fingers.

He would have cut the man down, but Horusel swarmed over him, and for the next few heartbeats they wrestled this way and that amidst a maelstrom of squealing blue and white guardsmen. Trinesh thought he saw Saina leap through the door and into the fray, then Chosun after her.

Horusel's dagger clattered against Trinesh's cuirass. Something was wrong with his sword-arm. He struggled to bring the blade around and set it against the straining sinews of the *Tirrikamu*'s neck, but his muscles refused to obey. The stench of sweat filled his nostrils, and he was surprised to find that he was dizzy. Had he lost so much blood, then? He did not think so—he did not even remember being wounded! He got his left hand free and clawed at Horusel's staring eyes, an ignoble trick, but then how much more ignoble would it be to die?

He felt as though he were as far away as the moons. Kashi, Lord Vimuhla's red moon of fire and blood, loomed above him, and he scrabbled to catch it. Gayel, the green moon,

must not have risen yet. Kashi bellowed and retreated back
out into space. Farther, farther, beyond the sun, beyond the
four planets, beyond the luminous spheres wherein dwelt the
omnipotent gods. . . .

Farther.

Trinesh winged away into a black and trackless sky.

He was disappointed; this was not the sort of afterlife the
priests had promised after all.

16

The footsteps grew louder, racketing away into the shadows like the tympani of an advancing army. Aluja had no choice: the metal walls kept him from taking any other shape; he must meet his visitors as himself.

He had no idea how long it had been. After Ridek left, he had husbanded his strength, performed mind-exercises to keep from thinking about food and drink, and cursed himself for all kinds of a fool.

The Baron would be angry indeed, and now Ridek would not be the only one to be punished. Concealed somewhere within the most secret recesses of the fortress of Ke'er were kept the *Gayu*, the matrix patterns that held Aluja and others of his species in bondage to the master of Yan Kor. Created for the Baron by Lord Fu Shi'i, those delicate linkages resembled flower-shaped grids of interlocking golden filaments—on this Plane, at least. A *Gayu* could be broken, which caused its subject's death on several Planes if not on all. Worse, it could be distorted, and that inflicted agonies that no dweller upon just one Plane could ever imagine or endure.

The Baron might not do that to a loyal servitor, but Lord Fu Shi'i would have no qualms about it.

Lamps and torches, unnecessary in the soft, unchanging light of the sorcerous globes illumining his prison, came nearer. They stopped, bobbing and swaying, before the adjoining cell, that in which the dead Shunned One lay.

"Hold!" That was Ridek's voice! "Wait here. The mage Aluja will wish to prepare himself to greet you." That was clever! The Mihalli repressed a surge of pride, almost as though the boy were his own offspring.

A woman said something in a foreign tongue, arising-falling language full of vowels. It sounded like Saa Allaqiyani.

Ridek's black poll appeared around the corner of the cell. He grinned when Aluja glided over to meet him. Then he stooped and concentrated upon a massive silvery key. The door opened.

"All hail, Aluja!" the boy cried. He flung both arms up so that his long mantle swirled out like the wings of a *Hu*-bat. Aluja saw what he was about at once. Cleverer still!

The cloak hid the Mihalli as he emerged from the cell. By the time it had settled down over its wearer's shoulders again, those in the dimly lit corridor behind the boy saw only a gentle, elderly, human scholar dressed in a tattered brown robe, a sage with a beard as long as his forearm and feeble, pale-veined hands. Surreptitiously Aluja adjusted the semblance to include a bulging forehead and bushy eyebrows; his red-glowing eyes were the one feature that no Mihalli shapeshifter could change, and these folk might have heard the legends.

"Oh, master Ridek," he whined.

"The Governor of this land graciously permits me to free you." Ridek motioned him to maintain the disguise.

"I give thanks, Lord, both to him and to you."

Was he overdoing this display of senile gratitude? He

squinted over the lad's shoulder and saw two women in the passage beyond. Farther back a squad of blue-and-white-liveried soldiers waited nervously with a middle-aged man wrapped entirely in what resembled bandages of coarse ebon cloth. One of the women wore a puffed, flounced, gray skirt, an overblouse of smoke-hued gauze, and a bird's-head mask of ashen feathers. The other was not masked, and her garb consisted of an overtunic of green with a sash of orange-red fastened diagonally across her breasts with jeweled brooches. Beneath these upper garments he caught the gleam of chaised and engraved dress-armor. Aluja had seen enough of the Planes of Time to recognize Engsvanyali garb. If this were ancient Engsvan hla Ganga, then his interplanar senses must have been asleep when he chose this particular Nexus Point!

There was something familiar about the second human female. His eyes snapped back to her face, and he almost shouted for joy.

The woman in green was the Lady Deq Dimani.

He essayed a dotard's stagger—and found that it was not much of a pretense after all. Hunger, thirst, and the discomfort of sleeping on the bare metal floor had taken their toll.

"Most noble sage." The Lady Deq Dimani came up to join them. Ridek must have warned her in advance. She gestured, and one of the soldiers edged forward with an ewer of water and a platter of food. Aluja ate without even noticing what it was.

"Oh, Aluja!" Ridek clutched his hand. He knew enough not to show surprise at the feel of aged, papery, human skin instead of the Mihalli's own smoothly textured hide. "You are safe? I could not come before—"

"No matter now. Where are we?"

"Mihallu—a place where they think the Engsvanyali still live. The ruler here calls himself the *Gaichun*—that means 'governor.' He says that he serves the Empire of Ganga. Nobody dares tell these folk that the Priestkings have been dead for centuries! It's like living in the past!"

The story poured out in a rush, but Aluja cut him off. Well he ought to know of this strange relic of a land! Mihallu had been the home of his people before the Priestkings' legions brought slaughter and devastation along with the glories of human civilization. This was not a good place for one of Aluja's race.

He bent close to Ridek. "Do you still have your staff?"

The boy smiled. "He holds it." He jerked a thumb toward one of the waiting guardsmen. There were advantages to being a prince upon the white *Klai Ga*!

"And the 'Eye'?"

"Here. In my belt-pouch. Do you want it back?"

"Not now. Keep it. My own powers are greater." He raised his head. "Come, both of you stand close to me. Now that I am out of that metal dungeon, it is only a matter of a moment until I can create a Nexus Point. Then we are gone—home to Yan Kor."

The Lady Deq Dimani shook her head. "The scholar Thu'n—you remember him, Aluja?—and the Lady Jai Chasa Vedlan are still captives of the Tsolyani who brought us here. I do not leave without them."

"I shall return alone later."

"No. Take Ridek and go. Come back for me."

"That I cannot. I was commanded to find you."

"And so you have. I am in no danger—now—and I will not abandon my comrades. I brook no argument!" She nodded toward the other woman, who still stood farther back with the black-clad man and the soldiers. "This lady, Dayetha Fashkolun, is the *Gaichun*'s best translator of Yan Korayni. She is charged with our safety. She says that Thu'n and the Lady Jai cannot be far away."

Hearing her name, the woman in gray bowed. She had a pallid, pasty complexion: probably a native of one of the towns on the western shore of Lake Parunal. Her ancient, aristocratic Engsvanyali name did not match her features at all.

Aluja considered. "Well, quickly then. Where are your companions?"

The Lady Deq Dimani lifted her chin toward the man in black. "He is Shakkan, the seniormost of the *Gaichun*'s agents in the spy-labyrinth they call the *Ochuna*. His people reported two incursions there a *Kiren* or so ago: one from the High General's Palace of Ever-Glorious War, and the other from this direction—the *Gaichun*'s stronghold. He says that the first is the Tsolyani party: either they seek me or else they try to conceal Thu'n and the Lady Jai. The second group is led by Prince Tenggutla Dayyar, the *Gaichun*'s son. What he does in the *Ochuna* at this hour is unknown."

The woman in gray said, "Shakkan humbly adds that the two parties met in an abandoned section of the *Ochuna*. Some now come this way, while others have gone elsewhere. As yet he knows not whither."

"Tell him to take us to the girl—the young, pretty one—not the soldier women. Say also that we would remain unseen."

The *Gaichun*'s agent set a fast pace. They descended the staircase Ridek had almost entered before, then passed through more corridors, passages up, others down, rooms and halls and winding tunnels, until at last they reached the level of the black fungus. Aluja felt a pang of something close to sorrow; his ancestors had grown this curious parasite as decoration for the walls of their homes. It had never been intended to serve as a cloak for secrecy and treachery!

Shakkan came to a halt and spoke. The interpreter said, "No lights. They are forbidden in the *Ochuna*."

"Tell him that the rules are changed," the Lady Deq Dimani replied sweetly. "We proceed." The man adopted a hurt expression, but he obeyed.

They halted, Shakkan nearly invisible in front of them, black upon black, then the two women, Aluja, and Ridek. Their six-man escort brought up the rear. The spy whispered something in Tka Mihalli.

The translator woman said, "He urges you to let the guards

go first; he perceives strangers ahead, and we cannot allow you to come to harm.''

The precaution was too late; their lights had been seen. A voice from the darkness called in Tsolyani, "Who is there?''

Aluja pushed Ridek behind him and raised his blue globe, the "Ball of Immediate Eventuation.'' The soldiers took up positions for a cautious advance, and for a heartbeat there was confusion as they rearranged themselves. The Lady Deq Dimani remained in front, ignoring the translator woman's pleas to let the escort go ahead of her.

"Tse'e?'' she shouted back. "Prince Nalukkan? Or 'sand-worm,' or however you name yourself! We are many. Come out and surrender, all of you!''

Ten paces ahead of them the old man appeared as if by sorcery from some near-invisible side-passage in the left-hand wall. He had retrieved his steel sword from Trinesh, and it gleamed like a crescent of yellow flame in the reflection of their lamps.

"Where are the others?'' the Lady Deq Dimani demanded.

He made a negative gesture and halted, facing them.

"Are you so heroic then, old sand-worm? Have you crawled out to die, to give your blood in exchange for that of the Vriddi of Fasiltum?'' She hefted her own weapon. "Let me oblige you.''

"I tire of running,'' Tse'e replied. He spread his feet apart in a dueling stance that was as rusty as his sword. "The *Hereksa* could not bring himself to kill you. I can. You endanger us all with your *Gaichun* and your plotting.''

She gave an unladylike snort. "How little you know!''

Aluja moved up behind the two women and Shakkan, Ridek close beside him. "Let me!'' the Mihalli hissed to the Lady Deq Dimani. "No need for you to risk your life!''

Ridek understood less than one word in ten of the others' rapid Tsolyani. He scrabbled for Aluja's "Eye'' within the fine leather pouch the *Gaichun's* tailors had given him. If his friends needed help, he would give it! The device felt slippery and damp as he fumbled it out, the dark red iris between two fingers and his thumb over the raised stud on its back. The slickness was probably the sweat of his own battle-fear. Why had the Ancients made their weapons so small and so awkward? He grasped it tighter, concentrated, and pointed it.

The *Ochuna* exploded into garish, scarlet dazzle.

"What have you done?" Aluja yelled. The Lady Deq Dimani screamed something too, and their escort echoed her with a shrill cacophony of shouts and questions in Tka Mihalli. Ridek heard footsteps blundering off into the tunnel behind him.

He stumbled against the wall, then yelped when something tiny and sharp, like a red-hot needle, stabbed his shoulder. When he could see again, he found Aluja crouching before him, his wide-dilated pupils as red as the blaze from the "Eye." The translator lay sprawled upon the black-carpeted floor, her bird-mask askew to reveal a tangle of gray-white locks beneath. The Lady Deq Dimani had thrown herself against the opposite wall; she nursed a darkening, bloody abrasion upon her temple. Only two of their guardsmen remained, both on their knees behind Ridek. Two more were visible farther down the passageway, but of the other pair there was no sign. Torches and lamps guttered on the floor all the way back to the last turning.

Aluja clutched his blue orb and peered at the elderly Tsolyani swordsman. The man had not moved. He still stood in combat stance: feet apart, blade up, and one bony hand held back for balance.

The Lady Deq Dimani rubbed at her bruise, decided that it was minor, and lifted her sword once more. "Well, sandworm?" she challenged.

Aluja crept forward to touch the man's blade.

It did not waver: it was as solid as though carved of stone.

"The boy—the 'Eye'—caught him full," the Mihalli said.

"Is he dead?" Ridek asked shakily.

"No. It is as I told you. He lives, but he is out of phase

with this Plane. You have only to click the 'Eye' at him a second time to free him from its hold."

"There is an 'Excellent Ruby Eye' in the treasury on my island of Vridu," the Lady Deq Dimani said. "Yet I have never seen it used." She felt of one fold of the old man's desert-cloak, then jerked her hand away in astonishment. "It is hard—frozen—but not cold!"

"Ai, none can touch him. No one can harm him, take away his belongings, or affect him in any way. Unless he is freed, he remains thus until the gods bring this cycle of time around again to start the world anew."

She did not understand. "Good! He is welcome to stand paralyzed thus—and may he suffer during each long moment of eternity! His slaughter of the Vriddi is well avenged." She looked into the stony, unblinking eyes. "Pain, old sand-worm, pain! That is my wish for your future!"

Aluja did not disillusion her. The Tsolyani would know nothing, feel nothing: perhaps a blink of bloody light, then, should some adventurer free him later on, life again without gap or discontinuity. The Mihalli had no reason to hate this man; let her think that her revenge was truly complete.

"My Lady." Dayetha Fashkolun pointed. "May we aid Shakkan?"

Ridek saw the spy for the first time, still black on black, but pressed against the wall of the *Ochuna*, open-mouthed and frozen, like some spidery insect preserved under glass.

The "Eye" had caught him, too!

Aluja held out his hand, and for the first time Ridek realized that he no longer held the "Eye." It had slipped from his grasp when he fired. The Mihalli himself discovered it, innocent as a stream-pebble, in a clump of sable-furred *Shon Tinur* on the floor. He clicked the stud, and Shakkan slipped down to lie wheezing and trembling upon the black carpet.

It took time to calm the *Gaichun's* terrified agent, to reassure the remaining soldiers, and to gather up their torches and lamps. No one looked directly at Tse'e, though the guardsmen cast sidelong glances and made furtive religious gestures as they passed his statue-still form. Ridek had to admit that the Governor's men were braver than he had credited: it was no shame to be frightened by all of this magic, these foreigners, and the strange wizard they had rescued from the metal dungeon. He whispered to Aluja, and the Mihalli quietly repaired his disguise: the planes of his face had begun to shift to an elongated snout. That would be all these poor troopers needed to send them screeching away in panic!

"My Lady," the translator suggested, "let us remain here while Shakkan seeks the rest of the old one's party—and perhaps gains news of Prince Tenggutla Dayyar's people as well. There are others of our agents in the *Ochuna*, and he can accomplish this alone quicker than we."

"As long as my comrades are found."

Shakkan prowled away. In less than a *Kiren* he was back with another behind him: Thu'n.

"My Lady! Oh, my Lady!" The little *Nininyal* scrambled past the black-swathed agent to fall upon the Lady Deq Dimani with squeals of joy. He looked behind her. "Who? Is it the boy?—Ai, it is Ridek, the son of the Baron Ald!" He stopped in dismay. "Alas! We shall all be impaled for this!" Ridek was suddenly reminded of his brother, Sihan.

"Calm yourself," the Lady Deq Dimani ordered. "Tell us where the others are—particularly the Lady Jai!"

Thu'n blinked beady black eyes at Aluja. "Ohe! A Mihalli! Is this the Aluja the Tsolyani mentioned?"

The creature could see through his disguise! Aluja's people had long suspected that a few members of certain other nonhuman species could do this, but there had been no proof until now. This was important, but it must be left for later.

The Lady Deq Dimani held Thu'n at arm's length and almost shook him. "Where are the others?"

The *Nininyal* clacked his beak, wriggled, gesticulated, and gibbered with what sounded like two tongues at once, thereby losing much of his narration in the telling. There had been a Prince, a fight, golden plates, and much running. The Tsolyani officer was unconscious—already dead?—and had been left somewhere to die. One of the soldier women remained with him. The others hoped to leave Mihallu with his, Thu'n's, assistance, but how this was to be managed was unclear. Later the *Nininyal* had gone with Tse'e while the soldiers went another way. None of this was overly intelligible.

The Lady Deq Dimani ended by seizing both of the *Nininyal*'s paws. "Where," she shouted into his big, furry ear, "is the Lady Jai?"

"Why . . . ?" Thu'n collected himself. "Why, she is upstairs—the Prince, the *Gaichun*'s son, the bejeweled one, took her to mate."

"To mate? As a concubine? A slave? —Or to rape?"

"Fa!" Thu'n squawked. "How should I know what you humans feel about such things? Too many silly distinctions! Rape—copulation—pleasure—fornication—sex—obscenity— you have more words for this one simple act than you have hairs on your heads! We Pygmy Folk see mating in a more balanced light. Ow!" He writhed as her nails bit into his wrists. "Ow! Fa!"

The Lady glared at him. That look, he knew, presaged a storm of monumental proportions. He would have essayed a sheepish grin, but his rigid beak would not allow it. He hissed weakly and cackled instead.

She swore angrily and rounded upon the startled interpreter. "So now we must invade the Prince's boudoir to get her back! Which way, woman—to the quarters of your *Gaichun*'s whoremongering son?"

Aluja intervened. "In the name of your Lord of Sacrifice, Madam, leave the Lady Jai for now! Likely she has already suffered indignities—and we cannot save her from what is done! Let me but return you to Milumanaya and Ridek to Yan Kor; then I shall come back for her, and the *Gaichun*'s heir will pay for his effrontery!'' He saw that she would not listen and tried another tack. ''The Baron needs you, Lady, to lead the attack upon the Tsolyani armies in Milumanaya. A victory there is worth a dozen maids, however noble!''

Her lips opened, then shut again in a hard, white line. ''The Lady Jai is important to me,'' she replied darkly. ''More than you realize.''

''I can guess. Flamesong.''

She glowered at him. ''A matter of mine, Mihalli, not yours! Keep your guesses to yourself! Come. I demand that we go to her. Now.''

The translator interrupted, saying, ''Shakkan is returned from the chamber at the end of this hallway, my Lady. He reports a foreign officer dead or unconscious upon the floor. A woman in armor sits beside him.''

The Lady Deq Dimani hesitated. ''An officer? The *Hereksa*? Trinesh hiKetkolel?'' She rubbed her bruised forehead in indecision. ''We will look there before seeking Jai.''

''But you just . . . ?'' Aluja began.

''If he lives, he may know more. Dead, he deserves at least a word of memorial, friend or foe, since he worships the Flame Lord and belongs to a good warrior clan. If indeed he be slain, we can still question the soldier woman.'' She looked from face to face. ''The Lady Jai can endure her Skein for a moment or two longer. Is that not what you just urged, Aluja?''

Without waiting for a reply she slipped past Shakkan and along the passage. At its end bronze hinges fixed to the side of a low archway showed where a door had once been. No panel hung there now.

''Tse'e—Lord? Thu'n?'' The voice from beyond the opening was a woman's, faint and soft.

''Saina?'' the Lady Deq Dimani called. ''Saina? I have soldiers—and others—here with me. Make no resistance, and no one harms you.''

She listened, but no sound came. Aluja grasped Ridek's

shoulder and pressed him against the side wall. The translator woman crouched beside them, and Shakkan motioned the guardsmen forward.

The Lady Deq Dimani uttered a scornful curse. She snatched a torch from one of their escort and marched straight on, into the room. They heard a jumble of conversation; then she reappeared and beckoned to them.

"The soldier woman—Saina—is injured," she said to Aluja. "The *Hereksa* is unconscious. Your so-noble Prince—" she almost spat at Dayetha—"stabbed him with a poisoned stiletto as he fought with Horusel—one of the Tsolyani subalterns."

The translator was bewildered. "Shakkan can summon aid. . . ."

The Lady Deq Dimani turned her back and re-entered the room, the others trailing after. The place had been a storeroom of some sort; empty chests and splintered slats of wood lay all about, a muddle of refuse and decay. Fortunately for the two Tsolyani against the far wall, the *Shon Tinur* fungus had not made serious inroads here.

Saina did not rise. She sat with her back against the grimy stones and menaced them with Tse'e's steel thigh-dagger. Trinesh lay curled next to her, his head upon a folded cloak, to all intents asleep.

Aluja glided over, hands open to show that he meant no harm. Saina's dagger-point swiveled to follow him.

The Lady Deq Dimani said, "Oh, put it down, girl. See to the *Hereksa*, Aluja." She added, "Please."

Aluja ignored the fiercely watchful gaze of the soldier-woman, left Ridek where he stood, and knelt beside the injured officer. He had no idea what to do. Some Mihalli were physicians as well as sorcerers, but Aluja had mastered only a smattering of the healing arts.

The Tsolyani was a rangy, powerfully built, young man, stern-looking and proud even in his present condition. Command, responsibility, and war: all shaped a person thus. Trinesh hiKetkolel had probably never been allowed to be a child but had been pressed into the warrior mold as soon as he could walk.

The Mihalli called for a torch and rolled the youth over upon his back. Broad, high cheekbones, reddish-copper skin, and a sharp, triangular chin betokened the warlike clans of western Tsolyanu, the Chakas probably, with just a hint of the more ancient aristocracies of the Dragon Warriors. The Tsolyani seemed to be asleep, his lashes black half-moons upon pallid cheeks. Only the slow beat of blood at his temples indicated that he lived.

"I think it is *Sha'u Nte.*" Aluja unbuckled the youth's breastplate to massage his chest. "That is a drug made by boiling the bark of a tree that grows hereabouts. My people used it to bring about visions and a sort of mental tranquility, but it puts humans into a trance for a time."

"*Your* people?" Dayetha Fashkolun puzzled.

Aluja had forgotten her—and Shakkan, and the soldiers. It would not do to have them flee from a dreaded Mihalli in terror now. He checked his human disguise. "A manner of speaking," he temporized.

"Cure him," the Lady Deq Dimani said shortly. "We—" she broke off, then continued in a different tone—"Aluja. . . . Best see to the woman first."

He looked. The Tsolyani girl sat in a widening pool of dark blood.

"Take Ridek out." He did not wait to see if anyone obeyed. "What happened, woman? Where are you injured?"

Saina said, "No. Attend to Trinesh—the *Hereksa.* In the fight—Horusel cut me—the inner thigh—I don't think he really intended it."

Thu'n peered over Aluja's shoulder. "Tse'e—the old Tsolyani—bound her leg tightly with a cloth. But she has lost much strength."

Saina's lips trembled, and she licked them with a tongue as gray as ashes. "No matter, I said. See to Trinesh."

"He comes to his senses even now." Aluja pulled her

sopping kilt aside. The gash was terrible: from just above the knee up almost to the groin. Did not humans go into shock from wounds like this? That must be why she seemed to feel no pain. He knew so little about their physiognomy! He turned his head to address the Lady Deq Dimani. "It is serious. We must summon aid."

Saina smiled. "No need, whoever you are. I am a soldier, and I have seen wounds like this before. A few minutes, a *Kiren* or two, then death as the blood flows away." The dagger slipped from her fingers, and she laid her hand upon Trinesh's arm instead. "Tell me: should I sing my death song now? I am not a very good singer, you know." She tried to smile again.

Trinesh stirred, groaned, and woke. He yawned. "Where—?"

The Lady Deq Dimani put out a hand to help him, an unusual thing for a matriarch of Vridu to do. "Look to Saina," she said.

"Trinesh? *Hereksa*? Oh, I am sorry. . . ."

He sat up. One glance and he knew. "Saina!"

"I tried, *Hereksa*. When Horusel would have slain you after the drug took effect—"

"We must have help!" the Lady Deq Dimani snapped at the translator. "The *Gaichun's* physicians? Come, woman!"

Dayetha Fashkolun shook her head. The bird's-head mask was in her way, and she wrenched it off. "They could be summoned, Lady. But I think it is too far—too late."

"Aid me, *Hereksa*. Give me words for my death song." Saina's eyes wandered about the dusty little room. "I had hoped—I would have been a good wife, *Hereksa*, not a first wife but a good second, or third. . . ."

He understood. "Oh, better than second. First."

He hated himself for the lie. It was ignoble to lie to a fellow-worshipper of the Flame, and thrice as base to lie to one who was dying.

His little inner voice would have much to say to him later. Even Aluja knew: no low-clan girl could ever be accepted as the first or second wife of a Red Mountain clansman. Whatever the boy or the girl might wish, such a thing did not happen, not in Tsolyanu, not in Yan Kor, not in any one of the Five Empires. A low-clan bride was acceptable as a concubine, or as a minor wife after the husband had achieved his status. The same was true in reverse for a high-clan *Aridani* woman who married a low-clan husband: he could never be first, and any children by him would be taken into the wife's lineage and clan rather than his.

Trinesh fumbled for the few catechisms he had learned in the temple school. "*Otulengba, Vimuhla, Hlatsalkoi, Noktel-modalisakoi hiwisu . . .* 'All hail, Vimuhla, the Flame, Great and Powerful Conflagrator of the Universe!'" He could remember no more. The drug seemed to have dried his throat, and the words refused to come.

Saina took his hand, and he exclaimed at the chill upon her fingers. She sighed. "In this land I would have been an Engsvanyali noble lady. Not as pretty as these Yan Koryani doxies, but more than the skinny bone-bags who dwell here." She struggled to sit erect and began to croon in a toneless whisper. She broke off. "Oh, if only I could make a beautiful death-song! What will the Flame Lord say when I reach the gates of His paradise bellowing like a *Tsi'il*-beast in rut?"

Trinesh turned blindly to the others. His limbs were as weak as reeds. "Get out, all of you—please!"

They did so.

"How is the woman?" Ridek asked. No one replied, and they took the boy back up the corridor, out of hearing. After a time the young Tsolyani officer emerged alone.

"I am ready." He had donned his breastplate once more, and he held his archaic visored helmet in the crook of one arm. "Your prisoner, Lady."

They walked in silence. Now and then Shakkan muttered in Tka Mihalli, and Dayetha passed his instructions on to the Lady Deq Dimani. The *Ochuna* was utterly still, sable-draped, a mournful place to die. They all shared the same thoughts.

Trinesh said, "The Flame—any flame—would have been so much more noble for her." The Lady Deq Dimani nodded.

At length they came to a vast, high-vaulted hall, roughly circular in plan, festooned with soot-hued *Shon Tinur*, and floored with head-high mounds of earth, stones, and broken tiles fallen from later edifices that had been built above. Here and there a floor of red and white mosaic showed through from beneath the clutter.

The translator said, "This chamber is named 'The Elliptical Veil,' the Gods alone know why. Here the *Ochuna* ends. That stair leads up to Prince Tenggutla Dayyar's apartments." She glanced around, then donned her mask. "There will be guards—soldiers—servants—"

"Prince Tenggutla Dayyar must summon his best," Trinesh declared gravely. "He will need them." As though from nowhere, Saina's short *Chlen*-hide sword appeared from beneath the helmet he carried.

No one had thought to disarm him. Yet no one objected.

They avoided the heaps of plaster and broken bricks fallen from the ceiling and picked their way across to the other side. There, massive pilasters opened into niches as black as the *Shon Tinur* itself. The translator indicated that the stairway lay in one of these.

Aluja stopped and scuffed at the cracked flooring with a sandaled foot. "What name did you give this place?"

"In the *Gaichun*'s archives its full title is 'The Elliptical Veil of the Myriad Worlds,' " Dayetha replied.

The Mihalli growled something and scraped harder. Whorls, circles, odd geometrical shapes, and interlocking curlicues appeared, faded white upon red, beneath his feet. The symbols were linked into bands which must once have run all around the floor in a spiral or in concentric circles. Many areas, including the center of the chamber, lay buried beneath rubble a man-height deep.

Aluja toed one visible section and recited, "*Alünu Meya tri Zhawai Nakoluvre.* . . ."

"What are you about?" Thu'n worried.

"These marks. This mosaic is a writing in my language. The *Gaichun*'s palace must be built upon the ruins of one of our council halls, a place of the Mihalli of old. . . ."

"We have no time now!" The Lady Deq Dimani clawed her heavy tresses back with impatient fingers.

"*Khu Nökekhrü.* '. . . And from hence the fourth Plane, and so to the Pylons of the Barrier . . .' " he continued to read, ignoring her.

Ridek went to help, prying up flat chunks of tile and plaster with the butt of his staff. More of the red and white mosaic showed beneath.

"As the Lord of Sacrifice burns!" the Lady Deq Dimani fumed. Their escort must have surmised by now that Aluja was no ordinary human sorcerer, and only the paralysis of terror kept them there. The interpreter chittered at them in Tka Mihalli; warning or reassurance, the others could not tell. Thu'n left Aluja to dig and paced from niche to niche, peering into each in turn. Only Trinesh stood still.

"This," Aluja announced, "is indeed a Hall of Myriad Worlds."

"The Flame sear you!" the Lady Deq Dimani cried. "What do you mean? —And what is that to us now?"

"A focal point—a place from which one who knows the way can travel directly to any place on any Plane, wherever an open Nexus Point exists. An intersection of many lines—of weak spots in the skins of reality that surround the island-universes. . . . Like bubbles in a bath of oil, with filaments linking them here and there. . . ." Aluja stumbled over the concepts. No human tongue could express exactly what lay here, and he abandoned the effort. "Find the Lady Jai," he said. "Then I can take you directly to any receptive Nexus Point within the spheres: to Milumanaya, to Yan Kor— anywhere that is not sealed and warded! Without hindrance, without traversing Planes where dangers await." His human form shimmered, wavered, and then solidified again, but he paid no heed. "Four such halls we had upon this Plane—only four. One was destroyed, melted into vapor by the catastrophe that created the Plains of Glass during the Latter Times. Three still exist, but they are far from here—in your spatial terms. Ohe, our histories speak of four, but this chamber is a fifth!" He seemed almost beside himself. "A fifth, lost even to the legend-singers . . . !"

Trinesh had not moved from the center of the cavernous hall. He stood now with his back to Aluja and the Lady Deq Dimani.

"Greetings, Horusel," he said.

17

The veteran *Tirrikamu* emerged from one of the side niches, Dineva and the two crossbowmen just behind him. Chosun, Chekkuru, and a group of five or six of the Prince's guardsmen were visible farther back in the darkness, and Trinesh thought to see the sheen of Okkuru's chain harness there as well.

"Chekkuru!" Horusel roared. "That one first—the old man! He's their mage!"

The priest lifted his arm, but the Mihalli was faster. His globe swung up, already glowing with a malignant azure light. There was no visible manifestation, but Chekkuru made a whinnying sound and toppled over backwards. Trinesh did not see what happened to him thereafter. Horusel was already closing for combat, and Trinesh himself was the nearest.

The guardsmen of both sides advanced as well; magic and alien beings might terrify them, but this was their own kind of battle, and they were by no means cowards. The *Ochuna* had doubtless witnessed scores of just such deadly little skirmishes over the centuries. Ornate falchions at the ready, they yelped shrill battle cries and trotted forward.

Shakkan's black-swathed shoulder blades spurted red. He threw up his hands and crumpled. In front of him, Mejjai bent methodically to rewind his crossbow. Arjasu was there too, pausing to look for a better target. The snap of his weapon was lost in their shouting, but Dayetha Fashkolun doubled over, mouth open wide, fingers clawing at the red-feathered quarrel in her belly. If Arjasu had been seeking the Lady Deq Dimani, he had chosen the wrong woman.

Horusel's rush carried him on right into Trinesh. The younger man was ready; they clashed together and swayed, nose to nose, for the space of two long breaths. The poison had left Trinesh weak, and his stockier, heavier opponent strove to trip him. He slid backwards, braced again, and shoved. Horusel shifted to the right and let Trinesh stumble past, only the backplate of his armor saving him from an awkward backhand blow as he went by. He slithered to his knees in a heap of earth and sharp-edged tiles, fell, rolled, and kicked out. His boots encountered empty air.

From out of nowhere something struck Horusel a glancing clout upon the left shoulder. He cursed, turned, and then smashed down with his stubby, scallop-bladed short sword at a new attacker rushing in from his flank.

It was the Yan Koryani boy. And all the lad had for a weapon was a black wooden cudgel! Trinesh shouted, but he was too late.

The blade hit the upflung staff. It should have sheared it in two and gone on to cleave the boy's skull. Instead, the *Tirrikamu*'s weapon seemed to glide *around* the target, a complicated, curving path never mentioned in any manual of dueling. Astonished, Horusel struggled to control his swing, leaped away, and returned for a straight-armed stab. This time his blade flickered sideways like a fish swimming in a stream; it missed the boy completely.

Trinesh was on his feet. "Here, Horusel! I am here!" he cried. "Why slay a boy when I am the one you seek?"

The *Tirrikamu* swerved around and met Trinesh' charge in a clatter of armor and weapons. The floor here was smoother—the red and white mosaic—and Trinesh's training had the advantage. A thrust, a parry, a slash, and the older man retreated, panting.

"Out of the way, boy!" Trinesh had no idea whether the youth understood Tsolyani. He feigned a wide blow, reversed, caught Horusel's blade and knocked it aside. He felt his own point bump along the fluting of the man's cuirass. Horusel ducked his head and lurched forward to grapple, his favored style of brawling.

Trinesh's backhanded chop caught him across the ornate cheekpiece of his Engsvanyali helmet. The armor of the Legion of the Storm of Fire would have held up, but the High General's gift was intended for ceremony. The *Chlen*-hide plate crumpled, and Horusel uttered a single, short, cawing shout. He staggered, lost his balance, and sprawled across the Mihalli inscription on the floor. Muscles cracking, he clambered to his knees. His helmet's chinstrap had been cut through, and the gilded burgonet slipped off entirely and went clacking and bouncing away across the mosaic.

He made the mistake of glancing after it.

Trinesh's next blow landed at the juncture of neck and shoulder, just above the chaised rim of Horusel's pauldron. The *Tirrikamu* coughed, slumped forward, and clawed at the awful red wound opening just beneath his ear.

He kicked and then lay still.

Trinesh gulped for air, but found that it stank of battle: metal, and leather, and blood, and sweat, and entrails, and dying. Farther off, shadows leaped and pranced in the fitful light of the escorts' torches. He heard shouting, clangor, and the screeching birdlike warcries of the *Gaichun's* troops. Then giddiness overcame him, and he knelt to recover.

He sensed someone beside him and hurled himself aside.

The boy's black staff whistled over his head. The lad had more courage than sense!

Before he could react, a shadow loomed up behind the boy: it was Chosun. Trinesh had no breath with which to cry a warning, but it would have been useless in any case. Yet the big soldier made no attempt to strike. Instead, he came forward, hands held wide to show that he meant no harm, and stooped to haul Trinesh erect. The Yan Koryani princeling backed away, wide-eyed, into the darkness.

"You wounded, *Hereksa*?"

"No—I don't think so. . . ."

"Sorry. This shouldn't have happened." Chosun's homely features were twisted with remorse.

"No help for it now. Who—who wins?"

"Think they do. The Lady. Magic."

Trinesh understood: the mysterious Aluja.

"The boy," he wheezed. "Get the boy, and she may yet give herself up. He's important to her."

Chosun peered about. "No boy now. He's run off—over there, I think, toward her." He pointed with his sword. "We can't beat 'em, *Hereksa*—not with a sorcerer on their side. Best we run."

"No. We must see." That was the least they could do.

They skirted head-high piles of rubble. It took less than five short sentences to tell Chosun of Saina's fate and another three to describe the boy's curious staff. Then they came out between two jagged tumuli of broken masonry and saw torches ahead, stuck into the damp, mold-fragrant earth. Trinesh pulled Chosun to a stop behind a hillock of rotted bricks.

Twenty paces away, the Lady Deq Dimani stood in the midst of an open space, the sorcerer and the boy beside her. Two of her Mihalli guardsmen were inspecting a body: Mejjai, Trinesh thought. Dineva squatted nearby under the eyes of a third soldier. She wore no helmet, and her lank, stringy hair tumbled down in a black cascade over the fingers she pressed to her face. She must have suffered a blow to the head. There was no sign of Arjasu or Chekkuru hiVriddi, nor could they see Thu'n.

Okkuru the translator ambled up out of the shadows and bowed. What he said was inaudible, but the Lady Deq Dimani made an imperious gesture. He shrugged and sat down beside Dineva. After all, the ex-slave had no stake in this fight; he did not care who won, and she would need his services as a translator, now that poor Dayetha Fashkolun lay either dead or badly wounded.

"Tse'e?" Chosun asked.

"Vanished." Trinesh had not seen the old man since their first battle in Chunatl Dikkuna's unpleasant little cell.

"I think Chekkuru hiVriddi is dead. And good riddance."

"I know. I saw him fall—sorcery. We should look for Chekkuru. I think he had the magical weapon the Prince was going to give me." He was struck by another thought. "And Arjasu? What happened to him? He's neither fool nor coward."

Chosun made no answer. Trinesh led the way between gigantic blocks fallen through the ceiling long ago from some less-ancient structure above.

They found Chekkuru hiVriddi almost at once.

The priest lay amid the rubble, his shaven head cradled upon one outflung arm. Chosun put a hand to his breast and murmured, "He lives, *Hereksa*. It's like he's sleeping." He grinned wolfishly. "Lazy like all priests! Ought to kill the bastard!"

"No. Leave him. Look for his weapon."

They searched the moist, clayey earth in front of him, around him, and then in wider circles. It was Trinesh who came upon the Prince's "Eye," half buried in the mold-streaked soil. He waved it at Chosun, who went off to reconnoitre from behind a hummock of debris.

"Cha!" the *Tirrikamu* grunted. "They're getting ready to move: the soldiers to the front and rear, Dineva and the translator man with the Lady and the others in the middle."

"Going up into the palace, probably. After the Lady Jai."

"How good is the 'Eye'? We can ambush them if you like."

He had no clear idea what the Prince's weapon did. More, he tended to put little trust in such esoteric devices. He thought furiously. If they attacked now and somehow managed to win against all odds, the Lady Jai would still be a prisoner above. He doubted whether he and Chosun could rescue her by themselves. On the other hand, if they let the Lady Deq Dimani leave to get the girl, she would have no reason to return here. They could follow at a distance, of course, but . . .

The decision was made for him. Shouting erupted ahead, and the escorts' torches scattered red-orange light in wild gyrations. Concealment forgotten, Trinesh straightened up to look.

The Lady Jai Chasa Vedlan had just emerged from the niche in front of the party.

She appeared unharmed. Her long, wavy tresses hung loose over a dark mantle of some sort. From the copper-gold gleam of her limbs beneath it, Trinesh suspected that it was her only garment. The Lady Deq Dimani went forward as though to embrace her but stopped five paces away, held out her hands, and said something in her harsh language.

The girl shrugged and dropped her cloak. She was indeed quite naked. She kicked the garment disdainfully aside with one bare foot, then stood silently, as though waiting for something. The Lady Deq Dimani spoke again, and Trinesh looked about for Saina to interpret for him.

There was no more Saina. Grief struck him with full force, and he almost cried out. He grimaced and bit his lip. After all, a warrior-child soon learns to postpone mourning; either that, or one can never be a soldier. Thus his preceptors had taught him in the clan-house training yard long ago.

The Lady Deq Dimani gestured. Okkuru sang a few words to the accompanying guardsmen, and one of them stripped away Dineva's short mantle and tossed it to the Yan Koryani girl, who put it on. The purpose of all this dressing and undressing was mystifying.

Chosun pulled Trinesh down beside him. "Look at their magicker, *Hereksa*."

Aluja's form seemed to shimmer in the torchlight, and Trinesh squinted. No, the graybeard was still the same. He had drawn a little apart from the others, though, the Yan Koryani princeling beside him. "It looks as though he wants no part of the Lady and her maid."

"There was something about him. . . . What's he seeking on the floor?"

"Something dropped? A weapon?" Then Trinesh remembered the white symbols of the mosaic and the words Aluja had uttered in an unknown tongue. A spell?

The old mage held out his arms, revolved slowly, and pointed. A dim, pale oval wavered before him in the air. It was of no color or definable substance, and its center was a black maw that yawned open upon unguessable vistas beyond.

Trinesh had heard of Nexus Points.

"We attack—now! On my signal!" he commanded. They could not let the Yan Koryani leave. He was no longer quite sure why, but this was no time for heart-searching! He gave his little inner voice no opportunity to comment.

He ran forward, stumbling and slipping upon the stones and moldering clay. Chosun vacillated; then Trinesh heard him lumbering along behind.

The *Gaichun*'s soldiers had had enough of sorcery for one night. They retreated from Aluja's sorcerous oval, wailed in their own language, and fled, tossing weapons and torches aside as they ran. Okkuru hurled his beast-mask helmet away and scrambled off after them as well, leaving Dineva alone in the midst of the open space. She glanced about dazedly, then bent and retrieved one of the soldiers' falchions.

The two Yan Koryani women stood transfixed: for all the Lady Deq Dimani knew, the dim shapes clattering toward her might be the High General's whole dainty Legion of the

Seekers of Indelible Victory, all two score of them! She sent a furious curse after her escort and thrust the Lady Jai toward the flickering Nexus Point doorway where Aluja crouched with the boy.

The "Eye" was an oily pebble in Trinesh' fingers. He held it out at arm's length before him as though it might explode—and what good would an extra pace do him if it did?—and thumbed the little stud once, twice—he did not know how many times.

Nothing seemed to happen. The damned "Eye" had no effect!

The wizard held up the ball-thing he had used on Chekkuru. Trinesh was directly in its path, and he threw himself down headlong into the rubble. The *Shon Tinur* grew here, and he ploughed into it and sent up a cloud of crackling black threads, like dried grass. A horde of tiny ebon-cased beetles squirmed away in all directions. Incongruously he thought: so *that's* what the little horrors look like! Then his outstretched elbow scraped stone, and pain burned along his arm. He somehow kept his grip on the "Eye," and he knew that he still had Saina's sword by the hard lump of its massive hilt pressed between his stomach and the ground.

He heard more shouts and raised his head. The wizard hovered beside the oval door into Other-Space, but the blue globe lay dull and lifeless before him on the broken mosaic floor. He slumped, both six-fingered paws over his face.

Paws?

Trinesh stared. No senile oldster stood there now but rather a tall, gaunt, gangling creature, dark-skinned and beast-muzzled! A nonhuman, an alien of some kind! Having heard only the tale-tellers' weirdly distorted descriptions of the Mihalli, he had no idea what it was.

Had he known, he might have joined the *Gaichun*'s troops in flight, nobility or not!

The Lady Deq Dimani faced Dineva across five paces of littered floor. The soldier-woman still appeared stunned, and she made no move other than to lift her sword in defense. The Lady Deq Dimani seized Jai's wrist and half led, half dragged her toward the Nexus Point, shouting something to the wizard-beast and the boy at the same time.

Trinesh scrambled up to his feet, wasted precious breath in one last war-whoop, and charged. He hoped Chosun was with him.

The Lady Deq Dimani turned, blade glinting in the bloody shadows cast by the scattered torches. "Only you, Tsolyani?" she jeered. "You and Chosun?"

Something whickered out of the darkness, and Trinesh heard a hard, smacking sound, like a club striking metal plate. The Lady Deq Dimani spun about, glanced down in astonishment, then stumbled back. A stubby crossbow quarrel stood out from her right shoulder pauldron, scarlet feathers against gray steel.

Arjasu had found his mark.

The Lady Deq Dimani let go of the girl to clap her hand to the shaft. She shrieked in Yan Koryani, then dropped her sword to reach for the boy. Another bolt hissed out of the shadows. The boy raised his black staff to knock the missile aside as one might bat a ball. The quarrel did not waver from its course, however, as Horusel's sword had done; it flew straight and true, missing the boy's forehead by no more than a finger's breadth, and he recoiled, away from the woman. Arjasu must be cursing himself for missing so easy a target!

The Lady Deq Dimani yelled again, then seized the alien magician and strove to propel him bodily into the Nexus doorway. He twisted free and held out his oddly jointed arms to the boy. The Lady left him no choice: a better grip upon the leather harness he wore, a violent jerk that must have cost her much pain, and then both she and Aluja tumbled back into the Nexus Point in a tangle of limbs and armor. There was no sound of their striking any ground inside.

Chosun and Dineva reached the two remaining Yan Koryani simultaneously from separate directions. The girl would have followed her mistress through the portal, but the *Tirrikamu* seized her around the waist and easily cast her aside. Dineva momentarily had her hands full: the boy was brave! He struck at her with his staff, dodged, kicked, and nearly succeeded in making his escape. At last she got him by one arm, wrested the cudgel away, then held him tightly to her armored breast until he stopped struggling.

All of this Trinesh saw from the corner of his eye as he plunged forward after the Lady Deq Dimani. He almost followed her into the Nexus Point, thought better of it, and hurled himself to one side just in time. He fell in a clattering heap almost at Dineva's feet.

Why was the *Aridani* woman so tall? He realized that he knelt upon the ground before her. Her? His eyes told him that three thin-faced soldier women stood there! Bemused, he pitched forward upon his face.

Fatigue had joined forces with the Prince's poison to defeat him at last.

He woke to find his head in someone's lap. Alas, it was Dineva's bony hip that supported his skull and not the Lady Jai's more delightful anatomy. He coughed, gasped, and licked his lips. He wanted water, but he doubted if anyone had brought any. Conversation bumbled around and above him like the buzzing of *Chri*-flies.

"—The damned girl." Chosun sounded as though he shouted through a waterfall. "Hoi! Here, the *Hereksa*'s back!"

Arjasu's smoother, higher voice answered him. "Make no mistake. I'd as soon slay the wench and the brat now and be done. Then we can decide whether to follow the Yan Koryani woman through her magic door or trust ourselves to the tubeway car and Thu'n's golden plates."

"The Nexus Point?" Trinesh contended with a throat as dry as the Desert of Sighs itself. "It's still there?"

"Don't try to talk yet," Dineva replied from above him. "The Lady Jai says you somehow sucked all the magic juice out of their accursed wizard. He could neither destroy the portal nor alter it, and there it hangs." He felt, rather than saw, her arm go up to point off over his head.

"Mejjai's dead," Chosun said simply. "So's the translator woman and some of their folk. The rest ran off. The Lady's gone through the portal with her monster, but we've got her maid and the Yan Koryani boy. And here's Thu'n. He hid in the ruins and now comes to join us. If we can get to the tubeway car, the Prince's discs will take us back to—uh— where did you say?"

The little *Nininyal*'s piping voice sounded muzzily from behind him. "The nearest I can make out is Tathurel, proba- bly the city you Tsolyani now call Thri'il. Then there's Somujrasa, which might be Sunraya, and a dozen other un- named marks between." Chosun pulled Thu'n out so that Trinesh could see him from where he lay.

Did Tumissa appear on any of the tubeway discs? His teacher in the temple school had said that the Engsvanyali had called it To'om Ssa, and before that, during the First Impe- rium, the city had been To'om Unessu, "the Place of the Crag." His head ached. It would be so good just to go home. But that would make him a deserter, of course, a shame to his clan and a traitor to the Petal Throne: a felon, a candidate for the "High Ride" on the impaling stake!

No, that would not do. There had to be a prettier Skein for Trinesh hiKetkolel of the Red Mountain clan!

Trinesh asked, "You, Thu'n. Why did you come back to us?"

He expected hesitation and a devious reply, but the *Nininyal* only said, "I cannot return by myself. Any method of getting home is better than none. And I'm no soldier; you Tsolyani have no quarrel with me, nor I with you. My race is neutral in your war."

Trinesh refrained from mentioning the Baron's two well- paid and very ferocious Pygmy Folk legions, the food and material aid they provided, and their scholars—and spies— who performed tasks for Yan Kor. Still, the Imperium did not wage war upon traders, travelers, and other noncombatants, not even when it was locked in battle with their governments. That would not be noble.

"The greedy little beast wants to sell the discs," Arjasu snickered. "A fortune! And the temples of Tsolyanu are far wealthier than those of Yan Kor, Saa Allaqi, or any other land you can name! Cha, *Hereksa*, never accuse the Pygmy Folk of philanthropy—or loyalty!"

"My people—" Thu'n began.

"Oh, la! *Chlen*-shit!" Arjasu swam around into Trinesh's vision, crossbow cradled under one arm, his fancy Engsvanyali armor streaked and smudged with clay and bits of *Shon Tinur*. He had probably applied that camouflage deliberately, though to do so was ignoble for a soldier engaged in honorable battle.

Trinesh sat up and leaned dizzily against Dineva's mail-clad flank. He looked about. Three paces distant Chekkuru hiVriddi snored peacefully upon the faded mosaic.

Chosun followed the direction of his gaze. "Can't wake him," he said scornfully. "Thu'n, here, says he'll come to by himself. Not that I care."

Trinesh picked himself up, his knees creaking audibly as he did so. Any more of this life and he'd be ready for a funeral pyre and a memory-niche in the mausoleum of his clan!

A little way off, Lady Jai Chasa Vedlan sat together with the unknown Yan Koryani boy upon an eroded ceiling cornice. Arjasu stalked back to watch them, but neither showed any signs of flight. Trinesh shuffled over to the girl. She hugged Dineva's mantle to herself and turned her head away.

"And your story?" he rasped. "Quickly."

She made no reply, and he wanted to shout obscenities into her sweetly placid face. Her indifference would try the patience of a god! He caught his breath and strove for control. "Scorch the world! You *will* speak! Else I let Arjasu and

Chosun have their way with you—and then Dineva, who knows just where and how a woman can be hurt!"

He had no intention of allowing any such ugly Skein, and she was probably aware of it. Yet he had to say the words, if only to impress his followers.

She surprised him by answering. "I—I escaped from the Prince and returned to join my Lady. The rest you know." She added, "Do not hurt the child. He is no threat to you."

"Damn the child! —Who is he?"

"His name is Ridek. I think that he understands only a little Tsolyani. He is a—the son of—a noble clansman of our people."

Later he would explore that. Now she interested him more.

"Your cloak." He waved a trembling hand at the garment. "It conceals you much less than the one you were wearing. Why did you change it?" He found it advisable to keep his eyes averted from the vision of long, golden calves and thighs she so casually displayed.

She made a little face.

"Here, *Hereksa.*" Chosun held out the mantle the Lady Jai had discarded in exchange for Dineva's.

Trinesh examined it: rich, heavy, dark brown fabric, all embroidered with golden thread and sewn with glittering discs in delicate floral whorls. He sniffed. The cloak smelled of fire, and its lower borders were burned and scorched, the lining there blackened and crackling. He hurled it at her.

"Explain."

She gave him a slight smile. "It is damaged. I tipped over the lamp while the Prince was—was busy with me."

"You *what*?"

"The oil lamp—one of those massive bronze things with many little bowls and wicks. I drew it over upon him. Then I came here."

"By the Fortieth Aspect—!" Chosun guffawed. "You roasted the filthy *Chlen*-turd? Slew him?"

She shrugged. "I don't know. The chamber was on fire when I left."

Dineva jerked her head up sharply. "Lanterns, *Hereksa!*" They all swung around to look.

"Ohe!" someone called from beyond the hillocks of masonry and rubble. "Ohe, Tsolyani?"

"Chunatl Dikkuna," Chosun whispered. Arjasu stooped to cock his crossbow, and the others snatched up their weapons. After a moment's consideration, Trinesh indicated one of the escorts' swords to Thu'n, who went to pick it up.

"Ohe! Well done!" Lamplight made a yellow halo around the Salarvyan's shaven pate. "The Yan Koryani women are taken? I have a warrant here from the High General—the Priestkings did provide their legions with special powers when the security of the state was in jeopardy . . ." He edged forward, a shade too cautiously, Trinesh thought. Armor and weapons glinted behind him.

"Is Tse'e—the old man—with you?" Trinesh called.

"Ai, here he is." Chunatl beckoned, and the soldiers opened ranks to let the elderly renegade through. Tse'e's steel sword dangled loosely in his hand, and he seemed confused. Chunatl took his arm to aid him.

"Beware, Tsolyani!" the Lady Jai murmured. Trinesh swung back to stare at her. "This Chunatl Dikkuna must have an 'Excellent Ruby Eye'! That was what we used to defeat Tse'e. We left him a frozen statue, out of phase with this Plane. A second charge is required to release a victim from its power!"

It was the longest speech she had ever made to him. Trinesh dared not stop to wonder why she chose to warn them. "Who has the 'Eye' I fired at the wizard?" He kept his voice low. "Give Chunatl Dikkuna a shot of it—now!"

Chosun fumbled at his belt pouch.

"Here, my friends!" the Salarvyani cried. "We want no violence!" He glided forward again, left arm around Tse'e's stooped shoulders, and right hand out and open. "Peace,

Tsolyani! You have done well indeed! The Yan Koryani women and their little pup are retaken, eh?" He blinked owlishly. "Where is the Matriarch of Vridu? I see only the girl and the youth."

"She's gone," Trinesh retorted. "Back to Ganga." Let him chew on that!

"No matter. Come and claim your reward! The *Gaichun*'s palace burns; we hear that Prince Tenggutla Dayyar is naught but a cinder within it; and the High General takes command! You shall be honored, given the yellow *Klai Ga*, and your mouths shall be stuffed with rubies! The defeat of the wicked pretender, Captain Harchar, is assured!"

So now the pirate was a "wicked pretender"; woe to those who hoped for constancy in politics! The High General's agents were apparently still unaware of the invader's abrupt change of plan!

"And the *Gaichun* himself?" Trinesh feared Chosun would drop the little "Eye." He had never been dexterous.

"Soon superfluous to smooth government."

"As we shall be," Dineva warned.

Chosun's huge fingers tightened, and he glanced over at Chunatl. The Salarvyani seemed to notice nothing; he gave Tse'e a fatherly push toward his comrades, and his left hand appeared over the old man's shoulder. Something gleamed there, a dull, glassy red.

He squeezed the device and beamed expectantly at them. Then he jabbed his thumb at it again and again.

Nothing occurred.

"Out of power!" Chunatl squalled. "Charge! Kill them!" He forgot that he spoke Tsolyani and had to jabber the order again in Tka Mihalli.

Arjasu's crossbow bolt took him squarely in the breast. Chunatl dropped without a word.

"Still we are outnumbered!" Thu'n moaned.

It was true. This time the High General had sent a force large enough to accomplish the task, with or without Chunatl

Dikkuna's magic—or his treachery. There must be two dozen high-crested helmets out there!

"Into the Nexus doorway!" Trinesh commanded.

"No—! What if it opens upon Ke'er?" Dineva cried.

"I doubt that it does." The Lady Jai surprised them once more. "Aluja first intended to return the Lady Deq Dimani to Milumanaya, then back to Yan Kor with Ridek—the boy."

"The Baron's own bedroom would be better than dying here in this hole," Trinesh grumbled. "The midst of a Yan Koryani encampment! —The Flame Lord's freezing hells! Anywhere! —Through the portal!"

Two soldiers had halted to attend to Chunatl Dikkuna. The others began to spread out. Trinesh glimpsed the tall plumes of an officer behind them in the darkness. The High General himself? "Shoot the damned 'Eye'-thing again," he ordered. "Over there!"

They did not wait for results but backed toward the glimmering oval in the air. Was it fainter now? Trinesh stopped to pull the Lady Jai to her feet. Her fingers were as cold as poor Saina's had been.

"So this is how you persuade us to go to your Lady!" he husked.

She turned and smiled at him, as gentle as his own clan-sister, Shyal.

"The priest—?" Arjasu interrupted. "Chekkuru? What to do with him?"

"Heave the Flame-burned bastard through! I'll not give them the joy of slaying any of us!"

In the midst of the turmoil Trinesh had forgotten Tse'e. The old man had turned, raised his fine steel sword, and begun to chant his death-song. To disturb him now was the ultimate discourtesy.

To hell with him too! Everything!

Trinesh collared him and pushed him, protesting volubly, blade waving, after Dineva and the boy into the strange, colorless doorway. Chosun took the Lady Jai's arm and hustled her through as well.

The others were gone. He sucked in the dank, mold-smelling air for the last time, and made the unmistakable three-fingered sign of the Flame Lord in the probable direction of the High General. Then he staggered over the threshold of the portal himself.

And was borne away into nothingness.

18

ale coins upon a money-changer's black cloth. Big ones
and little ones, in no discernible order, of no measurable
size and of no hue that human eyes could see. Were the
small circles really small, or were they farther off than the
larger ones? Were they fixed in the abyss, or did they wheel
like the moons and the planets?

The dully shining ovals surrounded Trinesh completely.
All of them, those in front, in back, above and below, left
and right, were equally visible at once! It was as though he
were a spherical eye, focused simultaneously in all directions.

A god must have this sort of vision!

It was horribly unsettling.

He could neither see nor hear his companions; yet they
were there. He had only to think, and his thoughts became
sparkling bolts that sped away into the illimitable void. Chosun
was nearest: a presence, a rough, warm, prickly, sentient
tree-trunk that smelled of woodsmoke and sang like green
leaves. Dineva was sandier, thicker, murmuring as a spring

freshet mumbles and chuckles between its banks on its journey to the sea. The boy was an attenuated reed, a smooth-barked branch; the Lady Jai a whispering pillar of cool, adamantine fire-fronds; Arjasu a jumble of glowing rings and rods—

He had to stop. This was no place for human perceptions, or for human minds.

"There!" he cried, and watched the word become a great, complex, golden droplet of candle-wax spattered upon the canvas of Otherness. "There—the biggest portal—!" Sapphire crystals hurtled away, thundering and smoking, as fragrant as fresh rain, to become sigils of coruscating glory.

The nearest—? —Nexus doorway approached. Or did they approach it? Or neither.

He was through. Gravel under his knees, air in his tortured lungs—had there been none in Other-Space? —real darkness, sharp pebbles against his outflung palms. Nothing had ever felt so welcome. A stir behind him, and Dineva tumbled past to sprawl face down against a slab of gritty sandstone. She lay trembling, clasping the earth as a swimmer clings to a raft in a maelstrom. Chosun followed, eyes screwed shut and mouth open in a comical "Oh." The rest came after, ending in a heap of armor, bodies, and limbs: like jumbled corpses upon a battlefield, too newly dead to salute Missum, the Lord of Death, when he came to free their Spirit-Souls for the long voyage to the Isles, the Paradises of Teretane.

No one moved for a time. Then Thu'n got his bowed, furry legs under him and arose. He seemed the least perturbed by their sojourn among the Planes Between.

"Ohe, *Hereksa*," he called as he panted. "Down there."

Trinesh heaved himself up onto one elbow and looked. They had emerged upon a slope: wind-worn pinnacles and squat, rugged bluffs above them, a dark plain below. A few steps to their left, and they would have plunged down into a gully. On the right, cracked and jag-toothed layers of eroded rock climbed up and away in a steeply angled giants' staircase.

Spread out upon the black mantle beneath their heights, where the *Nininyal* pointed, he saw a collar of twinkling rubies, a multitude of gems that glittered red and orange and amber upon sable velvet. The dark center of the circle was filled with sharp-edged, boxlike shadows.

"A city," Dineva exclaimed. He had not heard her come up beside him. "A city, and an army encamped without."

"You were right. That may well be Ke'er down there."

"Ke'er?" the Yan Koryani boy said unexpectedly. "Not Ke'er. Ke'er is upon the sea. No sea. No rocks . . ."

"Ai," Tse'e put in. "Ke'er's a seaport, and there's nothing this high behind it." He held up a sprig of some grasslike plant. "This is *Chi'omiq*. It grows wherever it can find shelter against the winds of the Desert of Sighs. We're back in Milumanaya."

"Ready your weapons, then," Chosun declared gloomily. "If the Lady Deq Dimani and her monster came this way, then that is probably the bivouac of her Legion of Vridu below us—or that of her brother, the Fishers of the Flame!"

"But did she emerge here?" Trinesh wondered. The quavering, shimmering oval portal still hung in the air behind them, and he set his followers to searching around it. They found no footprints; they themselves had churned up the sand in front of the Nexus Point, and the rock farther away was too hard to show anything.

Trinesh gave it up. "We'd best go down. In the dark their sentries can't see us, but we can identify them. Then we can choose: sing our death-songs and die, or walk back through the desert to our own lines."

"The sun, thirst, hunger—a barefoot girl, and a child?" Arjasu scoffed.

"What else? As I said, reconnaissance first. Then we decide."

The descent was not difficult. Gayel's horned crescent

presently rose to guide them, and they negotiated the boulder-strewn slope by her greenish light.

Trinesh took a last look back to fix the location of their Nexus doorway: from below, the hollow in which they had emerged looked like the lap of an old crone asleep beside a staircase. His clan-mother's slave, Uja, had kept the night watches thus, ostensibly guarding the way up into the loft in which all the children of the Ketkolel lineage slept. Her real task, however, had been to keep them from slipping down again upon various nocturnal escapades. Poor Uja! She had died of some ailment of old age just after he had become a man and moved into the warriors' quarters below. Three of his clan-mothers had contributed a silver *Hlash* or two for her cremation, but there was no memory-niche for her, not for a slave. If he survived this, he vowed to hire a priest to recite the Solace of the All-Embracing Flame in her memory—

Priest? By Lord Vimuhla's Fire! Where was Chekkuru hiVriddi?

He whirled and put the question to the others. No one had seen the man since Arjasu had bundled him into the Nexus portal. They halted in dismay. Was there time in Other-Space? Would Chekkuru awaken to scream and go mad in the alien dark? Would he perish for lack of air? Or would he float, silent and sleeping, until the sun set upon the last day of the world?

No one knew. They dared not go back for him.

Saddened and a little frightened, they plodded on.

The watch-fires were more distant than they had appeared from above. Their elevation was not very high after all, no more than a shapeless, black smudge upon the horizon when Gayel set, and Kashi, the red moon, climbed up into the sky to take her place. Trinesh judged it to be about three hours after half-night when they halted in the shadow of a leaning stone monolith to take stock of the encampment. From their walking pace, he estimated that the sun had been down perhaps two hours when they emerged from the Nexus doorway. The Milumanayani skirmishers employed by both sides made their sorties at just this time, and the sentries would be at their most vigilant. They must approach cautiously or risk being slain before any questions were asked.

Trinesh quickly made his dispositions. Arjasu, their best scout, would reconnoitre, while the others made sure that the Lady Jai, Thu'n, and the boy stayed put and gave no alarm.

The Lady Jai's bare feet were bleeding, and Dineva tore strips from her own tunic to bind them. The Yan Koryani boy added his longer, heavier mantle to Dineva's to keep the girl warm. It was the boy who worried Trinesh: he looked like just the sort of plucky little daredevil who would chance escape and cry a warning. At his age life still seemed so permanent, so durable, so unending! How impossible that anything could cut it short! He reminded Trinesh of himself at a younger age.

By the Flame Lord, he must be getting old, indeed!

They spent a *Kiren* or so watching and listening but heard only the barked watchwords of the sentries, unintelligible at this distance. No music, no singing, no clatter of artisans repairing weapons and accouterments.

This must be a weary army, a grim and determined army—or a defeated one.

From somewhere within the circle of watchfires came a thudding sound, followed by a faint, hushing whisper: artillery, a mangonel, most likely. That meant that the city within the crescent of campfires was unfriendly and under siege. Artillery fired at night usually signified a long leaguer, serving more to demoralize the besieged and make them keep their heads down than to do damage.

"No sieges anywhere near Fortress Ninu'ur," Chosun said. "May be some up by Sunraya. —And no Yan Koryani sieges of our positions that I've heard."

"No help for it." Trinesh replied. "We have to go down in order to find out." He motioned to Arsjasu.

The crossbowman had most of his armor off and was

sifting dust over his curling black locks. Trinesh had never really looked at Arjasu; a soldier was a soldier. Now he saw how handsome the man was: his face resembled one of the God-Emperors portrayed on old coins. Yet there was something incomplete about Arjasu, a dead note, like a *Sra'ur* with a missing string: a cold, closed sort of man, a scroll that could not be read. Surely Arjasu had a clan, a lineage, possibly a family. He was a ten-year veteran, and he might have served other enlistments before this one. Army life warped people, Trinesh thought; war was the most callous and barren mistress a man could have. The humdrum ennui of barracks officialdom, the hardships, the insecurity, the danger, the casual loss of friends: these things hardened a soldier's skin, turned it into a carapace as tough as an *Etla*-crab's, and left the Spirit-Soul a tiny, wary—and often fearful— observer peeping out from within. Arjasu's shell was nearly perfect; it was dubious whether he could now emerge to love anyone or anything. Trinesh' own little inner voice said something, but he did not want to listen.

"Keep these quiet." Arjasu stabbed a finger at their three captives. It was noteworthy that he addressed Dineva rather than Trinesh himself. She was Arjasu's match for simple, cold-blooded soldiering. Dineva made no answer but caressed the blade of the heavy falchion she had picked up from the *Gaichun*'s routed troops.

Tendrils of dawn mist caressed the crossbowman's legs as he tramped away: "Earth-smoke," the soldiers named it.

He was gone for less than a *Kiren*. Then they saw him coming back. He walked erect, and he was alone.

"Who—?" Tse'e began.

"They're Tsolyani, *Hereksa*."

"We can go in then!"

The man's expression cut their jubilation short. "I—don't know. They're Tsolyani. But they're all dead."

"How can that be?" cried Chosun. "Not all, surely! Some may be, but dead man don't tend watchfires!"

Arjasu sat down upon one of the boulders at the base of the stone pillar and laid his crossbow beside him. "Dead, all of them. But not dead." He looked about. "They're undead, *Hereksa*, troops who move and walk and fight but no longer breathe." He uncocked his weapon and put the fat-bodied quarrel back into the leather quiver that hung at his hip. His fingers shook. "They're all dead men."

Trinesh stared around the circle of stunned faces. "Exactly what do you think you saw?" Tales of ghosts and the undead were as common as chaff on a threshing floor in the dormitories of the temple school. The legends of Chmur of the Hands of Gray and Siyenagga the Wanderer of Tombs were enough to make any youthful devotee of bright-burning Lord Vimuhla forgo sleep for a month! Yet they were only tales; nothing in Trinesh's experience had ever indicated otherwise. Certainly not out here, in the midst of a desert, during a war!

Arjasu only shook his head.

"Damn it, man! There may well be corpses over there, perhaps set upon the perimeter to dupe the foe into thinking there are more besiegers than there are—or to make the accursed sand-worms waste arrows. But somebody lit those fires, somebody fueled them, and somebody let fly with a mangonel no more than two *Kiren* ago! Somebody living."

"Not necessarily," Tse'e said slowly. "There are stories— some more myth than history—of undead troops. Emperor Hehejallu, 'the Dark Moon,' and certain others who favored the Dark Trinity of the Lords of Change—Lord Sarku, Lord Hrü'ü, and Lord Ksarul—were said to have made use of them. The two Empresses, Vayuma Su and her daughter Shaira Su, fought what almost amounted to a religious civil war in order to send them back to their crypts beneath the City of Sarku. According to the treaty Empress Shaira Su, 'the Divine Daughter of Thumis,' made with the hierophants of Lord Sarku in 975—"

"Myth indeed! *Chlen*-shit!"

"We have the tale, too!" Thu'n piped. "No more undead,

not under any circumstances, not for any reason. As an historian, I ought to know. Your Empress Shaira Su made it an amendment to the Concordat the Engsvanyali compelled all the Temples to sign in order to keep the peace.''

"—And yet no interference with the inner sanctum of Lord Sarku's great shrine in His own city," Tse'e went on. "The Empress let the undead return there, rather than see the Imperium brought down in chaos!"

"History! Myth! Legend! Stories to make the brown-robes' peasants soil their kilts and pay their tithes!" Trinesh peered uneasily over his shoulder at the watchfires, somehow malignant now and not reassuring at all. "And even so, who would risk breaching an Imperial Edict—or the Concordat of the Temples—to bring them forth here? In Milumanaya?"

"You have never met my youngest nephew," Tse'e answered. "Prince Dhich'une. He fancies himself another Hehejallu or a Kurshetl Nikuma, 'the Viewer of Night'; or perhaps a Tontiken Rirune, 'Slave of Demons' or a Durumu, 'the Copper Blade of Sarku.' Were he to ascend the Petal Throne we would witness more than a legion or two of undead warriors!"

"As the Flame burns pure!" Trinesh snarled. "This cannot be! We marched into Milumanaya through Thri'il and the Pass of Skulls, and we would have heard of such monstrous legions. Yet there were no rumors—nothing!"

"The undead require neither bread nor boots." Tse'e held up a gaunt finger, skeletal enough in the half-light to make Dineva flinch. "They may have traveled overland, through the barrens where neither Tsolyani nor Yan Koryani go—or they may have come sealed in coffins carried on *Chlen*-carts and marked as armor or crossbow quarrels. Lord Sarku's creatures do not care."

"But why?" Dineva's tone told Trinesh that superstitious dread was not limited to worshippers of the Worm Lord.

Unwillingly, he himself saw the glimmer of an answer. "With Prince Eselne in the west, and our own brave Prince

Mirusiya here on the eastern front, what glory is left to Prince Dhich'une? He may want a cup of the stew as well.''

Tse'e nodded.

Chosun grumbled, ''Undead or just corpses, what do *we* do about it?''

The big *Tirrikamu* had a way of striking right to the heart of such practical problems.

''None of the Legions fielded by the Temple of Sarku or His Cohort, Lord Durritlamish, has artillery,'' Tse'e pondered.

''So any artillery Cohorts must be from some other unit?'' Trinesh took up the thought. ''Living troops?''

''Probably still friendly to Lord Sarku's cause, but alive. Yes.''

''Bring the *Nininyal*, the Lady Jai, and the boy. There's nowhere else to go. We can't walk off blindly into the desert.—And I think we've lost the Lady Deq Dimani and her creature.'' That meant no promotions, no rewards, and much explaining, but at least they were alive and hopefully close to people who might aid them. The besiegers were still Tsolyani, whatever God they worshipped, and that meant living masters someplace in the camp. He beckoned to Dineva. ''Where's Arjasu?''

''He prays,'' the woman said. ''Shouldn't you?''

They skirted the sprawling encampment. Its silence now seemed due to something other than sleep, and they walked as warily as though in the presence of the Worm Lord Himself. From a distance they could see the sentries, cloaked, motionless, watchful, and grim. Were the passwords they called formed with living lips, or were they uttered with the aid of the darker energies of the Planes Beyond? ''Earth-smoke'' flowed along the hollows to hide their features, as did the visors of their horned helmets, but Trinesh imagined that he saw the white of bone, the gray of mortifying flesh, and the cerements of the tomb. The devotees of Lord Sarku painted their faces bone-white, he knew, and those men might well be living, weary soldiers, fellows with clans and families, dozing, cold, and dreaming of home.

Yet as they drew nearer he did not think so. Arjasu was too good a scout.

"There, *Hereksa*!" Chosun crowed. "That man—he's different! His helmet has another sort of crest! And he's moving, scratching himself!"

"I see him too."

Another thump and a hiss came, much nearer now, and they watched the great stone ball fly up to glitter for a moment in the dawning sun, arc, and descend again. There was a distant crash.

"Ohe! Hoi! Tsolyani!" Dineva did not wait for a command. "We are Tsolyani!"

Heads popped up. The sentry raised a curve-bladed sword. Someone shouted, and others replied. A man bearing a torch, unneeded now in the charcoal dawnlight, left his post to gaze out at them from behind a round leather shield.

"Who are you? Your Legion?"

"Trinesh hiKetkolel, *Hereksa* of the Legion of the Storm of Fire. And you?"

"The Legion of Mengano the Jakallan," the other called back. "Twelfth Imperial Artillery. —Come forth and we don't skewer you!"

Never had the soft and lilting accents of Jakalla sounded so sweet.

The crowd had grown to a good three score before they reached the headquarters tent. Some cried questions; others pointed and plucked at the unfamiliar armor Trinesh and his companions wore; and a few offered *Chumetl*—the salted and hot-spiced buttermilk preferred in Tsolyanu—wine, water, and food. They halted to salute the tall *Kaing*, the plumed standard of their hosts' Legion, in the center of the tent-square, just behind the first rows of squat ballistae and square-framed mangonels.

Then the sentries led them inside, into canvas-smelling dimness.

The man who arose to greet them was a *Kasi*, a captain of a Cohort. He had the straight, delicately modeled nose and fleshy lips of a southerner: almost feminine, were it not for his square-cut black beard. Trinesh judged his age at about forty summers by the threads of white in his hair and the silvery patches at both temples. He was a career soldier—his stained leather tunic and scuffed campaign boots attested to that—and he had obviously just arisen. At the moment he was scrabbling about among the welter of documents that overflowed from the rickety camp table in the center of his tent.

"Direnja hiVayeshtu of the Green Malachite clan," the officer said, once Trinesh had introduced himself and his three troopers. "I have the honor of being the *Kasi* of the fourth Cohort of the Legion of Mengano the Jakallan. I find no dispatch announcing a visit from Storm of Fire." He smacked his lips ruefully. "Not that headquarters might remember to send me any. Have you reported yet to General Qutmu?"

"Sire?"

"General Qutmu. Qutmu hiTsizena, the new general of the Battalions of the Seal of the Worm, the Ninth Medium Infantry."

"I thought—"

"That old Qurrumu hiKhanuma was still in charge? He retired last year to tend his worm-crop in the City of Sarku, and Prince Dhich'une popped this toady of his into the slot. General Qutmu's in command of this miserable siege."

"Uh, yes, Sire." The *Kasi* was looking at him expectantly, and Trinesh stumbled on. "We're from Fortress Ninu'ur, Sire. We were lost in the desert, and now we seek to rejoin our unit." How much would this prosaic-looking artilleryman believe?

Direnja hiVayeshtu eyed them keenly. "Not deserters? I've nothing against you, and I'd hate to turn you over to Qutmu's wormy lads! But there are some—" he glanced toward the back of the tent "—who take considerable joy in watching the impalement of deserters."

"No, Sire. We fought the Yan Koryani at Fortress Ninu'ur, took it, and then became—ah—separated from the rest of our folk."

"Cha! Whatever." Direnja hiVayeshtu gave his scrolls a last desultory poke. "Well, you won't find 'em here at Pu'er."

"Pu'er?"

"Pu'er, *Hereksa*!" Dineva murmured. "Didn't somebody lay siege to Pu'er last year? I don't think it fell, though."

"Ai, Pu'er." The *Kasi* scowled, made a ring of thumb and forefinger, peered through it in the direction of the city, and spat. The obscene gesture conveyed a great deal. "Seal of the Worm and Scales of Brown—two of Lord Sarku's best Legions—tried to take it and failed. No artillery, no engines, and no timber anywhere within two hundred *Tsan* to make 'em. Stupidity! They gave up. They ate their supplies, ate the forage, ate the bodies of the dead, ate the peasants and all their children to boot—and left!" He slapped a palm upon the table. "Left it to us, the proper folk, to finish. Artillery and sappers. General Mengano sent us out from Thri'il, and we've a Cohort of Vrishtara the Mole's diggers over yonder behind the mangonels. We'll crack the nut, and then their undead—" he flicked a quizzical eye at Trinesh. "—You've seen, eh? You know? Fa! Their dirty undead can clean up the job and bring greater glory to the Petal Throne thereby!"

"Ask them where they acquired their armor," another voice asked, a woman's. Trinesh had not seen her reclining upon the *Kasi*'s sleeping mat in the shadows behind him. She sat up, stretched, and began wrapping an emerald-green skirt about her ample hips. Little silver chains jangled at her wrists and ankles, and her slightly slanted eyes still bore streaks of black *Tsunu*-paste.

Trinesh knew a devotee of Lady Dlamelish when he saw

one. The most sensual of the five Lords of Change of Pavar's pantheon, the Goddess loved the pleasures of the body and the hedonistic Now above all else. This woman was neither young nor old, a bit too plump for Trinesh' taste (a picture of poor Saina flickered among his thoughts), and much given to paints, powders, and strong perfumes. She lifted her loose, heavy tresses to clasp a collar of green-dyed *Chlen*-hide about her throat; its glyphs and symbols indicated a priestess of some sort, probably of one of the junior Circles.

"Ah, yes. Your armor." The *Kasi* raked them all with another glance.

"Took it from a cache we found at Fortress Ninu'ur, Sire," Trinesh improvised. No one would argue that: it was steel, far more costly than the harness issued by his Legion. He made out the glint of a tiny turquoise phallus on a silver chain at the captain's throat; the man, too, was a worshipper of the Emerald Goddess—or of Her Cohort, Lady Hrihayal. Both deities loved the pleasures of the senses. This *Kasi*, of all people, ought to sympathize with a rich bit of plunder!

Direnja hiVayeshtu grinned. "You've just these three soldiers, *Hereksa*?"

"Yes, Sire. We lost a few."

"But you picked up a few trinkets, eh? The armor? This girl? Yan Koryani, by the look of her."

"The maid of the enemy commandant at Fortress Ninu'ur," Trinesh replied easily. "The boy's a slave—useful."

"As you say. And the old man? —And that? The *Nininyal?*"

"The man's Tsolyani, a hermit who helped us in the desert. The other's a scholar of some kind. Surrendered and offered to join our side. We were taking him to General Kutume, Sire."

"Would you sell the girl?" the woman purred. "One of our senior priestesses, the Lady Anka'a hiQolyelmu, is at Kankara, just up the road, on her way to take charge of our temple in Sunraya. She'd like her."

The *Kasi* showed white teeth in a broader smile. "Save

religion for later, Mashyan! Sex and sacrifices after breakfast!
These folk have journeyed a long way. I'm not sure, but I
think Fortress Ninu'ur lies about a hundred and forty *Tsan*
southwest of here.''

The woman, Mashyan, went to the Lady Jai, pulled her
two cloaks aside, ran emerald-lacquered nails over the girl's
limbs, and admired her openly. She exclaimed at the strips of
bloody cloth Dineva had used to wrap her feet.

''A long walk through the desert, dear! We must remedy
that. Scars will spoil your value. Does she speak Tsolyani?''

Trinesh fixed the rest of his party with a warning eye.
''Not much. I'd not wish to sell her, though—a gift for my
clan-sisters. Uh, Sire, you did mention food?''

The *Kasi* shouted, and orderlies hurried in with *Chumetl*,
cakes of fresh-baked *Dna*-bread, a bronze cauldron of fiery-
spiced Jakallan stew, and the remains of a haunch of *Hmelu*.
He watched while Trinesh allocated eating places to his party.
The Tsolyani might not be as fastidious as the lords of ancient
Mihallu, but it was still mandatory to eat upon daises set in
tiers according to one's rank, even if these were no more than
several layers of carpets, a stairstep arrangement of earthen
platforms, or squares scratched upon the bare ground. This
was important, therefore: a gaffe here might just convince the
Kasi that they were deserters, unfamiliar with the usages of
Trinesh's Red Mountain clan. Too big a mistake, and they
could be hauled off as spies.

Direnja hiVayeshtu himself squatted crosslegged upon his
sleeping mat, the highest of the impromptu daises; Trinesh
and the priestess, Mashyan hiSagai, decided that their status
was about equal and seated themselves upon the carpet underneath the mat, the next lowest; then came Chosun upon the
rough reed matting that underlay the carpet, and below him
upon a raised section of the earthen floor were Arjasu and
Dineva. The others were relegated to the still lower area near
the entrance of the tent. Trinesh was relieved that Tse'e made
no objection; it would be hard to explain the presence of an

unknown Prince of the Imperium, the half-brother of the Seal
Emperor himself, to this simple artilleryman!

The food was plain camp fare, but to Trinesh it was a
banquet. The esoteric delicacies of Mihallu were as dead
leaves when compared with these familiar dishes. They ate
hugely, while Direnja hiVayeshtu and his priestess looked on.

Trinesh wondered whether the *Kasi* still suspected them to
be deserters. He did not press the matter, but his remark
about General Qutmu hiTsizena was worrisome: sooner or
later they would have to report. Only the senior commander
could grant them permission to leave for Kankara or wherever
General Kutume and their Legion were currently reputed to
be.

Then there was the Flame-damned priestess. Her basilisk-
gaze never left the Lady Jai. She might want the girl for
herself—devotees of the Emerald Goddess and Her Cohort
were given to such predilections—but Trinesh doubted it. A
very pretty, noble, captive maiden made an excellent offering, and had not Mashyan hiSagai mentioned the Lady Anka'a
hiQolyelmu? Even in Tumissa Trinesh had heard of that one:
second or third in the Empire after their High Priestess, the
Lady Timuna hiReretlesa, was she not? And devoted to very
odd rituals? A nice gift to her could mean a rung or two up on
the ladder of promotion within the Temple.

His little inner voice fussily insisted upon drawing a parallel
between that last thought and Trinesh's own plans for the
Lady Deq Dimani. He glowered to himself and forced his
attention back to what the *Kasi* was saying.

"—There's room in the guest-tent." Direnja hiVayeshtu
wiped his fingers upon the little towel the orderly held out to
him. "We've had only a courier or two during the past
month. Nobody of any consequence since the end of last
year."

"The end—?" Trinesh was confused.

"Ai, since the Emperor's Accession-day on the tenth of
Dohala."

This could not be! "Sire, what—uh—is the date? We've been in the desert a long time."

Direnja hiVayeshtu exchanged glances with his priestess. 'Um—today's the eighteenth, I think. The eighteenth of Shapru."

Dineva gasped, and Chosun cried, "The year?"

Puzzlement and suspicion successively crossed the *Kasi*'s bearded features. "Why, 2,362, of course. You couldn't have been out in the wilderness *very* long. Without provisions?"

"Five months—and more," Arjasu whispered. "How? It was Pardan when we left! We spent only a night in Na Ngore, several hours in the tubeway car—a six-day or so in Mihallu."

"The Nexus Point," Thu'n cried shrilly. "Sometimes they open into the same place but across the Planes of Time! We're only lucky that we didn't come out farther up or down the timeline!"

"Deserters!" Mashyan tossed her black locks and shrieked with delighted laughter. "La! I guessed it! You've no choice now, love! Everybody saw these rogues come in, and General Qutmu'll feed your eyeballs to his worms if you don't turn them over to the guards!"

"No—no, we're—" Trinesh stammered. Oh, to the icy hells with it! "Sire, please listen to me. You won't believe our story, but I swear by Lord Vimuhla's Eighty-Seven Greater Aspects that what I say is true!"

He was right. Neither Direnja hiVayeshtu nor the priestess Mashyan hiSagai believed a word of his tale. At least the *Kasi* had the decency to display a little regret when the soldiers came to lead them away.

19

The Lady Jai Chasa Vedlan strolled gracefully across the sun-baked square in front of the slaves' stockade. Ridek watched her stoop to enter the Tsolyani *Kasi*'s tent. She wore an ankle-length skirt and a short blouse, both green and both very becoming, given her by the priestess Mashyan hiSagai.

She seemed to have gone over completely to the enemy. He spat a thick globule into the dust.

Three days he had spent grieving for Aluja and the Lady Deq Dimani, then another three pining for Ke'er and his family. Thereafter he strove to shut off the tears and force himself to accept the unhappy present. He did not succeed, of course. One six-day was not enough, nor was one year, nor even one aeon. Yet his tutors had praised the resilience of the young, and they had not been wrong. The noble children of Yan Kor were steeped in fortitude, endurance, and patience; those three stepping stones lay at the threshold of the "Way of Nchel." He would recover, and he would live, whether as the son of the Baron of Yan Kor or as a slave who cleaned latrines and ate offal.

Ridek Chna Ald was determined to survive. He was also resolute in his intention to escape. The Weaver of Skeins would have to be dissuaded somehow from using the drab threads of slavery to make Ridek's tapestry!

The Lady Jai had apparently taken the easy road: sleep with the Tsolyani *Kasi* or with the slatternly bawd who passed for a priestess—or both—and lick the scraps from their plates. Let her! She might come of noble lineages, but she apparently lacked courage. Ridek would waste no tears upon her.

The life of a slave was hard, far more onerous than the tasks and tests his father's teachers had set him. Ridek's hands and feet blistered, bled, and hardened, and he thought his bones would crack with the endless digging of saps and trenches. His fellow prisoners would have covered for him, he knew, and even the Tsolyani guards might wink at an extra rest period down in the pits where their officers could not see. He was stubborn in this, too, however: he would do his share and ask no favors. Would his father have done less?

Vrishtara the Mole's overseers were not harsh, as slave-masters in the Five Empires went, but they did demand a healthy return on the crusts of bread and brackish water they invested in their prisoners. The Yan Koryani and Saa Allaqiyani soldiers were accustomed to toil; most had been peasants at home and knew what it was to sweat. They were thus little different from the Milumanayani villagers who had eked out a bare subsistence in this awful land before the war. Those poor creatures, too, worked without protest. The nomadic tribesmen of the Desert of Sighs were another matter; they worked and died, or they refused to work and died anyway. For them the end was the same.

Unfortunately, it was not quite the end for everyone. That was the terrible part of it.

Ridek had not believed the senior Yan Koryani officer

among the prisoners, a *Ghitaa* of a *Tlümrik* of five hundred, the equivalent of the Tsolyani *Kasi* of a Cohort. This man, Shekka Va Kriyor, told him that those who died were used as food.

"The undead eat the corpses?" Ridek cried.

"Not the undead," the *Ghitaa* replied somberly. "Those eat nothing. It is the living who enjoy a haunch of red meat now and then: the fiends of Lord Sarku's Battallions of the Seal of the Worm—and sometimes of the Legion of the Scales of Brown as well. The custom is ancient in the Kraa Hills around the City of Sarku. As the worms consume corpses in the tomb at the behest of the Worm Lord, so do His two-legged devotees. It is ceremonial, a ritual of identity with their deity."

Ridek was revolted to the core of his being. Thereafter he remained in the midst of the crowd of prisoners whenever the soldiers in brown-lacquered armor and skull-helmets came to inspect their captives. Some were taken away, and they were not seen again.

Later Ridek inquired further from Shekka Va Kriyor. "They do not make them—us—into undead, then?"

"No, boy," the man said. "It's no easy process to make a dead man walk. It's an honor, moreover, for a warrior of Lord Sarku's faith to return and fight for Him again. They don't take others—except as sacrifices."

"But what joy can there be in joining the undead: to shamble mindlessly along, to eat nothing, to live a half-life of bare awareness?"

"Such are only the lowest of the Worm Lord's servants: the *Mrur* and the *Shedra*. A favored minion is made into a *Jajqi*, a creature possessing intelligence, a will, and certain other powers. A *Jajqi* may live—as they speak of life—forever. Consciousness, the survival of the intellect, and the preservation of one's powers: these are the promises Lord Sarku dangles before His followers."

"But—but not to come forth by day, not to be accepted

among the living—to dwell always amid bones and sepul-
chres . . . !''

"Oh, the undead can indeed walk in daylight—you'll see
them when General Qutmu orders the assault upon Pu'er.
They do not like the light, but they can function in it. Folk
say that a *Jajqi* can imitate the living to such a degree that
you would not know he—it—was dead. They move freely
among us." Shekka Va Kriyor chuckled. "Within the Inner
Citadel of the City of Sarku there are many *Jajqi*, and they
are said to be more honored there than the living."

Ridek shuddered and went back to digging with renewed
vigor in the trench he had been assigned.

The long line of mangonels behind him fired another volley, their thick, vertical beams thudding against the leather-
padded rests in a cadenced drum-roll. The stones, rough-hewn
into balls by the masons, whistled overhead, and even their
Tsolyani guards ducked. Ridek raised his head to watch the
dust-clouds rise from the dun-hued city wall across the dry
fosse some two hundred paces away. Last night Oghan Chai
Vidur, who had once served as an artilleryman in the *Gurek*
of the Clan of the Second Moon, said that the wall would fall
within three days. He and some others of the prisoners wa-
gered breadcrusts upon the exact hour.

And then what? Ridek straightened up, leaned on his crude
mattock, and ran a dry tongue over cracked lips. The sappers
would withdraw, the creaking siege towers would trundle
forward, and this trench he was digging would swarm with
armored soldiers, some living and some otherwise, on their
way to make the final assault.

One after another, the big stone-throwing ballistae on Ridek's
left hissed and vomited destruction at the city. He dived into
the trench. The crossbow-like contraptions fired smaller balls
than the mangonels, but their trajectories were flatter and
hence more perilous to anyone in their path. The little bolt-
firing ballistae were silent this morning; the garrison of Pu'er
no longer put their heads up to provide targets.

"Hoi!" their leather-armored guard shouted. "Work! Dig!" Those words and some cheerful obscenities were all the Yan Koryani he knew.

Ridek dusted off the remains of the *Gaichun*'s elegant green tunic. He had paid the price for his brief sojourn as a prince! When the *Kasi* had first ordered him thrown into the slave pen, he had almost been stripped of this garment by his fellows. He had speedily learned that there is no aristocracy among slaves. It did not matter that the tunic was cut in Engsvanyali fashion and was neither Yan Koryani nor Saa Allaqiyani. It identified him as one of the soft officers' sons who went on to become staff officers in the Baron's army. He had met their ilk so many times at his father's court that he tended to sympathize with the rough, simple soldiers. A few of the female captives had made him different offers for his tunic, too, and were it not for Shekka Va Kriyor, he might have ended as somebody's fancy boy!

A poor Skein that would have been for Ridek Chna Ald!

The *Ghitaa* had taken pity upon his youth and inexperience—there was no other explanation for it—and had included him in his circle of lesser officers and older troopers. Ridek had enough sense not to divulge his true name. The ransom of a son of the Baron of Yan Kor would make any Tsolyani rich, and the sacrifice of such a prize would doubtless rejoice their Gods and hasten their victory. He dared not confide in anyone, not even Shekka Va Kriyor: there were probably spies in the stockade, while others might sell him for freedom—or even a breadcrust. Henceforth he was Dokku Khessa Tiu to his own folk as well as to his captors. He hoped that his ancestors in the Paradises would pardon the deception; his personal servant in Ke'er, whose name and lineages he thus borrowed, would not mind.

The Lady Jai emerged from the *Kasi*'s gray canvas tent in the company of the priestess Mashyan. The two women picked their way along behind the mangonels where the artillerymen strained at their winches. They paused before the wooden cage in which the Tsolyani who had brought them from Mihallu were imprisoned. Ridek was too far away to see, but he thought that the Lady Jai spoke to the man—the *Hereksa*.

The fate of those four was even less appetizing than Ridek's. General Qutmu's staff had swiftly condemned them as deserters, after which General Vrishtara's sappers erected a cage and four stakes in the square before the headquarters tent. The impalements were delayed, however, to await the arrival of professional executioners from Kankara. One of Ridek's fellow captives, Kai Vrishn Tlarik, who had lived in Tsolyani before the war, said that there was some special clan, devoted to Lord Vimuhla's ferocious Cohort, Lord Chiteng, which performed this function for all felons in the Empire. It was a matter of religion as well as of the state: the executioners worked always in parties of four because of some obscure doctrinal reason, and no one else was permitted to impale a criminal. General Qutmu had fumed, rumor had it, and demanded swifter justice, but the *Kasi* of artillery—whose Legion's prisoners they technically were—held out for the strict observance of legal protocol. The wretched *Hereksa* and his three soldiers thus had perhaps two more days to live.

Ridek had not seen either Tse'e or Thu'n after the *Kasi* had ordered them arrested. The old man was Tsolyani but neither soldier nor slave; there was no charge against him, therefore, and he had probably wandered away into the desert or found acceptance among the artisans and camp-followers who hovered about the army like *Chri*-flies. The *Nininyal*, on the other hand, had been taken somewhere else.

Where Aluja—poor Aluja—and the Lady Deq Dimani were he had no idea at all.

The afternoon passed in a blaze of early spring heat. A volley of fire, followed by shouts and jests as the city's defenses crumbled, then silence. Then another volley. The crenellations were gone, and plumes of dust drifted up from the wall below. Even from this range Ridek could see cracks and fissures spread across the masonry like a network of tree roots. A thump, a crash, and the Tsolyani artillerymen whooped and cheered. The tents off to Ridek's right remained silent; somewhere over there the undead waited, as patient as the Worm Lord Himself, for the clarion that would summon them forth.

The work-party returned to the stockade at sundown, passing the second shift on its way to carry on their task by torchlight. The pen stank of sweat and excrement. Ridek knew better than to fight for the chunks of *Dna*-bread the Tsolyani cook threw over the palisade into the enclosure. He waited, and at last a pale Saa Allaqiyani youth tossed him a thick red-brown crust. The fellow had favored him before, and Ridek suspected that eventually payment would be demanded in a coin he had no intention of giving. He responded with a curt shrug of thanks and was relieved when Shekka Va Kriyor came over to sit beside him.

"Tomorrow, boy," the *Ghitaa* said. "Then we sit back and watch 'em go over the walls and fight like *Ghar*-lizards mating in a riverbed." He showed chipped, yellow teeth in an uneven grin. Shekka Va Kriyor was as homely as a clay idol, a tenant farmer from Tleku Miriya in eastern Yan Kor. He had been wounded in the face at the first Battle of Mar, and the scar where his left ear and part of his cheek had been gave him an appearance not unlike one of the undead themselves.

"Afterward?"

The older man let out a long breath. "They take me back to Tsolyanu, I guess. A field-slave—not pretty enough to be a house servant. Maybe somebody'll buy me for sacrifice. Then I'll see how well I've learned our 'Way of Nchel.' I've thought a lot about it. . . ."

Ridek did *not* want to think about it. He asked, "The rest of us?"

Shekka Va Kriyor rubbed his stubbled chin. "You must

have clan. I saw from the first that you're no poor farm bumpkin. Tell the Tsolyani that your people will ransom you. The greedy bastards'll ship you home in the next exchange.''

"Why? When you and so many others are enslaved or slain! Why should I be otherwise? Should I not seek the 'Way of Nchel' too?''

"Cha! You're too young. A long life. Home. Your clan-mothers'll find you a wife or two.'' The *Ghitaa* stirred restlessly, a shadowy hulk in the gathering dusk. "Now Besa there, the little girl from my *Gurek*, she'd want you.''

Ridek was grateful for the reassurance of the man's jibe. "She'll have to wait in line.'' He smiled back. "I've my own plans.''

"Then live 'em, boy. No 'Way of Nchel' for you!''

They sat together in silence for a time. Then the *Ghitaa* said, "Escape. That's another Skein.''

"I'd chance it.''

"Look, you. The desert is as much death for us as it is for the Tsolyani. The sand-worms'll gladly slay us both. Still. . . .''

"When? How?''

Shekka Va Kriyor seized Ridek's face in one callused vise of a hand and pulled him around to peer into his eyes. The stink of his breath—or of the still festering wound in his jaw—was sickening. "Hoi, hoi! A word to the Tsolyani and we're meat on the Sarku lads' platters! One whisper, and you're spitted first!'' He relaxed his grip. "Your clothes, your hands, your fine speech all say you're somebody's son. Somebody important. Now that doesn't move me the length of a *Shqa*-beetle's tiny twig, but I've five brats at home your size, and it's them I remember whenever I look at you, boy. Why your *Chlen*-brained parents let you join the army makes me wonder! —And may the gods give the Baron Ald Ahoggya piss to drink for starting this buggering war!''

Ridek almost laughed. "He'd probably like that. As for me, I can take care—''

"Of what? Your pretty arse? The target of that plummy

Saa Allaqiyani dildo over there! Him and a dozen others, were it not for me and my troopers!"

"I—I thank you—"

"Cha! Thank the gods instead. Just be nearby when I shout."

They curled up on the dry sand to sleep. The Saa Allaqiyani importuned Ridek with delicate gestures and whispered something sibilant in his singing language, reminding Ridek of the Tka Mihalli of Ninue. Shekka Va Kriyor gave the youth a look that would have withered a *Sro*-dragon, and he went away.

Lanterns flared amber to dazzle his eyes. He awoke to find three of Vrishtara's barrel-chested guards opening the crude wooden gate. A fourth man stood there, an officer, possibly a *Kasi*, in gleaming brown-lacquered armor. The visored, flanged helmet bore a skull-crest of bleached *Chlen*-hide.

He burrowed down behind the *Ghitaa*'s massive torso.

"Why now of all times?" he heard one guard complain. Ridek's Tsolyani had improved enough to follow the simple exchange.

"Here is my—" the officer used an unknown word. Copper-trimmed vambraces flashed yellow-orange in the buttery glow.

The other held out a hand, received a document, and pretended to read. He was probably no more literate than a sand-worm! "Over there, I think."

The guards picked their way across the compound, halberd butts at the ready.

"Here. Behind that man." The officer's bony finger pointed straight at Ridek.

"No! Damn it," the turnkey protested. "The boy? There's a lot of work left in that one—Sire."

"Read."

Shekka Va Kriyor loomed up before them. "Take me instead," he stammered in broken Tsolyani. "Me, I go. Bigger. Better! Tasty!"

The skull-painted face beneath the helmet rim only grinned. "The boy."

Shekka Va Kriyor moved, and the halberds jabbed at him. "Not the boy! No boy!" he roared. And charged.

It was no contest. The sapper guards yelled for reinforcements, the big Yan Koryani fell like a *Tiu*-tree beneath their clubbed weapons, and the rest of the prisoners shuffled back out of danger. A soldier pulled Ridek to his feet, kicked him efficiently, and jerked his hands up behind him. He felt the bite of thongs about his wrists.

Then he was dragged out into the tent-lined square.

Torches, lanterns, passwords, a whirl of shadows around leaping watchfires, dust, and the stink of fear. His own fear. Someone rose up before him, another death's-head, and he heard an exchange of salutes.

They bore him past the bivouac of the Battalions of the Seal of the Worm, past General Qutmu's elegant tent with its lanterns of copper and sepia-hued glass, past the areas between the tent-rows where dun-armored troopers squatted to sharpen their weapons, past the *Chlen*-carts and the jumbled, tarpaulin-shrouded supply dumps.

Into a place that was silent: tents in which nothing moved, watchfires that lacked the throngs of raucous soldiers and whores about them, empty camp streets that were unlittered and unlighted.

And dead.

Dim shapes sat around those fires, to be sure. He saw helmets that had been old when the Second Imperium was young, upcurved pauldrons of rusting steel, capes and mantles streaked with grave-hoar, spears and glaives and pikes and other weapons of designs so antique that they no longer had names, and shields embossed with dread Lord Sarku's wriggling, serpentine worm. He smelled rot and decay, not strong, but omnipresent, the sweet-sick stench of things long entombed. There were faces, too: most were skeletal and fleshless, but some still showed bloated and gray, stamped with the rictus of death—and of unnatural life.

Ridek screamed.

"Enough," his captor snarled. "I take him from here." He halted at one of the watchfires, its light spilling from his mailed shoulders like rich, red blood.

He heard mutters of willing, uneasy assent and the tramp of retreating boots.

Then he was alone, with the undead all around him.

His captor spun him about, and he felt a knife nibbling at his bonds. Over his shoulder he saw the man lift off his copper-chaised skull-helmet with his other hand. The face beneath it was very similar to that of the young Tsolyani *Hereksa*, Trinesh hiKetkolel.

Ridek gaped. Then the nose lengthened, the eyes spread apart, the jaw grew longer, the skin darker. Fangs emerged to project like downward-curving scimitars over blackish lips.

It was Aluja.

One of the dark-shrouded undead arose from the motionless group seated about the fire and limped toward him.

"Here's the Lady," Aluja said. "She's wounded. We must get her to—"

Ridek did not hear the rest; his cries made even General Qutmu's staff officers look up from their dinners.

Aluja shook his beast-head in frustration. "I never know how much you humans can bear! We Mihalli have no fear of dead bodies, not even when animated by power from the Planes Beyond. Such entities are naught but multi-planar foci within the continuum."

"Jargon!" the Lady Deq Dimani snapped. "You could have used some gentler method of getting him out of the Tsolyani slave pen!" She kept one arm about Ridek but favored the other beneath the tattered blue-black cloak she wore. Aluja had taken the garment from one of the uncomplaining undead; it stank, and there were dark-crusted stains upon its folds.

"How? I can fool humans in a marketplace, a crowd, or wherever there are foreigners and strangers. But an army? I don't know their passwords or salutes or—or anything. I had no time to master the background. Nor is my Tsolyani native enough: more than a barked command, and somebody'd want a look. The next thing would be one more Yan Koryani spy wriggling on a stake!"

"Where—how—?" Ridek managed. He was growing calmer.

The Lady murmured something soothing, but Aluja intervened. "He's ready to talk—stronger than you think: less than I had guessed but more than you credit him."

"He's only a child!"

The Mihalli spared her a critical glance. "How little you know the capacities of your own species, Madam. Now if you had children of your own. . . ."

He was not prepared for the furious glare she flung at him.

"We Mihalli are hermaphrodites," Aluja protested mildly. "I have myself given birth to two children—and fathered others. I do not understand!"

She clenched her teeth. "There are other matters to discuss. As soon as Ridek is able."

The boy hugged himself tightly to keep his hands from trembling. He said, "I'm all right now. How do we get out of this camp?"

"See? I—" Aluja thought better of his comment just in time.

She faced the boy. "Leaving's easy. Some garments from—from these poor creatures, Aluja as a Tsolyani officer, a password overheard, and we're out."

Ridek arose to peer anxiously at the silent warriors seated about the watchfire behind her. "They—they do not see us? They do not object if we—you—take their clothing?"

"No. They are the lowest form of the undead: *Mrur*. A few are *Shedra*, who are a trifle more aware. They respond to commands from their officers, the *Jajqi*, Lord Sarku's elite."

"I—I know. Someone else told me."

"So. We must avoid the *Jajqi*, for they are as clever as they were in life." She hugged her wounded arm to her breast and rocked to and fro.

Ridek noticed her injury for the first time. "How badly are you hurt?"

"Not much. A crossbow quarrel through my pauldron and into the shoulder-muscle."

"She must have help," Aluja contradicted her. "I thought we might obtain it within Pu'er. Last night I crept past the Tsolyani siege lines into the city, but the garrison has neither food nor medical supplies. Their sorcerers save their healing magic for the battle to come."

"They refused? They won't help us?"

"They would—gladly. But they urged us not to enter Pu'er. If the Tsolyani mount an assault, we might not get out again."

"Find a Nexus Point," Ridek suggested earnestly. "Use your powers! Return us to Ke'er!"

The Mihalli shook his alien head. "I no longer can. I have never seen the like of that weapon the Tsolyani employed there in Ninue. I can change my shape, but the rest of my energies are drained as empty as a drunkard's flagon! I am like a child—a human. I do feel my strength seeping back, but very, very slowly."

"The 'Eye' you took back from me? Your globe-thing? My staff—it did not deflect the crossbowman's bolt after the *Hereksa* fired his device at me."

"All are depleted, useless. My 'Ball of Immediate Eventuation' is a dead cinder somewhere on the floor of the Hall of the Elliptical Veil."

"The—Nexus doorway through which we came?"

"Gone. They do not remain long. Now I can only sense Nexus Points, not summon them—not until I am more recovered."

"We must try for my brother's encampment," the Lady

Deq Dimani interrupted. "He and his *Gurek* are somewhere north of the *Sakbe* road, in the mountains behind Kankara."

"But you are wounded. Can you travel?"

"She thinks she can," Aluja said curtly. "She is determined."

"Of course. I am a soldier, after all. I have endured wounds before!"

The Mihalli cocked his head. "The Tsolyani supply carts come and go. It's about sixty *Tsan* from here to Kankara: four days' journey. An injured soldier woman—a foreign mercenary, mayhap? —a captive slave-boy, and perhaps a merchant from neutral Mu'ugalavya or Salarvya. Some of these sad undead still wear the ornaments of the tomb: armlets of gold, collars, necklaces, amulets. We can easily glean enough to pay some carter or suttler."

"It is Kankara or surrender, Ridek," the Lady Deq Dimani said. "You know what that means."

He did, in all its dreadful reality. "Can we find your brother and his *Gurek*?"

"We must. Aluja tells me that there may also be other Mihalli at Kankara. We have agents in the Tsolyani camp there."

"If I can find them, we are gone," the Mihalli said. "Home, Ridek!"

"There's someone I must rescue first," he declared. "From the Tsolyani prison stockade—a *Ghitaa* named Shekka Va Kriyor. Wait—why him alone? We can help them all escape!"

Aluja only looked at him.

"We cannot," the Lady said regretfully. "You are no Hrugga of the epics, Ridek. You are more important than a *Gurek* of good troops. No, do not gainsay me! Think, and you'll realize why."

It was true.

"Then we depart." Aluja stood up to readjust his disguise.

"There is something I must do, however," the Lady added casually. "The rumor you heard in the camp market—about the gift the priestess Mashyan makes to her superior in Kankara?

If the Yan Koryani girl is really the Lady Jai, then I cannot abandon her.''

"You mean that you will not. I think I can guess your purpose.''

The Lady Deq Dimani wrinkled her nose at the redolence of death that clung to her cloak. ''It will take but a little time—long enough to give an instruction.''

"We cannot stop to play dangerous games!''

"I plan no such. Only a word or two with the harvester when the crop is ripe.''

The Mihalli shook his head so violently that his masquerade slipped, leaving his face an unpleasant mixture of human eyes and nose but an elongated Mihalli fanged jaw. ''No, I say! A quick look for another Mihalli at Kankara. That is all! If we find no one, then we seek your brother's troops.'' He turned away to repair his features.

Ridek considered; then he said, ''I agree with Aluja. Neither Shekka Va Kriyor nor any missions at Kankara. Not now. First you must be healed, Lady, and I—I would return to Ke'er. I am a Prince of Yan Kor and my father's son. This is my command.''

Aluja smiled at the Lady Deq Dimani over the boy's black head, a look that held more of respect than amusement.

In answer she only bared her teeth and wound the grave-stained cloak the tighter about her wounded arm.

20

O n the following morning, the twenty-ninth of Shapru, a
section of the ramparts of Pu'er gave one last despairing,
dust-choked, mumbling, roar and collapsed into the fosse.

The camp came alive. Trumpets bawled, soldiers streamed
past the cage in which Trinesh and his companions were
imprisoned, artisans scrambled about, bearing ladders and
mantlets and heavy-bladed axes, and the slaves, servants and
camp-followers scurried to get out of the way.

As the sun thrust up above the haze the Legions' sorcerers
took their places upon the wooden platform General Vrishtara's
sappers had built for them, divided themselves into their
offensive and defensive contingents with much good-natured
raillery, and awaited orders. Each Legion fielded its party of
trained military spell-casters. All of an army-group's special-
ists operated together as one powerful unit during a battle:
half erected a defensive shield over their own troops, inciden-
tally damping out all personal magic and even those devices
powered by energies from the Planes Beyond; the other half

then collaborated to probe and smash through the enemy's shields with destructive spells. Battlefield sorcery tended to be quite spectacular—and very terrible if pressure and exhaustion caused one's shields to fail. Trinesh well remembered the skies above the battlefield at Mar: flickering, lowering lightnings of sparkling scarlet; miasmas of demoralizing fear; clouds of noxious gases; and illusions of demons and horrors designed to confuse and terrify. None of these things could do real harm as long as the defensive shields held. He knew of unpleasant historical occasions where they had not.

Sorcery was of vital importance to siegecraft in the Five Empires also. Without protective wall-spells, a city would quickly find itself with no fortifications left. The temples charged exorbitantly for the process, but thereafter a town's defenses were proof against personal spells, devices employing forces from the Planes Beyond, and the cruder but more potent enchantments of the military magical contingents. Even a smallish city like Pu'er was warded in this fashion. Everyone benefited: the temples profited from refurbishing older wall-spells and applying new ones; each city's rulers and clan-masters slept more soundly; and the artillery Legions had something useful to do.

The little bolt-firing ballistae kept up a steady, rattling bombardment all morning. As the sun neared its zenith, General Qutmu hiTsizena and his staff paraded portentously between the hulking mangonels to take their places upon the command dais. Red copper and bright gold gleamed there amid armor like the brown carapaces of *Aqpu*-beetles, the gaudy plumes of the *Kaing*-standards, skull-crested helmets, and the gray sheen of precious steel. Trinesh looked in vain for Direnja hiVayeshtu; he had probably not been invited. The artillery's work was mostly done, for now, and no mere *Kasi* would be asked to join the august company of generals and higher staff-officers, the *Dritlans* and the *Molkars*, observing the assault.

By noon the rickety, leaning beffroi-towers crouched hungrily along the edge of the fosse, and flights of arrows arced up and then down again in a whispering rain of death. Another *Kiren*, and the first columns of assault troops emerged from between the tents, their skull-helmets swarming like white-knobbed insects along the trenches and over the filled-in ditch to wash against the sloping plinth of the wall beyond. From this range it was impossible to tell, but Arjasu swore that these were the undead: stolid phalanxes of dull-gleaming weapons, cloaks the color of grave-earth, shields bearing unknown, time-dimmed blazons, and armor of styles now seen only in faded murals and the mausoleums of the dead.

Iridescent green beetles appeared along the top of the ruined parapet. Siege ladders arose, and white skulls met emerald crests there in one continuous, surging, roiling line. A roar went up, a monotonous, prolonged, fearsome "aaaaah." Gongs boomed—the Yan Koryani preferred them to trumpets— and the white-topped dots retreated to flow down and back.

The gongs clamored defiance.

General Qutmu lifted his baton, and fresh troops poured forth. These were clearly living men. A drum began a staccato *tiktikit-tiktikit*, and more dust drifted away on the breathless air. A trumpet squalled, and another shrieked in urgent answer. Copper and silver and gold and brown mingled with the azure of the Tsolyani Imperium. Trinesh heard hoarse cheering and smelled leather and sunlight and sweat and fresh-cut wood and baking sand. Other, deeper, drums picked up the cadence: the bronze-hulled *Korangkoreng*, the gigantic wardrums of the Tsolyani Legions. Tall ladders stretched clawing fingers above the haze. Something cracked like a whip of thunder; ravening light sprang out of the sky above the Battalions of the Seal of the Worm. The sorcerers swayed and chanted in unison upon their platform, and the lightning growled in sulky fury and slid away harmlessly to the north. In reply, a cloud of brown vapor arose to hover above Pu'er's squat towers, but this, too, dispersed and swept off in rags and tatters as though blown by the wind. Yet the air was still.

White and brown and blue met green again at the top of the shattered battlements. The solid, droning "aaah" became a shriller paean of yelping war cries, then the darker, clattering cacophony of battle. Skull-helmets tumbled down, but the Yan Koryani line along the battlements was left noticeably thinner. The Tsolyani flowed back in disarray, their ladders toppling with them, one after the other. Taking a well-defended wall was no easy task, Trinesh knew.

General Qutmu knew it too. The drums stopped, only to resume with a different, slower rhythm. More brown-lacquered squadrons appeared at the edge of the tent-city: the heavy-armored troops of the Legion of the Scales of Brown. It seemed that Lord Sarku's minions intended to wipe out the stain of last year's broken siege in one single, crushing escalade.

More silent contingents came forth, passed between the waiting phalanxes, and plodded away toward the wall. The undead did not retreat, nor did they falter. Their commanders— the intelligent *Jajqi*, Arjasu said—marched with them. Ladders were raised yet a third time, and those who had died once long ago in the Worm Lord's service did so again.

Only a handful of green plumes still showed upon the ramparts.

The drums sang, *tiktikit, tik-boom-tik; tiktikit, tik-boom-tik*. A screaming clarion split the air, and the heavy infantry rolled ponderously forward. More magic grumbled and shuddered. This time something exploded in a froth of pallid smoke along the parapet, and little green beetles flew up to become red-winged birds before tumbling back down to the stones below. A keening, moaning, belling roar of victory arose from a multitude of Tsolyani throats. The copper-trimmed helmets bobbed and danced below the walls, then surged up and over in a milling, struggling horde. Now no more green beetles were to be seen. The archers spilled down out of their towers to join the melee; all that Pu'er contained was plunder for the seizing. The sorcerers broke ranks to rest and to watch, and the phalanxes of undead halted in silence, almost indistinguishable from the tawny gray desolation of the desert.

General Qutmu turned and descended from his dais amidst the plaudits of his officers. There would be fighting within the city, of course, and some of the foe might hold out for days amid the ruins, in the towers, and in the ancient central citadel. Yet the city was his.

Pu'er had fallen.

Trinesh felt Dineva's thin, muscular arm about his shoulders. She babbled something jubilant about the battle, but he did not listen. His sunburn still hurt, and he pulled away. Victory was contagious, undead or no, but this was hardly an occasion for rejoicing; the four gaunt stakes in front of their wooden cage bore witness to that!

Trinesh looked again for Direnja hiVayeshtu and saw him this time, standing upon the timbered framework of one of the massive mangonels. The *Kasi* had not been unreasonable, all things considered. In fact, he had displayed more kindness than many others might have done in his place. He had provided food from his own rations, and he had left Trinesh and his companions their kilts, although their armor and other possessions were confiscated, of course. He had also supplied a roll of matting wherewith to keep off the worst of the sun. Mashyan hiSagai had argued for stripping them all naked and chaining them in the latrine-pits, but the artilleryman remained resolute in spite of all her blandishments. These soldiers came of good clans, he said, particularly Trinesh's Clan of the Red Mountain, and dignity demanded courtesy. He was only a military man doing his duty as he saw it; the penalty for desertion was severe enough without going beyond the letter of the law. Trinesh was grateful. Few Tsolyani minded nudity, but there was an important and none-too-subtle difference between wandering about one's clanhouse unclad and being exhibited in that condition like a slave or a *Hmelu*-beast!

Trinesh would have a little more sympathy for those in like circumstances in the future.

If there *was* a future. That seemed dubious in the extreme.

The fighting continued all day, more troops moving up to the city as the dead and wounded were brought back. Trinesh wondered idly whether some of the slain would know life of a sort again at the hands of the Worm Lord's brown-robed clergy.

After a time there was nothing more to see, and he squatted upon the planked floor and adjusted the mat to shield himself from the hazy, biting sunlight. Chosun dozed, as he had ever since they were put here; Dineva recited prayers; and Arjasu sat and stared out at the world with the blind look of a killing machine that has nothing left to slay.

In the afternoon there were victory offerings to Lord Sarku and the other gods, singing, rejoicing, and extra measures of wine. Pu'er was not a rich prize, as cities went; Sunraya had held a thousand times its meager treasures. Yet the Worm Lord's Legions rejoiced as though they had sacked Ke'er itself. Prince Dhich'une's adherents had had few victories to celebrate during the past year or two.

Sunset brought visitors. Three men and one woman pushed their way through the thronging soldiers to stand before their prison.

"We," said the eldest, a sallow, plumpish man in a flowing, shapeless robe of purple and orange, "are the *Mrikh*, the Four sent by the clan of the Company of the Edification of the Soul."

"No!" Chosun's head snapped up sharply.

"It is so. I am Miga, this is Hargai, the lady is Sihal, and my fourth colleague is Aritl. We are all of the family of hiBashuvra, there being but one lineage in our clan. Tomorrow, at the conjunction of Kashi and the planet Ületl, we shall perform our offices."

"The horoscope is appropriate," the second man, Hargai, said. "Red Kashi since you are followers of Lord Vimuhla, and brown Ületl in honor of Lord Sarku, who has condemned you. There is also a 'Glance of Brightest Joy'—an aspect of 120 degrees—from Gayel, the moon of Lady Dlamelish, whom your accusers serve. All is loving and auspicious.''

"The best moment occurs at four minutes after sunrise," the woman stated. She was middle-aged, with worn, lumpish features that might have belonged to one of Trinesh's clan-mothers.

"General Vrishtara's people make such nice stakes," the fourth member of the *Mrikh* observed admiringly. "White-washed stone platforms, sturdy ladders, and all the needful."

The horror of their fate became apparent.

"You . . . ?" Trinesh got out.

"All is proper," the sallow-faced man said kindly. "We have brought a pot of red paint so that you may adorn your bodies with the symbols of the Flame—you do all worship Lord Vimuhla, don't you?"

"And after it is over, we shall see that you are cremated," Aritl, the fourth of the quartet, added. "Hargai, here, knows the rites of your faith. It is easier when one does not have to scour a city to find a priest of the correct temple."

"If you would all stand, please," Miga suggested. "We must see that the crosspieces are affixed to the stakes at the proper heights for your bodies. It is neither noble nor aesthetic to have you sliding all the way down the stake and thrashing about at its base."

Trinesh discovered that his knees had turned to water. His bowels threatened to follow suit. "There is no—no hope . . . ?"

The woman shook her head so that the gray-black bun of hair at the nape of her neck bobbed to and fro. "La! Of course not. —And don't worry, young man. We've done this service for ten score others. It only hurts when the stake first slides in through the organs. With a little care it can be made to pass directly up through the heart. It's soon over when done skillfully."

Someone was sick. Trinesh was relieved to find that it was Chosun and not himself.

"They're not manacled, Miga," the third man exclaimed. "Will that not be troublesome?"

"I fear so," the first replied gravely. "It won't do to have them windmilling about and kicking. The soldiers must remedy that in the morning."

The woman smiled. "Here is your *Kasi* with your dinner. May the Flame Lord take you into His incandescent Paradise. Till dawn, then." The four bowed and departed.

Direnja hiVayeshtu himself pushed the tray through the slot in the door. "Not much time left. Eat what you can." The spicy fragrances of his Jakallan dishes were wasted upon those in the cage.

Trinesh turned away, and Dineva made a miserable sound in her throat.

"We are not deserters!" Chosun cried in a choked, desperate voice. The *Tirrikamu* had no fear of death in battle, Trinesh realized, but this sort of relentless, inescapable—and undeserved—doom seemed to unman him completely.

"Of course you are. Mashyan was right about that."

Trinesh said, "As I told you—and as you admitted yourself—we *asked* to return to our Legion. The Flame burn you, would deserters do that?" He himself felt better arguing, quarreling, shouting—anything—than when left to contemplate those four neatly hewn stakes.

"If only you'd been cleverer! A stupid story about monsters and magic doorways! Who's ever seen such marvels? Did you expect me to believe your epic? Nearly six months in the desert, strange clothes, well-fed, and fancy steel armor worth a tax-collector's teeth! Cha! The spoils of war have been a soldier's right since the days of Hrugga himself, but absence from duty is either heedless greed or ignoble cowardice! Your men could have died at Fortress Ninu'ur, *Hereksa*, for lack of your leadership!"

"We did not leave there of our own will!" Dineva shouted.

"So you said, over and over. Yet you did not convince General Qutmu's officers. Even so, I never wanted this for you." The *Kasi* glanced back at the silhouetted stakes behind him. "Any believable little lie, and I'd have let you off, but your silly fable hardly gave me a choice. And then Mashyan's testimony did you no good either. La, she gets all warm and excited at executions. Mashyan should have been a priestess of our Goddess's Cohort, Lady Hrihayal, who enjoys pain and other curious entertainments."

"Ai, enjoys!" Trinesh said gruffly. "Enjoys our captive, the Yan Koryani girl!"

"As you enjoy our steel armor!" Dineva accused. She made an obscene gesture.

"Leave us be," Trinesh sighed. "What's done is done. The Weaver of Skeins knows when a tapestry is spoiled."

"It was General Qutmu." The *Kasi* seemed eager to make amends. "Even if your own Legion had been there to speak for you, it would have been difficult. Qutmu hiTsizena hates your General Kutume, your Prince Mirusiya, and your Flame itself. Fire does not sit well with his undead monsters."

"Oh, *Chlen*-shit. Go away."

"Look." Direnja hiVayeshtu sounded both resigned and frustrated. "I can't help you, that's certain. But if you managed to escape tonight during the celebrations and the confusion, I'd tear up your writs of conviction—see to it that you weren't pursued."

"Why, damn it, *why*?" Chosun roared. "Why torment us now?" His huge hands made the bars creak.

"Mashyan leaves within the hour. She's taking the Yan Koryani girl off to present her as a delicacy to Lady Anka'a. There's no one to see, to report. By the Emerald Goddess Herself, I value fine troopers, fighters loyal to the Imperium— and you, like me, come of a decent clan, *Hereksa*. I'm neither zealot nor martinet, and whatever cruel little games Mashyan plays, I am convinced that our Lady Dlamelish prefers warm, living bodies to dead meat stuck up on poles!"

In spite of himself Trinesh felt a stab of warmth for the artilleryman. There were moderates, it seemed, in more than one place in the Empire.

"The guards are going to be drunk later. If your mountain-ous *Tirrikamu* here can break the bars, you're free and away."

Trinesh spat. "He's already tried."

"It's the best I can manage." Direnja hiVayeshtu stroked his beard. "If I open that door I'll take the 'high ride' instead of you. The Skein is as it is woven. Do what you can."

He turned on his heel and left them once more to themselves.

They had not long to wait. Their third visitor was the Lady Jai Chasa Vedlan. She had been to see them before, but this time she came alone, without Mashyan hiSagai.

She wore traveling boots of dark green leather, a panelled, tight-fitting skirt of green and white *Firya*-cloth laced up the left side to display a teasing gleam of smooth thigh beneath, a silver-tooled cincture about her waist, and, as a concession to the obsessive modesty of Yan Koryani women, a short blouse that covered her breasts. A mantle of thick, velvety, sea-green *Hma*-wool swung from a chain about her throat, and she had found a little skullcap of emerald-dyed felt upon which scrollwork designs were picked out in metallic threads.

"La," Trinesh observed wryly. "A Yan Koryani princess comes to see the *Kuruku*-beasts."

"Not the funny little 'gigglers' of the forests! More like caged *Zrne*, all wild and snapping."

"Ai, *Zrne* who are soon pelts upon the hunter's trophy-wall." He motioned Dineva and Chosun back. "Well, what would you? A delightful gloat? A tear-stained farewell?"

She looked down so that he could not see her face.

More gently, he said, "I never did you ill, Lady."

"No."

"And now you go to follow a Skein worse than any I would have woven: a dainty gift to the orgiasts of the Temple of Lady Dlamelish! You, who rejected my advances, those of my men, and even of a Prince of Mihallu—ugly little fop! You were better off with me."

She hesitated. "That may be. I refused you, Trinesh hiKetkolel, but not entirely of my own desire."

"What do you mean?"

"I told you before. Certain responses are—are barred from me, walled away from my Spirit-Soul."

He knit his brows into a single black bar of puzzlement.

"I am not my own person. You did not guess?"

He did not understand. Her physical charms had dazzled him, as had those of various other ladies elsewhere on other occasions. And that, his clan-masters said, was what came of a surfeit of romantic poetry! He squinted to see her expression in the play of light from the watchfires across the camp plaza.

She tugged at the hem of her little blouse. "The Jai Chasa Vedlan you seek is an ordinary clan-girl, taught to play the *Sra'ur*, sing a ballad, sew, embroider, and host her husband's friends. She has a steady hand with the servants and might be a fair mother to her children."

He essayed a grin. "That is wrong?"

"No, but that girl is only a part of me, *Hereksa*."

"And the rest of you? I do not see—"

She glanced up, so that her eyes flashed red with firelight. "The Lady Deq Dimani serves our god, 'the Lord of Sacrifice,' which is but another name for your Vimuhla."

"What has her religion to do with you—us?"

"Hear me through. The first part of me might have welcomed you—in peaceful times even been glad of you, Trinesh hiKetkolel."

He opened his mouth, but she made a brushing gesture in the air.

"It is the second part that holds me in thrall, an accursed, horrid slavery more oppressive than any you can imagine. You have heard of the Priest Pavar, he whose codifications underlie all of our modern theologies?"

"Of course. Every schoolchild knows."

She seemed determined to tell him anyway. "Once, long ago at the very end of the First Imperium, the Priest Pavar lived upon the Isle of Ganga in the southern sea. It was he—and his disciples, and the many who followed them— who brought about the end of that age and began the Priestkings' Empire of Engsvan hla Ganga. Pavar was cast in the rigid mold of the scholiasts, the temple sophists: neat, precise, balanced, and impassioned with symmetry. He proposed—discovered—invented, some say—the ten gods we still worship: five of Stability, and five of Change. He also defined the ten Cohorts who serve those gods: lesser deities who share something of the essences of their Master or Mistress."

"I know all that!" He mocked her. "Even we benighted Tsolyani recite our catechisms!" Her preaching, lecturing tone nettled him. Did she intend to convert him to some obscure Yan Koryani creed—on this, his last night of life?

"What you may not realize is that Pavar's obsession with harmony left no room for deities beyond his ten. There were—are—more: the Pariah Gods. Village crones still frighten children with tales of such as She Who Cannot Be Named—"

"Cha! Then I'll name her: the Goddess of the Pale Bone! And the One Other. And a half dozen other devils, demons, and bogeys besides!"

She shrugged away his ridicule. "The fisherfolk of my Lady's Isle of Vridu told tales of the Pariah Gods long before the Vriddi of the Legion of the Searing Flame sought refuge there."

"The terrors of superstitious old women—!"

"Not so. One of the most crucial questions of theology."

"Oh—fa!"

Cosmic doctrines bored him utterly. His teachers in the temple school had despaired, and his rump still smarted in memory of their persistent switches. He wished she would get on with it. Tomorrow—no, later this same day, for it was after half-night—he, Trinesh hiKetkolel, would suffer great pain. Then he would cease to exist: a thought no human mind can contemplate in its entirety. Nor was he completely convinced of the promises of the paradises the priests held out before the faithful.

He gave her a tired, angry look. "Say how this connects with the Lady Jai Chasa Vedlan."

"You have heard the story of the Battle of Dormoron Plain, in which nine of the gods fought against the tenth, Lord Ksarul? Nine gods brought their minions to battle; yet when he was defeated and condemned to sleep forever, *ten* walls were built around the Blue Room in which He was imprisoned. The tenth wall is that of the One Other, the least inimical of the Pariah Gods."

"I know all that. The epics—"

"They speak truth."

"The gods exist, then? As they are depicted in the legends?" Trinesh had never before realized that his religion consisted largely of conformity. He mouthed the words, practiced the rites, and followed along in the footsteps of his forefathers. But now, here, when it came to real belief, he was amazed to discover himself a skeptic!

"Of course. They are gods to humankind; yet They are only beings upon a much higher rung of the cosmic ladder. As you are to the little *Dri*-ant who touches its antennae to the toe of your boot, so are the gods to us. That is from the Scrolls of Pavar."

"For a simple clan-maiden, you have all the worst traits of a philosopher!" he said, jeering. Before Fortress Ninu'ur he would have extricated himself from this god-struck girl as graciously as possible. Such women were common as candle-ends in the temples. Did not the priesthoods rule the hearts of the credulous with this sort of mythical claptrap?

Now, however, he was not so certain.

"At Dormoron Plain each of the gods did battle against Lord Ksarul with a weapon of his or her choice. Lord Hnalla struck with His Supernal Light of Myarid Brilliances; Lord Thumis with His Wand of Gray—and so for the rest. Lord Vimuhla, alone, possessed no arms beyond the Raging Flame of His own Being, and that was not enough. It was the One Other who placed a weapon in His hand.''

"I never heard that.'' He was mildly interested in spite of himself. "A column of ravening fire—that is what our scriptures say Lord Vimuhla used.''

"That was its shape then. Once Lord Ksarul was defeated, this weapon was not returned. Lord Vimuhla loved it so greatly that He concealed it upon one of the Many Planes.''

"And I suppose you found it?'' He could not resist a small, cynical jab.

"No. The ancient mages of Vridu did. They enshrined it, venerated it, guarded it, and built a mighty sanctuary to contain it. —Until the One Other found the strength upon this Plane to come and steal it back.''

A flippant comment came to mind, but the girl was so deadly serious!

"His—its—servitors seized it from its guardians' keeping. Later, when my Lady's Vriddi ancestors settled upon Vridu, the first dwellers told their priests the tale. They made inquiries, but by this time the Ensgvanyali and afterwards the first Emperors of the Second Imperium had razed the temples of the Pariah Gods and slaughtered their adherents and driven their priesthoods from the land.''

"The Emperor Trakonel I, 'the Blazing Light.' Was it not he who finally destroyed the sect of the One Other?''

"Yes, he.'' She twisted at a lock of her hair. "All traces of the Flame Lord's weapon were lost, but in the time of my Lady's maternal grandmother the scholars of Vridu discovered where the sacerdotes of the One Other had hidden it. Only now, when the positions of the moons and the planets are correct and the time has come, did my Lady Deq Dimani endeavor to regain it.''

Her reference to astrology reminded Trinesh of the unhappy events awaiting in the morning. He shivered and asked, "And has she?"

"It is so. She has found it—and learned to wield it. The hilt of this weapon, Flamesong, lies ready to her hand."

He could not help laughing. "Oh, *Chlen*-shit! We searched your elegant Lady from crown to heels in the tubeway car! —And I've seen her as naked as a whore's bare arse there in the pool in the deserted palace in Ninue! If she carried any hilt, it must have been—"

"Trinesh. *I* am that hilt. I am the pommel, and I am the blade. I myself am Flamesong."

He could only goggle at her. He must have snorted since Dineva made a questioning sound, and Chosun stirred behind him.

"She chose me, took me to the ruined temple of the One Other in the hills behind Fortress Ninu'ur, and there she changed me from the clan-girl I was to the divine weapon I now am. The Lady Deq Dimani selects her targets, aims me, and strikes. I can no more resist her than a sword can disobey the hand that wields it!"

"Lady Jai," he said, as gently as he could. "Whatever you think, whatever spells she used to twist your mind, you are no sword. You are quite human—and very much a woman." He reached through the bars and took her hands. She did not draw away, but her fingers were again as cold as her northern seas. "A charming, lovely clan-girl, a maiden who can play the *Sra'ur* and sing. . . ."

"You are skilled with maidens, Trinesh hiKetkolel. Were I what I was, you might have cozened me into your embrace. I could have responded to you—or to any decent warrior-husband—had it not been for this—this burning brand within me."

"Cha! You a sword? Flamesong? Lord Vimuhla's own fiery, seething, raging Fire? The Lady seeks to conquer all the world with you! La, you are a blade to daunt armies indeed!"

"Recall Balar. And Prince Tenggutla Dayyar. It was I, as Flamesong, who slew them. By my conflagration."

"Nonsense! Accident—coincidence! Your Lady has worked some illusion to make you think that they died by this—this cosmic magic!" He had not yet fathomed the precise cause of the crossbowman's demise, but she had explained that of the Prince herself. He saw nothing very fantastic about either.

"Believe me."

"Come!" he taunted. "Burn away the lock of our cage! Melt General Qutmu's dandified copper armor down to slag! Rage among the undead and the soldiers; turn the night of Pu'er into day for your Yan Koryani army!"

"I cannot. I am not so commanded."

"Ohe, a good excuse!"

She bit her lip and glared at him. "I—I cannot. You are to die on the morrow, and I cannot use my power to free you—even if I would." He thought to detect a note of real sorrow in her tone.

"Then why tell me this tale now, of all times?"

"So that you will understand. So that you may die knowing that the little clan-girl truly did not turn away your advances—not of herself, not of her own will." She sounded brittle, almost tearful, and he softened toward her. "But you do not believe me, Trinesh hiKetkolel of the Red Mountain clan. You are blinded by your limited, petty, mundane experience. You can no more understand than—than—"

"Than a fish can sneeze, as we say in Tumissa."

She did not smile. "What I have said cannot harm my Lady's purposes. You must die, and she goes on to wield me, her Flamesong, against higher targets. The Kasi's coarse priestess gives me to the Lady Anka'a hiQolyelmu. But that one will not waste me in some carnal ritual! No, she in turn curries favor with those mightier than herself. Have you heard that Prince Mirusiya and his generals lie at Kankara? I have learned that the Yan Koryani retook the wretched town of Mar, and that your Tsolyani only lately got it back again.

This is therefore the best occasion for gift-giving. The Lady Anka'a will offer me to Prince Mirusiya. He it is who will receive me, and he it is who will perish! Your Prince and all about him!''

Whatever he thought of her delusions, an assassination attempt was very possible. "And how do you propose to do this thing?" he inquired sarcastically. If she would tell him, they might trade that knowledge for their lives—a very slim hope, impossible with General Qutmu but more likely with the *Kasi*. "The Prince has guards, attendants, sorcerers with powers that make your Flamesong seem no more than the clay amulets the hawkers peddle in the temples!"

"Flamesong is not detectable, save by sorcery of the highest order—and only then if it be suspected."

"Oh, the Prince's folk *will* suspect. You won't get near him, not alone. Princes must take their pleasures in front of their guards and mages—the price they pay for royalty! Even if he beds you there'll be a score of chamberlains and servitors standing about to watch, to fawn, to applaud—" He could not repress a chuckle.

This time she smiled with him. "Chekkuru hiVriddi accused Tse'e—Prince Nalukkan—of a massacre in Fasiltum many years ago. Prince Mirusiya hiTlakotani was raised in that city by the Vriddi clan, and he will remember the young woman who led the rebellion. He will recall Elara hiVriddi.''

The Lady Deq Dimani had mentioned that name once, and the elders of his Red Mountain clan had spoken of her as well. When the revolt of 2,340 ended with Prince Nalukkan's ghastly slaughter, she and several others of her Vriddi hotheads had been frozen in the stasis of the "Excellent Ruby Eye,'' sealed into blocks of adamantine cement harder than any stone, and then immured in the Lower Catacomb of Silent Waiting beneath the Emperor's impregnable citadel of Avanthar. Her awful fate was meant as a lesson to any other aspiring rebel—but twenty-two long years! Impalement would have been far kinder! He felt icy fingers upon his heart.

"Prince Mirusiya adored Elara hiVriddi, though she was older than he." The Lady Jai retreated a step, thrust her fingers into her tresses, and pulled them back from her face.

His eyes mirrored his puzzlement.

"The Lady Deq Dimani chose me, Jai Chasa Vedlan, for just one reason, *Hereksa*. I come as near to an exact resemblance of Elara hiVriddi as any woman can. Prince Mirusiya will know this face, and he will remember this body. He will take me. He will welcome me. He will dismiss his servitors when I plead that I am ashamed before many and would be alone with him in his bed! After all, what harm can a little Yan Koryani clan-girl do? Flamesong requires only a moment to strike, and then your Tsolyani will learn what it is to mourn a master!"

She bent closer, kissed him lightly upon the lips, and said, "Were it not for Flamesong, Trinesh hiKetkolel, I might have loved you. I am no *Aridani* warrior-woman, but we both are spawned of warrior clans."

Then she went away.

No one slept. Dineva prayed incessantly, Chosun and Arjasu pondered their Skeins in glum silence, and Trinesh prowled back and forth at the front of the cage. He tried the bars, the lock, the beams of the ceiling, and even the planking of the floor a dozen times, but nothing availed. The *Kasi*'s invitation to escape was written upon sand! Given a six-day, they could saw away the lashings with a stone, dig a tunnel, or—he forced himself to smile—learn enough sorcery to magic themselves out of here. But the dawn was too close; just outside, those four stakes pointed up like skeletal fingers beckoning them away to the afterlife to come.

Gayel rose, swept across the sky swathed in veils of emerald radiance, and set. Shichel, the Goddess Avanthe's azure-blue planet, and Riruchel, Lord Karakan's blood-red orb, followed her. Maleficent Ziruna, Lord Hrü'ü's distant eye of faint-glowing purple, hovered just above the horizon to peep into the world. Ületl, the nearest planet to Tuleng, the sun, was late, as was Lord Vimuhla's smaller orange-red moon, Kashi.

When those last two met in the heavens, the *Mrikh* of the Company of the Edification of the Soul would return, and they would die.

Their fourth visitor was Tse'e.

The old man was not alone; another stood behind him in the shadow of the *Kasi's* tent. Trinesh went to grasp Tse'e's dry, wrinkled fingers in his own clammy ones. He wished that his hands would not tremble so.

"You have come to say farewell?" he began.

"Not quite." Tse'e pulled away to fumble at something that jangled.

The door swung open.

Trinesh stared. Then Arjasu rose, lithe as an arrow, and slipped past them, out of the prison to freedom. Chosun lifted his shaggy brows unbelievingly, and Dineva's litany choked off in mid-syllable.

"Who—? How—?"

The second man shambled forward: a muscled, shaven-headed soldier with a lantern jaw and small, pouched eyes like a *Chlen*-beast's. He was attired in a leather tunic and artilleryman's boots. Not recognizing him, Trinesh looked a question at Tse'e, but the old man was already inside helping Dineva to her feet.

"Hoi, *Hereksa*!" The newcomer spoke in a gravelly whisper.

"Who—? I don't know you."

But he did. The voice was that of Okkuru, lately First Translator to the *Gaichun* of Mihallu! Trinesh had never seen him without his mask.

"Get your shit-smeared arses out of there!" Okkuru ordered cheerily. "Not much time. The guards are peaceful now, but they do have to make a round sometime. Then they give the alarm or mount the 'high ride' themselves!"

"But—?"

"La! No fear, *Hereksa*. Three gold bars and a necklace of

rubies as big as a *Sro*-dragon's scaly balls! They'll take their time inspecting the scenery with the camp trollops this night!''

"Three gold bars—?"

"Ai, and another *Chlen*-cart full where those came from. I told you I had put away a few trifles for myself. Now I need some stout lads to help me carry it all off to Sunraya—or somewhere I can spend it!''

Trinesh found that gathering his wits was no easy task. "You—you followed us, then, through the Nexus doorway?"

The translator's teeth gleamed in the shadows. "That I did. Soon as you left. Met this one—" he wagged a thumb at Tse'e "—in the merchants' camp yonder. Figured you'd help a poor wanderer—you being good soldiers and all. You could wangle me a pass or two and keep me from being confiscated for the glory of the Imperium, as the army politely puts it. Never thought to see you squatting there waiting to be buggered by a stake, though!''

"The *Kasi*?"

"Four gold bars, a solid gold candlestick, and a big brassiere-thing all set with little sparklies for his lady's drooping udders!'' The man stifled a guffaw. "Your armor and things're there, just inside his tent—and he's sleeping the sleep of the blessed Doomed Prince Himself. He won't wake up—he said so himself. You could dance on his head!''

Things were becoming clearer. Yet there was one question he felt he had to ask: "Did you speak to the *Kasi* before or after he talked to me tonight?"

"What? Why, after. Just now, in his tent."

Trinesh found this oddly comforting. His illusions about the existence of nobility could remain intact—almost. It would be disheartening indeed if everyone were ignoble: venal, grasping, and unprincipled. Direnja hiVayeshtu had succumbed to Okkuru's gold, it was true, but only after first suggesting escape on his own, without thought of reward.

Somehow this did not seem quite so blameworthy.

"On—out," Arjasu hissed.

Their belongings were exactly where Okkuru had promised: their armor and weapons, Prince Tenggutla Dayyar's "Eye," everything. These they gathered up and then trotted swiftly between darkened tents and campfires that were only smoldering embers and dim, red coals. A sentry called a challenge, and Okkuru advanced to reply. He returned, and they moved on.

"Bastard wanted a handful," the translator grunted ruefully.

By now Trinesh knew what he meant.

The edge of the camp was mantled in blackness. An ungainly *Chlen*-cart waited there; its driver, a pompously efficient man in the livery of one of the carters' clans, emerged from behind its head-high wheels and bustled over to them. Behind him, a *Chlen* stirred and groaned like the opening of a gate into hell. Trinesh had had some experience with these ponderous, armored, six-legged monsters before: they could be ridden but were so slow and uncomfortable that no one did so. The carters' clans therefore employed them to pull the monstrous carts that, along with slaves, were the major means of transport in the Five Empires. Other than *Chlen*, there were neither riding beasts nor draught animals on Tekumel.

"A little stop in the hills first," Okkuru grumbled. "Couldn't carry all my baggage by myself, you might say."

Tse'e came up to Trinesh. "Whither from here, *Hereksa*? Kankara's nearest behind us. Or ahead, to Sunraya? Or down to Slankar and back to the Pass of Skulls through Dhair and Fort Omor? You know this region better than I."

Trinesh had not had time to think. Now he must decide. "Whatever this—this mad slave says, he'll not live to wallow in his gold if we go northeast to Sunraya. There's likely fighting there, and without orders and identities, we'd soon be taken. —And," he added, a trifle hopefully, "not every soldier will accept a bribe."

"Of course. Then?"

Trinesh drew a breath. "My—our—Skein lies with the

army, with our Legion. If we do not rejoin it, we are indeed deserters—criminals, felons—"

"And ignoble. That, I think, is the thing that would trouble you most, Trinesh hiKetkolel."

He grimaced. "As you say." He thought of something. "By the Fiery Flame! We must get to Kankara! The Lady Jai—! She told me of some insane magical assassination plot against our Prince Mirusiya!"

"Prince Mirusiya—? Ah, people spoke of him in the camp," the old man said. "One of Hirkane's litter of brats, suckled by the Vriddi of Fasiltum."

"So he is." Trinesh was not used to this tone when speaking of Imperial Princes.

"I do not recall the boy. The Vriddi must have concealed him under another name. Some of the children of each Emperor are declared at birth, you know, while others are entrusted to the temples and high clans to be kept secret until their patrons deem the political climate right to trot them forth. When I was last in the City of the Chiming Skulls, the circumstances were—different."

Trinesh was embarrassed. He said, "In any case, we may regain our status—a reward—by foiling this stupid plot."

Even as he spoke, he realized that his feelings were woefully confused. He could not just let the Lady Jai try her Flamesong upon Prince Mirusiya. She might have next to no chance of killing him, but any attempt—success or failure—meant an agonizing death for her. If only he could dissuade the girl! But the Lady Deq Dimani had convinced her that she was truly the Flame Lord's weapon, and he doubted whether sweet reason—or anything short of stunning her with a club—would persuade her to abandon her plan. Damn all fanatics anyhow!

"The Prince is at Kankara," Tse'e was saying. "The gossips mentioned certain of his officers with him, possibly your General Kutume. That is where you must go."

"Good. But you? Okkuru?"

Tse'e looked away. "Why, we travel thither with you."

"Why? You risk arrest. And he as well."

The old man avoided Trinesh's eyes. "I no longer care. I promised the slave a reward."

"What reward?" He found he already knew. The man who delivered Prince Nalukkan hiTlakotani to the Petal Throne would assuredly live to enjoy his wealth into a pleasant old age.

"That Skein will *not* be woven," Trinesh stated with finality.

"It must be. It is the price I offered to make the greedy Okkuru spend his gold to save you."

"To save us? As the Gods live, *WHY*?"

"You were good to me, Trinesh hiKetkolel. You behaved with honor and nobility, and you were wrongfully condemned for desertion."

"It means your death!"

"Should a Tlakotani be less noble than you? You have taught me something, young man. We both belong to warrior clans."

Others had made much the same statement before on this same night.

Again, it gave him no joy whatsoever.

21

"Six months? It's been six months?"

"Six months since what, Lady?" The Milumanayani officer prodded the charred remains of a sand-clam out of the embers with his spearpoint. It was too hot yet to crack, and he blew upon it heavily.

"Since the month of Pardan—since we left. . . ."

The man glanced at her in puzzlement, then hammered at the shell with a rock, broke it open, and offered Ridek the steaming brown mess inside. "Ai, Lady. It's Didom now." He had no idea what she was talking about.

"The war? The—*Gurek* of the Fishers of the Flame? Their General, On Nmri Dimani—my clan-brother?"

"Ohe, you've been in the desert a good while, then. The General's gone, off into the barrens. The Fishers of the Flame had their chance at Mar: caught Mnashu of Thri'il with his finger up his arse. Trapped the Tsolyani between their troops and some of the crossbowmen of Tleku Miriya's second

Gurek. Pounded 'em badly, almost destroyed their Shen auxiliaries—almost won.''

"What happened?" Ridek asked. The clam-thing tasted better than it looked.

"We emptied Mar to fight Mnashu: General On Nmri Dimani's folk, some of the Saa Allaqiyani of Siu Kaing's *Gurek*, archers from Makhis, some of my Milumanayani irregulars and nomads as skirmishers. We knew the Tsolyani had a relief column moving west along the *Sakbe* road from Sunraya to Mar, but we didn't guess how close it was—neither we nor they had any flying Hlaka scouts. The Tsolyani force-marched and came up from behind just as we were dusting Mnashu's lads. Rather than get hit in the rear, General On Nmri Dimani pulled out and ran for the hills. Mostly we lost just mediums, some of Siu Kaing's heavies, a batch of useless nomads—"

"May the Lord of Sacrifice roast my cowardly brother!" Ridek caught the glitter of angry tears on the Lady's cheeks.

"No cowardice, Madam." The officer clacked his tongue reproachfully. "He fought well—until the Tsolyani relief troops arrived to step on his tail."

"May he die thrice over for that! No rear scouts! No garrison to hold Mar! No reserve!" She beat her good fist against the gritty boulder upon which she sat.

"You don't know where the Yan Koryani have gone?" Aluja changed the subject. Tonight he wore the seamed brown features of an old campaigner, a subaltern of the Lady Deq Dimani's *Gurek* of Vridu.

"Tlekara, Manuker, Valarash maybe. Somewhere in the barrens north of Mar."

"And your people?"

The man scowled and spat into the fire. Two more sand-clams lay cooking there; he turned these over and banked hot sand and coals around their ridged shells. "Mostly we just sit—harass the Tsolyani—skirmish—see to liaison with your people north of here. We were part of the Sunraya garrison, Lady. Firaz Zhavendu's troops. You know what that means.''

Old Firaz Zhavendu had been fairly loyal to Yan Kor; his son, Firaz Mmulavu Zhavendu, hated his father and coveted the throne of Milumanaya for himself. Firaz the Elder had perished when the Tsolyani took Sunraya last year, and at that time his ignoble son had been on the Tsolyani side. Firaz the Younger then betrayed the Tsolyani at Mar, recanted—enticed by gold and a promise of the governorship of Sunraya when the Tsolyani were done looting it—and had probably switched sides more than once since. This bedraggled officer and the fifty or so dispirited troopers with him in this mountain hideaway were dead men in Sunraya. Only the Baron of Yan Kor could help followers of the elder Firaz now; they had nowhere else to go.

They could therefore probably be trusted—a little.

"You can't make it to Tlekara," Aluja told her. "The color of that hole in your shoulder worries me." The bruise on her forehead where she had scraped against the *Shon Tinur* in the *Ochuna* was of growing concern as well. It was becoming darker and uglier. The fungus might be poison to humans, or, worse, it might even thrive in such a wound.

Ridek reached out and took her hand. It was hot and dry. Too hot and too dry.

"You need a doctor," the Mihalli said.

"Go into Kankara? Will the Tsolyani ask no questions? Will they treat me? Heal me? Smile and bow and let me go again?"

"You could—"

"Play the part of a naked captive in chains? A slavegirl? A harlot? I refuse, Mihalli! I'll act none of those roles! Dignity—nobility—you cannot comprehend!"

"You prefer to die?" he asked bluntly.

She set her teeth and stared off into the night.

"The Lady's tired," Ridek murmured to the officer. "She—we—all need a place to sleep." He was exhausted as well, too weary to think any more of the jolting baggage cart, the oven heat of their four days on the road, the pain he had seen the Lady Deq Dimani endure. The trip had been torture, more harrowing, almost, than the trenches of Pu'er!

"Over here." The officer raised his stubbled chin and squinted down into the hollow behind their aerie where his followers clustered around their own tiny campfires, concealed by the jagged ridge-crest from the Tsolyani in Kankara on the plain to the south below them. He gabbled in his own tongue. Ridek looked alarmed, and the man smirked. "I told 'em I'd disembowel anybody who touches her."

Aluja spread a grimy leather desert-cloak for the Lady beneath an outcrop of crumbling shale and covered her with a borrowed mantle. They heard the hiss of indrawn breath as she lay down: her injuries were more painful than she admitted.

"What can we do?" Ridek asked when the Mihalli had returned to their fire.

"Sleep. Tomorrow—"

Ridek sniffed. He caught the officer's eye. "Send someone to tell her brother. He may not come himself, but he will surely send a physician or a spell-caster with healing magic."

"It's too far, boy." The Milumanayani captain pulled at his drooping moustache. He had a rakish appearance, the look of a man just energetic enough to exert himself for food, animal pleasures—and plunder. "More, the wastelands north of here are too vast and too hot; only an *Alash*-snake could sniff out water there! —Oh, my tribesmen could reach General On Nmri Dimani, all right, but I don't trust them any more than the Tsolyani do. We were city-folk in Sunraya, as different from these sand-worms as steel from stone."

Aluja came to Ridek's assistance. "There will be gold. Reward enough to set you up on a farm in Yan Kor—good land, animals, a house."

The officer pondered. Then he felt about within his own desert-cloak and withdrew a ring hanging from a chain about his throat. "Hodal will be back soon. He sells *Chlen*-hide

armor and weapons to the Tsolyani in Kankara. The guards
know him, and he can pass the three of you through their
lines and into the town without trouble. We've got some
people down there: a magicker, merchants, a few soldiers,
nomads, a spy or two. This ring'll make you known to them.
They can get your Lady to a doctor if anybody can. That'll be
quicker than finding her brother.''

Aluja took the little gold ring. The dangers of the captain's
plan loomed as large as Thenu Thendraya Peak. The Lady
Deq Dimani and Ridek would give themselves away, disguise
or no disguise; Ridek spoke only a little Tsolyani, for one
thing, and though the woman was better, her harsh, burring
accent still smacked of Yan Kor. What made it truly impossible was the ingrained, unconscious, aristocratic arrogance
that both his charges had suckled with their mother's milk.
Five sentences, and any half-awake Tsolyani sentry would be
bellowing for impalement stakes! The Lady refused to play
the part of a captive or a slave, and Aluja could not fault her
for that. It was equally unthinkable for him to let Ridek essay
such a stupidly perilous role.

No, he himself must go for help, and he must go alone.
The boy and the Lady Deq Dimani would insist on accompanying him if he tried to explain. Aluja therefore resolved to
leave while they slept, before first light.

The conversation began to echo, to wash over Ridek's
head, a monotonous susurrus of waves in some lost cavern of
the sea. He was weary to the bone, yet he could not sleep. He
left the Mihalli and the captain and went to stand upon the
rock spur that overlooked Kankara in the valley beneath their
eyrie. Torches and watchfires turned the Tsolyani camp there
into a sorcerer's cabalistic diagram. The entrenchments around
the perimeter were concentric orange-red circles within which
neat grids of saffron lanternlight marked the streets of the
great tent city. Strings of bright-hued lamps, red and green
and golden beads upon black velvet, surrounded the makeshift marketplace and beckoned the troops to food, to liquor,

to women, to the stalls of the merchants, to the priests and soothsayers and amulet-sellers,—all of the trappings of a mighty army. Off to the southeast, the ruined and despoiled town of Kankara itself was an empty blot of onyx darkness. The only illumination within its shattered walls came from the central administrative buildings; the rest had been destroyed, looted, wasted by both sides, until nothing remained but rubble and the memories of its forlorn ghosts.

Beyond the camp, two straight lines of watchfires and torches marched away along the course of the *Sakbe* road, one westward to the Pass of Skulls, Thri'il, and the Tsolyani Empire; the other northeast to Mar and Sunraya and thence to Saa Allaqi and Yan Kor. Ridek's lessons had had much to say about the *Sakbe* road network. The forgotten kings of the First Imperium had begun it; later the Engsvanyali had extended it into every corner of their enormous and unwieldy realm; and the masters of the Five Empires, the present-day inheritors of the Priestkings' magnificence, now maintained most of these thoroughfares, although those in the hinterlands were often no more than overgrown, winding giants'-walls of tumbled stones and debris. A well-maintained *Sakbe* road was almost a civilization in itself: three tiers of stepped pavements, the lowest and broadest for commerce, the next highest for troops and officials and notables, and the narrow, topmost level for messengers and those aristocrats who preferred walking to the bouncing, jolting, slave-borne palanquins that were the fastest means of travel on Tekumel. Guard towers and garrisons, platforms with accommodations for spending the night, peddlars and hawkers and whores and entertainers of all kinds: one could spend a lifetime on a *Sakbe* road and never descend to the rutted secondary arteries that joined it to the villages of the countryside.

This *Sakbe* road had once carried the goods of the Five Empires past little Kankara. Now the creaking *Chlen*-drawn wains and the coffles of bearer-slaves who jostled one another upon its lowest tier were laden with the paraphernalia of war rather than the produce of peace; soldiers tramped its second level instead of traders; and the wind-scoured, crenellated topmost walkway knew only the feet of messengers, officials, and generals bent upon the destruction of Yan Kor.

It was a sobering sight: a runic circlet of glittering flame-opals with two strands of rubies reaching off along the mountain-chain, humped shadows invisible in the night. A collar fit for an Emperor! A collar indeed, but a slave-collar meant to lock around the neck of Ridek's father, the Baron Ald of Yan Kor.

Ridek let his gaze slide back to the lights in the midst of the murky emptiness that had been Kankara. Down there, in that lamplit building— "palace" was too high a word for its mud-brick, splotched, and ruinous mediocrity—slept the man who would clamp this collar about his father's throat: Prince Mirusiya hiTlakotani. He was the enemy, the son and heir of the Seal Emperor of Tsolyanu, the jeweler who had forged that collar, and the slaver who would lead Yan Kor back into the captivity it had known long ago before the Tsolyani Imperium had lost its grip upon the north.

Ridek would go into Kankara with Aluja and the Lady Deq Dimani. He would bide his time—even accept captivity and slavery again if he must. People spoke of Ridek as a child, a twelve-year-old boy—soon thirteen, if six months had really passed since he had left Ke'er! —yet he was still only a helpless white counter upon the board. The Lady Deq Dimani had said that he was more important than a *Gurek* of soldiers, but that was only because of his value as the Baron's son. He might well become a black counter on his own, if he lived to grow up, and if Yan Kor won this war or obtained an acceptable peace.

He decided that he was not willing to wait.

He would slay this overweening Mirusiya if he could. Was that not a noble Skein? Was his life not a worthy exchange for that of a Tsolyani Prince, the foe of Ridek's homeland? Was it not better to become a mighty black counter now when he had the chance? A black counter for perhaps only a moment before the Tsolyani cut him down, but a black counter nevertheless, one the Seal Emperors of Tsolyanu would remember until the gods put final quietus to this cycle of time!

He would kill Mirusiya.

Ridek steeled himself, made his vows, and sat gazing down at Kankara until Aluja came to lead him off to sleep.

Hodal, whoever he was, did not come, but sunrise did bring an unpleasant surprise: Aluja was gone.

There was no help for it, nothing to do. The Milumanayani captain listened politely, made reassuring noises, and went away. The Lady Deq Dimani cursed and uttered words that Ridek had heard only from serfs and scullions. Nothing availed. They both understood why Aluja had done as he did, but that did not make it any more tolerable. In the evening the captain returned to urge patience and to announce that one of his sand-worms would indeed seek out the Lady's brother, a journey of many days.

They waited.

The following two days were anxious and tedious; there was no word from Aluja. The Lady's shoulder wound grew better, healed, and became less inflamed. The bruise on her forehead did the opposite: it pained her less, but the bluish-black, veined shadow spread over her cheek, squeezed around her long-lashed eye, and sent tentative fingers down her jaw toward her throat. The captain shook his head and uttered encouragements, but Ridek was not deceived. She grew visibly weaker, and he suspected that she could no longer see from the eye thus embraced by the discolored, puffy flesh.

Hodal arrived on the third day, a sinewy oldster with a face as sour as cheap wine. He announced that Aluja, now a lowly Milumanayani warrior in the pay of Firaz the Younger, was in contact with a physician who was a friend of Yan Kor. As soon as the doctor could find an excuse to leave the camp, he would come. They had to be satisfied with that.

On the fourth morning Ridek awoke to laughter, shrill voices chattering in sibilant Milumanayani, and the burned-fish redolence of cooking sand-clams. Ten paces away, the Lady Deq Dimani sat crosslegged upon her desert-cloak combing out her locks as best she could with her good hand.

"Nomads," she warned him. "Be cautious."

The captain's scruffy soldiers were crowded about something down in the hollow behind their lookout post. Ridek used sand to make his ablutions, adjusted the remains of the *Gaichun*'s tattered green tunic, and scrambled down the slope to see. He paused to offer the Lady Deq Dimani his hand, but she refused with a grimace that swiftly became a smile.

The Milumanayani officer met them halfway down. "As you requested, Madam," he said formally. "My sand-worms intercepted the Tsolyani a *Tsan* or two outside Kankara. Lost three—and one good soldier as well—but we rescued your comrade for you. There was no girl—another party had taken her into Kankara separately, a gaggle of soldiers and a priestess of the Goddess Dlamelish, the scouts say."

Ridek would have questioned him further, but the Lady hobbled on past into the throng below. The soldiers parted before her, and he saw whom the nomads had brought.

It was one of the Pygmy Folk. He peered. The stance, the splotchy gray and black fur, the mottling on its beak: it was Thu'n, he who had accompanied them out of Ninue!

Surprisingly, the little nonhuman did not appear at all pleased to be rescued. If anything, he was outraged. Two gaunt, sun-blackened tribesmen laughed and lurched and swung to and fro from his furry arms, dodging his snapping beak and wildly kicking, sharp-clawed feet. Bloodstains and torn desert-cloaks attested to the effort it had taken to subdue him.

"My Lady!" Thu'n squalled. "My Lady! Oh, help me!"

She rounded upon the captain and his soldiers. "What has been done to him?"

"Nothing—uh—Lady. Nothing," one replied. "The sand-worms only follow their custom."

"What custom?"

Thu'n shouted, "They took my golden discs, my Lady! My discs—the ones the Prince gave me in Mihallu—!" He broke off.

"The Pygmy Folk love gold!" She snapped her fingers imperiously. "Give him back his wealth!"

The captain issued stern commands. Some of the nomads grinned, others sniggered, and only the eldest, a blackened skeleton of a man, had the grace to look apologetic.

The officer translated. "He says he cannot. In the Desert of Sighs all property belongs to everyone alike—whoever asks must receive."

"I have already had too much experience of their laws in Na Ngore. Tell him we want Thu'n's property back. He has need of it. At once."

A babble arose, which the captain quelled by laying about him with the flat of his sword.

"He says that this is no longer possible, Lady," he panted. "The little beast had a handful of golden discs—coins, perhaps—and the maidens of the tribe fancied them for bangles and necklaces."

"Where are these 'maidens'?"

"In the desert, I suppose. The nomads did not bring their womenfolk here."

She swiveled back to Thu'n. "Let them keep your coins. I shall give you gold aplenty when we reach my brother—or Yan Kor."

"Never! You do not understand—" Again, Thu'n seemed at a loss to explain the importance of his missing discs.

Some of the tribesmen scowled. A few fingered bone-tipped spears, and the Milumanayani officer retreated a pace or two.

"The old man says he can have 'em back if he can find 'em." The captain hawked up phlegm, visibly unwilling to do more.

Thu'n was released, still hopping and fuming. He went to

each of the nomads in turn, made demands, and held out his hand. No discs appeared.

"Give these sand-worms breakfast," the captain ordered. He addressed the Lady Deq Dimani. "The girls'll hang the little beast's precious discs from their ears and noses. If ever he sees one, he can have it back for the asking." He chortled. "And more besides. Their hussies earn their keep by serving the needs of the Tsolyani army—and ours as well."

L ater, when the captain's troops had eaten, and the no-mads, too, had been fed outside the camp, Ridek went to relieve himself in the rocky gully behind the campfires. One of the tribesmen awaited him there, a skinny, starveling youth attired in the voluminous leather cloak that was the sole and universal costume of the Desert of Sighs.

"What do you want?"

The other shook long braids that stank of *Hmelu*-fat and showed straggling teeth in what could be interpreted as a smile.

"Off! Away! I have nothing for you!" He was not afraid; help was but thirty paces away.

The nomad made an unmistakable gesture, one that repelled Ridek more than it shocked him.

"Go away before I—!"

The Milumanayani reached down, caught the hem of the poncho-like cloak, and raised it high. The naked, scrawny body thus revealed was indubitably female.

"*Tupazhes?*" the girl said. "*Tupanges tlu?*" She repeated her gesture.

Between her flat, big-nippled breasts swung a golden disc the size of Ridek's palm.

He pointed wordlessly. She simpered and slipped the disc and its thong off over her head. "*Lufajes mtu,*" the girl said, and handed it to him. She grinned expectantly.

He had nothing to give her in return—most certainly not what she asked! He grinned back. "Thank you—uh—thank you." He indicated the captain's campfire back on top of the rise and grabbed himself by the ear, as a mother does a naughty child. "They're calling me," he improvised. And fled.

Ridek found Thu'n seated by the fire moping over a mound of empty sand-clam shells. He sat down beside him. "Would you tell me something?"

The creature fixed him with one sharp black eye but made no response.

There was no other way; Ridek plunged into the heart of the matter. "Why," he asked, "did you so willingly go over to the Tsolyani in Ninue? And later at Pu'er?"

Thu'n flicked a glance over toward the Lady Deq Dimani who dozed upon her desert-cloak in the shade of the outcrop.

Ridek continued doggedly, "The captain said that you were chatting merrily with the Tsolyani soldiers when his folk rescued you. That you did not aid in your escape. That you actually resisted until you saw the Tsolyani must lose. That only then did you attempt to slay one of the foe with his own dagger and cry out allegiance to Yan Kor."

"All false—the errors of desperate men!" Thu'n said grumpily. "And how does this concern you?"

"The Lady considers you a loyal adviser, yet you seemed very eager to exchange her green for Tsolyani blue."

"Go away, child. The Lady is aware of everything. She makes no accusation; why should you?"

"I have heard my father say that the greatest loyalty dwells in the breasts of children and old women. If people are not faithful, then I do not help them."

"Help? How can you help me? By not tattling to the Lady Deq Dimani? Cha! You profit nothing thereby! She employs me as a scholar, an historian, one who reads ancient tongues and pores over scrolls. I *work* for her, boy! I am neither liegeman nor slave, and my loyalties are my own."

"My concern is not with the Lady." He withdrew the golden disc from within his tunic. "I weave my own Skein:

my friends I help, my foes I disdain, as my father says. Are you friend or foe?"

Thu'n leaped up to thrust one grasping paw at him across the fire. "That is mine! Give it here, child!"

"It was given—freely—to me." The circumstances did not merit repeating. "I may give it away again. But only to a friend."

Thu'n cursed and clacked his beak. The Lady Deq Dimani raised her head to look over at them, and he subsided. "To the Deep Hole with your silly human 'nobility'! Even for a human you are naïve—childish—unlettered in the world!"

"Lettered enough to read the word 'friend' and tell it from 'foe.' "

Thu'n flexed his clawlike fingers, ran them through his grizzled gray-black fur, and sputtered.

Ridek took pity upon him. After all, how much of a hero had he himself been? Had he fought to the death when the Tsolyani took him in Ninue? Had he tried to slay the *Kasi* or his other tormentors at Pu'er? Had he even refused to work when they turned him into a slave? Hrugga of the epics indeed! There were always necessities, exigencies, reasons, and qualifications to everything. He was fast learning what it was to live in a world where no color was pure, where Lord Hnalla's white shaded imperceptibly into Lord Hrü'ü's purple, and where loyalties and ties and bonds were forever tangling in shifting webs that defied unsnarling.

He dropped the disc into Thu'n's leathery palm.

For a moment the creature blinked at him, his gray-white beak agape in what might have been either astonishment or joy. Then his eyes narrowed as he held the disc up to the light.

The Milumanayani girl had pierced it for a neck-thong. She—or a comrade—had also punched many other little holes in it: a phallus, the primordial symbol of fertility, crosses and crescents and circles, the glyphs of some unknown desert deity. The whorls and symbols its ancient makers had inscribed upon it were obscured and lost.

Much to the startlement of the rest of the camp Thu'n threw back his head and uttered a long, ululating howl. It was thus that Ridek learned that the Pygmy Folk cannot cry.

During the afternoon of the fifth day a boy, a *Chlen*-hide tanner's apprentice not much older than Ridek himself, brought the news they had dreaded to hear. The youth displayed the captain's little ring and said, "Hodal asks you to come. Your friend—the nomad—has been arrested by the Tsolyani. He got a message to Hodal first: bring the woman and the boy to Kankara. The physician waits to treat her, and there is another agent whom you are to meet. Can you return with me now?"

They could. It was a grim and solemn trip down through the dry, bracken-covered scarps and gullies to the bustling encampment below.

22

The tent flap opened from darkness into a medley of yellow lamplight. Blinded, Trinesh stumbled upon the figured Khirgari carpets that made pools of cyan and amber and carmine and orpiment and viridian upon the sandy floor. He squinted and managed to avoid the heaped dais-pyramids of smaller rugs and druggets, each surrounded by its own foothill-range of cushions and hassocks and bolsters and backrests of carven, ivory-limbed *Ssar*-wood. Amid the carpets, like pagodas rising out of a rainbow-hued garden, stood enameled chests, filigreed taborets, and trivets upon which burnished, fat-bellied censers gleamed with the brightness of golden moons. There was too much to see, more than the senses could take in at once: draperies, banners, tabards, a jungle of colours and fragrances and intricate shapes. In one corner, against a tapestry overflowing with the stately figures of the Gods advancing into battle upon Dormoron Plain, Lord Vimuhla's Holy Flame quavered upon a portable altar of red-veined carnelian. Trinesh stopped to blink and rub his eyes.

In front of him, General Kutume hiTankolel gave the appropriate fist-to-breast salute to the man seated at the campt-table in the center of the tent. General Kutume and General Kadarsha hiTlekolmü, Commander of the Legion of the Searing Flame and now *Kerdudali*—Senior General—of the eastern armies under Prince Mirusiya himself, were old friends.

General Kadarsha looked up. "At this time of night? What is this you bring—an armed insurrection?"

Trinesh's superior sought a carpet-dais of suitable height. He found it, pulled a fat cushion around to lean upon, and sat down. "Just a few of my lost troopers—veterans of that fiasco at Fortress Ninu'ur last year—with a tale that deserves a rendering by an epic-singer." A wave indicated the three men and one woman with him; these he gestured to sit where they were, by the door. The other two—the spindling, lean-fleshed old hermit and the ugly slave—he had left outside. Their apparent status did not merit an audience.

Trinesh had not revealed Tse'e's identity, nor had he mentioned Okkuru's unexplainable wealth. To do so was to assure the impalement of both men, as well as the speedy confiscation of the slave's gold. The aid those two had rendered him and his comrades at Pu'er deserved whatever reward he could contrive. If they desired his silence, they would have it, even if the Flame Lord Himself were to decree otherwise! He could only pray that Tse'e had put aside his suicidal plan to surrender himself in exchange for Okkuru's freedom—and that the latter, in turn, would keep his riches safely out of sight until Trinesh found some means of getting him away from the encampment.

Kadarsha stood up, scratched the small of his back against a tent-post, and pushed away the parchments his staff-*Dritlan* had spread in front of him. "Enough for tonight, Kambe," he grumbled. "Even a bad epic is better than your funereal dirge of debits and requisitions and roster-lists."

The Senior General was taller by ten finger-breadths than most Tsolyani: a powerful man, once slender, but now softer and thicker in the wrong places from good food and easy travel in a general's litter, rather than army rations and "the pauper's palanquin": a pair of serviceable feet. Kadarsha's face was unusual, a trifle foreign-looking, with a broad forehead and wide-set eyes, the white lines of healed battle scars, and faint creases at the corners of his mouth that spoke of the encroachments of time, laughter, and not a few sorrows along the way. General Kutume was smaller and more debonairly handsome, as Tsolyani tastes went, but he was clearly of a different breed, one far commoner in every army: a soldier devoted as much to purses and haggling and documents as to swords. Both were about thirty years of age, and both were numbered among Prince Mirusiya's "new men," his comrades in the Legions before his Vriddi patrons and the Omnipotent Azure Legion, that corps of special servitors closest to the Emperor, had pulled him out of obscurity and announced him to be a Tlakotani, a Prince, and one of the heirs to the Petal Throne.

"Sing your epic, soldier!" the Senior General grunted. He sat down again, drew his legs under himself upon the carpet-dais, and adjusted the folds of the dark orange night-robe he wore. From the inner chambers of the pavilion behind him a child crowed and giggled; it was said that this Kadarsha was devoted to his priestess-wife, the Lady Oyaka hiTlekolmü, and she, in turn, was an abject slave to her two sturdy twin sons.

Trinesh did as he was told. It took a long time, and before it was ended the Senior General poured goblets of amber-hued *Mash*-brandy for them with his own hands. Both Generals were said to be familiar with matters of sorcery; both were moderates in the service of the Flame Lord; and both were reputed to be reasonably noble, as "high folk" went.

Most importantly for Trinesh, neither would dismiss his adventures as a fable or a deserter's glib alibi.

If only Trinesh could relax and yet stay awake! The trip north from Pu'er had been arduous—awful! There had been questions and retellings and reports to be tediously copied by the Legion's pokenose, busybody scribes. In turn, he had been informed of the recapture of Fortress Ninu'ur by the Yan Koryani and the deaths of Vinue and many of the troops of his *Kareng*. Fressa and Charkha had escaped, as had his own body-slave, Bu'uresh; General Kutume promised that he would be reunited with these three presently, as well as with other survivors of his unit. The Tsolyani had subsequently taken Fortress Ninu'ur back and razed it to the ground in a frenzy of vengeance, but Trinesh could no longer rejoice even in that. He was drowsy, fatigued beyond imagining, and yet stretched so taut that the blood thrummed in his temples like the drone-strings of a *Sra'ur*. Dineva leaned on Chosun's thick shoulder behind him, while Arjasu sat apart, eyes glazed, and fingers still unconsciously caressing the crossbow that General Kadarsha's guards had made him leave outside with them.

"The Lady Deq Dimani," the Senior General mused. "I met her once—twice—a long time ago."

General Kutume said, "Your Mihalli, *Hereksa*: you did not see him or the Lady again after they passed through the Nexus portal ahead of you?"

"No, my Lord."

"I wonder if he could be the same Mihalli spy General Kaikama's watch seized a night or two back? The one involved with the Mu'ugalavyani physician?"

The Senior General rubbed at the pale scar-lines upon his cheek. "We left the good doctor free to run, but on a very short tether: a juicy *Hmelu*-beast to entice more of the Baron's spies. I can have that tether shortened—or call for the butchers if need be." His robe rustled as he turned to his *Dritlan*. The barracksroom tongue-waggers said that it was upon this solemn, eager-eyed youth that General Kadarsha piled most of his paperwork as a farmer loads a cart with *Chlen*-dung. "Kambe, see if our bait has tempted any other prey."

"I think the Lady Deq Dimani will seek out the doctor, Sire." Arjasu ventured. "She'll be wounded: my bolt took her in the shoulder. And she may have the Yan Koryani princeling with her."

"His name is Ridek," Trinesh added. He could not recall whether he had included that detail in his report.

He was unprepared for the two generals' reaction.

"Ridek?" General Kutume cried. "The Baron's eldest son bears that name!" General Kadarsha set down his goblet with an audible *clack*, almost breaking its stem.

Trinesh said, "The Lady Deq Dimani and her maid showed great deference to the boy." He was too exhausted to remember more. The scribes had the rest of it down in their Flame-burned, ink-blotted scrolls anyhow.

"Bestir yourself, *Dritlan*!" the Senior General ordered. "A full watch! And none of your usual army ninnies! Alert the Omnipotent Azure Legion's people—and the Prince's!" He rubbed a hand across his lips. "It cannot be. The Baron's boy is—what?—eleven, thirteen? What would he be doing in Mihallu?" The *Dritlan* hovered first on one foot and then the other by the door.

"He or some other Ridek. It's worth discovering." General Kutume leaned over to inspect Trinesh's Engsvanyali armor, dusty, scratched, and a little dented though it was. "A fine harness, *Hereksa*. A good specimen of the style of Ssirandar the Twelfth."

"You—you would know, my Lord," Trinesh stammered. He could guess what was expected. "I—uh—hoped to offer it as a gift to the Legion."

"Do so. A noble benefaction. —And then we shall not dock your pay for the Legion armor and weapons you left behind during your heroic wanderings." The General showed white, even teeth in a pleasant smile. Trinesh wondered whether he was serious. The camp jesters made much of General Kutume's almost sacrilegious devotion to material prosperity.

"The girl—this 'Flamesong'—an attempt upon our Prince's life?" Kadarsha muttered. "She has as much chance of success as the Baron has of pissing on the Petal Throne in Avanthar! Yet we should see to it."

"The Lady Anka'a had her audience yesterday, Sire," the *Dritlan* stated. "Prince Mirusiya still lives."

"The Yan Koryani woman may not have found her opportunity yet," General Kutume said. He turned away reluctantly from a scrutiny of the armor of Trinesh's companions. "His Highness is likely still awake. Do we disturb him? The later the hour, the more zealous his Flame-scorched Vriddi guards."

"Let the Vriddi be, Kutume. We have to settle with them if ever we hope to see Prince Mirusiya ascend the Petal Throne! East and west, we make up our quarrels, or we all go down tangled in their snares like a *Zrne* in a hunter's net!"

This was clearly a recurring and unhappy topic. Trinesh's clan-elders had expressed these same yearnings for unity within the Flame Lord's faith piously and often—while at the same time decrying the haughty intransigence of the Vriddi clan. The struggle between the eastern Vriddi and the great clans of the western Empire was older than the Second Imperium itself, but now the winds of politics bore just the faintest scent of reconciliation: Prince Mirusiya had been raised among the Vriddi but his army friends were mostly westerners. If anyone could bring the clans together it would be he.

"Up!" General Kadarsha commanded. "Kambe, see to the physician. Bring him and any women and boys who call upon him to the Prince's quarters at once." He stripped off his night-robe and shouted for body-servants to aid him with his dress armor.

They tramped past campfires, tents filled with sleeping troops, and dumps stacked high with sacks and bales and kegs, the grist of the army's mill. Sentries challenged and saluted; scribes and functionaries stood back to bow and ogle after them; and throngs of soldiers and camp-followers pointed and whispered. The pinnacles of power were not entirely pleasant, Trinesh decided. To be a perpetual cynosure for all eyes would soon grow tiresome indeed.

The fallen walls of Kankara swept by, jumbled stones and sharp-angled silhouettes in the night. The ugly little gate-house was roofless now, but there were torches and troopers on watch upon its ramparts, men of mighty Vimuhla's favored Legion of the Lord of Red Devastation. Other than these, the Flame Lord's elite, few still dwelt within the town. They passed the Prince's ceremonial palanquin in the central square, itself as big as some looming, fanciful castle, its lacquered and gilded wooden daises shimmering green with Gayel's eldritch moonlight. Three reliefs of eighty porter-slaves apiece were needed to carry it, and these now slumbered in huddled clumps beneath its sculptured, beast-headed carrying-poles like corpses upon some chaotic battlefield.

Then there were more lamps, torches, guards, and attendants as they clattered up the steps of the dismal mud-brick "palace" that had once housed all there was of Kankara's city government.

General Kadarsha wasted no time with the Prince's staff. A sketched salute, a greeting or two, and they entered the hall the Imperial entourage had commandeered for a temporary headquarters. It was very like Fortress Ninu'ur; this place was bigger, and someone had made attempts at murals and dadoes upon its crude mud-brick pilasters, but it still stank of animals, smoke, and straw in spite of all the household slaves could do with their brooms, mops, perfumes, and incense. Whatever happened, however long Trinesh might live, those smells would forever remind him of wretched Milumanaya.

The Senior General conferred with the hawk-nosed Vriddi guards at the foot of the circular staircase leading to the story above. An aide appeared, and they were allowed up.

The antechamber at the top of the stairs had but one tiny, round-headed window. It was stuffy with the mingled odors of candle smoke, oiled weapons, leather, and *Hruchan*-reed paper. A bevy of scribes crouched over their inkpots along one wall, and three more Vriddi warriors slouched by the inner door, resplendent in Imperial blue but with the symbol of Lord Vimuhla's Holy Flame emblazoned upon their steel cuirasses.

"Tlangtekh, Te'os, Zaklen," General Kadarsha addressed each bodyguard by name. The last of these stepped forward, consulted a scroll, and gestured at the three officers in the liveries of other Legions who squatted there upon the carpet-daises to await the Prince's pleasure. The Senior General made some curt reply Trinesh could not hear, and the soldier bowed.

"He's with Karin Missum," Kadarsha told Kutume. "Still, he'll see us."

The inner chamber had originally been the sanctum of some petty city-official. It measured perhaps eight paces wide by twelve long and was completely windowless, as breathless and hot as a baker's oven. The Prince's furnishings were richer in quality but sparser and more austere than those of General Kadarsha's pavilion. Before his Vriddi patrons had proclaimed Mirusiya a Prince, he had been a soldier's soldier, the gossips said, and his tastes would forever bear the stamp of army regimen.

Two servants puttered about silently at the rear of the room, and a silver-haired harper sat crosslegged in one corner. Trinesh was surprised to see that this last man was a Milumanayani nomad from the deeper reaches of the desert. The harp the man was tuning was not of Tsolyani manufacture but was the tasselled, gaud-bedecked instrument of the tribes. The fellow was blind, his eyes almost invisible beneath a thick crust of scar tissue, the final stages of *Alungtisa*, the horrible eye-malady so common in the Desert of Sighs. Folk said that the Prince collected legends and epics of the gods; if he listened to the nomads' caterwauling for musical rather than historical reasons, then the musicians of Tsolyanu would have to shut up shop should he become Emperor!

They made obeisance, faces pressed into the lush scarlet pile of the Khirgari carpet just inside the door. General Kutume snapped his fingers softly, and they rose to kneel before the man who might one day sit upon the Petal Throne of Tsolyanu.

Three men sat within the circle of warm, yellow light shed by the bronze candelabrum in the center of the room. He who occupied the topmost level of the carpet-dais wore only a soldier's white kilt, with a dark blue shawl wrapped carelessly about his shoulders for warmth. A gilded replica of the Seal of the Imperium on the patchy plaster wall behind him haloed his shoulder-length black hair with an aptness that was probably unintentional but might have been his advisers' calculated method of awing visitors. An altar to Lord Vimuhla stood in a niche below the Seal, a second underscoring of his allegiances.

This was Prince Mirusiya hiTlakotani.

In his mid-thirties, this man could have been a Vriddi indeed, a true scion of the clan that had raised him. The aquiline nose and sharp-cut planes of his cheeks were common enough among all of the old aristocratic clans, but the deep-set, brooding eyes resembled those that looked out from the portraits Trinesh had seen of the Vriddi overlords of Fasiltum, the "City of the Chiming Skulls." Mirusiya stood a full head taller than Trinesh, the equal of General Kadarsha himself. In other respects the Prince differed subtly from his Senior General: his features were harsh where Kadarsha's were gentle, stern where the other's were scholarly, and commanding where Kadarsha appeared determined at best. One might willingly serve either man, Trinesh surmised, but the Prince would command obedience through a charisma akin to that of the heroes of the epics, while Kadarsha would need persuasion and cajolery to hold those who followed him.

There was another comparison to be made. Trinesh had once seen Prince Eselne, Mirusiya's elder brother, during the annual "Fete of the Might of Heroes," celebrated by Lord

Karakan's Temple in Tumissa. Proclaimed a Prince at birth, Eselne had always known what it was to rule, while the Vriddi, for political reasons known only to themselves, had not told Mirusiya until he was an adult and an officer in a Legion with battle experience under his belt. Both were soldiers, both were strong and decisive, and both were noble in the warrior's sense of the word. Both would govern well. Yet folk said that Eselne relied too heavily upon advisers from the old Military Party and the Temples of the war-gods of Stability, Lord Karakan and His Cohort, brave Lord Chegarra. It was also rumored that he was not overly clever: "the Chlen-beast in azure robes," as some named him. Should he ascend the Petal Throne, the aristocrats and the priesthoods would pull the strings that made the Empire dance. On the other hand, Mirusiya was perhaps *too* severe and soldierly: too blunt, too self-reliant, and too quick to answer swords with swords. Both would build armies such as the Imperium had not seen for three hundred years, not since the halcyon days of Emperor Gyesmu, "the Iron Fist." Eselne's soldiers would guard his sponsors' interests and would see battle only if other stratagems failed. Mirusiya's armies would never sit idle; they would certainly march, and thereafter the frontiers of the Five Empires would be altered, one way or another, for centuries to come. He was the only choice for Trinesh's clan—for all those who served Lord Vimuhla and His Cohort, Lord Chiteng—and even among Eselne's current backers there were those who swayed away from him and toward this candidate of the Flame. Trinesh was satisfied with what he saw here tonight; his clansmen had made the right choice.

Trinesh knew one of the two others with the Prince: General Karin Missum, "the Red Death," who had previously commanded Trinesh's Legion of the Storm of Fire and was now in charge of the Legion of the Lord of Red Devastation—a fanatic to lead fanatics! He was short, squat, as massive through the chest as a *Tsi'il*-beast, with a face like some dour icon painted upon rumpled leather.

The third occupant of the dais-pyramid was slender, balding, clean-shaven, and as smoothly urbane as Karin Missum was not. This was a man who kept secrets, dark currents beneath serene water. His bland features were a better mask than any fabrication of wood or metal, and only his hands, stiffly poised and tense in his lap, hinted at what lay within. General Karin Missum wore scuffed battle armor, but this other was attired in the orange-red vestments of a priest of Vimuhla of the middle Circles.

"General Karin Missum you know. Lord Huso hiChirengmai you may not." The Prince's features gave nothing away. "Lord Huso is the Preceptor of the Society of the Incandescent Blaze."

Trinesh started—and felt Chosun and Dineva stir behind him. Lord Huso hiChirengmai was the leader of the faction of zealots within the Flame Lord's Temple that favored decisive—and sometimes violent—political action. This was Chekkuru hiVriddi's mentor. Trinesh ought to inform him of poor Chekkuru's fate, but now was not the time. With any luck, he could put off the telling until the Legion's ponderous network of scribes and reports made it all unnecessary.

"Mighty Prince," the Senior General began. "If you would hear this soldier's story."

"Stories I have aplenty, Kadarsha." Mirusiya managed to sound amused, patient, and harassed all at once. He pointed to a heap of glittering stones upon a square of reed matting before him. "I am being instructed in High Cartography. These gentlemen offer a plan for our summer campaign."

The Prince seemed embarrassed. Karin Missum ought have cleared any such proposals through the Senior Gen and his staff first. Here, once again, was the perpetual tu war between moderation and zeal.

Trinesh spared one curious glance for the odd-shar stones. He had seen the art of High Cartography in school at Tumissa. One stone of appropriate color and texture symbolized each geographical region; this was carved with innumerable tiny lines, grooves, indentations, and protuberances representing the particulars of that place: its contours, cities, roads, rivers, villages, mountains, and much more. An adept could feel of the stone, "read" it with eyes, fingers, and even the tongue, and know what it contained. Trinesh's tutors said that the Ancients had made better map-stones, ones that were "alive" with sorcerous power from the Planes Beyond. Those sang in the mind of the one who held them, displayed mental pictures, and provided a thousand other details. Alas, the languages of the Ancients were lost, and the millennia had so altered the face of Tekumel that much of what a "living" map-stone related was as mythical as the paradises of the gods. Still, even the modern map-stones were superior to the paper maps the merchants used: boxes and squares connected with straight lines and annotated with scribblings concerning routes, distances, and the minutiae of commerce. A mountain upon a merchant's map was at best a crude circle; upon a map-stone it was a tiny knob surrounded by incised symbols that an expert could translate into heights, peaks, valleys, ground cover, passes, springs, wells, and habitations. One had a choice: squares upon paper or the difficult art of High Cartography; humankind made no other maps upon Tekumel.

General Kutume said gravely, "My *Hereksa*'s tale concerns your own safety, mighty Prince."

"Oh . . ." Mirusiya sounded more bored than dismayed. "Let him reel it out, then."

Trinesh told his story yet another time, feeling General ʼarin Missum's unwinking gaze fixed upon him as he spoke. ⸙re disturbing, however, were Lord Huso's eyes, like two ⸙sin's needles concealed in velvet. He finished, lamely ⸙h, with an account of the Lady Jai Chasa Vedlan's plot. ⸙d already made up his mind about that: he could not ⸙girl, not and remain true to his personal nobility, his

Legion, and his Imperium. She had said that she would not—could not—give up her insane plan, and he saw no way out of the dilemma. He consoled the plangent cries of his little inner voice with one last, faint hope: Senior General Kadarsha might listen to an appeal for mercy. So might General Kutume—there was always Okkuru's gold. The Prince, also, impressed him as stern but fair. The other two in this room would certainly hand her over to the Company of the Edification of the Soul or sacrifice her out-of-hand in the Flame.

If only he did not have to make his plea before General Karin Missum and this ice-eyed fanatic, Lord Huso hiChirengmai!

"A girl?" The Prince picked up a map-stone of delicate-veined rose quartz from the pile and rubbed a hand over its striations. Those callused fingers could probably no more read the minute symbols of High Cartography than an Ahoggya could sing! "A gift from the Lady Anka'a hiQolyelmu?" He sighed. "I am so tired—I forget—I have no time for women now, not even to honor the gifts every temple, clan, and petty lordling within a thousand *Tsan* thinks vital to bestow upon me. One would think a Prince did naught else save populate the Empire with his own seed!"

"Ah—mighty Prince—she said you—you would know her . . ." This was the hard part, and he stumbled over the formal Tsolyani pronoun employed solely for heirs to the Petal Throne.

The Senior General helped him. "The *Hereksa* reports that the woman resembles one whom your Highness knew in childhood: the rebel, Elara hiVriddi."

"Who? Elara? I—I recall her well." The Prince strove visibly to shift from the present to the past, to another identity and a Skein of Destiny that had belonged to a different lifetime.

"She—the Lady Jai—said you would be—uh—attracted, mighty Prince." Trinesh had no idea how to phrase this tactfully.

"I would—I was. At the time." Prince Mirusiya looked through him, past him, at a world that was gone.

"The girl must be stopped." General Kadarsha's tone was sharp. "If she's a danger, we'd best—"

"—Put her where she does no harm," General Karin Missum finished for him. Lord Huso's higher, mellower voice chimed agreement.

The Prince hesitated. "There's little likelihood of peril. This chamber is defended by more enchantments than Avanthar itself. Not even Subadim the Sorcerer could cast a spell here, though he had Origob the Prince of Demons and all his hosts to aid him!"

"Still. . . ." Lord Huso was on his feet, turning round and round, eyes shut and lower lip clenched between his teeth. "I sense nothing now."

"Te'os!" the Prince called. The bodyguard appeared in the doorway, and Mirusiya beckoned him over. "See that the Yan Koryani girl gifted me by the Temple of Dlamelish is brought hither. Gently. Do not alarm her." Over the babble of protest the Prince said, "We shall never know what fine threads the Baron and the Lady Deq Dimani would weave into my Skein unless we see her. And, Te'os, send my house-sorceress, the Lady Arsala, to me!"

"Is this wise, mighty Prince?" General Kutume objected.

"This is no battle between honest warriors!" Lord Huso was still more vehement. "You risk your life—the Imperium—your Temple—for naught!"

The Prince shot him a sardonic glance. "La! You yourself sent the Lady Arsala hiChagotlekka to me, good priest! A perfect guardian, you said, one so versed in defenses and wardings and perceptions of the Planes Beyond that I would be swaddled in protections like a *Dnelu*-egg in its cocoon—safer than in Lord Vimuhla's lap!"

"Mighty Prince! That is not fair! I spoke of common sorcery, not of weapons of the gods!"

"Who knows whether this Lady Kai—Jai? —has such a

weapon? She may be as addled as a sand-worm too long in the sun!" He pressed big, splay-tipped fingers together until the knuckles cracked. "I will learn!"

Trinesh was horrified to hear his own voice blurt, "Is it that you really desire to look upon this Elara hiVriddi once more, mighty Prince?"

Mirusiya had turned his back to stand before the altar-flame. He did not seem to notice who had spoken. "So it may be, my friend."

General Kutume was scowling at Trinesh. Fortunately the door opened.

The woman who stood there was a gaunt, emaciated priestess in the orange-red, ankle-length skirt and short tunic of the Temple of the Flame Lord. A streak of pure white swept back from the parting in her hair to be lost in the graying locks that spilled free over her bony shoulders. The scholars said that the gods put such streaks into the hair of creatures for whom They had special tasks, as a scribe marks an important word in a scroll with colored ink.

"My Lady Arsala," the Prince said.

"Lord?" She wrinkled her high-curved forehead and drew the dark wings of her brows together. "There are others here. I recognize Generals Kadarsha, Kutume, and Karin Missum. Another? Lord Huso. And four more. Them I do not know. And two servants—and yet another. . . ."

It dawned upon Trinesh that the woman was blind. Unlike the harper, this was no case of *Alungtisa*; the priestess's empty eye-sockets were filled with orbs of milky glass!

She came to him and put cool, parchment-dry fingers to his face. He gulped and would have pulled away, but she gentled him with a smile. "Do not fear, young man—soldier. This blindess is of my own choosing. I gave up my worldly sight the better to perceive the energies of the Many Planes. I see auras, powers, minds, and souls, rather than the veil of sensory illusion that beclouds the vision of you with eyes!"

Dineva made some sound, and Trinesh guessed that she

was praying. He watched as the sorceress moved to touch Chosun's plump, sweat-slick cheeks, then Arjasu's coolly handsome features. From him she swiftly drew away. "Four soldier-folk," she intoned, "no better and no worse than their fellows: more here, less there, one more kind, one more cruel, one more afraid. . . ."

A pent-up pressure in his lungs warned Trinesh that he was holding his breath. He expelled it in a ragged gasp that was as much fear as relief.

The Lady Arsala turned to face the Prince. How she saw him—and what she saw—Trinesh could not imagine. "Mighty Prince, you summoned me?"

The Prince licked his lips. He, too, was obviously ill at ease with this strange seeress. In short, chopped sentences he told her of the Lady Jai and her threat.

" 'Flamesong?' Lord Vimuhla's blazing sword? Unlikely. I would have said impossible, but I read neither ignorant superstition nor deception in your soldiers here. The young man who tells the tale may be wrong—the girl could have duped him for reasons of her own—but he does not lie."

"Persaude the Prince that this is too perilous a game, my Lady," Lord Huso urged. "The girl must be seized, exorcised, made harmless!"

"Punished, you mean, Lord Huso. Put to the question, tortured, then sacrificed in Lord Vimuhla's Flame. I read the real meanings behind your words all too well!"

The priest's lips worked, and Trinesh wondered if he were casting a spell to bar the woman from his thoughts.

The Lady Arsala smiled.

None of them heard the door open again. The bodyguard named Zaklen cleared his throat, abashed at his intrusion. "Mighty Prince," he said, "there are two outside who say they must see you—that they bring matters relating to—to your present concerns."

"Send them in."

Trinesh recognized Okkuru's bulk and his slyly obsequious

grin even before the translator reached the circle of light around the candelabrum. Tse'e was with him, as diffident as ever.

Damn the slave—and the old renegade! Utter fools!

General Kutume's features took on a bright red flush. "Who let this—these—?"

Tse'e asked gently, "Mighty Prince Mirusiya?"

"I am he."

The old man narrowed his one good eye. "I had thought that I did not remember you, but I was wrong. You were named Torisu—Torisu hiVriddi."

Puzzled, the Prince lowered his arm, already half raised to summon Zaklen back. He made a questioning sound in his throat.

"Listen! Hear me out before you call your guards!" Tse'e touched thin fingers to his face as though begging Mirusiya to look closely upon him. "I am your father's half-brother, Nalukkan hiTlakotani. You are my clan-nephew."

The Prince opened his mouth, then shut it again. A wild, scraggly, barefoot old dotard, a Milumanayani sand-worm in a ragged desert-cloak!

He burst into peals of delighted laughter.

"Hear me, nephew. Shall I name your clan-fathers and mothers? Arinu hiVriddi, Dlerüssa hiVriddi—"

The laughter stopped. "You cannot be who you claim."

"I am as I say." Tse'e extended a hand from beneath his stained and filthy garment. "Call for the sword I surrendered to your soldier at the door." Something in his tone must have carried the ring of Imperial command, for, rather to his own amazement, the bodyguard found himself laying the weapon on the carpet just inside the threshold.

General Kutume picked the blade up and wordlessly passed it forward. Tse'e—Nalukkan hiTlakotani—pointed, and the Prince himself twisted at the pommel knob. It came free in his hand. The hilt and guard slid off after it, and they all beheld the golden Seal of the Imperium worked upon the tang.

"You see?" Tse'e said simply. He put the weapon back together and laid it by his side.

Trinesh moved through the ensuing confusion to take Tse'e's hand. "No 'nobility' drives you, old man," he observed sadly. "No high purpose! It is death you seek!"

"A fugitive's every breath denies nobility, friend. Now it is time for the Weaver to hem my Skein and remove it neatly from the loom." He brushed aside Trinesh's restraining touch. "Prince Mirusiya—Torisu hiVriddi—when last you saw me I stood in the burned-out shell of the Vriddi clanhouse in Fasiltum. My troops had finished assembling our captives, and you clung to your clan-mother's skirt, a big-eyed *Hu*-bat, to watch them go. You spat curses at me and wept for those whom I took away to suffer punishment in Avanthar."

"I—I remember," the Prince husked. It was as though he dug down through layers of stubborn, frozen rock to tap Lord Vimuhla's smoldering fire-stone beneath.

"The rest I will tell you—if you grant me time before you send for the *Mrikh* and their impaling stake." He drew the Prince aside toward the altar, but Trinesh could still just hear them.

Mirusiya's jaw was ridged and white. "I—uncle—if you *are* my uncle—" He paused for a space of ten heartbeats. Then: "I hated you!"

"So you still must. So you should. It cannot be otherwise. Within you there is a Vriddi; a man does not easily cast aside the nurture he suckles with his nurse's milk, not even when the emissaries of the Omnipotent Azure Legion come to lay the mantle of the Tlakotani Emperors upon his shoulders and hail him Prince."

No one spoke. It was long before the Prince himself broke the silence:

"I hated you when you ravaged our city—I was too young to die for Fasiltum then. I despised myself for being a child! I hated you for what you did to Elara and the others. Then I hated those 'tame' Vriddi who took me, reared me, and taught me to abandon any hope of reprisal, any retaliation against the Imperium—against the omnipotent God-King in Avanthar!''

"Then you must have hated yourself all the more when you found that you yourself were no Vriddi but a Tlakotani, the son of that very Emperor who had earned your hatred!''

"Yes.''

"As did I, boy. As did I, when the Omnipotent Azure Legion came for me, long ago. I, too, found it hard to accept my Skein.''

The Prince could make no reply.

"That is the way the Seal Emperors of Tsolyanu are made. The best of them are smelted from the ore of adversity, forged upon the anvil of strength, tempered in cunning, and quenched in blood. Thus do the Tlakotani ensure the perpetuation of their dynasty and of the Second Imperium. Thus they guarantee a driver who can manage his beasts, a master who has known the whip and hence knows well how to wield it. Such a one rules the better. Thus, too, is the danger of weak heirs lessened: it is harder for a spoiled princeling to take the reins from a stronger parent and mire the cart of the Empire in the mud of decadence. You will see, you will learn.'' He bobbed his head in a mock bow. "Ohe, you will make a fine Emperor!''

Mirusiya gave him a black look. "Our *Kolumejalim*, the 'Rite of the Choosing of Emperors,' has never assured Tsolyanu of a brave, kind, or even an efficient emperor. La, the Imperium has rarely lacked for folly!''

The older man shrugged. "No system delivers perfection. Even with sound *Chlen*-beasts and a sturdy cart, the driver may still be an idiot, a rogue, or a madman, in spite of his clan's best efforts to teach him otherwise.''

"You are glib, uncle. What was done to the Vriddi cries out for more than excuses!''

"What, then? Tears? Guilt? Self-loathing? Retribution? Punishment—death and more death? Those hold no life for the future! They are withered rootlets, seeds that cannot grow. Alas, this is the lesson we forget first: we think to take vengeance for history, then to expunge it, ignore it, cast it aside, rewrite it, give its mistakes different names and joyously proclaim a newer, better day to come! We relive the stupidities of our ancestors with all the placid equanimity of a *Chlen*-beast who thinks each step round the threshing circle takes him on to a fresh pasture!"

"Uncle, I am no philosopher—"

"But you are an intelligent man, one who holds the shaping of the world in his hands. The solution, nephew, is not revenge upon the past but construction for the future. The bricks and beams one uses must come from whatever resources the age provides, but the mortar—the cement that holds the edifice together—is *Khomoyi*, 'noble action.' That—and hard work—are the principles a ruler needs!"

" 'Noble action?' Of course. . . . A warrior is immersed in 'noble action' from birth! I do not take your meaning."

"Your young soldier there, the *Hereksa*, thinks nobility consists only of some stern and crusty warrior's code: iron laws that call for blind heroism and blood in answer to blood."

"And is he wrong? The Vriddi taught me the same."

"Not entirely. But *Khomoyi*—'nobility'—is more than heroism. The noble being—man, woman, or nonhuman—seeks to learn who he is and where he fits into the Weaver's tapestry. When he has understood his role, he makes his nature manifest before all without hypocrisy or self-deception, saying, 'Thus am I, and so be it.' He prosecutes his beliefs: he *acts*. The ignoble person is false, indolent, and quick with apologies and alibis; he lacks identity and purpose as an army falters without its standard. He is passive and weak: he accomplishes little that will make him remembered by the centuries to come. The priest of Lord Vimuhla sacrifices victims in the Flame, and this, for him, is noble; it is what he believes with all his heart. Lord Thumis's gray-robes abhor living sacrifices, pick their gentle *Tetel* flowers, seek wisdom, and aid all who ask—again a noble Skein. Lady Avanthe's flock—of whom I once was one—yearn for peace and the forging of bonds with nature, with those other life-forms with whom we share this world, and with the cycles of the crops and the rains and the year. The followers of Lady Dlamelish dance and copulate and pursue their transitory pleasures; they are noble as well, as long as they make no pretense otherwise. The *Zrne*, 'the Barbed One of the Forests,' pounces upon its prey and hence is noble according to its own dim understanding. A *Zrne* who does differently—there are those in the zoological gardens in Avanthar that come peaceably enough to take food from their keeper's hand—is ignoble; it has surrendered to ease and sloth and a life of being other than its nature." The old man sighed. "Your *Hereksa* is noble, nephew, though not quite for the reasons he thinks."

"Cha! There must be true—honorable, justifiable—reasons for not doing as one preaches!"

"Of course. But those each Spirit-Soul must examine for itself."

Prince Mirusiya pondered. "Were *you* noble, uncle, when you slaughtered the rebels of Fasiltum?"

"No. I had not thought—I had not yet looked to see who I was. Now I have learned that I am no executioner, no follower of grim and blood-stained Chiteng, nor even of Lord Karakan, the Master of Ever-Glorious War. When I was assigned to quell the rebellion at Fasiltum I was only a young man obeying orders, one more blind to himself than your priestess is to the colors of the sky."

"And would it be noble for you—for another—to do the same again?"

"I have sought within me. Another might act as I did and be noble according to his own nature—a fiercer and more warlike man. But not I."

"Are you noble now, uncle?"

"I hope to be. —And I am the happier for it."

The Prince shook his head. "We must thank the gods that few practice nobility in this strict sense of yours, else the smooth running of the Imperium—of any organization—would swiftly become impossible! We would founder in introspection as the Milumanayani tribes do in their endless voting and debating!"

Tse'e sighed and turned his one good eye upon the others in the chamber. "You may be right. Each to his own Skein. Come, no more words now. I am done: your captive—or rather brother Hirkane's, if he wishes me carried to Avanthar for execution."

"No. . . ."

The old man laid a hand upon the Prince's arm, unthinkable to any lesser being. "We can speak more later, when these fine soldiers of yours are elsewhere upon their rounds." He scratched beneath his desert-cloak and grinned lopsidely. "Ohe, one last matter: this slave, this Okkuru, claims the reward for delivering me to the impaling stake."

The Prince glanced toward the back of the chamber. "A slave turns you in? A slave?"

Okkuru had the excellent wisdom to fall upon his face and grovel.

"Is there a difference? Would it have been better if this Hereksa here had brought me? Or one of your elegant generals? Okkuru behaves with nobility: he makes no pretense. He is what he is."

"The Flame melt your nobility! No slave lays hands upon a Prince of the Imperium and lives! Not even a Prince who is a fugitive—not even one who goes disguised as a sand-worm!"

"Oh, Chlen-shit, as the Hereksa says!" Tse'e made a wry face. "You are very much a creature of your upbringing, nephew. Think of nobility—"

"I'll consider your philosophy, uncle; that is the most I promise. In the meantime I obey Imperial law. For now, for me, that is *my* nobility." The Prince's cheeks were suffused with fury, and the snap of his fingers was very loud. "Take this slave out! March him to the perimeter of the camp and turn him loose! His life is his reward!"

Okkuru ground his nose into the scarlet carpet. His hairy haunches quivered in the air, and from someplace underneath his bulk they heard a muffled groan as of a *Chlen*-beast giving birth.

"He has a cart, only a little cart, full of supplies, nephew," Tse'e pleaded patiently. "Why not at least let him take that?"

Prince Mirusiya's eyes were cold lightning. "He may have all he can carry upon his own back. No more! The cart is doubtless army property, as his supplies are assuredly pilfered from our commissary. General Kutume, confiscate whatever the wretch cannot load upon his own shoulders and see him past the sentries. Let no one aid him!"

Okkuru uttered one last bleat of abject despair. The Prince opened his lips to speak, saw Tse'e's face before him, and shut them again. Zaklen bellowed for an escort, and General Kutume followed the slave out.

Prince Mirusiya returned to the altar to stand ruminating before its ruby flame. Whether he communed with his fierce and implacable God or whether he meditated upon the lesson he had received this night, none but he could say.

23

The giant Milumanayani held up the fat, pink-white grub, clucked with gustatory anticipation as befitted a true connoisseur, and dropped it into the stewpot. As big as a log of wood, the thing splashed steaming brown gravy up over his wrist. He swore, licked his fingers, and said, "A sandworm tastes as sweet as human flesh, they say, but only if it's marinated for three days in *Mash*-brandy!" Sharp teeth, like a *Zrne*'s, glittered as he grinned. "This bugger'll delight even the most discriminating palate! You'll see when it's served to the Emperor in Avanthar!"

"Not so!" Trinesh's senior clan-father, old Morudza hiKetkolel, scoffed. He sat with Trinesh beside the fire. "He'll get off—Prince Dhich'une is every worm's friend!"

"Not this time! We have him as plain as Thenu Thendraya Peak! The 'high ride' awaits. Dhich'une can whine and wheedle and piss his kilt, but he can't save him."

The fire sent up a cloud of smoke and sparks, and the scene drifted away upon the breeze. The Milumanayani dwindled to be replaced by Prince Mirusiya. Trinesh's clan-father became the Senior General, Lord Kadarsha hiTlekolmü.

Trinesh sat up. The sleep-demons had stolen a march on him: he had dozed—and dreamed—without realizing it! He was surprised to find Chosun's hand pressed against the backplate of his armor, quietly supporting him so that he might not slump over and embarrass himself before the Prince.

General Kadarsha was saying, "—Qutmu has friends in the City of Sarku, clansmen, priests—some of the Emperor's chamberlains in the Court of Purple Robes within Avanthar itself. . . ."

"Cha! What good will they do when your troopers here bring evidence of undead soldiers at Pu'er? The law forbidding that is as solid as the Petal Throne itself! Qutmu has broken that law—on Dhich'une's orders or of his own will, it makes no difference."

"We knew of his undead before—"

"I was not officially in command of our eastern armies then—nor was I at Kankara, just a few *Tsan* away from Pu'er, with agents and emissaries who can be sent down to catch the worm-sucking monster in the very act! General Kutume's troopers here are witnesses; I shall speedily have a dozen more—and maybe a captive *Mrur* or *Shedra*—or even a *Jajqi*—to dance at Qutmu's trial as well! The trap springs shut! I have the authority to impale Qutmu hiTsizena on the spot."

"Yet you said you'd send him to Avanthar . . . ?"

"Exactly. I shall *not* impale him here. He goes to my Imperial father at Avanthar for two good reasons: first, though I have jurisdiction, I won't punish a General of the Empire without obeying every last cantlet of legal protocol. Secondly, I want the entire nation to see Qutmu dragged to the stake, a shame to his patron—my youngest half-brother, Prince Dhich'une! La, he'll wriggle like one of his own worms and crawl to the bottom of Lord Sarku's deepest hell to escape the disgrace! We'll get the credit for exposing this flagrant breach

of law and tradition, and our credibility among the Temples—
those of Change and of Stability alike—will ascend to the
heavens like the sun! Eselne will never catch up after this, not
even if he captures Ke'er and roasts the Baron Ald on a spit
before the gods and all their creation!''

Trinesh looked muzzily around. The room was the same:
the Senior General and the Prince near the candelabrum,
Karin Missum and Lord Huso with their heads together in one
corner, and Tse'e—the familiar name would not go away—in
communion with the blind priestess before the Flame Lord's
altar. As he watched, the old man's skinny hand reached up
past her shoulder to lay another twig of long-burning *Tiu*-
wood upon its fire.

The Prince and his uncle had certainly struck mutually
sympathetic chords here tonight; it could thus be a long time
before Mirusiya got around to sending Tse'e to Avanthar. An
heir who neither relinquished the Gold nor took part in the
Kolumejalim—nor perished gracefully if he lost—*had* to be
punished, Trinesh knew; this was one of the perils of Imperial
glory. Yet a prisoner might die of old age—and in very
pleasant circumstances—before his case was heard, particularly if a strong-minded Prince such as Mirusiya hiTlakotani
kept muddying the bureaucratic waters.

General Qutmu hiTsizena's Skein of Destiny was more
predictable; it was also shorter and much less to be envied!

Trinesh hunched around to peer behind him and discovered
that his legs had gone to sleep. Dineva and Arjasu squatted
against the back wall. La, those two were probably as numb
as his own feet, paralyzed with awe at their proximity to all
these puissant lords! A servant knelt beside them to offer a
tray containing a clay jug of *Chumetl* and a pewter pitcher of
wine. The harper was still in his corner, silent and unnoticed,
his pot-bellied instrument across his scrawny knees.

It had been the creaking of the door that had awakened
Trinesh. The *Dritlan*, Kambe, stood there.

Kadarsha beckoned, and the young officer said in a hushed

tone that still carried to every ear in the chamber, "Sire, we have the woman and the boy."

Heads turned, garments whispered, and armor scraped and rattled. Trinesh shook himself to clear away the last webs of sleep.

It was indeed the Lady Deq Dimani, the Yan Koryani princeling with her. The woman's head lolled, and her body dragged limply between the two soldiers in the Senior General's livery who dumped her down upon the scarlet carpet. For a moment Trinesh thought she had been beaten; then he saw the bloated ruin of her face.

They had not bothered—had not needed—to bind her.

Trinesh had seen her wounded by Arjasu's bolt in Ninue, but the ghastly disease that now turned her beauty into horror had nothing to do with that. Both eyes were swollen nearly shut, her temples and cheeks showed blue-black beneath her damp, sticky tresses, and wherever the ulcerations had not yet spread her skin was flushed bright with fever.

"The boy put up a nice fight," Kambe reported in his most militarily correct voice. "We have the physician, too, if you want him, Sire. And I sent over to General Kaikama's headquarters for the Mihalli."

The Lady Arsala gave a soft cry and went to the prisoners. The boy's wrists had been tied with a length of *Daichu*-fibre cord. She touched him upon the forehead, just between the eyes, and he relaxed.

"A knife, please, General Kadarsha. He will make no trouble." She took the proffered dagger and cut the boy free.

"Ridek?" the Senior General said. "Ridek?"

The boy raised his head. "I am Dokku Khessa Tiu." He glanced at the priestess, then at the Lady Deq Dimani. "No. The blind woman reads minds? So?"

"She is a seeress, yes. Deception is useless."

"Then you know us." He straightened up and continued, proudly and distinctly, in his broken Tsolyani. "I do not shame my lineages further. I am Ridek—Ridek Chna Ald, eldest son of the Baron of Yan Kor. I will not ask to be ransomed. If my father offers it, I shall refuse. Sacrifice or slavery: those are your choices for me."

"An honored captive, then." Kadarsha smiled at him. "One whose noble word is acceptable as his parole."

"See—see to her," the boy rasped. He trembled, and his thin features were pasty with sweat, yet he managed to hold his head high. Trinesh marveled at him—and wondered how he himself might have behaved at his age in a similar situation.

The Lady Arsala had already taken the Lady Deq Dimani's unprotesting face between her hands. She shut her eyes and said, "Fevered. Hot. A foreign thing within her. Not a wound, not an arrow—that was there, but it is healing. . . ." The blind, glassy orbs swung up to seek Kadarsha. "Herbs, medicaments, bandages. All in my chambers—one of you!"

The Senior General pointed, and the servant set down his tray and hastened off.

Kambe stood aside to admit two soldiers. Between them, manacled, gagged, and blindfolded, was the alien Trinesh had last seen in the *Ochuna* in Ninue.

General Kaikama's soldiers had not treated the Mihalli thus because of any delight in cruelty. Some enchantments required gestures, substances and words, but others could be cast with the mind alone. A skilled mage needed only to see the target to hurl a psychic spell. Trinesh also caught the gleam of a metal collar about the creature's neck: a sorcerer could not wear metal or carry it upon his person unless it had been appropriately constructed to act as a conductor for the energies of the Planes Beyond. Other metal objects randomized those forces and caused malfunctions or even the death of the spell-caster. No, the Mihalli had been bound in this fashion out of fear—and the utmost respect for the danger he posed.

The creature made himself as comfortable as he could upon the carpet. The boy slid over and murmured something in

Yan Koryani into his pointed, short-furred ear. Lord Huso would have intervened, but the priestess waved him back.

"He has no spells to cast," she chided. "Only words of consolement." She could not see the look of baffled rage upon the priest's sleek countenance, but it required no psychic power to guess its presence. "The woman, too, is defenseless, my Lord. Yet if you are afraid, I can lay an enchantment of immobility upon her . . . ?"

Lord Huso glared and retired, discomfited.

Kadarsha came to stand before the Lady Deq Dimani. "Will she recover? Can you cure that—whatever it is?"

"I think it likely. It is some manner of parasite, a fungus. I have both medicines and spells that may succeed."

The Lady Deq Dimani spoke for the first time. Her jaw was so badly puffed that it was hard to recognize her words as Tsolyani. The blackness had begun to envelop even her gums and tongue.

Kadarsha leaned closer.

"Who? Aluja?" He glanced at the Lady Arsala and followed her nod. "He is here. He is—as well as can be."

The servant returned with the priestess's own serving girl and a brass tray heaped high with a jumble of vials, jars, and rolls of white *Firya*-cloth strips.

The Lady Arsala held the woman, embraced her, murmured softly, and applied her arts. The others gathered behind to watch. There was no visible change, but the Lady Deq Dimani sighed and sank down upon the figured carpet.

"Do all that is needful for her comfort," Kadarsha ordered. Trinesh wondered at his tone: he had mentioned meeting her before, had he not?

"If this be truly the Matriarch of Vridu, then Tsolyanu's omens are auspicious indeed, mighty Prince!" Karin Missum said. He spoke with growing jubilation. "Her *Gurek* of Vridu— and her brother's Fishers of the Flame—will think long before attacking when she's shackled to a hurdle before our Legions! Why, we may even see Vridu's troops retire from the war—break their alliance with the Baron—start an exodus of other city-states that will decimate his ranks like an earthquake!" He made a shaking gesture with both brawny hands. "We shall march to Ke'er through the crumbling towers of his empire, a ruin which his petty clan-chiefs and town-governors will scurry to abandon before the roof falls in completely!"

"You rejoice before the building has quivered even once, my Lord!" Kadarsha retorted dryly. "She is but one: her clan will quickly select some younger sister, a niece or other kinswoman. Vridu belongs to Yan Kor, and naught can change that—saving this wondrous earthquake of yours!"

The Lady Deq Dimani leaned forward as though to speak, but words refused to come. Her long tresses swung down to curtain her face. The seeress pushed them back again and began snipping away her stained under-tunic to get at the crossbow wound in her shoulder. After a moment the Lady sagged against the physician's arm.

"She sleeps," the Lady Arsala whispered. "We can hope for some improvement when she wakes again."

The Prince himself cut short the babble of argument that arose to fill the room. "You all presume too much! First she is made well. Then she goes to Avanthar, as is customary for any captured Yan Koryani general. There she may choose ransom, sacrifice, imprisonment—or she may follow their 'Way of Nchel' and become as limp as a dead eel! Those decisions are hers—and my Imperial father's."

Undaunted, Karin Missum sat back down, Lord Huso behind him. The Incandescent Blaze Society could bring many pressures to bear, even upon an Imperial heir. Especially upon one whose support stemmed from the Temple of the Flame.

"Mighty Prince," Kambe said from the doorway. "Te'os is here with the Yan Koryani girl. He begs forgiveness for the delay, but you ordered that she not be alarmed. The chamberlains understood that you wished her for your bed tonight, and they took their time adorning her."

"Bring her in."

"My Lord!" Karin Missum and Lord Huso protested again in unison.

"Let her come. We have better sorcery in this room than anywhere outside of Avanthar, and I would rather take the risk myself than see her demon-sword scything down my army! —Not that I think she can."

"You are well defended—" Lord Huso began.

"Precisely. I shall meet her on her own terms—"

"As a noble warrior feels he must," Tse'e flung in sarcastically. "Yet you carry your blind nobility too far! This is foolhardiness!"

"Should I then submit myself to a painful death, as you would do, uncle?" the Prince shot back. "A hero's code or a suicide's—is there so much difference?"

"Mighty Prince." Kadarsha went to whisper in Mirusiya's ear. The latter frowned, seemed to consider, and then made a slashing gesture of frustrated acquiescence.

"Oh, very well, I yield to your concession," the Prince groaned. He removed his blue shawl and wrapped it about Kadarsha's shoulders. "Let us see if Flamesong can tell a prince from a general. You—" he pointed at Trinesh "—keep the boy from giving our little masquerade away. I doubt whether he understands all we say, but I want him kept quiet. Here, take my uncle's sword."

"She—Flamesong—may know!" Lord Huso remonstrated fiercely.

"How? When the Lady Anka'a presented her to me I was twenty paces away, attired in Imperial regalia, a plumed helmet as high as a *Tiu*-tree on my head, and surrounded by two hundred officers and courtiers! Kadarsha is as tall as I am, and he can play the part. I doubt she could recognize either of us face to face! La, as I recall, during the entire ceremony she did not raise her eyes to me even once—I

thought she was a meek little clan-girl, as bland and unentic-
ing as *Kao*-squash pudding. . . ." He ended on a softer note,
". . . I did not think to look for Elara hiVriddi."

"She may see minds!"

"If she has all the powers you fear, then we had best flee
Tsolyanu or hide our heads in the cesspits beneath Avanthar!
Is she then Lord Karin Missum's mighty, metaphorical earth-
quake? Cha!"

"Clear the chamber of these others, then!" Lord Huso
pleaded.

"And thereby alert her? The Lady Arsala stands ready—as
do you and my bodyguards." He signed to Kambe. "Now."

The *Dritlan* opened the door. Te'os hiVriddi entered, followed by the Lady Jai.

By their own flamboyant standards, the Lady Anka'a's
costumers had made her beautiful indeed. The Lady Jai's
tresses were lacquered and looped about with silver links, her
cheeks touched with copper-red *Aunu*-pollen, and her eyes
lengthened with dark *Tsunu*-paste. Powdered gold had been
sprinkled over designs painted upon her limbs with an adhe-
sive made from the *Voqu'o*-plant to cover her skin with
arabesques and traceries from her bare shoulders and high-
nippled breasts down to the silver girdle clasped about her
waist. Streamers of translucent *Thesun*-gauze hung from a
collar of emeralds to tangle with the tabards of her sweeping,
panelled skirt of rippling green *Güdru*-cloth, the finest fabric
made in the Five Empires since the days of Engsvanyali
splendor. Her legs displayed more gilded patterns, all the way
from her silver-lacquered sandals to her thighs and the one
sleek hip visible beneath her gown. Turquoises, beryls, opals,
and malachite dripped from her wrists and throat, her ears,
her ankles, and every finger and toe.

The Goddess Dlamelish's Temple had expended much wealth
upon this peace-offering to the Flame Prince. Trinesh found
the effect elegant but florid and overdone.

The girl glided forward to halt before the tall candelabrum.

She kept her eyes demurely fixed upon the carpet a pace or so in front of her.

Trinesh was struck with sudden dismay. She had only to turn her head to recognize him, Chosun, Dineva, and Arjasu! How stupid! He had not thought to remind the Prince of this, and none of the others had remembered either! It was too late to warn anyone now, and he signaled unobtrusively to Dineva and Arjasu to keep well back in the shadows by the door. There was no way to hide himself and Chosun, however: they were as conspicuous as two *Chlen*-beasts in a meadow! He could only pray that the Lady Jai would remain as diffident as he had known her—that she would not look up!

"The Lady Jai Chasa Vedlan," Te'os announced in over-formal tones.

Kadarsha spoke from the highest carpet-dais: "You look upon Prince Mirusiya hiTlakotani." He made a sweeping gesture that she would interpret as pointing to himself. To his right behind him, the true owner of that name stood in watchful silence.

The girl saw the Lady Deq Dimani curled beside the blind priestess, then Ridek beyond. Her eyes traveled up past the boy's head to Tse'e's glittering sword, then over to Trinesh's appalled face.

She knew him at once.

The Lady Jai smiled, a tender and loving smile, full of yearning and enticement, temptation and promise and desire. Trinesh had seen her so only twice before: once after Balar died, and then again when she had descended from Prince Tenggutla Dayyar's apartments in Ninue.

"I see that you already have been told of me, mighty Prince," the Lady Jai said.

She did not change, did not transform herself into the column of ravening flame Trinesh had both expected and dreaded. She only smiled, glowed with all of the charm of a maiden in love, and advanced a pace.

"No!" the Lady Arsala shrieked. She leaped to her feet. Karin Missum was before her, sword raised. Lord Huso clenched his teeth and made diagrams in the air. The others fell prone or scuttled aside.

"It profits nothing," the Lady Jai murmured. "Mighty Prince, we shall not lie together tonight—no embrace of joy, no union of our bodies. Yet we shall at least touch lip to lip."

Kadarsha seemed frozen. He stared, struggled, and lifted one hand. He held some device, an "Eye," probably. Trinesh fumbled in his belt-pouch for the one Prince Tenggutla Dayyar had given him.

"No spells, no magic, no machines, no swords," the girl crooned. "They are futile against Flamesong. Lord Vimuhla's weapon is mightier than all." She held out her hands to Kadarsha.

The gauzy draperies smoked, flared, and dropped from her arms in a swirl of gray ash. The collar, the girdle, her bracelets and rings, melted and dribbled away to become white-hot lumps upon the carpets. Fire sprang up there in a score of places. The silver chains in her hair became bright rivulets that trickled down over her naked shoulders. Her tresses fell free about her but did not burn. Trinesh felt heat like that of a smith's forge: a sustained, growing, roaring conflagration. It was hot but not unbearable: its energies were somehow contained and fed back again out of the room into the Planes Beyond. Flamesong consumed only those things which were in direct contact with the girl's body. From Trinesh's distance—three paces—its burning was more of a passion, a tide of sensual fervor within himself, than the blazing calefaction of any mortal fire. He sensed his loins thickening, his manhood rising.

Naked, the Lady Jai went forward, a lover eager for her beloved.

Karin Missum slashed at her, struck, and stood amazed as his fine steel sword disappeared in a spray of molten silvery dew. Some of that deadly rain fell upon Lord Huso, and he screamed and lurched aside.

The Lady Arsala mouthed the words of some spell. The Lady Jai shrugged, turned, and touched a single, slim finger to the woman's tunic. Cloth crackled and burst into red tongues of flame. The priestess jerked backward, rolled, doubled up, and beat at her breast like a *Qasu*-bird who blunders into a watchfire.

Others sprang in to strike: Kambe, Te'os, Zaklen, and the other bodyguards from outside the door. Some she slew, and others she left charred upon the smoldering carpets. Trinesh saw Dineva fall, clutching an arm that was blackened and blistering. Chosun swung the heavy candelabrum, a giant mace near as heavy as a man, only to see it touch her skin and explode in a shower of liquid bronze.

Kadarsha still hesitated. The girl's eyes had not left his. It was as though he were transfixed, ensorceled. The Prince, behind him, moved to thrust him aside.

Trinesh still held Tse'e's sword. At his feet, the boy, Ridek, batted at a drop of molten metal that sizzled upon his ragged green tunic. The Mihalli had rolled over and was struggling with his bonds; there was no time to see, but Trinesh thought that someone else knelt there beside the creature.

The Lady Deq Dimani caught his attention. She was awake, sitting up, her hands clawing at her cheeks as though she would pry her swollen eyelids open by sheer physical force.

"No, Jai!" the woman shrieked. "That is not Mirusiya! Kadarsha—I know him! I have seen him before!" She repeated her words in guttural Yan Koryani.

For the first time the girl faltered. She slowed, swerved to look, and opened her lips. Her eyes were blank ovals of fire, her mouth the ravening maw of some flame-belching furnace.

Trinesh pressed the stud of Prince Tenggutla Dayyar's "Eye."

She staggered. He could feel the blaze within her dim, then

leap high again; it was as though a door had momentarily closed upon an oven.

"No, Jai! Not Kadarsha!"

Trinesh fired his "Eye" a second time. The room swayed, darkened as does a new-poured ingot when water is splashed upon it, and righted itself again. The "Eye" grew hot in his fingers, and he almost let it fall. The Lady Jai turned to stare straight at him. There was death in that gaze. She swung back to Kadarsha, then twisted to her left, toward Prince Mirusiya.

"Yes! Yes, he!" It took no knowledge of Yan Koryani to interpret the Lady Deq Dimani's cry.

Kadarsha took two paces forward.

He embraced the girl.

If he screamed it was lost in the white-hot shriek of steam and flame that poured up from where he stood. The choking stench of roasted flesh and burning entrails filled the room and was just as quickly gone as all that had been Kadarsha hiTlekolmü became first a contorted, blackened shell, then a cinder, then a storm of pale ashes.

It was over within a single heartbeat. A dusting of white floated down over the flaming carpets.

Something smashed against Trinesh's thigh, and he stumbled back. The boy! No, it was another, the dark-furred nonhuman. How had he freed himself?

Now he saw that there were two such aliens. One was still bound, but the second seized the Yan Koryani princeling and thrust him headlong into the colorless mirror-oval of a Nexus Point portal that flickered upon the wall beside the Flame Lord's altar. The creature picked up the Lady Deq Dimani and wrestled her into the opening, then returned to drag the remaining Mihalli after himself as well.

"Jai! —Flamesong!" the woman called shrilly, "Follow us! Now!"

Of those still unharmed, Trinesh was the closest to the Nexus Point. He yelled something and stabbed blindly at the second Mihalli's retreating back. He heard a cracking, rattling crunch, and wood splintered under his blow. The harp! The blind nomad had been a Mihalli, his red-glowing eyes disguised in the only possible way, beneath the hideous scar-tissue of *Alungtisa*!

Trinesh turned and cast about for help. Other figures were visible in the choking smoke and Flamesong's incandescent glare, but he could not see who or how many. He hesitated, but the heat was too great to bear. He coughed, screwed his streaming eyes shut, and hurled himself after the four Yan Koryani. He did remember to shout, "After me!"

24

The heat—battle-madness, divine passion, or the very real agony of burning—dissipated almost as quickly as it had come. Trinesh found himself on his knees upon a paving of black-flecked gray stone. A corridor descended in front of him in gradual stages to be lost in the murky gloom ahead, its neatly mortared masonry walls lit at intervals by torches in cressets. The ceiling was vaulted, and moisture plashed in puddles upon the flagging.

Was this Ninue again? It was certainly not the *Ochuna*. Nor, praise to the Flame Lord, was it one of those Demon Planes where poisonous vegetation vied with more mobile inhabitants to discommode the traveler. More than one epic described such mordant events!

If the second Mihalli were a Yan Koryani agent, then he could hazard an excellent guess as to his present whereabouts. This gave him small comfort.

He looked around. Two paces behind him, up the shallow staircase of the passage, the Nexus Point hung upon the right-hand wall, an alien and colorless doorway to Other-Space. Ten more paces beyond the portal, a verdigris-stained portcullis of thick metal bars blocked the tunnel completely.

That direction was closed, then.

Yet where was the boy? The Mihalli and his living burdens? Trinesh turned back to squint down the corridor but could see no sign of them. They had preceded him by no more than two minutes at most. Yet that would probably suffice to travel far enough down the dimly lit stairstep-passage to be lost to view, if one knew where one was going.

And now that he was here, just what, exactly, had he planned to do?

Escape did come to mind.

He inspected himself. Aside from a few bruises and a white blister upon his left thigh between his tasses and his knee where a drop of molten slag had landed, he was unhurt, saved by his Engsvanyali armor. He'd be damned if he'd meekly surrender it to General Kutume after this! He rose, leaned on Tse'e's steel sword as an old woman does her cane, and stumbled up to put his head cautiously through the Nexus doorway.

Flames. An inferno. Smoke, fire, leaping figures. Shouting. He could distinguish nothing. Nor could he see Flamesong in the midst of the conflagration.

He wrenched himself back as two—three—blackened shapes came tumbling through the Nexus door. He was too late; they knocked him flat, sending the breath rattling from his lungs. The first was Chosun, the second Arjasu, and the third, who leaped over the others like a nimble *Atlun*-spider, was Tse'e.

Trinesh crawled out from beneath the tangle, grimly contemplated a new roster of abrasions, and examined the newcomers. Chosun's armor was starred with golden sun-blaze spatters of what had recently been the bronze candelabrum. He had no helmet, and his round, neckless head was scorched and blistered, yet he seemed to feel no pain. Arjasu was unharmed; he had not attacked Flamesong. His crossbow had once more been left outside with the Prince's guards, and the short dagger he still wore at his belt would have been as feeble as a *Hruchan*-reed—as were all their weapons! Tse'e's desert-cloak was burned through in a dozen places, but the leather had protected every scrawny part of him save for his balding skull. Several angry burns there would require attention later.

"The others?" Trinesh panted.

"The Prince got out through some secret door in back," Arjasu reported smoothly. "Karin Missum and his priest fled through the front entrance—Dineva too. I saw somebody helping her, Kambe maybe. At least one of the thrice-damned, useless Vriddi bravos escaped as well. The rest—?" He sketched the Flame Lord's sign in the air with three soot-smeared fingers. "They're probably sipping molten fire-stone in one of mighty Vimuhla's ecstatic, white-hot paradises by now!"

"The Senior General's dead," Chosun added unnecessarily. All of them had seen him die.

"General Kutume returned just after the fire started," Arjasu continued with military precision. "He was howling for buckets and water, but those of us on your side of the room couldn't get across to him." The crossbowman fingered a seared spot on one cheek. "Aside from General Kadarsha, we may not have lost much."

"He was enough," Trinesh sighed gloomily. He did not want to think now of the political and military ramifications of the Senior General's brave self-sacrifice. More, the most urgent question still remained:

"The Lady Jai—Flamesong?"

The others exchanged uneasy glances. "The room was a furnace, *Hereksa*," Chosun muttered.

Trinesh came to a decision. "Time we got ourselves away—I heard the Lady Deq Dimani calling the Lady Jai to follow. If we stay here or try to go back now, we may run headlong

into her Flamesong—more morsels for her feast!'' He set the
example himself by striding off down the passage.

They had not gone more than a hundred paces when a flare
of crackling yellow-white light behind them announced the
advent of Lord Vimuhla's mighty weapon herself.

Tse'e halted to look. ''She's not human any more,'' he
marveled. ''More like the 'column of candent Flame, a funeral pyre upon which all foes are consumed,' as the poet
says in 'The Lament to the Wheel of Black.' Thus was Lord
Vimuhla's weapon at Dormoron Plain—'' Trinesh seized the
collar of his desert-cloak and dragged him away. There was a
fascination for all ages and sexes in Flamesong, it seemed.

A larger darkness appeared ahead. The corridor opened out
into a chamber before them, and Trinesh slowed to take
stock. His little band was mostly unarmed. He still had
Tse'e's steel blade, but he counted himself their best swordsman and hence did not offer to return it to the old man. Both
he and Arjasu had daggers—useless as feathers, probably,
against whatever inhabited this hole: monsters, soldiers, demons, or the gods themselves! Chosun and Tse'e had no
weapons at all.

Arjasu was the most skilled with missiles, and Trinesh
handed him Prince Tenggutla Dayyar's ''Eye.'' As he instructed the crossbowman, it had done something to Flamesong
back in Kankara and possibly to the Mihalli in Ninue, but he
still had not fathomed precisely what.

He explained his plan. ''We watch for the Lady Deq
Dimani, her two Mihalli, and the boy. We can't fight them,
not if they have sorcery. Instead we hide or run, stay out of
the Lady Jai's—Flamesong's—way, and wait for a chance to
run back up the passage. Pray that the Nexus Point doorway
lasts until we reach it. By that time the fire in the Prince's
chamber should be extinguished, and we can slip back
through.''

''If we catch the Lady Deq Dimani off guard—'' Chosun
suggested optimistically.

"Recapture her? Slay her? Small chance of that!" His hopes for gold and promotion had long since gone a-glimmering. The Baron's son, the Lady Deq Dimani—even Okkuru's gold, now doubtless confiscated by an amazed and joyous General Kutume—all were shadows, dreams, fantasies as far-fetched as those of a gambler who has already lost his last *Kaitar* to the *Kevuk*-dice!

An obscenity rose to his tongue, but that, too, was futile.

They came to another gate, a threaded, circular tunnel of bronze barely a man-height high and almost five paces in length. A plug of great size hung upon massive hinges beside the aperture, ready to be swung into place and screwed shut with a wheel. An identical wheel was visible on the inside of the door-plug; once within, one could at least emerge again. Both hinges and wheels gleamed bright gold with recent usage.

Someone came this way. Often.

Whoever it was, he or she—or it—had built to last. And to keep some other very powerful thing either out or in.

The chamber beyond the entrance-tunnel was cool and shadowy, lit from above by a wavering green phosphorescence. Colossal pilasters marched away into obscurity, but they did not support the roof. These columns were stumps: old, worn, pocked, corroded, and coated with vermilion and indigo encrustations that hid whatever inscriptions or designs they might once have held. The floor crunched underfoot. Washed in the undulating, citrine glow, it resembled the floor of the sea.

Which it was. A scalloped *Faru*-shell protruded like a miniature pink pyramid from the sea-wrack by Trinesh's boot.

He raised his eyes. The luminous emerald ceiling could well be water. That shadow which glided over their heads was no bird, no winged *Sro*-dragon! Circles of pallid luminescence spotted the beast's flanks like the portholes of a foundered ghost-ship, and its ribbed flukes raised roiling eddies of smaller, silvery fish with their passing.

He swallowed hard and gave Tse'e a sidelong glance. This place resembled Na Ngore, but the look the old man sent back told him that he, too, had divined the nature of their surroundings. It seemed expedient not to mention it to Chosun or Arjasu. This was no habitat for humankind!

Now he could make out other constructions farther on within the gloomy chamber: broken, blue-gray walls whose angular carvings were blotched with corals and the empty skeletons of pallid sea-growths; rows of pedestals from which disfigured statues gazed sadly down, heroes wounded not by war but by time, the Ultimate Victor; trapezoidal doorways that did not use the arch; titanic blocks of porous stone half-sunk beneath the sand; and friezes blurred and rubbed soft by the relentless caress of the sea.

There was air here; his lungs told him that he still breathed. He had not become a fish! The sorcerous energies needed to keep this place secure against the pressures of the ocean must be potent beyond imagining!

Yet they were not really very deep: a shimmer of sunlight filtered down to them through the layers of green water, and back in the direction of the way they had come, he perceived a tenebrous mass, a looming wall, that must be a headland rising up out of the ocean into the world above.

Glitter caught his eye. He waved the others down behind a hedge of lacy, brittle, alabaster-hued limbs. There was a clearly defined path through the ruins straight ahead, but that was the likeliest spot for guards. He signaled Arjasu and Chosun to scout to the left, while he and Tse'e went to the right.

They skirted two pylons of ocher-mottled stone, then took shelter again behind an enormous lump of greyish coral the size of a vintner's wine-cask. Just ahead, three broad tables stood before a forest of spiky, sky-blue branches: trees from some drowned and forlorn landscape, or the up-jutting ribs of a sea-monster. These tables, however, belonged not to the deeps but to the upper world of light and air: they were carved of sorrel-hued wood, dark-varnished and scarred with use, as prosaic as any of the furnishings in Trinesh's clanhouse. Objects were heaped in disarray upon them, a *Mnor*'s-nest of shapes, hues, and materials.

Trinesh surveyed the nearest table, that on the right. Its contents looked like weapons: he made out a sword-hilt, another complex blade with many points and barbs, a big round object that could be the head of a mace, a gauntlet, a heap of rusted links—a mail hauberk? —and a score of other military oddments. Loot from these sunken ruins? Plunder from ships cast away at sea?

The objects on the central table were different: a farrago of metal parts and pieces, whorls, strands, devices, tubes, enigmatic boxes like those they had found in the tubeway car they had taken from the Ssu, and shiny tools. In a cleared space at the front of the bench he saw six small ovoids the size of *Dlel*-fruit pits.

He blinked.

Those were "Eyes," identical to Trinesh's own, though doubtless built to perform different functions! Two had been separated into hemispheres, and these were surrounded by a fuzz of silvery filaments. Other tiny parts lay ready to hand beside them.

Excitedly, Trinesh pointed out the devices to Tse'e.

"A few scholars can repair 'Eyes,' " the old man whispered. "But no one knows how to construct them. That skill was lost after the Latter Times."

Trinesh had heard only vague mention of that fabulously ancient period, and it showed in his face.

Tse'e glanced around but saw no imminent danger; neither Flamesong nor the Lady Deq Dimani's party was in view. He dug himself a hollow in the dry sand. "Listen, then. The Latter Times followed the Time of Darkness as twilight succeeds a storm before the night. It was during the Time of

Darkness that the lamps in the sky were blown out—have you heard that at least? It is mentioned in the 'Hymn to Na-Iverge,' the recension of the twenty-third Engsvanyali dynasty. In any event, Tekumel was sent into an eon-long convulsion of upheaval and cataclysm—no epic says how or why—and so ended all alone, save for its sun, its four sister-planets, and its two moons.''

"Company enough, one might think."

"But not what had been before. Once, in Avanthar, I saw a book inscribed upon leaves of imperishable metal such as the Ancients made. It had been translated into the tongue of Llyan of Tsamra, thence into Engsvanyali, and so into Classical Tsolyani, which all of us Imperial children were taught to read. That text detailed the paroxysms of the earth and the sea, the cyclones and torrents, the fall of cities, and the termination of the world as the Ancients knew it. It spoke of the decay of knowledge, the enclaves of artisans who grew ever fewer and could obtain neither materials nor power for their machines, the fossilization of learning and its transformation into cant and ritual, and the dissolution of the ties that bound Tekumel's peoples—human and nonhuman—together. The indigenous races, 'the Foes of Man,' the Hlüss and the Ssu, poured forth from the reservations where they had been contained, and they wrought vengeance upon those who had wrested their world from them. As that book said, 'Once the wan, slow afternoon of the Latter Times had begun, it endured for millennia without counting, until the final sunset brought the shadows and the end of the day.' ''

Trinesh grew restive. "But those 'Eyes'?"

"Ai, they appear to be under repair by some artificer who knows his craft. The Temples of Lords Thumis and Ksarul are best at such gimcrackery." Tse'e paused to consider. "Yet this is certainly no jack-priest's magic-shop!"

"Cha! Why build such mechanisms when spells are available?"

"Why, indeed? Once the technique of drawing energy

from the boundless stores of the Planes Beyond was discovered, it profits little to fuss with metals and glass and mechanical tricks. An 'Eye' is stronger than a spell, but each must be individually constructed for its purpose, and that requires more art—and scarce materials—than does a spell learned by rote. If one has the psychic ability, the training, and the *Pedhetl*—'' He noted the pained look on Trinesh's face and took pity. "The *Pedhetl* is a mental reservoir found within each animate being; the energies of the Planes Beyond seep through the 'skin of reality' to fill this basin, and one whose *Pedhetl* is capacious can then utilize that power to trigger spells drawing still greater forces from outside this Plane. Why labor to create an explosion with alchemical powders—I have seen it done—when any temple adept can make a much louder bang with the force of his mind alone?''

"Then? Why 'Eyes' at all?''

"I think they were developed before the Ancients knew how to exploit the energies of the Planes Beyond. And, as I said: they are stronger in their one limited effect than most spells. Moreover, they can be employed by anyone: a child, a fool, a person with no ability or *Pedhetl* at all!''

"How ignoble,'' Trinesh mused. "To deprive the sorcerer of his uniqueness, to put magic within the reach of any idiot who acquires a device! I myself have pushed the stud of an 'Eye,' and it gave me no sense of accomplishment or dignity thereby. If swordsmanship were like an 'Eye,' then any herd-boy would be the equal of mighty Hrugga himself! Fa!''

"The scholars concur. They wag their beards and shake their wise heads; yet it is clearly easier to fire an 'Eye' than to master the arcane lore of sorcery. Don't you see?''

Trinesh did. He was also reminded to look for their foes and so put his head up above their coral refuge. At this distance, he could not distinguish what rested upon the leftmost table, but Arjasu ought to be in a position to see that. On the other side of the jagged vertebrae of the ridge before which the three tables stood he noted something else: a row of golden helices upon pedestals, involuted three-dimensional patterns of what appeared to be metal rods. As he watched, these revolved slowly, caught the light as they swung this way and that, and turned themselves inside out in eye-hurting optical illusions of lines and spaces.

He opened his mouth to make these new mysteries known to Tse'e, but he was interrupted. A voice, feminine and weak-sounding, called something in Yan Koryani from behind them.

Flamesong!

No, it was now the Lady Jai Chasa Vedlan. She came picking her way down the central path, a naked, pretty, and very human clan-girl who stumbled over the sand like some tipsy handmaiden at a Jakallan orgy! She was clearly near collapse.

An answering shout came from in front of him, and he swung back to see one of the Mihalli emerge around the end of the jag-toothed wall of blue-white bones—or coral, or whatever it was. The creature went to her, gathered her in its oddly jointed arms, and bore her to the open area before the work-tables. Whether this was Aluja or the erstwhile harper from Prince Mirusiya's chambers he could not say.

The boy, Ridek, came forth as well. Then the Lady Deq Dimani followed, leaning upon the arm of the second Mihalli. She gestured, and the boy took up a garment—a russet worksmock or tunic—from the left-most table and went to drape it about the girl's shoulders. The older woman limped over and embraced her, as Trinesh had seen her do in the *Ochuna*. She drew the Lady Jai down, stroked her hair, and murmured to her in Yan Koryani. The girl appeared dazed, sick, and confused, and her body shook with weeping.

Did Flamesong debilitate its bearer—eventually destroy the feeble, mortal "hilt" with which it must be wielded in this Plane? Or was her weakness due to the "Eye" Trinesh himself had fired at her?

Trinesh felt a pang of sadness: not for Flamesong, certainly, nor for the suffering of the Lady Deq Dimani. He was sorry for Jai Chasa Vedlan. It was as she herself had said: under other circumstances she might have loved him—as he assuredly could have loved her in return.

Fingers clawed at his arm. Tse'e hissed, "Flat! Someone else comes!" He jerked Trinesh down so violently that he bit into powdery, brine-tasting sand.

Footsteps crunched along the central path and stopped perhaps ten paces away. Trinesh dared not raise his head to see. He and Tse'e ought to be near-invisible lying prone behind their giant *Kao*-squash of coral.

He heard a shout and then a garble of unintelligible Yan Koryani. One of the newcomers was a woman, another a man. The boy, Ridek, cried something; the man replied in a sharp, staccato voice almost as high; the woman added a word or two in a rich contralto different in pitch and intonation from the others; then one of the Mihalli spoke at length. These people knew one another! Presumably they were explaining how they came to be in this bubble-chamber beneath the sea. The conversation went on and on.

Trinesh could stand it no longer. He ventured a look.

And found himself staring at the glinting point of a steel sword not a hand's breadth from his nose.

He let out a wordless yell and fell backwards over Tse'e.

There was shouting. Tse'e's sword was knocked from his grasp, and he could only flail and kick at his attacker. Hands pulled him roughly to his feet, and he felt the ice-keen edge of a blade at his throat.

He stopped struggling.

A slender, clever-eyed, smallish man in a loose, brown tunic and leather boots stood before him, disheveled and panting. Beside him, two paces away upon the sand, Tse'e knelt clutching at his abdomen. Trinesh could see no blood. One of the Mihalli ran light-footed over to menace them with a claw-bladed cutlass from the table. Over his shoulder Trinesh glimpsed a feminine face, harsh but exotically beautiful, light-complected, straight-nosed, and proud. This, then, was the woman who had crept up to ambush them. Her lips were drawn back in a grimace, and the dagger she held had a businesslike sheen to it.

A vision of Horusel threatening the Lady Deq Dimani in just this fashion in the tubeway car rose to mind. That seemed so long ago! He sighed and held his hands out from his sides in surrender, as she had done then.

Where was the Lady Deq Dimani? He sought and found her still slumped beside the Lady Jai, one hand pressed to the bandage the blind seeress had applied to her face.

Was she pleased at this turnabout? He could not discern her expression. Nor Jai's.

The woman with the knife stepped around him, and he saw that she wore a belt of animal hide with the fur still attached, leather leggings, and, incongruously, a Yan Koryani over-blouse and fringed skirt of silky *Güdru*-cloth. Her hair was caught up in a net of lacquered leather cords.

What sort of odd, tribal war-witch was this? He knew so little of the peoples of the Baron's realm.

The man snarled something in Yan Koryani that sounded both harsh and commanding.

The Lady Deq Dimani raised her head. "He is Tsolyani, my Lord. Use that tongue, and likely he'll answer you."

The other raised an eyebrow. "Tsolyani? He followed you through Gireda's Nexus Point?"

The Mihalli before him held out what looked like a shape-less chunk of grass-green stone and growled something in Yan Koryani. This must be Gireda; Trinesh was beginning to recognize the slight individual differences between him and Aluja.

"Ah. A symbol of High Cartography depicting Yan Kor." The brown-clad man waggled his fingers in a beckoning gesture, and the creature laid the rock upon his palm. "An old one, made back before the Tsolyani Emperors lost the north. It shows the long tunnel from the Citadel of Ke'er down to the sea but not this chamber. That was not built then." He gave Trinesh a harder look. "Engsvanyali armor. You must be the hero of Ridek's tale."

"I am Trinesh hiKetkolel, of the Red Mountain clan, *Hereksa* of the Legion of the Storm of Fire."

"Cha! Such punctilio! Aluja says that you possess a most useful 'Eye.' May I have it, please?"

"You fail in courtesy, Sir. You are?"

The other pursed thin lips. "I? I am Lord Fu Shi'i, the Baron's adviser, and this gentle maiden is the Lady Si Ziris Qaya, matriarch and chieftainess of the Lorun tribes of the north. The 'Eye,' young man!"

"It—is—was lost at Kankara. I dropped it." Lying to an avowed enemy was not ignoble.

Lord Fu Shi'i adopted a sorrowful look, but the woman smiled, reminiscent of a fanged *Zrne* about to receive its dinner. She was tall, broad-shouldered, and obviously skilled with either the dagger or the long sword that hung from her baldric.

The little man frowned, drew a diagram in the air, and muttered words. Trinesh discovered that he could no longer move or speak. Even in distant Tumissa folk had spoken of Lord Fu Shi'i; the Baron's chief counselor was said to be a most puissant wizard, but no one had come close to the reality of it! The spell had seemed effortless, as casual as drawing breath!

"Search him. And the old Milumanayani—" The Lady Deq Dimani murmured, and Lord Fu Shi'i's eyebrows rose still higher. "A Prince? Nalukkan hiTlakotani? I knew him once." He examined Tse'e again. "Ohe. My memory grows dim over the years. You are indeed he, the bane of the Vriddi, the butcher of Fasiltum! The Lady Deq Dimani may have more to say to you later."

They would be kept, then, for ransom or sacrifice. He was not sure which of those two unhappy dénouements he himself would choose when the time came, but there would be oppor-

tunity enough to think upon it in the prison to which he and
Tse'e would likely be sent. At least death upon a Yan Koryani
altar was not shameful, unlike the impaling stake at Pu'er!

That reminded him of something: where were Arjasu and
Chosun? He was facing the wrong direction to see their
presumed hiding place, but they must be out there somewhere! Lord Fu Shi'i's prowling warrior-woman had found
him and Tse'e easily enough—la, like two sand-clams bask-
ing at their ease in the sun! —yet she had missed the others.

Could their comrades rescue them?

He doubted it. The most he dared hope was that his two
soldiers might avoid capture. If they could reach the Nexus
Point, they were safe and could report to Prince Mirusiya.
But was the portal still open? Probably not: after all, Lord Fu
Shi'i and this Lorun wench had come down by that passage,
had they not? The mage would surely have dealt with any
Other-Planar doorways encountered en route.

The woman ran her hands over them, efficiently and rudely.
She shook her red-glinting black locks.

"Naught. Let me slay them. Why waste the Baron's time?
He will only worry." She spoke Tsolyani slowly and con-
temptuously, as though she wanted Trinesh and Tse'e to
appreciate their melancholy Skeins to the utmost.

Lord Fu Shi'i stood close beside her. "I know you, my
Lady," he replied in a voice low enough to be inaudible to
the other Yan Koryani behind him. "You would slay this
pair. Then you would dispatch the boy and the Lady Deq
Dimani as well. You would have me slay Flamesong—or
dispel her to her own Plane. Thereafter the Lady Mmir dies,
and you, my Lady, become the successor to Ald's lost Yilrana
in all things: in the Baron's bedchamber, in his heart, in the
councils of his generals, and among the clans of Yan Kor. A
Lorun triumph—and a Skein as transparent and blood-scarlet
as a goblet of Mu'ugalavyani red glass!"

She licked her full lower lip. "You have said that you
work better with Sihan than with this *Thargir* warrior-pup,

Ridek. You have filled Sihan's soul with cruelties and terrors, the better to knead him upon your potter's wheel! Now is the time to use that clay! The Baron has already ordained forty days of mourning for his lost son; why compel him to cancel such poignant commemorations?''

"So the boy stays dead. I was right, then. La! Let no one accuse the Lorun of fidelity: you are as duplicitous as the Pygmy Folk!'' Lord Fu Shi'i stroked his chin and chuckled. "Thereafter Yan Kor soon rejoices in a new princeling, eh? A child by you, the Baron's wife—no longer 'the Princess of the North' but its queen.''

If Lord Fu Shi'i accepted the woman's proposal, there would be no ransom or honorable sacrifice for Trinesh and Tse'e. They would die here in this secret workroom beneath the sea.

"Your Mihalli are slaves to you alone, my Lord. They cannot tell, nor even hint at, what transpires here unless you give them leave. A nice tapestry, a credit to the Weaver of Skeins, as these southerners say. We Lorun blame our destinies upon other gods.''

"The deities of your Cold White Land? Were-beasts, faceless monsters, the archetypes of your savage shamans?''

"Better than those who live beyond the northern ice, on the other side of Tekumel: those things whom *you* serve, my Lord! Those who would see Yan Kor, Tsolyanu, and all the rest of humankind go howling down to dance before the Lord of Death!''

Lord Fu Shi'i returned her only a bland and pleasant smile. "I agree to your plan. Do as you would.''

The Lady Si Ziris Qaya said, "So. First we shall have a look at this Tsolyani soldier's innards!'' She raised the dagger, and Trinesh could make no move to thwart her.

There was movement. He heard, rather than saw, Chosun's lumbering, *Chlen*-beast charge across the cavern. Arjasu was there too, the "Eye" clenched in both fists, pausing to aim

and fire, then zigzagging forward after the *Tirrikamu*. The
weapons piled on the right-hand table were their goal.

The Lorun woman whirled, her dagger in her left hand in
lieu of a shield and her sword already out and ready. Tse'e
suddenly erupted into action; Lord Fu Shi'i's spell had either
missed him or had been ineffectual. He swarmed over the
woman from behind, and she staggered, yet did not fall. The
Mihalli, Gireda, dropped his cutlass and flourished his blue
ball, seeking a target. The boy, the two women, and Aluja
were on their feet as well. Lord Fu Shi'i grunted in surprise
but seemed unafraid. He stood back, shook himself to settle
his tunic upon his shoulders, and wove a spell-pattern with
nimble fingers.

Only Trinesh was compelled to stand immobile, a piece of
decorative statuary, while his companions fought for their
lives! He strained each muscle in turn and was rewarded with
a tingling sensation in his fingers and toes.

The spell was dissipating!

Chosun reached the right-hand table, snatched up a huge
mace that bristled with steel thorns, and hurled it at the Lorun
woman. She dodged, but Tse'e's weight and flailing limbs
dragged her almost to her knees. She slashed down beside her
thigh with her dagger, and the old man fell away, red staining
the mottled brown of his desert-cloak. Chosun wasted no time
but selected another weapon from the table, a thick chopper,
very like the axe-sword of the reptilian Shen or the *Chidok*
the Livyani preferred. He advanced to do battle.

Trinesh had unbalanced himself in his struggle. Slowly,
majestically, he toppled forward to mash his nose in the sand
and lie supine almost beneath Lord Fu Shi'i's polished black
boots. He heard shouting, the clamor of melee, the clash of
Chosun's heavy weapon against the Lorun girl's lighter blade,
and the shuffle of feet as the combatants feinted for advantage. Here he had a nobleman's seat at the arena and yet
could not see the gladiators!

In fact, the reek of brine and gritty sand in his face gave

warning that he would soon suffocate unless he could rid himself of this accursed spell! He increased his efforts.

From directly above him Lord Fu Shi'i cried out, more a wail of anguish than a scream of pain. Trinesh could not see the cause. He guessed that Arjasu's "Eye" had done something, though he had no idea what. He gasped and discovered that he could open his mouth—which promptly filled with sand. More usefully, he was able to roll over.

He sat up.

Lord Fu Shi'i stood over him, eyes wide and staring as he sketched invisible runes in the air. Had the crossbowman missed, or was the mage immune to the "Eye"? Trinesh had no way of knowing, but he knew how dangerous the Baron's adviser was reputed to be. He cast about for a weapon, saw nothing, and struggled with limbs that were as heavy as waterlogged wood. Cha! He still could not stand up!

He crawled over and butted Lord Fu Shi'i from behind with his helmet-crest.

It was enough; the sorcerer yelped and whirled upon him, enraged. At least the incantation had been disrupted!

Now Trinesh perceived the hilt of Tse'e's sword protruding from the sand a pace to his left. He stretched out a hand and scrabbled for it. He need not have bothered: Lord Fu Shi'i took note of Trinesh' determined face and scuttled off to a safer distance.

Trinesh assessed the situation. Chosun and the Lorun woman were locked in melee, sweat-glazed and streaked with sand as they battled to and fro. Directly in front of him the Lady Deq Dimani had risen, dragging the Lady Jai up as well. She waved her good arm and cried words at the girl. Aluja crouched beside them, one restraining hand on Ridek's arm.

Trinesh arose upon legs as stiff as *Tiu*-logs. Lord Fu Shi'i stood poised for flight, but Arjasu blocked his path, the "Eye" still aimed at him.

Trinesh was directly in the line of fire.

His limbs were brittle crystal; he could not even dive for

cover. The glassy iris of the device winked at him like some evil, one-eyed beast, and his stomach congealed. He was as good as dead!

Trinesh saw Arjasu's thumb tighten once, twice, upon the stud.

There was no effect!

He still lived! Indeed, he was amazed to discover that he felt better than ever!

Lord Fu Shi'i howled again.

Gireda, the Mihalli with the blue-glowing sphere, appeared at the edge of his vision. Aluja gesticulated and cried something in their lilting, warbling, nonhuman tongue, and the creature halted, his weapon half raised.

Trinesh lifted Tse'e's sword to meet him. Astonished, he watched Gireda point his weapon not at Arjasu nor at Trinesh himself, but at the Lorun woman! Its beam of twinkling, pearl-blue radiance struck her like a bolt from a ballista. She threw up her hands, and her sword spun free; then she stumbled back to crumple in a rag-doll heap beside the central table. Chosun lowered his blade to gape at the Mihalli.

"Tsolyani! Tsolyani!" Gireda cried shrilly. "Not me—not Fu Shi'i!" The creature addressed Arjasu and not Trinesh. "Behind us—those devices! Those golden whorl-things!"

The crossbowman faltered, confused.

"The *Gayu*, Tsolyani! Free us!"

Trinesh followed Gireda's pointing finger. Two or three of the strange helices had already been hit; they were dark and had ceased to revolve. More metallic volutes glittered there behind the vertebrae-like ridge.

Still Arjasu wavered, undecided. He looked toward Aluja, then back to Gireda.

Trinesh sprinted forward to snatch the "Eye" from the man's hand. He aimed and fired. Two of the constructions dimmed, flashed with tiny sparkles, and died. He went down the row, clicking the "Eye" until all of the helices were dark.

He saved his final shot for Gireda, but it was not needed. The Mihalli cast his blue globe away upon the sand and spread his six-fingered hands.

"Leave be, Tsolyani," Gireda said. "I do not use my magic against you. Aluja told me of the strange 'Eye' you carried, and I brought you here with just this purpose. I knew when you arrived, where you hid—I had only to find a reason to cause you to use your weapon upon the *Gayu*, the snares built by Lord Fu Shi'i to hold me and my comrades in servitude. Now we are free!"

Trinesh took no chances: he fired one last time, not at Gireda but at his globe. The thing turned dark and became a ball of dull, cloudy glass, as empty as a lamp without oil. Trinesh aimed the "Eye" at the Mihalli but did not shoot.

Gireda's expression changed. "We are free—free!" he marveled. He felt of his limbs, his face. He exulted, rejoiced, flickered, and became a succession of beasts and beings. He elongated, shortened, stretched and shrank, and danced like the pale blue flame above an alchemist's crucible. He vanished, then reappeared. "Free!" he sang, and became a black stick-figure upon a banner of bubbling yellow. "Free!" he cried, and gamboled upon a nimbus of scarlet scintillations.

He sprang forth into a thousand dimensions all at once. He was gone.

Lord Fu Shi'i retreated, away from Trinesh and Arjasu, away from Chosun, who had stooped to see to the Lorun woman. His lips were contorted, and he mouthed incantations; he fumbled with a welter of amulets and periapts which he drew from his garments. None of these produced any result, and he flung them aside one by one. Chosun rose and stalked purposefully toward him, hefting his monstrous cleaver as he came.

Lord Fu Shi'i squalled one final curse and fled back toward the entrance to the sea-chamber.

Trinesh turned his attention to the others. Aluja and the boy had drawn apart from the two women. The Lady Deq

Dimani leaned against the massive worktable, long legs braced to hold herself erect, her head back and her breasts heaving. He followed her eyes over to the Lady Jai.

He knew at once. The girl was radiant, lovely, full of animation.

She was becoming Flamesong again.

"No! My Lady!" Aluja's pleading cry made the older woman turn her head. "Not here! It is too dangerous!" She ignored him and motioned to Jai.

Trinesh pressed the stud of the "Eye." At this range he could not miss. The Lady Jai staggered. Tiny tongues of flame licked her outflung arms, caressed her thighs, touched her hair with cusps of blazing yellow-orange fire. The worksmock she wore was gone within the instant, and she flexed her naked limbs with sensuous delight.

He clicked the "Eye" again, but this time it did nothing. Was it exhausted, empty of power?

He no longer cared.

There had never been anything more glorious than Flamesong, not since the Egg of the World was shattered upon Thenu Thendraya Peak, not since the immortal Gods had warred upon Dormoron Plain. Trinesh did not need to touch her. It was as his Tumissan court-poets declaimed in their lyrics: one look, and the lover's loins turn to coals of fire, his heart to flame, his soul to incense that must burn itself to ashes in order to pleasure the nostrils of his beloved!

Flamesong gazed upon Trinesh. He moved forward, a humble *Karai*-beetle rejoicing in its imminent, gladsome doom in the candle flame! Armuel the Verse smith had never rhymed it so sweetly! The Bard of the Age, Mikkonu of Butrus, could not have immortalized it with greater eloquence! Wondrous-tongued Elue must throw away her sonnets and begin anew! He, Trinesh hiKetkolel, now experienced in the flesh all of that painful, heady, rapturous, divine bliss to which those poor versifiers might aspire but could never attain!

His joy was wondrous. He was transported, exhilarated. Beyond the crude, physical couplings of the Goddess Dlamelish, beyond the cold glories of Lord Hnalla's Pure White Light—beyond the Flame of Lord Vimuhla Himself!

There was a note of disharmony.

For an instant torn out of time he perceived the face of a much less splendid being amid the rapture of Flamesong: the Lady Jai Chasa Vedlan. She cried soundless words to him, her lips wide and distorted with terror, her eyes imploring, her arms out to warn him, to ward him off, to push him away. Then she was Flamesong again, and his ecstasy returned with redoubled fervor.

A pace, another, and he felt her heat. His body shuddered as he reached involuntary climax, then relaxed. The lascivious, searing, delightful agony began to build all over again. He knew now how Kadarsha had felt.

There was a second disharmony, a melancholy chord in this paean of exaltation. Furious, helpless, he felt his attention dragged forcibly away from the goddess in front of him.

Tse'e crouched there. He clawed at Trinesh's shoulder with one skinny hand, the other pressed to his red-sodden breast. The old fool was singing his death-song again! Trinesh slashed at him with his own steel sword. He missed, but it did not matter. Flamesong was too near, too resplendent. She reclaimed him utterly.

"Go!" Tse'e gasped to Aluja. "Take Trinesh—the boy, the others. I will delay her!"

Flamesong had begun to assume her final form, the mighty column of roaring incandescence of which the epics sang. Tse'e looked up. The ceiling, the unthinkably ponderous, immeasurable weight of the ocean above them, sagged and trembled. Lady Avanthe, Tse'e's own goddess, ruled the waters, as she did the seasons and the crops and all that was life. She hated fire.

He squinted with his one good eye and walked forward.

Chosun's well-planned blow caught Trinesh neatly upon

the crown of his head just where the steel of his crested Engsvanyali helmet was thinnest. Aluja swung around, gestured, and brought forth a Nexus Point.

"No!" the Lady Deq Dimani implored him.

Aluja glared. "No more!" he snarled. "No more! Flamesong belongs not to mortals but to the gods! You have gone too far! She is lost to you!" He seized the woman and thrust her into the Nexus doorway. Then he took Trinesh from Chosun and pushed him, stunned but still bedazzled, through after her. He motioned, and the rest scrambled to follow.

Aluja hesitated for a last look. Tse'e—no, give him his true title, the noble name his Imperial father had bestowed upon him: Nalukkan hiTlakotani, Prince of the Petal Throne—stood before Flamesong, arms open, feet wide-spraddled, his one good eye alight with the knowledge that now the Weaver would end his Skein with the nobility for which he had yearned all his life.

Flamesong embraced him and roared high with fiery triumph.

The roof groaned and bellied down above her.

The Mihalli could save neither the Lady Jai nor the old man. Regretfully, he stepped over the verge of the Nexus Point himself.

He was just in time.

25

"I have seen no other 'Eye' like it," Aluja said. The magenta sun was westering now, dulled and dim, a dying coal. He held the device up to catch the rays of the second sun, a marigold-yellow orb bigger in size and appreciably warmer. Their hues had led Chosun to call them the "*Dlel*-fruit" and the "*Mash*-fruit," and these names had stuck during the three long—oddly long—days of their stay upon this alien world to which the Mihalli's Nexus doorway had brought them. Even the Lady Deq Dimani had emerged from her grief long enough to smile.

Trinesh took the "Eye" back. "It sucks Other-Planar power from its target?" He would never be comfortable with sorcery.

"Yes. From any mechanism fueled from the Planes Beyond. It also drains such energies from an animate being's *Pedhetl*. Do you know what that is?"

He did not answer. The word reminded him of Tse'e, and he did not want to remember.

"The *Pedhetl* is like a pot set beneath a leaky roof; when

emptied, it soon fills again. After you struck me with this 'Eye' in Ninue I could neither change shape nor cast spells. The first ability quickly returned, but the second took days.'' Aluja pinched thumb and forefinger together as though firing the device. "Had you done thus to a human mage, he would have been as empty as a beggar's bowl for a six-day—perhaps a month or more. We Mihalli have larger reservoirs—*Pedhetl*— than your species, but even so this weapon would wreak havoc upon us.''

"The 'Eye' grew hot when I used it upon Flamesong.''

"Of course. The Other-Planar energies by which she manifested herself upon Tekumel were immensely powerful. Whatever she was—demon or demi-goddess—your 'Eye' siphoned off no more than a portion of her presence each time you hit her. Yet I doubt that it could have emptied her, even had you fired a hundred shots. It took the mighty waters of the Northern Deeps to vanquish her and expel her from your Plane. The Baron must have witnessed a maelstrom in the ocean below Ke'er that will keep him marveling for a time indeed!''

"This—this 'Eye' is very rare?''

"The rarest. Alas, its charges are now exhausted. It is useless—unless you were to find a 'Thoroughly Useful Eye,' which is what the Ancients called that variety they made to recharge depleted devices. Such replenishers are less common than this one of yours. They were delicate, and most have now failed or are lost to us.''

"Still, this 'Eye'—call it the 'Eye of Imparting Other-Planar Impotence'—can be recharged?'' Trinesh was half minded to fling the thing over the edge of the bluff upon which they sat. The red-green bracken covering the alien landscape below was a fitting repository for something so repugnant to his warrior traditions!

Aluja made the strangled coughing noise Trinesh had learned to interpret as laughter. "I do not know. It might imbibe all the power you put into it, swell up like a puff-bladder, and occasion a serious dehiscence in the continuum!''

Trinesh grimaced and put it away in his pouch. ''Whatever *that* is! I shall keep it then.''

Did the scholars of the Flame Lord's Temple possess a—what was it?—''Thoroughly Useful Eye?'' If so, they might want this one—and pay handsomely to get it. Let the priests worry about poking holes in the cosmos! His little internal voice would have uttered a sharp protest, but he savagely slammed a mental door shut upon it. He was weary of sorcery and enigmas and all rest of the baubles of the Flame-scorched Ancients!

'' 'Eyes' were created as tools,'' the Mihalli continued placidly. ''Most had obvious, workaday purposes, and it was only after the Time of Darkness that the lords of the Latter Times had their savants devise new ones with unusual functions—some appealing to very perverse tastes. It is to this second period that your 'Eye' belongs.''

''Would that none of them had survived!'' Trinesh grumbled. ''What good is a warrior when battles are as easily won by deviants and weaklings?'' He leaned over and spat into the red-flecked brown soil.

Aluja raised his long head. ''It is almost time.'' The two suns made a double halo around him, blood-red on one side and amber-gold on the other. ''When the shadows merge into one, I can return you to Tekumel. The—'' he fumbled for a word ''—the alignments of the Planes will be exact, and you will reappear shortly after you left—in your own places.'' His tone was determined; this time he would make no mistakes!

Trinesh glanced down at their campsite in the glen behind the promontory. The pool, the lean-to, the cooking fire, all were tranquil. Chosun sat upon a log there, ostensibly on guard though Aluja had sworn that this world held no inhabitants: ''a gentle place, near the farthest apex of the cardinal conflux,'' he had styled it, mystifying everyone but himself. He was correct; they had seen nothing larger than the rodent-things Arjasu shot for dinner with his improvised pellet-crossbow.

Ridek's shining black head appeared in the entrance to their shelter, then the Lady Deq Dimani's. Chosun arose to greet them, but Arjasu was not visible.

"You still insist?" Trinesh said. "The Petal Throne will pay handsomely for the woman. —Oh, take the boy home—but give the Lady to me. She is an officer of the Baron's army and Tsolyanu's foe."

"She offers much the same for you," Aluja replied archly. "No, don't bother bidding! We Mihalli are not business-folk. We neither buy nor sell, nor do we hold auctions like the slavers of your human markets. She—all of you—go home."

This was the hardest part for Trinesh—and apparently the Lady as well—to comprehend. Everyone had needs. If the Mihalli did not desire gold, then they ought to want other things: food, land, power, wisdom—something! Nonhumans! Cha!

Indeed, the Mihalli were more alien than Thu'n's Pygmy Folk. The little creature's avarice had earned him no more than a long walk home across the Desert of Sighs—or possibly a less arduous post in Prince Mirusiya's entourage if the Tsolyani sentries had not slain him on sight! Thu'n's motivations were intelligible. So, to a greater or lesser degree, were those of the other nonhuman races: the Shen, the Pe Choi, the Hlaka, the Pachi Lei, or even the rank-smelling, uncouth Ahoggya.

Aluja's race, on the other hand, shared few emotions with humankind. After hunger, sex, and a desire for security, the Mihalli traveled off in other directions. They felt no affection as humans knew that sentiment. He and Gireda had made it easy for Trinesh to follow them to Ke'er—the green mapstone had facilitated the focusing of the Nexus Point—and Trinesh had then used his "Eye" to destroy Lord Fu Shi'i's cruel *Gayu*, thus freeing the twenty or so Mihalli held in bondage to Yan Kor. The action profited both Trinesh's and

Aluja's people; nothing was owed, therefore, as the Mihalli understood the concept of indebtedness. No thought of gratitude crossed Aluja's mind, much less of payment. He did thank Trinesh, yet this was visibly no more than politeness, lip-service to the expected human response. Gireda, who had also benefited from their efforts, had not paused to offer even that courtesy. He had simply vanished.

Were the Mihalli ignoble? Their humanoid form and obvious intelligence made it easy to expect too much of them. They were alien. Still, Trinesh thought, any species ought to respond to affection, and in this Aluja seemed truly unnatural. The most glaring instance was the casual way the Mihalli had hurt Ridek. As soon as they were settled upon this empty world, Aluja had declared in front of everyone that once the boy was safe in Ke'er, he would depart and never see Ridek again. That was unexpected; even an adult would have been taken aback at his abruptness. One did not dismiss friendship as nonchalantly as one brushed dust from one's boots! Not if one were human. . . .

When Trinesh and the Lady Deq Dimani later reproached Aluja for his callousness, the creature responded with puzzlement. His people were the *Chri*-flies of the Many Planes, he said: they fluttered here and there, observed, tasted, enjoyed, and then danced away to seek ever newer sensations. To be tied to any one Plane, even momentarily, was as constricting to them as shackles to a human. He intended no coldness to Ridek—and in truth felt the same affection for him that a Mihalli parent did for its own child—but that was very little when compared with human attitudes toward parents, children, and families. There were no permanent bonds: one went one's way, did as one wished, cooperated or not as whimsy dictated. Intellectually, Aluja's words made some sense to Trinesh and his companions. At a deeper, emotional level, they were incomprehensible. The nature of the Mihalli mind remained obscure.

Aluja's willingness to return them to Tekumel also had no connection with either kindness or camaraderie. It was a means of setting the Skeins straight, laying out the threads, and repairing the rips and tears created by Flamesong's intrusion into their Plane. When this was done, he would go his way.

Yet, Trinesh asked himself, in the last analysis, were the Mihalli really so very different from humankind? Ridek was too young to see the selfishness that cemented human dealings: treaties and policies, friendships and social bonds, marriages and families—even protestations of love! Self-interest was humankind's greatest god; the true altruist, the martyr, the philanthropist who made no display of his giving—those were rarer even than Trinesh's "Eye!"

Cha! He was fast becoming a thoroughgoing cynic! It was not Ridek's idealism that showed the flaw; it was Trinesh' own nature, his lack of trust! Did he not have the evidence of Tse'e, Saina, the Lady Jai, General Kadarsha, and even poor Horusel, who had died for what he sincerely believed? Trinesh' little inner voice would doubtless harp upon those examples until it wore him into the grave proving that the world was not completely venal. Whatever their various—and oft-times opposing—objectives, those folk had behaved nobly; they had set aside their personal interests to serve what they considered higher goals. That, he supposed, was the ultimate purport of Tse'e's counsel to Prince Mirusiya. That was the best a limited, fallible, and very insecure little creature like Trinesh hiKetkolel could hope to accomplish.

He had much to ponder.

Someone hallooed, and Trinesh got to his feet to reply. Chosun clambered up to the top of the bluff, red-faced and puffing. Behind him came Ridek and the Lady Deq Dimani. The shadows cast by the two suns were well nigh one, and it was time to depart.

The woman was beautiful once more. Whether through the

Lady Arsala's doctoring or Aluja's sorcery, the *Shon Tinur* had receded to become only a dark shadow upon her cheek and temple. That, too, would vanish in time, the Mihalli said. Bronzed by the waning red sun and washed with gold by its mate, she was lovely as an arrow is lovely: graceful, sleek, and purposeful. Their sojourn here—days, months, in Tekumel's time? —had done her good.

She and Trinesh had not spoken of their mutual griefs and shadows. Yan Kor and Tsolyanu, the deaths of friends, the hatred her Vriddi ancestors bore for the Petal Throne—all of those stood as firm as the walls of Avanthar between them. Even were they to be breached, dismantled, and made fair, one insurmountable rampart would still remain: the Lady Jai Chasa Vedlan. He himself could never forgive the Lady Deq Dimani. Jai's sad wraith came with the sleep-demons to hold out yearning arms to him, begging him to take her to Tumissa and give her the love and security he and his clan might have provided. The little clan-girl had been made to bear too great a burden—indeed, how many mighty warriors or learned mages could have supported the intolerable presence of Flamesong?

No, the Lady Deq Dimani had much to answer for. Her vaunting ambition, her ancient hates, her heedless desire to win Yan Kor's war with the aid of terrible powers from the Planes Beyond—all were dust when compared with the Lady Jai. The Lady Deq Dimani mourned her, Trinesh knew, but did she have the honesty to face her guilt in the girl's death—even to herself, in her most private moments? Did Jai's ghost visit her, too, to point a finger of accusation? That he doubted; Jai had adored her mistress, obeyed her, and done all that she commanded. She had been unselfish and loyal.

Even when it meant her own sacrifice, her own death.

Nobility . . . !

The Lady Deq Dimani still limped a little. She picked her

way across the rough stones to Trinesh and Aluja, then halted for a last view.

Trinesh greeted her with careful formality. "My Lady."

"*Hereksa*." She seemed hesitant.

"You return to Yan Kor."

"Or to Milumanaya. And you to Tsolyanu? Or Kankara?"

"My place is with my Legion and my Prince."

"As is mine with my people."

She brushed her long tresses back from her cheeks with the graceful gesture he had come to know. "We may meet again—on the field of battle. As once I promised General Kadarsha."

This touched something within him. "Yes. Kadarsha." He clamped his lips shut.

Her eyes glinted yellow in the feeble sunlight. "I—met him once, long ago, in the Chakan forests. I invited him to come to Vridu, to be my consort, chief among my harem of men. But he would not tolerate a matriarchy."

"I can understand that. Nor could any Tsolyani male."

"It is no shame in our northlands."

"No more than were I to invite you to become my chief wife in Tumissa, not a protected little clan-girl but an *Aridani*, my equal . . ." He cursed himself; this bottle he had meant to leave sealed forever!

She gave him a little half-smile. "We are both of warrior clans."

He did not want to hear—especially not this! The ghosts of Tse'e and the Lady Jai still hovered too close.

"We are not soft, gentle, staunch, peaceable people such as the adherents of Lady Avanthe or Lord Thumis," she went on. "Our nobility is not the pursuit of quiet dignity, the round of the year, the sowing and the harvest, the birthing of children, the building of clan and nation and religion. We are warrior-folk: two *Zrne* who battle over their prey and mate only when one or the other howls for quarter."

"As you say." He bit his lip. There were doors here that he did not wish to open. More, he was no longer sure. Trinesh hiKetkolel of the Red Mountain Clan had much thinking to do before he—and his little inner voice—decided what really lay within himself. He turned to Aluja. "Where is Arjasu?"

The Mihalli gave a rippling shrug. "He chooses to stay."

"What? But—"

"He requires healing, just as the Lady did, though his injury is not of the body but of the Spirit-Soul. Such a wound is worse: it festers and is harder to cure. Solitude, peace, and contemplation are his medicines; time is the physician." Aluja swung around to scrutinize the cloud-daises of mauve and burgundy heaped high upon the horizon. "When he is recovered I shall return for him. His Skein, too, must be rewound and woven anew."

Trinesh understood—partially, anyway. He asked, "Then we are ready? Come, Ridek, it is home to Ke'er for you. Your father will be overjoyed."

The boy grinned nervously. In his accented Tsolyani he said, "At first. Then he will be very angry."

"If Lord Fu Shi'i lives—" the Lady Deq Dimani murmured in an ominous undertone.

"My father—and I—will deal with him. If he managed to rescue the Lorun woman before Flamesong brought down the ocean upon her, then the two of us will see to her as well." He shot the Lady Deq Dimani a sidelong glance; she, too, would have to curb her single-minded zeal and her willfulness if she wanted to maintain her status at the court of Ke'er.

The boy was strong. Should Ridek Chna Ald survive, he would become a power indeed! He possessed many of his father's better traits, and he had not suffered the terrible trauma of the soul that had so marred the Baron. When Ridek took up the "Amethyst Sceptre of the Clans United," Tsolyanu would face an implacable foe. Perhaps—just perhaps—something could be done about that first. Prince Mirusiya was not stupid; there might be—must be—a way to turn Ridek, and through him Yan Kor, into an ally.

The Nexus Point appeared. They saluted one another and passed through it.

Trinesh gazed down from the dry, sunbaked scarp upon the *Sakbe* road. There was Kankara! Beyond, the serpentine column of the army wound along the sere roadway to Sunraya for the opening of the spring campaign. He looked upon the dusty squares of marching troops, the nodding plumes of the *Kaing*-standards, the potpourri of multi-hued uniforms and emblazoned shields, the glittering spear-points and the sheen of armor. There came the gaudy litters of the officers and the folk of the Imperial household, then the plodding *Chlen*-carts, top-heavy with baggage and provisions. In the rear, like *Dri*-ants swarming across the plain beside the buff-and-brown roadway, followed the settlers, slaves, servants, whores, merchants, and all the rest. In the midst of the van the pinnacles, banners, and awnings of Prince Mirusiya's magnificent palanquin showed gold and azure above everything else like the palace of one of the gods. Even from this distance Trinesh could hear the deep, sonorous roll of the marching drums, the bray of horns, and the shriek of flutes.

This was familiar. This was home.

He took a step and found Chosun beside him. Another pace, and the events of the recent past began to recede. Another, and they became memory.

They would fade. But never completely.

"Report to General Kutume, *Hereksa*?" The big man sounded as happy as Trinesh had ever known him.

"What else? We've a war to fight."

"Ai, and a little business back in Kankara." The *Tirrikamu* rubbed his shapeless lump of a nose. "Okkuru and I—uh—hid some of his wealth while you were busy reporting to the scribes, right when we first arrived from Pu'er. It's likely still buried under the floor of the tent where they put us. The guards won't let Okkuru back into camp—not after the Prince almost gave him the 'high ride' and packed him off into the desert with General Kutume as a personal escort! La, if we can get leave for a day or two . . . !''

Trinesh's mood improved. "No chance of that! General Kutume'll suffocate us under documents, ring us about with scribblers, and have us picking fly-turds out of his *Chumetl* for a month for being absent without permission! If Okkuru is still about, we can divide the gold with him later—after all, we've earned our shares of it, too! But we'll have to come back for it.''

"Ohe, after we take Vridu," Chosun questioned slyly.

"Yes, all of Yan Kor. I, Trinesh hiKetkolel, intend to be a general myself someday."

He would not speak of the Lady Deq Dimani. Chosun noted this and asked no more.

"A noble Skein, *Hereksa*. But I recall what you said in Ninue about a soldier's wagon." The *Tirrikamu* stroked his jaw philosophically. "Money's only one wheel. The other three are your clan, your friends, and the good graces of your superiors. Those're what roll you on to glory."

Trinesh laughed. He could smell the dust, the leather, the spices, the perfumes, the sweat, and the stench of the great army.

Chosun added, "And as that Mihalli-creature, Aluja, said: at least we're freer than we were, out of the grasp of at least *some* of the greedy buggers from the other Planes!"

His words cast a slight shadow over the sunny landscape.

"Ai, *Hereksa*. He said we should keep *all* of the meddlers from the Planes Beyond away from Tekumel—his own folk included! Play our own game and not let the big gamblers from outside bring in their dice! Fight our own wars, solve our own problems, and weave our own Skeins ourselves. Human Skeins in human hands! Worship the gods but be ready to toss 'em aside when we find we've become damned well as mighty as they are!''

Trinesh turned to raise a quizzical eyebrow at him. ''That last advice you had best forget,'' he said sternly. ''That's heresy, and those like Lord Huso will fry your liver on their altars for it!''

Chosun guffawed and kicked at a clod of earth.

They trudged on in companionable silence.

Come to think of it, the Mihalli's counsel did make a goodly amount of sense at that.

About the Languages

Much of the following material has already been published (*The Man of Gold*, DAW Books, Inc, 1984), but it seems unfair to require readers to rush out to buy a copy of that book in order to see how the names occurring in *Flamesong* are pronounced. Hence this section.

Those who have never been bitten by the "linguistic bug" are invited to ignore everything after this paragraph. Say the names as you think fit. Their pronunciation is of no import to the story in any case.

For those who *are* interested, suffice it to say that the human inhabitants of Tekumel are indeed descended from Terran stock, although the setting of the story is immeasurably far in Earth's future, after humankind has acquired interstellar travel, met the Pe Choi, the Shen, and other star-faring species, and wrested Tekumel from "the Enemies of Man," the Hlüss and the Ssu. The languages of these remote offspring are thus distantly related to ours, as English is to Sanskrit, but at such a time-depth that they have become as different from English as Chinese, Mayan, Arabic, Cree, or Swahili. The one constant in historical linguistics is change: unstoppable, frequently unpredictable (though various laws can often be adduced *post facto*), and sometimes quite surprising. The developments, alterations, minglings, and diversions undergone by our twentieth-century tongues in order to become Tsolyani cannot be chronicled here. The essential fact is that the languages of the humans of Tekumel are still phonologically, morphologically, and semantically similar enough to our own to make a story about their speakers intelligible.

Even so, over millennia, that leaves a lot of leeway . . .

Tsolyani, Mu'ugalavyani, Livyani, Salarvyani, and Yan Koryani—the languages of the Five Empires—belong to the Khishan linguistic family. They trace their descent back to Engsvanyali (the tongue of the Priestkings of Engsvan hla Ganga), thence to Bednalljan Salarvyani (spoken by the rulers of the First Imperium), possibly through the little-known dialects of the Three States of the Triangle, and eventually to Llyani. Before that, no one can pierce the mists of history back through the Latter Times to the days of the Time of Darkness, and thence to the language(s) of the highly technological cultures that existed before that inexplicable cataclysm.

(The causes of the Time of Darkness—when Tekumel was cast into its own lonely pocket dimension, together with its sun, moons, and sister-planets—will *not* be explained here. They comprise the ultimate, innermost mystery of Tekumel, and their unfolding will be set down at the appropriate place in the series of novels I am now writing.)

To return to the languages: of the Khishan family, Yan Koryani differs most from the others; it is in turn related to the tongues of some of the other northern states: e.g. Milumanaya and Ghaton. Mu'ugalavyani and Livyani are closer to Tsolyani—as close, perhaps, as French is to English—while Salarvyani is more distant and more "archaic" in the various features it preserves.

Trinesh hiKetkolel's Tsolyani is not difficult for English speakers, although it does contain a number of unfamiliar sounds and combinations. It is important to note that each letter always has *just ONE* pronunciation: e.g. *s* is always *s* as in "sip" and never *z* as in "dog*s*"—or *zh* as in "plea*s*ure." This is true both of consonants and vowels.

The following consonants are pronounced much as an English speaker might expect: *b*, *d*, *f* ,*g* (always "hard," as in "go"), *h*, j (as in "Jim"), *k*, *l*, *m*, *n*, *p*, *s*, *t*, *v*, *w*, *y*, and *z*.

The *q* is a problem; it is a "back-velar *k*," as in Arabic "Qur'an" or "Qadi." Those unfamiliar with this sound may pronounce it as an ordinary English *k*—not a *kw* sound, as in "quick" or "quote."

The Tsolyani *r* is like that of Spanish "pero." When *r* is doubled (i.e. *rr*), it is trilled: Spanish "perro," or as *r* is "rolled" in Scotland. For example, *Tirrikamu* is "teer-ree-KAH-moo."

The glottal stop (') is common between vowels: e.g. *Tse'e* ("tsay-'AY"), the Milumanayani form of Tsolyani *Tsire* ("tsee-RAY"), which means "to be outside" and hence "foreigner." The glottal stop also occurs after consonants, as in *Dhich'une* ("theech-'oo-NAY"; see the following paragraph for *dh*). In some languages, too, it glottalizes the following consonant: e.g. *N'lüss* ("n-'LÜSS"), and *Thu'n* ("THOO'N"). *Thu'n*'s name is cognate to Tsolyani *thu'in* ("thoo-'EEN"), which means "old (of persons)." In these cases, this "catch in the throat" is a bit difficult for those unaccustomed to it.

The digraphs (sequences of two consonantal letters used to represent just one sound) are: *ch* as in "chin"; *dh* as in "thee" or "this" (thus keeping it separate from *th*; see below); *gh* as in Arabic "ghazi" (a velar voiced fricative—English speakers can get by with an ordinary "hard *g*" as in "go"); *hl* is a "voiceless *l*," as in Welsh "Llewellyn" (the other *h*-initial digraphs all represent pre-aspiration: e.g. *Hnalla* is "h-NAHL-lah"); *kh* as in Scots "loch" or German "ach"; *ng* as in English "sing" (and *ng* can occur at the beginnings of words!); *sh* as in "ship"; *ss* is a retroflex voiceless sibilant found in Sanskrit but not in any modern European language: the tip of the tongue is turned up to make an *s*-sound against the back of the alveolar ridge; *th* as in "thin"; *tl* as in Aztec "atlatl" or "Tlaloc"; *ts* as in *fits* (again this is found in word-initial position); and *zh* as in Russian "Zhukov" or English "pleasure."

Other sequences of two consonantal letters are pronounced as written; this applies to two *identical* consonants as well: e.g. *Llyani* is "l-LYAH-nee," *Mmir* is "m-MEER," *Nalukkan* is "nah-look-KAHN," etc. An English-speaker may have trouble with *nmatl* (a species of fish found in Salarvyani coastal waters), or with *Nmri* (one of the lineage-names of Deq Dimani's brother).

The vowels are likely to be difficult, too, but this is due more to the confused writing system of English than to anything in Tsolyani. The vowels, with one exception noted below, are pronounced as in Spanish: *a* as in "father"; *e* as the "ey" in "they"; *i* always as in "machine"; *o* as in "no" or "oh"; and *u* as in "flute" or "Zulu." In English spelling, these might appear as "ah," "ay," "ee," "oh," and "oo." The vowels of "cat," "above" (either one), "pet," "pit," or "law" are not found in Tsolyani, although Yan Koryani has them: e.g. *Belket*, which sounds like "BELL-kett," and *Ele* which is "EH-lay." There are two common diphthongs: *ai* as in "I" or "bite," and *au* as in "cow" or "how." Other vowel sequences (e.g. *ua, ue, uo, iu, io*) are all pronounced as written: e.g. *tiu* is "TEE-oo," and *Ninue* is "nee-noo-AY." There are *NO* "silent letters" (e.g. the "e" of "above"); *EVERY* letter—vowel or consonant—is pronounced. For example, *Nere* is "nay-RAY," *Kutume* is "koo-too-MAY," *Na-Iverge* is "NAH ee-vayr-GAY," etc.

The one non-Spanish vowel is the *ü*. In western Tsolyanu this is the "umlaut *ü*" of German "für" or "über," while in the east it is pronounced as a high-back (or central-back) unrounded vowel not found in any European language, but which does occur as the "undotted *i*" in Turkish. Some practice is necessary, therefore, to pronounce *Hrü'ü* properly; an English-speaker might get by with something like "h-roo-'OO." *Bey Sü* is approximately "bay soo."

Word-stress—"accent," as some may call it—is important in Tsolyani, just as it is in English (which confuses everybody by not writing it at all: compare "PER-mit," the noun, with "to per-MIT," the verb). Properly speaking, this feature should be shown by an "accent mark" upon the stressed vowel, but diacritics would detract from the story, clutter the page, and also be prohibitively expensive to publish! "Accents" are therefore omitted. A person learning English cannot guess from the letters alone whether to pronounce "syllable" as "SILL-uh-bull," "sih-LAH-bull," or even "sih-luh-BULL." In the same way one cannot tell whether *Mirusiya* is "MEE-roo-see-yah," "mee-ROO-see-yah," "mee-roo-SEE-yah," or "mee-roo-see-YAH." The third of these is correct, but without diacritics there is no way of knowing.

The "accent-problem" becomes clear when one looks at some of the proper names used in the story: *Trinesh* is "TREE-naysh" (the second syllable like the first part of "nation"); *Saina* is "SAI-nah" (the first syllable like "sigh"); *Dineva* is "dee-NAY-vah"; *Horusel* is "HOH-roo-sayl"; *Chosun* is "CHOH-soon"; *Deq Dimani* is DAYK dee-MAH-nee" (*Deq* rhymes with "drake," but the final *q* is "special," as described above). *Jai Chasa Vedlan* is "JAI CHAH-sah vay-DLAN," with *Jai* again rhyming with "sigh." *Ridek* is "REE-dek"; this time the Yan Koryani *e* is not "ay" but the "e" of "deck." *Si Ziris Qaya* is "SEE ZEE-rees KAH-yah" (again note the *q*). *Na Ngore* is "NAH ngoh-RAY," etc.

As can be seen, the stress-accent does not always fall upon the same syllable: *Trinesh* is always "TREE-naysh" and never "tree-NAYSH." *Avanthar* is "ah-vahn-THAHR," *Eselne* is "ay-sayl-NAY," *Ahoggya* is "ah-hohg-GYAH," *Tekumel* is "TAY-koo-mayl," *Thumis* is "THOO-mees," *Vimuhla* is "vee-MOO-hlah," *Tsolyanu* is "tsohl-YAH-noo," and *Avanthe* is "ah-VAHN-thay." These are relatively easy, but some words are stressed in odd places for English speakers: e.g. *Ninu'ur* is "nee-noo-'OOR," *Mu'ugalavya* is "moo-'oo-gah-lahv-YAH," and *Salarvya* is "sah-lahrv-YAH." The adjective-forms made from some of these are more as an English-speaker might expect: e.g. *Salarvyani* is "sah-lahrv-YAH-nee" and *Tsolyani* is "tsohl-YAH-nee."

The prefix *hi-* "of" is pronounced "hee-." It is equivalent in lineage-names to German "von," and it is never stressed: e.g. *Mashyan hiSagai* is "mahsh-YAHN hee-sah-GAI," *hiKetkolel* is "hee-KAYT-koh-layl," and *Chekkuru hiVriddi* is "CHAYK-koo-roo hee-VREED-dee."

There is also a "secondary stress" in Tsolyani: a vowel that is less loud than that which bears primary stress, but which is still louder than others in the word: e.g. *kolumejalim*, which might be represented as "KOH-loo-mayl-JAH-leem." This can be ignored by all but the purists—and for those few lonely people, a grammar and dictionary of Tsolyani are available in print; see below.

Several languages have word-*tones*, like Chinese. The tongues of the Aom ("ah-OHM") family, such as Tka Mihalli ("t-KAH mee-HAHL-lee") and Saa Allaquiyani ("Sah-AH ahl-lah-kee-YAH-nee") are two of these. Both Tsolyani and Yan Koryani lack this feature, and Trinesh and Ridek thus hear these languages as "sing-song," "warbling," "lilting," etc. *Klai Ga*, for example, has a rising tone (like "yes?") on *Klai* and a low, level tone on *Ga*.

The language of the Mihalli—the original, nonhuman inhabitants of that land and not the descendants of the Priestkings' settlers—is just barely pronounceable by humans. The Mihalli words quoted in the story are an approximation at best. Even *Aluja* ("ah-LOO-jah") contains a sound our speech-organs cannot quite encompass. Written Mihalli is known and understood by the scholars of the Five Empires, but most of them pronounce it about as accurately as many Classicists do Latin: Julius Caesar might think he was hearing Pictish. . . .

The tongues of the other nonhuman races are not pronounceable at all, nor can their written forms be learned. Phonological differences are minor when compared with their conceptual intricacies. Humans cannot even make a decent stab at *Thu'n*'s real name, for instance, and his language is more alien yet!

For those with an interest in the linguistics of Tekumel, a grammar and dictionary of Tsolyani were published in 1981 by Adventure Games, 1278 Selby Avenue, St. Paul, Minnesota 55104. This same address will also serve (as of this writing) to reach "The Tekumel Journal," a separate company which issues not only a periodical dealing with Tekumel but also a book on demonology ("The Book of Ebon Bindings"), a history of the Legions of Tsolyanu ("Deeds of the Ever-Glorious"), a language primer, war-game rules for use with miniature lead figures ("Qadardalikoi"), troop-lists for the armies of the Five Empires, and also the miniature figures themselves needed to play with the aforementioned war-game rules.

The role-playing game now exists in two forms: the earlier, simpler version ("Empire of the Petal Throne"), and a more complex set ("Swords and Glory: Adventures on Tekumel"). Volume I of the last-named work is a sourcebook for Tekumel's history, cultures, religions, languages, nonhumans, costumes, economics, customs, and much, much more. It is already in print. Volume II should be published by the time this novel appears: it comprises the players' handbook for the game. Volume III is still being written; it will be a manual for the use of game-referees. These role-playing game books (and accompanying maps) are available from Gamescience, Inc., 01956 Pass Road, Gulfport, Mississippi 39501, or possibly through local game and hobby shops.

DAW

A. E. VAN VOGT
in DAW Editions:

DAW

The really great fantasy books are
published by DAW:

Andre Norton

LORE OF THE WITCH WORLD	UE2012—$3.50
HORN CROWN	UE2051—$3.50
PERILOUS DREAMS	UE1749—$2.50

C.J. Cherryh

THE DREAMSTONE	UE2013—$3.50
THE TREE OF SWORDS AND JEWELS	UE1850—$2.95

Lin Carter

DOWN TO A SUNLESS SEA	UE1937—$2.50
DRAGONROUGE	UE1982—$2.50

M.A.R. Barker

THE MAN OF GOLD	UE1940—$3.95

Michael Shea

NIFFT THE LEAN	UE1783—$2.95
THE COLOR OUT OF TIME	UE1954—$2.50

B.W. Clough

THE CRYSTAL CROWN	UE1922—$2.75

DAW

DAW BRINGS YOU THESE BESTSELLERS BY
MARION ZIMMER BRADLEY

☐ CITY OF SORCERY	UE1962—$3.50
☐ DARKOVER LANDFALL	UE1906—$2.50
☐ THE SPELL SWORD	UE2091—$2.50
☐ THE HERITAGE OF HASTUR	UE2079—$3.95
☐ THE SHATTERED CHAIN	UE1961—$3.50
☐ THE FORBIDDEN TOWER	UE2029—$3.95
☐ STORMEQUEEN!	UE2092—$3.95
☐ TWO TO CONQUER	UE1876—$2.95
☐ SHARRA'S EXILE	UE1988—$3.95
☐ HAWKMISTRESS	UE2064—$3.95
☐ THENDARA HOUSE	UE1857—$3.50
☐ HUNTERS OF THE RED MOON	UE1968—$2.50
☐ THE SURVIVORS	UE1861—$2.95

Anthologies

☐ THE KEEPER'S PRICE	UE1931—$2.50
☐ SWORD OF CHAOS	UE1722—$2.95
☐ SWORD AND SORCERESS	UE1928—$2.95

Attention:

DAW COLLECTORS

Many readers of DAW Books have written requesting information on early titles and book numbers to assist in the collection of DAW editions since the first of our titles appeared in April 1972.

We have prepared a several-pages-long list of all DAW titles, giving their sequence numbers, original and current order numbers, and ISBN numbers. And of course the authors and book titles, as well as reissues.

If you think that this list will be of help, you may have a copy by writing to the address below and enclosing one dollar in stamps or currency to cover the handling and postage costs.

DAW BOOKS, INC. Dept. C
1633 Broadway
New York, N.Y. 10019